PLEASANT GROVE

Ricky Lindley

PLEASANT GROVE

1934-1948
The Early Years
A Southern Novel

Ricky Lindley

authorHOUSE®

AuthorHouse™
1663 Liberty Drive
Bloomington, IN 47403
www.authorhouse.com
Phone: 1-800-839-8640

First published by AuthorHouse   09/27/2011

ISBN: 978-1-4670-3736-5 (sc)
ISBN: 978-1-4670-3735-8 (hc)
ISBN: 978-1-4670-3734-1 (ebk)

Library of Congress Control Number: 2011916949

Printed in the United States of America

WELCOME TO PLEASANT GROVE

People ask where Pleasant Grove is located. It's south of Mayberry, just before you get to Valley of the Dolls.

I was haunted by this imaginary southern community for weeks. It crept into my mind and consumed my thoughts. It overwhelmed by heart and emotions. I had no escape, no rest and no peace.

I told my wife, Elaine, that I was going to write a novel. She wasn't shocked, amazed or amused. Her response was immediate and truthful.

"Ricky, don't you think you should read a book before you write one?"

"Oh, probably not."

And so it began. I plopped down in the kitchen at Kaitlyn's computer and set Pleasant Grove free. It had been held prisoner in Ricky's world too long. I felt like a racehorse was pounding on my chest until I began to write. My fingers became the hooves that set it free. The characters, their thoughts and their community bolted. I didn't have to coax it. I only had to hold on; it was out of control. Trust me. I didn't know what was going to happen next. At times my laughter made me stop writing and I would spend the rest of my day grinning. Other times I would be sobbing uncontrollably and have to walk away.

Pleasant Grove is inspired by true people in small southern communities. Devoy Lindley never knew what the rules were, so he made his own. He married Joyce Phillips and she lived by her young husband's rules instead of the neighbor's rules. This is not their story. It is the inspiration of their lives, their hearts and their community. It takes you behind closed doors and into closed hearts. It reveals secrets, hopes and dreams. It covers everything from the Holy Scriptures to holy shit.

Living in the Bible belt urges you to look at others through the eyes of God. Well, brothers and sisters, God sees it all!

What will your visit to Pleasant Grove be like? I quote my very good friend, Diana Wallace:

"OH, YOU JUST CAN'T IMAGINE!"

APRIL 25TH 1948

Edna May's Recovery
Sunday Morning at the Barn
Time for Church
Vinni Rises to the Occasion
Understanding Velma Stout
The Worship Service
Sunday Afternoon

APRIL 26TH 1948

The Overheard Phone Conversation
School Days
A Teacher's Wisdom
An Emotional End to a Long Day

APRIL 28TH 1948

An Appointment with Eloise
Time for Lidia's Hairdo
School Plans
A Bad Hair Day
The Letter
Gary and Edna Go to Lunch
Ms. Stout's Afternoon Class
Lidia Gets Ready for Greensboro
Vinni Goes to the Principal's Office
The Bus Ride Home
Mary May Gets Home
Wednesday Evening on the Farm
Lidia Arrives At Winterberry Court
Velma Stout's Phone Call

APRIL 29TH 1948

Plans for Vinni
Ms. Stout's Phone Call at School

Vinni and Mr. White
A Day with Margaret
An Evening with Genevieve

APRIL 30TH 1948

The Morning of the Lake Trip
George Leaves for Greensboro
Catching Up With Genevieve
The Tribe Leaves for the Lake
Vinni Meets Joy

MAY 1ST 1948

Across the Lake
Vinni Meets Joy

JUNE 1ST 1948
The Last Day of School

There is, on a rare occasion, an event that shakes the very stillness of a community. A rock plummets into a neighborhood, like into a pond, causing unexpected ripples and waves lasting for generations. On March 25th, 1934 such a rock fell into Pleasant Grove, North Carolina, a small farming community where life revolved around Matthew's Garage and Eloise's Beauty Shop, the Piggly Wiggly and First Methodist, the High School and the dairy barn. True to its name, life was indeed pleasant, coordinated by Southern manners and the expectations of others, where no rules were broken and Jesus was respected above all.

My, how things change.

MARCH 25 TH 1934

A Splash in the Community

"Oh, Mother, please. What can I say to my friends? At your age and I am nearly ten years old. Really, what were you and Father thinking, having a baby at this time in my life?"

Genevieve Davis, nearly ten in years and fifteen in mind, was a force to be reckoned with. Genevieve carried the name and features from her father's side of the family. French heritage was how she described it. Her blue eyes and blonde hair must have been carried on a strong gene outweighing her mother's Italian influence on her appearance. She looked just like her father. Genevieve was a whirlwind who stirred her parents' lives, giving them cause to wonder, "What were we thinking, having a baby at this time in her life?"

George was a dairy farmer, reared from generations of Pleasant Grove hardy stock and married to a most uncommon girl. He met Lidia when he was in the Foreign League after his senior year at Grove High. It was a moment in Capellini, beside a stone dairy barn where sheep were being milked to make cheese. George had hoped to find his future in the wisdom of the local cheese makers. Instead, he found his future in the burnt umber eyes of Lidia Salotti. It was the summer of 1922 and George Davis returned from Italy with his new bride.

Somehow that baby boy landed in the heart of the entire community. They were spellbound by his wondering brown eyes, eyes that looked for trouble the first time he opened them. He found trouble as soon as he could walk and by the time his second birthday rolled by, he no longer looked for trouble. He caused it.

JUNE 11TH 1939

A Summer Morning

"Giovanni, please darling, stay where I can see you this time. When you carried that snake up yesterday, you nearly gave me a heart attack."

Lidia was busy in the garden with five-year-old Giovanni at her apron string, or so she thought. She needed to finish picking the green beans and checking the squash before the men came in for breakfast. Giovanni, however, was much faster than his mother. By the time she had a handful of green beans, he had a handful of green bean vines from roots to blooms and was running across the garden, crushing everything in his path. Lidia made it back to the house just in time to help Genevieve finish breakfast, carrying a basket holding just a few green beans across her arm and Giovanni on her hip. He held tight to his bean vine in one hand and a turtle in the other.

"Thank you, Genevieve, I couldn't do it without you. George is on his way up from the barn and I haven't even started in the garden." She let Giovanni slide down to her knee and dropped him on the kitchen floor. His legs were at high gear in mid air and he hit the floor at full speed. "I'll finish the eggs while you set the table. Don't forget to set a place for Hurley. He's helping with the hay this week and he'll be here for every meal."

Hurley White was a black man with a tall, slender build and light complexion. He lived across the woods with his wife, Daisy, and three children. Roy was their youngest, two years older than Giovanni. Roy's two sisters were in the second and third grades. Daisy was an excellent cook and worked as a housekeeper and cook for Dr. and Mrs. Duncan and their daughter, Mary Alice. Hurley and Daisy were a kind and gentle couple with inviting smiles. Their three children were the same.

George and Hurley came in the back door and set a glass pitcher of fresh milk on the kitchen table beside the plate of hot biscuits.

"Please, Hurley, sit, Genevieve's bringing the rest of the food. Thanks for helping us, I don't know what we would do without you, truly, I don't. I think I'll roast a chicken for lunch." Lidia made everyone feel like family. It came natural to this gorgeous Italian lady.

It was different being at the Davis'. It was the way Lidia did things, the way she planted her garden in square lots instead of long rows letting bean vines climb up branches trimmed from the apple trees. She didn't go to The Farmer's Alliance Store to buy her garden seeds and plants. She brought her seeds with her from Italy. They were saved from year to year, for generations and the flavors they offered were from another world. Roma tomatoes instead of German Johnsons and wax beans instead of half runners. Flowers were planted with vegetables and baskets lined the rows instead of metal buckets. Her aprons were even brighter than her neighbors, made from fabric her grandmother loomed and dyed with vegetable dyes when Lidia was a child. Lidia's garden didn't look like a place of hard work and sore backs, it was more like a festival where you ran to claim your prize. There was something about Lidia. George had always known it. Even Hurley knew. Genevieve took great silent pride in it. All the neighbors admired it, but most refused to acknowledge it. Lidia didn't see the magic, because she created it.

Genevieve came in with the food, being careful to place every dish in its correct place. "I was reading that in New York at The Carlton, this is considered An American Country Breakfast and the very most important people in society rave about how wonderful it is. Except on Sunday, of course, when they have brunch. That's when they stay in late, reading the Sunday paper in bed, having their first meal at ten o'clock instead of seven. Then it's Belgian waffles with fresh fruit and whipped cream, or French toast with powdered sugar and link sausage, or Canadian bacon. I think they find some of our heartiest foods a little heavy. Oh, not because it isn't good, it is good, it's delicious. It's because they really don't work hard enough to rationalize eating such a breakfast. You know, life really is very different in New York. Somehow I think I would be right at home in that atmosphere. Don't you think so, Mother?"

"Oh, Genevieve, darling, somehow I think you're already there!" Lidia could barely keep up with her daily responsibilities, let alone take fantasy trips across the globe with Genevieve. It was exhausting to even talk to that girl sometimes because she was so involved in her dreams. You couldn't simply listen. You got caught up in the glory of it all and were only permitted to leave when Genevieve released you. She loved this about her daughter, knowing that a willingness to dream is what landed her in Pleasant Grove with the man she still adored and two beautiful children.

The family finished their breakfast. The milk glasses had only a white film left and the biscuits were reduced to golden brown crumbs scattered across the white tablecloth. The jelly and butter were ready to be returned to the refrigerator. Genevieve was up and promptly taking the plates away just as it was done at The Carlton. George and Hurley were heading out the back door and Lidia was trying to pry Giovanni from the high chair. Having Giovanni in a high chair was the only way to keep him at the table; he had long since been too tall for the contraption. He had tried to escape and was wedged between the strap that held him around the waist and the tray that held his brown chin where smears of jelly held onto bread crumbs. It was almost impossible to set him free. He was running in mid air, causing the chair to bounce across the floor, but he didn't cry or complain. Giovanni Davis lived for what was just ahead of him and never worried about the present. He didn't have time to worry about being stuck in the high chair when there was a cat on the porch with a tail long enough to get both his hands on.

Lidia finally freed the strap around his waist and before she could grab him, he slid down, hitting his chin on the tray and bouncing his head back against the seat just before he slammed onto the hard linoleum floor, missing the table leg by a fraction of an inch. The fall was so fast and dangerous that it seemed to happen in slow motion and somehow Lidia was unable to help her beautiful son. Before she could even react to the injuries the screen door was slamming behind Giovanni.

"Mother, do you think we could have our cloth napkins monogrammed? That way when we take our food to the church socials our napkins won't get confused with Edna May Crutchfield's napkins. I really do think that she ended up with some of our napkins at the last dinner. I guess it was because that daughter of theirs, Mary May, was screaming. Did you hear her, of course you did, everybody did. It hurt my ears, Mother. I don't mean it was uncomfortable, it really hurt them. I thought I was going to have to go to a specialist, but they got better. Why does that girl scream like that? She's the same age as Giovanni and he never screams. Even if he did scream, he wouldn't scream like that. Nobody could scream like that. I think she needs a spanking. Of course, you know, it's not the fashion to spank your children in some countries. I say they either need to move to one of those countries or spank her in this country. The screaming really did hurt my ears, Mother! I still may need to see a specialist, especially if she does it again."

Two Forces Collide

Just as Genevieve was drying the last plate, they heard the cat howling and screeching and immediately knew the source of its pain.

Lidia tilted her head towards the screen door and shouted, "Giovanni, dear, please let that cat go."

Little Giovanni let go. However, Lidia didn't realize that he had the cat in a full pivotal spin when she asked him to let it go. He released the cat and Genevieve caught a glimpse as it sailed past the kitchen window. She leaned up to see where it landed and spotted Edna May Crutchfield and her daughter Mary May getting out of their car. Edna May was carrying a pie. The cat landed just in front of Mary May and set her into a frenzied screaming fit. Giovanni immediately ran towards her to catch the cat. Inside Genevieve covered her ears and exclaimed something about her specialist. The shriek outside made it hard for Lidia to understand what she said. She could see George and Hurley across the pasture in the hay fields as they cut off their tractors and looked to see what was happening. Giovanni trotted up to Mary May.

Little Mary May's screams were past human; they were more on the electronic scale. Mary May could pierce the air waves with the frequency of an air raid siren. The screaming didn't scare Giovanni, just irritated him. He walked up to her and stood almost nose to nose, his little eyebrows scowled as he stared at her. Nobody had ever been this close to the scream center and he noticed something amazing. Mary May wasn't in a state of hysteria, fright or panic. It was more like she was performing a solo. When she screamed her eyes were very calm as they floated from one side to the other and sometimes up toward the sky. She was surveying the reactions, or damage as it was, to her unrelenting song. When she was out of breath and stopped to refill her exhausted lungs, she looked at Giovanni. He was so close that her eyes automatically crossed. There they stood, toe to toe, will to will, breath to exhausted breath, waiting for the other to react. There was tremendous power tied up in those two little people and everyone watching stood in silent anticipation, afraid to set off another alarm by speaking.

Edna May stood a few feet away with the fresh baked pie in her trembling hand, embarrassed by the performance, ashamed of being unable to control the unscheduled concerts from Mary May. Lidia was coming around the corner of the house with her heart pounding. She knew what Giovanni was capable of and how helpless she was to control his actions. Genevieve followed close behind, wiping her hands on the nicest dish towel she could find as she rushed out the door. The cat was on top of the barn. The audience waited for the next act in this drama and they heard Giovanni speak.

"Shut your mouth or I'll put a frog in it." This was not a threat; he was too young to know what a threat was. It was the only way he knew to stop this girl from singing her song again.

On the other hand, the thought of putting a frog in Mary May's mouth excited him.

Mary May closed her eyes in defiance, pursed her lips and with her hands on her hips announced, "I don't believe you and you don't have a frog, anyway . . ."

By that time the air under her nose smelled like the creek in the woods behind the barn. She opened one eye and saw only the back of a bull frog. She couldn't see the rest because it was too close to her mouth.

Just before Giovanni ran to see where the cat landed he had picked up his mason jar. It was sitting outside the kitchen door with enough water in it to keep his frog wet. He put the jar inside his overalls between the top snap and his little brown bellybutton. Leaving his frog behind would be like a pirate leaving his parrot on the ship.

The two stood in a face off, will against will, threat against threat, frog against lips. This was probably the first time in Mary May's life she actually had a reason to let out her shrill alarm and it was impossible to let go. Her lips quivered and her eyes darted frantically for help. The scream was swelling up in her throat like a geyser about to erupt. Giovanni stood in front of her, patiently waiting for the opening. Mary May's lips turned white as they held back the scream. Her cheeks filled with air and her green eyes were fixed on Giovanni's brown eyes, calmly staring back. Just when she thought all was lost and the song was about to be released for all to hear, Giovanni stepped back and put the frog in the jar. The scream was reduced to a puff of air that would blow out candles on a birthday cake and Mary May's little body slumped in relief. Giovanni had placed the jar back in his pants and was on his way to the barn, the confrontation already forgotten. He had another adventure in mind. No time to dwell on the past.

The Way Things Are Done

It had only been a minute since the cat had taken flight, but it seemed like hours for the witnesses. Lidia gained her composure and passed Giovanni as she walked toward Edna May, who had dropped the pie in her moment of weak helplessness.

"Dio, cio che a commotion! Povera donna, e necessario essere terrorizzati. Come posso io domare mio figlio bello?" Lidia often broke into an Italian oration when an unexpected situation arose and even though no one knew what she was saying, it was always the perfect remedy. Her Italian voice took the entire situation to another place and everyone regained control. "Mary, darling, why don't you go with Genevieve and let her show you some of those magazines from New York? I'm sure you two will have a great time while I help Edna with this pie."

Edna May was picking the pie up from the soft green grass. Luckily it had fallen straight down like a rock and not turned upside down. The crust was broken and the apples had burst through the lattice work on top, but it was still somewhat presentable.

"My goodness, I am clumsy today, I just dropped this pie right on the ground. It was just a surprise when that cat flew toward us and poor little Mary May was just sent into a tizzy. Well, my goodness those children of ours certainly are full of life. Whoever would have thought that a child would carry a frog around in his pants?! I think everything will be fine, the frog didn't actually touch her lips, not that I could see. I know, boys will be boys and all that, but what an imagination. Where did he run off to? Well my goodness, where are my manners? Let me tell you why we stopped by."

Edna May had a gift for saying the most cutting things simply by dancing around a subject. The fact was she had always thought Lidia and George Davis let their son run like a wild animal. She had said so at the last Ladies Missionary Society meeting at Pleasant Grove Methodist Church. She brought it up during a time of prayer concerns, "Hoping that the little boy wouldn't be led astray with no parental guidance in this evil world." It was easy to see where Mary May inherited her sense of drama. Her only chore was to learn how to be less direct in her presentations.

It was true, Edna May had a vindictive streak, but she was not a bad person altogether. She was acting out of hurt and disappointment. It was George Davis she had the highest regards for. It was in high school when she set her sights on him. He had always been the most handsome boy in the community and she had undeniable beauty and charm. Edna May was sure that one day she would be known as Edna May Davis. The romance, prompted by her parents, grew into nothing more than a couple of church socials and a high school dance that ended in the most awkward kiss imaginable. George never saw the kiss coming. Edna May planted it on his lips in a nervous spasm just as he was saying good night. The result was a question hanging in her mind: "Did he try to French kiss me?"

Left with a deflated ego because Edna May made the first move, George wondered if she told all the girls what a shy, horrible kisser he was. George left that summer with their relationship being, not of friends, but rather one of awkward acquaintances. Edna was sure that time apart would erase the childish past and two adults would start on a new romance when he returned from Italy. She spent her nights imagining how he would look when he returned with an Italian tan covering his beautiful features. She was sure that everyone would envy the beautiful couple as they listened to the Italian phrases they would say to each other. The only person she shared her dreams with was her best friend, Ruth Green.

By this time, Genevieve was upstairs with Mary May, hoping not to set off another screaming ordeal. Lidia was sitting at the kitchen table across from Edna May and the broken apple pie. "Well, as you probably know, we are having our annual bake sale and dinner auction at church a week from Saturday. I haven't seen you lately at our Ladies Missionary Society meetings and thought I would bring a pie over and invite you to help with the fund raiser. I understand how busy you are, with little Giovanni and all. Believe me, I don't know what I would do with a boy like that, but you handle it the best you can, I'm sure. Anyway, all us ladies will be baking desserts, pies and cakes and such for the auction and bringing covered dishes for the dinner. I know you aren't always familiar with the way things are done in this little farming community, you coming from Italy and all, so I thought I could help you with your choice of what to bring. I fixed this apple pie as an example of what brought the highest bid last year. Do you have one of our church cookbooks, Honey? I know you like to use those exotic herbs and such from your beautiful garden, but some of our congregation simply don't know what to think of such. Not that it isn't tasty, don't get me wrong, I'm sure it is to your family. We're just accustomed to more delicate flavors. Now, I will be baking all day Friday, so why don't you plan on popping over and we can fix all our dishes together? Of course, I know that little boy of yours would be just bored to death, so why don't you let him play with his father that morning? Anyway, I hope to see you Friday."

Lidia didn't have a chance to accept or decline her offer. Actually, it was more like a decree. Genevieve was upstairs watching Mary May curling the pages of her New Yorker magazine with her freshly licked little fingers when Edna May called for her to come downstairs. Mary May was trotting down the stairs with the magazine in her hand and Genevieve close behind her.

As they stepped into the kitchen, Mary May asked, "Mama, can't I just stay here while you go to the store? You can pick me up on the way home?"

The answer came like a shot, but it came from Genevieve instead of Edna May. "No!" As soon as she realized how it came across, the hostess began to explain why. "Oh. I have to meet some friends in a couple of hours and it takes me forever to get ready, but thank you for stopping by, Mary, and take the magazine with you, there's no reason you need to come all the way over here to look at it. I know you must be in a hurry, I know I am." Genevieve turned and dashed up the steps, leaving her mother to make her own excuse for denying the prolonged visit.

Lidia was more diplomatic. "Of course you can stay, I would love to have you. I'm roasting a duck with rosemary and thyme for dinner. You can play with Giovanni while I finish peeling the potatoes. After dinner he can take you to the stream behind the barn and show you where he catches his frogs. Edna May, I will see you as soon as you get back. Please, take your time, Mary will be in good hands with Giovanni. I'm sure they will get along beautifully."

Lidia was walking Edna May to the door as she recited Mary's agenda for the next few hours. Mary May was frozen in the kitchen, helpless, pale, breathless, like she was being sacrificed to a tribe of savages. Edna May was shortening her steps and looking over her shoulder at her pitiful daughter as Lidia's hand pressed against her back, leading her out the door.

Edna May had accomplished just what she wanted on the visit. Lidia learned how they did things in the little farming community of Pleasant Grove. It wasn't like Italy, but Edna May had taught her their ways very well and very quickly.

Mary May stood in front of Lidia helplessly as she heard her mother's car drive off.

The Dare

Lidia knelt down in front of Mary May, put her hands on each cheek and said "Mia principessa ottavino, you are a beautiful child with a beautiful spirit, full of life and fearless. I think we will become the very best of friends. Now, dear, what would you like for lunch? Giovanni loves hot dogs. If you like hot dogs, that's what we'll have. I think Giovanni would consider you his friend if he knew you fixed him hot dogs for lunch and dear Giovanni is very nice to his friends. Now, what do you think, mia piccolo principessa?"

Suddenly the fear left Mary May and she looked in Lidia's brown eyes and saw how beautiful she was. It would be nice to have Lidia as a friend, she wasn't like Edna May and she liked that. "I like hot dogs too, Mrs. Davis. Do you think Giovanni would mind if I helped? I really don't want to upset him, you know how he can . . . ." Mary May stopped herself from reciting her Mother's thoughts and began again. "Thanks for letting me help, Mama doesn't let me help in the kitchen, but I think it would be fun. I hope Giovanni likes them."

Lidia stood up and smiled down at Mary May. "Thank you for helping, Mary dear."

Edna May was under the hairdryer at Eloise's Beauty Shop, flipping through a Ladies' Home Journal, nervously bobbing her foot as she thought about her poor daughter. "Anyway, she was practically held captive and Lidia just pushed me out the door, I hope she's okay." She was finishing the story about her visit to the Davis' under the hairdryer. This gave her an opportunity to shout the information so everyone in the beauty shop could hear. "I like Lidia, she's very nice and George's family has always been our friends. I'm just not sure that little Giovanni can be trusted, he's just wild. Mary May was scared to death. I believe he really would have put that frog right in her mouth. It may have touched her lips. I hope she doesn't get sick and miss the bake sale and auction Saturday."

Eloise was putting a blue rinse on Velma's white hair and pretended not to hear the conversation. Everyone liked Lidia and it was impossible to get anyone to criticize her. Velma spoke up on Lidia's behalf. "Did you see her garden while you were there, Edna? I was over last week and it was just beautiful, looked like something out of a magazine. I'm not sure what everything was, but it sure was purty. She had flowers planted with her vegetables. Maybe I'll plant flowers with my vegetables next year. Well, Ed would probably just plow 'em up, so maybe I won't."

Velma and Ed Smith lived down the road from the Davis' and treated them like their own children. They were the first ones there in the fall when George's family needed help with the corn shucking and when the Davis children were born, they did all the milking for three days. Things seemed even more inviting since Lidia and the children were a part of the family. It wasn't the same since George's mother had died of a heart attack the year after he brought Lidia back from Italy and the fact that his father went to live with his sister in Greensboro added to George's responsibilities. Neighbors were a blessing.

"George's sister, Margaret, you know Margaret, Edna, brought his father to visit last Sunday and Lidia roasted the vegetables with the roast. Ed and I stopped to visit that afternoon and it smelled like a restaurant. We had a nice visit, but Mr. Davis looked frail. I think he's going downhill. He had a doctor's appointment on Monday, but I don't know what it was for. They have good doctors in Greensboro. I guess it was best for him to move, but we miss him." Velma's concerns and love were sincere and when she spoke she had respect.

"It's hot, it's hot, I think I'm done. I'm going to turn this thing off and you can brush me out when you're finished with Velma. I need to go, I bet Mary May is having a fit. Poor thing, I would be, too, no telling what that boy is up to. I just hope she's not sick." Edna May was fanning her red face and patting her hot rolled hair as she stood up and walked over to Eloise. She watched her finish setting Velma's blue hair. "I'm ready any time you are, Eloise. I stopped by the Piggly Wiggly before I came and my butter's getting soft."

Mary May had helped Lidia fix hot dogs for Giovanni's lunch. He appeared at twelve o'clock, Giovanni always knew when it was time to eat. He was surprised to see Mary May standing in the kitchen, but didn't really care one way or the other. "Please wash up for lunch Giovanni, dear, Mary helped me fix hot dogs for lunch. I think it would be fun if you and she had a picnic out by your sand pile."

Mary could hear Giovanni in the bathroom, splashing water and something banging, but couldn't imagine what it was.

"Here, Mary May, if you will take this tablecloth outside and lay it down for your picnic, I'll bring the food out."

Mary took the tablecloth outside and laid it on the ground beside the sand pile. It wasn't like her mother's tablecloths. It was covered with bright yellow lemons, eggplants and sunflowers with a cobalt blue scalloped border. Mary took extra time laying it on the ground, pulling on each corner until she could see the beautiful pattern like a painting on the green grass. It was a little uneven in the middle where a large root from the maple tree rolled across the ground. The shade from the tree made an extra pattern on the tablecloth and sand was dashed across one corner. Just as Mary May finished, Lidia appeared carrying a basket with heavy white dinner plates and hot dogs neatly rolled up in cloth napkins. In her other hand she carried a green glass pitcher of sweet tea to fill the matching glasses in the basket. Giovanni followed a few feet behind and plopped down Indian style on the tablecloth while Lidia set the plates down. Mary didn't know how to act and was very surprised that Giovanni did. He seemed very casual about the whole presentation, like this was typical for him. He looked very out of place, but felt very in place. Mary wished this was something she had at her house. Lidia finished placing the food and turned to go back inside without any instructions on how to be careful or nice or how to hold their glasses and not spill anything.

She just said, "Diverciteri senea litigare" as she walked back to the house.

George and Hurley were walking across the yard on their way from the barn. They had been repairing a broken belt on the hay bailer. They looked like giants from Mary May's viewpoint. Hurley was a little scary to her. Most people didn't have the respect for Hurley that the Davis' did and Mary May didn't have any reason to consider him a friend. Being around Giovanni and his family made her like Hurley, too.

Mary May looked at the tablecloth and food. Then she looked at Giovanni. She wasn't sure, but she thought he whispered a quick prayer before he bit his hot dog. They finished their lunch in silence with only occasional glances to each other. Mary May gave more than the occasional glance to the jar beside Giovanni holding the frog in shallow water. The frog seemed to fear Mary May more than she feared the frog. When they had finished their lunch, Giovanni walked into the sand pile and started digging with a metal spoon, throwing sand toward the tablecloth.

Mary May didn't want to speak, but had to ask. "Why didn't you put the frog in my mouth?"

Giovanni wasn't surprised at the question and answered as quickly as it was asked, "I was 'fraid you'd bite his head off."

"Oh." The answer seemed to make sense. "You know, in fairy tales, if the princess kisses a frog it will turn into a prince." Mary May spoke with pride, hoping that Giovanni would think that she had actually read the fairy tale. She hoped that Giovanni would be impressed, but he was not to be out done.

"If you kiss a frog, snakes will be afraid of you the rest of your life and bees will never sting you." He made the proclamation with such authority that Mary May believed him.

"I hate snakes and bees. I heard that a boy died in Jackson County from a bee sting."

Giovanni never looked up. "Want to kiss my frog so you won't die?"

Mary's eyes floated between Giovanni, the tablecloth and the jar holding the frog. "Do frogs have teeth?"

Giovanni's spoon stopped digging. "No, frogs don't have no teeth and they eat honeysuckle all day and kissing a frog is like eating sugar."

His tone was consoling to Mary's concerns. She stood up and walked over to the jar and picked it up. Giovanni took it from her, unscrewed the lid, reached in and pulled the frog out. The scene from earlier that morning was being replayed; Giovanni held the frog up to Mary May and looked at her with raised eyebrows.

What he whispered next put Mary May in a trance. "I dare you."

Mary closed her eyes tight, held her breath and leaned toward the frog.

Just before the lifesaving act took place, Edna May rounded the corner of the house and let out a scream that jolted both children. "What are you doing to her Giovanni Davis? You get that frog away from her, how dare you try to poison my daughter again. I never should have let her stay. Where is your mother?"

JUNE 18ᵀᴴ 1939

An Ordinary Sunday

"I think I'll wear my pink dress with the lace collar today, I haven't worn it in over a month. Did you see what was on the cover of _Vogue_ this month? It was a dress with almost the same fabric, not the same. It just looked the same and it probably came from France. France is the very center of style and I can't wait to go. Do you think I'll go to France someday mother?"

Lidia hardly had time to finish getting ready and be at church on time. Giovanni was already dressed and outside in the sandbox. George was dressed and sitting in the den, reading his Bible. He was preparing the Sunday School lesson he had to teach. Lidia trotted down the hall putting her left earring on. She made the familiar sound of high heels on wood floors that the family only heard on Sunday mornings. It was accompanied by the aroma of a chicken in the oven being slow roasted with herbs and vegetables. This Sunday morning held everything that would remain in the hearts of the family as a reminder of home.

"Giovanni, dear, it's time to go. Come get in the car. Have you seen my purse, Genevieve?" Lidia dashed back to the bedroom, grabbed the purse off the bed and trotted back down the hall. "Are my nylons straight George?" She stopped in front of George and stretched her calf for him to examine. George's eyes rose above the book of Mark and floated up and down his wife's beautiful tight calf muscle supporting a perfect figure draped in a rose color cotton dress. The smile rose from the right side of his lips and floated across his face. He couldn't stop a huge grin as his eyebrows rose in appreciation. "Oh, George, please, gli vomine sanno amare. Are they straight? Cosa faro eone te mio dolce amore?"

George stood up and followed his beautiful ladies to the car where Giovanni was patiently waiting in the back seat, holding a stick with a caterpillar on it.

The hot June air rushed in the windows as they drove down the road. It lifted Lidia's black hair in waves. Most women would have panicked if their hair was blown on the way to church, but Lidia didn't have one of Eloise's hair do's to protect. Her hair rested in heavy loose curls on her shoulders and nothing could undo what came naturally. If anything, the wind finished what God had begun.

Giovanni shuffled to his class. A pair of half round tables met to form a giant donut around the chair where his Sunday School teacher sat. The other children were already there, including Mary May, who stared at him with contempt and stuck out her tongue. Mary always knew when it was safe to make her move. She either needed to be under her mother's protection or behind someone's back. The magical day she had spent at the Davis's yesterday had been erased by the ranting of her mother the evening after. She now understood that Giovanni was a bad boy and it was his parent's fault. She had forgotten the kindness shown to her by Lidia. She was already planning the next time to release her ear piercing scream to prove that Giovanni's threat had no effect on her. Even so, there was a battle being set in her heart. There was something about Giovanni Davis that captivated that little girl. She had tasted just a little of his world and couldn't erase the fascination, from the colorful tablecloth to the magic in kissing a frog. How could any child be denied this world that welcomed her with open arms?

George stood in front of his class and asked if there were any prayer concerns. This gave Edna May the perfect opening for a not so well disguised complaint. "I think we need to remember the children in our church and community who are so easily led and influenced without parental guidance into sinful natures." As she sat back into her wooden chair she crossed her hands in her lap and lowered her head, hoping that everyone would come to the same conclusion. Giovanni Davis needed to be disciplined by his parents. The concerns that followed were more sincere; relatives who were sick, a man who had been in a car wreck, the need for rain.

"Thank you for your concerns. Could you open with prayer, Lidia?" George had not let Edna May's hidden agenda go unnoticed. He knew Lidia could certainly rise above the comment.

Hearing Lidia's accent still had a calming effect on people, even after all these years. "Heavenly Father, we thank you for those who are gathered here today, for the warm sun and cool breeze at night. Lord, we bring the mentioned concerns to you and lay them at your feet. We pray for the children, we accept the responsibility for their future. Please remind us daily that our words and actions are seeds sown in their hearts. Please help us guide and direct them. When we see their faces, you see their hearts. They are a blessing. For those who are sick and hurting, we ask for Your grace. For those who are lonely, we ask for Your presence. I ask a special blessing on George as he brings Your word to us; prepare our hearts, remove any malice and prepare us to receive the blessing you have for us today. We ask these things in the name of Jesus. Amen."

Lidia's prayer had softened the stone Edna had cast into her heart and humbled all the hearts in the class, perhaps with the exception of Edna May's. Most of all, it was the final witness that George needed to continue with the lesson.

"Thank you, Lidia. The lesson today is from the book of Mark." His words were accompanied by the sound of the electric fan drawing the fresh summer air through the open window.

Lidia was proud of George. He held onto the values and even the sheepish grin that he brought to Italy seventeen years earlier. Pleasant Grove was a different world, but Lidia had made it her world. She made it a better world.

Genevieve's class decided to meet outside under the oak tree. The shade provided a coolness that made the youth restless. Harold knew his students were more interested in what happened at the movies the night before than his lesson on the Prodigal Son. He gave a very brief lesson and left the remaining time for friends to be friends. There would be years ahead for them to learn about this lesson, but last night's memories were in danger of being lost unless they were shared and cherished.

Harold Wells was a young pastor, freshly graduated from Duke's Divinity School. He had the wisdom of an old heart and the heart of the youth. Only time would tell if he had the backbone to stand up to church politics. Unknown to him was a future where lambs could be fed to wolves. Things were not always pleasant in Pleasant Grove.

This was another typical Sunday. Most things were typical in the small community. After lunch, Lidia and Genevieve cleared the table while George lay on the couch and read the Sunday paper. It took Giovanni about three minutes to throw off his best clothes and jump into the overalls that had been kicked halfway under his bed. He grabbed his jar, spoon and willow stick and ran downstairs past his daddy. George was already asleep with the paper resting on his chest. The noises that defined the Davis house Sunday morning had yielded to the quietness that defined the Sunday afternoon. The only sound was the clicking dishes and splashing water from the kitchen. Even Genevieve was silenced by the relaxed afternoon mood.

It happened at three thirty, just as it had for the past seven or eight years. George opened his eyes and looked down across the paper resting on his chest. He was alone in the den, listening to the world outside the screen door. Lidia was swaying on the porch swing. He could hear the ice in her glass clicking as she shook the lemon to the bottom of her iced tea. Giovanni was making airplane noises and drumming his stick on something metal. George never tried to guess what was under his exploring son's control. He took a deep breath and folded the paper as he rose to his feet. He held his stomach muscles tight and arched his back, regaining the movement he had before his nap.

It was time to start milking. George couldn't allow himself the luxury of wondering what it would be like to have a day off. He was responsible for the cows and the crops, the hay and silage, the farm machinery repair and house upkeep. He felt like the entire care for his family rested on his shoulders, until he considered what Lidia did. He wasn't the only one rising with the sun and working by moonlight. The meals and clean clothes didn't magically appear, neither did the garden. George and Lidia had eased into a life of hard work and sacrifice before they realized it. If anyone had given them a description of their daily lives years earlier, they may have chosen a different road. Maybe they would have a life where love and fulfillment were available with an easier schedule.

It was hard to imagine life without the farm. The sun that cast shadows beside her father's stone barns in Italy was the same sun that dried the hay fields of Pleasant Grove. There was a silent understanding held by farmers. If a man's thankfulness and humility ever gives way to complaints and self pity, the farm would become his slave master. The only way for a family to live happily on a farm was to joyfully accept a life of sacrifice. It was that attitude that not only resolved their dependency on the land and family, but also their dependency on God. A life of sacrifice is only a burden if it is sacrificed to the wrong thing.

The Committee

"Hello, Margaret?" It was four o'clock and Edna May couldn't rest until she had called to set her hidden agenda for the trustees meeting at church that evening. "Oh, hello dear, this is Edna May Crutchfield. I know you haven't been coming to our church very long and I thought I would fill you in on what to expect at the meeting tonight. It's at seven, of course, because George Davis has to milk. I don't know why we have to wait on him, the minutes are available to everyone. Anyway, I am the recording secretary and there are several things on the agenda tonight. The front door at the church needs to be painted and we have to decide on a color. Most people think white is fine, and it is, unless you want to offer something different that draws people into the church. I have some information to share on that later. Some have had concerns about the cleanliness of the church and I must agree. There are professional services that do just this type of work. We cannot neglect the church's appearance and neatness any longer. I'm sure you will agree. There is also work that needs to be done at the parsonage. Evidently that strapping new pastor is not able or willing to care for the house we provide him. I hope the finance committee knows what we have to deal with. I know we are faithful tithers, as I hope you are. The Lord loves a cheerful giver. Well, that's just about all, I'll see you at seven."

Tom Adams heard his wife pick the phone up after the first ring, but didn't hear her say anything before she hung up. "Was that a wrong number?"

Margaret smiled and replied, "Yes, I think it was. I don't know who Edna May Crutchfield thought she was talking to!"

The Adams had moved from Chapel Hill to Pleasant Grove two years earlier. Tom had been hired as the editor of a local newspaper and had received advice from Edna May on several occasions about what the local community needed to hear. "Um," was Tom's response. Enough said on that subject. The Adams both graduated from U.N.C. and lived in Chapel Hill at 700 South Columbia Street while Tom was an assistant English professor. They were a very handsome couple who loved reading and sailing and often missed Sundays while away for the weekend. Edna May was no more than an aggravation for either of them. They realized she was probably envious and therefore tolerated her piercing comments. The fact that their son was a friend of Giovanni didn't help the relationship, either.

The trustees gathered at seven o'clock in the sanctuary. Harold left the door open as he arrived later than the others. "Sorry I'm late, I was visiting Grace and it ran a little long." He opened with prayer and turned the meeting over to Ed Smith.

"Thank you, Harold. Edna, will you read the minutes from our last meeting?"

"I will read them as quickly as possible, I know it's late to start a meeting and we do understand our pastor's other responsibilities."

Being pleased with her abilities to control the situation, put down other people and seem truly caring, Edna inhaled deeply and tried to read the entire summary in one breath. After finishing, she exhaled and panted like she had finished a race.

Ed took a deep breath himself and thanked her. "Is there any new business?" There were several moments of silence and Margaret looked around, expecting someone to mention something from the list Edna had recited earlier that evening. "If there is no business . . ."

Edna broke in, "Excuse me, Ed, but I have had several members mention some concerns to me. I feel like I should bring them before the committee." Everyone on the committee had seen this act before and knew they were about to be hit with a shower of Edna's wishes. The pastor could see everyone's eyes darting and meeting. He didn't understand what was happening. Harold had been their pastor only a few months and didn't have the history with Edna May Crutchfield necessary to read between the lines.

She began. "Well, several people have mentioned that the front doors need to be painted. It seems they don't give a very nice first impression to visitors. I must say that I agree and move that we repaint the front doors. Does anyone have a color they would like to suggest?" The members were relieved with the suggestion. If painting the front doors would satisfy her, it was a small price to pay for silence. "Margaret, have you seen any church doors on the Chapel Hill campus painted an inviting color?" She had set Margaret up with the previous phone call and now she was expecting her support. Edna had just visited Chapel Hill and noticed a red door on a small chapel at the Episcopal Church.

"Before we get ahead of ourselves, I think we need to revisit the request." Harold spoke up, seeing that everyone else sat in silence. "I recall my first visit here with the district superintendent just a few months ago and he commented on how well Pleasant Hill Methodist kept their church. He even mentioned your custom to repaint the front doors for the first Sunday when a new pastor arrives. I thought it was a wonderful welcome. The doors are already freshly painted and I see no reason to repaint. Perhaps I'm missing something in the request."

George added his support to the young pastor. "I move that the issue of painting the doors be tabled until next spring when we review the building committee's requests."

The motion was seconded by Margaret and passed by the majority.

"Well, I do hope the black marks on the doors caused by a child kicking them don't get any worse. This brings me to a second concern. The general cleaning of the church. People have noticed that it needs to be cleaned better. They don't think Grace is able to keep up like she did several years ago. Perhaps we should give her a rest."

Ed Smith spoke up with a comment that shocked everyone. "I couldn't agree with Edna more. To expect Grace, who is fifty eight years old, to keep this church spotless is unreasonable. She does deserve a rest."

Edna gave a great exhale, closed her eyes and bowed her head. "Thank you for understanding, Ed. I know that First Baptist uses Marley's Cleaning Service and . . ."

"Excuse me, Edna, I wasn't finished. In appreciation of Grace's service for over forty years, I think we should take up a love offering.

I also know that First Baptist has a fall clean up day where all the members come together and give the church a thorough cleaning from top to bottom. I agree with Edna that we have put far too much responsibility on Grace. Therefore, I would like to make a motion that we take up the love offering on the first Sunday and set a church building and grounds cleaning day the second Saturday in August."

George wasted no time. "I second the motion."

The motion passed without further discussion. Edna was too busy trying to capture the details in her notes to notice that the meeting had been quickly adjourned. The members were filing past her as she scribbled down the minutes.

A Hot Summer Night

It was eight fifteen when George pulled his Chevy pickup into the driveway. The kitchen was spotless, as usual, and he reached into the cabinet to get a glass for his iced tea. He carried the half full glass to the bedroom where Lidia was stretched across the bed in front of the open window. Her feet were floating off her side and her head rested on George's side of the bed. She was listening to an Italian opera record. Her eyes were closed and her arms were resting above her head on the white linen sheets. George set his glass down on the end table and she felt the mattress relax when George sat down on the opposite side of the bed. He was already undressed and fell back, resting his head against her waist. Her silk slip felt cool on his cheek as he remembered her calf stretched before him earlier that morning. He reached over her waist and held her little finger resting on her stomach.

"Your stockings looked fine this morning, by the way." He tilted his head up and watched her smile and shake her head. "Didn't you have anything to say about how I looked this morning, all dressed up in my white shirt and linen suit?"

He finished speaking with a smile. "I did it just for Edna May, you know."

Lidia rolled onto her stomach beside him. "In that case, I do have something to say." Resting on her elbow with the backs of her fingers on his temple, she leaned down and kissed him on his bottom lip and whispered. When she spoke her lips danced across his bottom lip and he was a helpless young man in her spell, not knowing what she said. "Ti amo George Davis. Tu sei il miglior amorte e vomo ogni. Donne vorreber buglio es jare mantenuta nelle tue. Braccia e nel tuo cuore ti reggero da grovane vome e lo faro in vacchiaro fin. Lanorte un devida, e ti amor stanoltte, mutilare come io amo te?" She stood up and let the silk slip glide to the floor.

All George could do was whisper, "Yes."

There was little room and her body pressed against his when she lay down beside him. He lifted the crisp white linen sheet and a cool breeze floated up from their toes across their bodies. The air escaped past their faces and Lidia felt the linen sheet float across her back. They slid together and the Italian opera orchestrated their motion. The movements took them back to a summer day in the Tyrrhenian Sea. They held together, their arms locked around each other's necks, his fingers were full of her thick black hair while the waves lifted them and eased them down again. The white linen sheets had them bound and helpless as a wave crashed into the knot that held them together. They inhaled and held their breath until they felt the wave break over their bodies and swirl past their legs, leaving them in a breathless embrace. They were left drenched inside and out, gasping for breath. They exhaled

49

and Lidia rested on George's chest. The rhythm of their exhausted breaths were in perfect time with the soft scratching of the opera that had finished, leaving the needle slowly rising and falling at the end of a song.

JUNE 23RD 1939

The Dreaded Phone Call

The week passed quickly as the Davis family worked in the June heat. Garden work was done by Lidia and Genevieve in the early morning while George did the milking and Giovanni slept. The mornings were cooler and usually covered with dew, making the chore of gardening almost unbearable for Genevieve. She had too much respect for her mother to complain about helping, but she couldn't control her frequent sighs and moans. Lidia's heart wanted to tell Genevieve to go inside before the garden work was finished, but she knew how important it was for her daughter to experience hard work. It would give her an appreciation for her accomplishment and an understanding of her parents' sacrifice.

June's harvest was displayed in baskets full of squash, zucchini, green beans, peas, okra, corn and herbs. The garden was a full time job from spring until frost. Having a garden was not optional. Everybody had one. Bounties were compared every time two women met. The volume of produce was the pride of every woman in the community. There was a constant flow of information about how many quarts had been canned, bushels had been picked, pints had been frozen and pounds had been dug up. The garden could drive a woman like a professional football coach might drive his players to endure hours under the sun so they could present their finest on the day of the big game. The big game for the women was the annual bake sale, dinner and auction, and the event was only two days away.

"Hello, Lidia?" The voice on the phone sent chills up her spine. It was Edna May calling to make sure Lidia would be able to spend the next day with her preparing food. Actually, preparing food that would be acceptable to the community, nothing with all those herbs and spices, something with a milder flavor. Lidia had heard the speech before and was resolved to spending the day with her. The only thing in the kitchen sharper than a knife was Edna May Crutchfield's tongue.

"Yes, Edna, I wouldn't miss it for the world. No, Giovanni will be staying with his father. Are you sure I can't bring a basket of herbs? Yes, you did tell me your apple pie brought the highest price last year. Oh, and the year before, too? You must be very proud, I am so lucky to have your help. Yes, nine o'clock will be fine, I'll see you then." Lidia dropped the phone receiver down and felt it hit in the pit of her stomach. "Chi donna odiose. Eva arroccato sempre tormen catrame mi? Povera maria e cosi una brava ragazza. Dio, Dio, Dio!"

"George, ask Hurley if Roy can come over tomorrow and play with Giovanni, I'll be at Edna's." This was a simple request and Lidia didn't realize how it would change their lives. Giovanni had always been in his own world, following his imagination, fearing nothing and always living in the next moment. The way his mind worked was very unusual and only understood by Lidia. He would plan his action, every detail would be considered. By the time he was actually doing what was planned, he didn't have to think about it. His action was like an instant replay, and as it was playing, he would be thinking about the next thing he would do. This made it impossible to get his attention or make him understand the result of his actions. His mind was always two steps ahead of his actions. However, his world, so far, was confined to his mother's world. Tomorrow that would change; he would enter his father's world. A man's world would create a new boy with a new future.

A New Friend

"Let's go, Giovanni." George was walking from the house to the truck and shouted out the order. He didn't know where his son was or what he was doing, but he knew he could hear him. It was like calling a faithful dog. It didn't matter what held his interest, he would always stop and run to his father at the sound of his voice. Giovanni had always ridden in the seat beside his father, resting on his knees with his hands on the dashboard, giving him a panoramic view. Today, as he ran from the sandbox toward the back of the truck, he noticed the tailgate was down. It was like an open door to a new world. Giovanni ran to the truck and with one hop, rested his knee on the tailgate and sprung into the bed. George didn't see him, but knew he had landed and drove down the driveway.

Giovanni rested on his knees and looked around, but the wind made his eyes tear up, so he lay down on his back. He rested his head in his palms and looked straight up. This was a world he had always lived in and never seen. He had always been amazed by the ground, water and leaves, insects and twigs. He never needed to look to the sky for adventure. Today he did. The smells and sounds were new. He was feeling things for the first time. The hay he played on in the barn was scattered under him. The smell was familiar, but it was mixed with the smell of gas from the engine. The vibration of the truck jarred his body, but his eyes rested calmly on the clouds floating above. He soon realized that he could use his elbows and arms as shock absorbers to stop his head from bouncing. The sun was casting a shadow from the cab that drifted across his body as the truck followed curves from left to right. He was being carried into a new world. He rested and let it happen. The sun was warm and his eyes were heavy, but he fought rest in fear of missing something. He lifted his head and looked over his bare feet past the tailgate. He could see what they were leaving behind, but he wasn't interested and only looked a few seconds. Giovanni was more interested in the sky. It was a world where you could see everything below as you drifted. No one could touch you. Regardless of what you did, they could only watch. He no longer belonged to his beloved earth. He belonged to the sky.

The clouds only crept by as George turned to the right. The sun came across Giovanni's right cheek and the vibration that jarred his body gave way to a slow, smooth roll down a sandy drive. His sky was hidden by a tangle of branches and leaves from a grove of oak trees that only allowed the sun to blink across his face.

Giovanni stood on his tip toes and looked across the top of the cab. He heard the truck door close and looked over at George. He didn't say anything or call for anyone, he just stood there and waited. Giovanni could tell his daddy was chewing on a toothpick by the way his ear rose when he held his mouth up on one side. He looked back across the top of the cab. He had never been here before. The house was very white and very small with a front porch offering shade to a black dog. He saw a clothes line tied to a white post disappearing behind the house. It held children's clothes, dresses, shirts and pants. It seemed strange to have such a white house and fresh clothes resting on a dirt yard. He could hear voices from the house and the screen door squeak when Roy ran out. He jumped off the porch in front of his daddy and Hurley followed him to the truck. Roy crawled onto the tailgate as Hurley's door shut and George backed the truck around. The men never looked to see if the boys were in the bed of the truck, they just knew.

"Hey." Roy was looking at the hay in the truck.

"Hey." Giovanni was looking at Roy. Giovanni returned to his position of lying on his back and Roy lay beside him. Roy had never seen the world from this position, he had always been careful to know where he was going. He had a sense to always know what surrounded him. His parents never talked about society and prejudice, they learned by living. He was like a mole, forging a path blindly, being guided by sound and vibrations, following what was comfortable. He had learned how to survive at this early age. Roy knew when he felt safe and when he felt uncomfortable, but he didn't know why. He felt safe with Giovanni.

"What's ya name?" Giovanni asked, never looking away from the clouds.

"Roy." He didn't reply with the same question. "My daddy works with your daddy."

"I know Hurley eats at our house sometimes. We like Hurley." There was an understanding between the boys; Hurley didn't work for George, he worked with him. Other people, less wise, thought Hurley worked for George.

"Are you Vinni?" Roy never understood what his daddy was saying when he referred to Giovanni, Vinni was as close as he could come.

Giovanni wasn't sure about the answer and didn't really care. "I guess. Would you like to be up in the sky with the clouds?"

"No." Roy had never considered being in the sky.

The boys rolled to their sides as the truck turned into Matthew's garage. All the farmers went to Matthew's for their mechanical work and it became the social hangout because he had a Coke machine.

"You boys want a Coke?" George was already grasping a handful of change from his overall pocket and heading to the Coke machine. He gave each boy a quarter. He lifted Roy first and let him drop the quarter in the slot. Giovanni opened the long glass door displaying a column of Coke tops and George grabbed one in the middle, jerking it out. The glass bottles made a loud crash as they fell back into place, causing the boys to jump and blink. George popped the metal cap and it fell off the pile of caps in the full metal box onto the dirt floor. George lifted Giovanni and repeated the process.

Roy had been to Matthew's garage before and knew there was a tire swing behind the shop. "Come on."

He headed out the large sliding doors and to the right. As they passed the corner, they saw a man standing with his hands on his hips, a cigarette in the corner of his mouth, looking at the top of the tin wall and peeing. The boys were surprised to see him. "Hey boys. What you up to?"

"Goin' to swing." The two continued down the hill. The tire swing was suspended by a large rope tied to the limb of the maple tree. It stuck through a hole in the top of the tire where a large double knot was tied. The leaves in the bottom of the tire were old and damp. There was usually water standing inside the tire, but the dry weather had even affected that. The smell of musty leaves mixed with the smell of dry hay made the boys feel comfortable.

Roy grabbed the rope on top of the swing with both hands and shot his legs through the hole. The limb bounced when he plopped down on the tire. "That man had a big dick."

Giovanni burst into laughter and Roy's head tilted back with a giggle. Roy had heard his teenage cousin use that word and wanted to use it himself. It was the perfect opportunity and perfect timing. Giovanni had never heard the word, but had no doubt what Roy referred to. The boys cackled as Giovanni pushed the spinning tire above the maple roots. The spinning and swinging left the boys dizzy and exhausted with little brown bellies full of Coke.

Roy picked up a little stick and put it in the side of his mouth. Then he walked over to the maple tree and pulled his pants down, revealing half of his butt and everything in front. He put his hands on his hips, arched his back and let the pressure of the Coke fly across the air. He tilted his head to the side and cut his eyes to Vinni. "Hey boys. What you up to?" Giovanni tried to hold back a huge laugh and his words broke through with a snicker. "You've got a little dick." Giovanni stood beside him, doubling the shower.

Giovanni had never had a friend like this. He had friends who were neighbors, ones he went to church with and friends because their parents were friends. Roy was his friend because of laughter and it was a friendship that would last forever.

The remainder of the day was filled with laughter and discovery, a trip to town, hot dogs for lunch and an evening playing in the barn. Giovanni's day ended the same way it started. He was lying in the back of the truck, holding his head in his hands, looking at the clouds. The evening sun was warm, his eyes were heavy and he fought sleep to avoid missing something, but sleep took over his tired little body. George pulled up to their house, picked Giovanni up and carried him in. He laid his son on the couch with hay stuck to his sweaty black hair. Lidia stood in the doorway from the kitchen and looked at her beautiful Giovanni. Little did she know, it was not the same child she had left earlier that morning.

JUNE 24TH 1939

The Big Day

The morning of the bake sale and auction had arrived, throwing the entire community into high gear. Any other day there would not be a minute available for anything other than housework, gardening and milking. Today, the entire day was available for the event.

"Genevieve, George will take you to the church and you can drop off the cakes." It was ten fifteen and she knew cakes had started arriving at the church at eight o'clock. Placement was everything if you wanted a winning bid on your cake or pie. Lidia's biggest concern was getting this day over. Impressing a local farmer with a cake was her last concern.

She headed upstairs to get Giovanni out of bed. He had never slept this late and she wondered if he was awake and up to mischief, or had escaped through the open window. A second story window was no match for Giovanni Davis. She opened his door and saw him fast asleep, one hand over his head and the other arm resting on the edge of the mattress. He had kicked his sheets off and the bottoms of his black feet were a filthy contrast to white linen. She stroked his black matted hair where a few oats from the hay still remained and he opened his tired brown eyes. This was the only time of the day when he was helpless, before he could form a thought of what to do next.

"You, dear boy, need a bath. I will run the water and after you brush your teeth I want you to scrub your dirty self clean." Yesterday he would have resisted, but today he was older, he felt like a man, or at least an older boy.

Lidia was drying the last of the breakfast dishes when George and Genevieve returned. She noticed her daughter didn't seem herself, not the usual drama. She had been out the night before with friends, maybe a boy had hurt her feelings. Genevieve was always willing to talk about New York, Paris, fashion and etiquette, but never about things that really mattered. The ordinary was just too ordinary for Genevieve Davis.

"I think I need to rest a while," she said and went upstairs. No mention of her symptoms, specialist, or the latest illness on the French Riviera. Maybe it was just her time of the month and she would never mention that.

This day seemed ominous to Lidia. Giovanni was clean, in his room and quiet, Genevieve wasn't herself at all and George would be around the house all day, waiting for the auction and dinner. She could feel something strange taking hold of her family.

"You can take the pickup to the church and Hurley can drop me off after milking." He could see the day's cooking hadn't brought Lidia any satisfaction and the kitchen was a mess without Genevieve's help. Lidia spent a lot of the day thinking about life when her daughter would be at college, only two more years. Was that the darkness that stood with her all day?

"I don't know what to wear, Mother. Everyone will be there, but I will have to help in the kitchen. An apron is too old fashioned, unless it's a chef's apron, the kind the chefs in New York wear. But I guess you would have to wear a chef's hat and that would just look silly. I do like those white knot buttons, or maybe a chef's jacket instead of an apron. No, I read where wearing a chef's jacket was like wearing a surgeon's scrubs. They really do deserve respect for what they do. I can't wear anything nice and I can't be seen in anything old."

Lidia was sitting in front of her dressing mirror and she saw the tears shine across her chocolate brown eyes. The whirlwind had just blown in and everything had fallen back into place. She wiped the tear rolling down her left cheek just before it reached her chin and walked to her bedroom door, leaning against the jamb. Her daughter was on the couch, wearing a plain blue sundress. Her legs were crossed and her foot was bobbing frantically. Lidia knew exactly what to do as she headed to the kitchen. She returned to the den carrying the tablecloth with sunflowers and eggplants that Mary May had used for the picnic.

"Stand up dear." She was shaking the folds from the tablecloth and folding the corners together, "Now turn around." Lidia draped the tablecloth around Genevieve's waist and tied the corners together below her back. "When I was your age I had to help serve at a birthday party for Antonio Vitaro. He was the most beautiful boy in Capalli and I refused to look like a milk maid, but couldn't risk ruining my only nice dress. So Nonna tied this tablecloth around my waist and sent me to the party. I felt like the most beautiful girl there. So will you."

Genevieve looked down at the beautiful design across the front of her dress and felt like royalty. "Oh, Mother, this is just the most . . ."

Then she stopped and turned to Lidia. Her tears spoke first and then her heart. "No, you are the most beautiful thing I have ever seen. It's you, mother, that makes me feel special, not the tablecloth." Something had happened at that moment, when Genevieve's heart changed her words. She realized all the things she longed to have, all the places she wanted to go, all the people she wanted to meet were just pictures in magazines and voices on the radio, but this was real and wonderful and in two years it would be gone. She stepped over to Lidia, put her arms out and just let her mother hold her.

The ladies had one table filled with auction desserts and a row of four tables were set to hold covered dishes for the meal.

"Oh my goodness, what have we here?" Edna May was in charge of the dessert auction table. Her apple pie was front and center with a golden lattice crust. "I don't recognize this dessert. What recipe did you use? Is it one I gave your mother yesterday?" Edna was looking sideways at the dish Genevieve was carrying.

She handed it over. "No, it's one of my grandmother Salotti's recipies, Zuppa Romana. Maybe it's in the church cookbook, I'm not sure."

"Um," was the reply, "I'll have to label this one." She sat the dish on the back left corner of the table as she headed to the kitchen for a pen and paper.

Families were in line to eat by five thirty, giving a donation at the table just outside the door as they entered and continuing to the covered dish table for their meal. There was a separate table of precut desserts to choose. The drink table was offering jugs of tea with sugar, tea with saccharin, unsweet tea and moderately sweet tea. The lemonade was almost gone. The children who arrived early with their mothers had drunk most before the guests arrived. Lidia's Sunday School class was in charge of refilling drinks and clearing plates. She was continually thanking people for their compliments on her dress and beautiful apron.

By seven thirty the meal was being completed and the dishes were either being put back into baskets and cardboard boxes or taken to the kitchen. People were picking their spots for the auction. Dr. and Mrs. Duncan were on the left side sitting with Margaret and Tom Adams and some of their friends visiting from Wilmington. George had arrived and sat a little closer to the front along with visitors from the community. The right side held most of George's Sunday School class, Velma and Ed Smith, Ruth Green sat with Eloise. Edna May stood beside a chair in the very back corner, giving her a clear view of everyone in the room. She looked across the tops of the matching hair dos by Eloise and admired her apple pie, front and center. The display looked like the other desserts had stepped back and bowed to the queen pie. The center of the room was left open so the teen Sunday School class could parade the dessert being auctioned to the crowd. It was a fashion runway for desserts. Edna had instructed the auctioneer where to start and how to move across the table, making sure her pie would be the last to go. She felt this would hold the crowd longer. The auction went as usual; chocolate pies and pound cakes brought modest prices from family members of the baker. Lidia's dessert remained on the back corner beside a piece of notebook paper torn in half with "Something Italian" penciled on it.

Genevieve was ready to take her next turn with a dessert when something went terribly wrong. She reached for a pecan pie and just before she picked it up, she turned pale. Her eyes rolled back and her head gave a spastic jerk to the right just before her knees buckled, sending her to the floor. Her legs were in a violent jerk and her jaw was clenched like a vice as her head shook, bouncing off the concrete floor. Lidia saw her fall, but the table blocked her view as she came out of the kitchen.

When she saw the convulsion she screamed for Dr. Duncan. "Steve!"

He was already at Genevieve's side, holding her head still until Fay, his wife and nurse, replaced him. George and Lidia knelt beside the doctor, watching helplessly. They had forgotten where they were until a scream broke the silence. It was Mary May standing at the door, letting out a scream causing everyone's shoulders to draw up and look in her direction. Giovanni was standing at the end of the dessert table and saw his father's eyes flash in angry rage at the outburst.

Without thinking, acting out of instinct and fear, he knew he had to stop Mary May. Giovanni grabbed a fork on the corner of the table and bolted towards Mary May as she continued to scream. His right arm rose from his side like the wing of an airplane, the prongs of the fork sticking out of his tight fist. Edna May watched from the corner she had pinned herself into as he lunged toward her daughter's neck. He was in mid-air when Ed Smith grabbed his waist and swung him away from Mary May's continuing scream. Velma slapped her hand over Mary's mouth and jerked her out the door.

Dr. Duncan immediately recognized the diabetic seizure taking place. Fay pried her jaws apart and Steve reached onto the table behind him. He sunk his hand into an apple pie and forced some into Genevieve's mouth with his fingers. Fay continued to hold her jerking head and Steve gently held her legs as the seizure subsided. George could see just enough through his tears to step forward and pick his daughter up.

Fay put her arm around Lidia as they trotted out behind George. "We'll meet you at the hospital."

APRIL 17ᵀᴴ, 1948

Genevieve's New Life

People's lives and futures changed that Saturday night. Seven years later, things continued in ways never imagined. Genevieve was a junior at The Woman's College in Greensboro. The discovery of her diabetes was more severe than first imagined. Genevieve was one of the most severe diabetics on the east coast. She was able to graduate from Grove High with her classmates; the school agreed to let her do much of her work at home. When Dr. Duncan gave permission, she was able to have work brought to the hospital during her extended stays.

Learning to manage and control her illness took a few years and delayed her enrollment in college. The family agreed to let her enroll at Greensboro if she stayed with George's sister, Margaret, and her husband, Daniel Long. George and Margaret's father had died the year after Genevieve's first seizure and their guest house was empty.

Daniel was an executive vice president for The Pilot Life Insurance Corporation. He and Margaret had no children and loved having Genevieve in their lives. Genevieve had lost her drama and zest for life, never knowing when the next seizure would fall on her.

The Longs had a beautiful home on Winterberry Court. It was a neighborhood just outside the Greensboro city limits, mostly occupied by doctors and business executives who could easily get to the hospitals and corporate offices downtown. 104 Winterberry Court sat on a hill. Whitewashed brick scaled the two story house with black louvered shutters that matched the side and rear doors. There was a slate walk that curved up the hill from the curb on Winterberry Court, the terraced steps landed on the two story front porch where Doric columns flanked a double front door with leaded glass. The lot sloped down to a stream in the rear where a full basement was bordered with a slate terrace. Most of their entertaining was done there, with the exception of their annual Christmas open house.

The carriage house where Genevieve lived was just to the right of the garage with a connecting breezeway. She remembered a time when living here would have been a dream come true, but now her illness overshadowed any hope of joy. Her family hoped she would soon step out of her depression. Genevieve did like living here. It was beautiful and the neighbors were kind. She often had meals with Margaret and Daniel. Their housekeeper and cook, Miss Mimi, cared for her just like she did her aunt, uncle and late grandfather. She led a quiet life, one that intrigued her classmates.

Just a Misunderstanding

They were lined up in the hall leading to the lunchroom. Mrs. Stout, the eighth grade teacher, had them file from the classroom in their seating order. As soon as she was out of sight they regrouped according to friendships. Vinni hadn't really changed in seven years, he had only intensified, not only with his mischievous actions and dislike for Mary May Crutchfield, but with his good looks, too. Vinni Davis was a thirteen-year-old boy who looked like a star from a mafia movie. His Italian features and olive skin set him apart from the crowd, making the girls want him. His boldness and wild mind made the guys want to be around him. Like it or not, Vinni Davis was unknowingly reshaping the community of Pleasant Grove.

The class had broken into two lines. The girls were first, leaning against the right wall. Where the last girl stood the guys started their line, leaning against the left wall. Vinni was always on the end where the girls were, for two reasons: he was the leader and he wanted to be near the girls. The shy girls gave awkward glances toward Vinni, but angry glares were passed between Vinni and Mary May.

She would never admit it, but Vinni was still the forbidden fruit she hungered for. Sometimes she found her eyes wandering up and down his white shirt and jeans from across the hall. Unfortunately, on this day, Vinni also found her eyes wandering up and down his white shirt and jeans. He turned his back to her, pretending not to see her gazes. He unzipped his pants and slipped his left hand down between his white shorts and open zipper. He could feel her eyes on his back.

"Is she still looking?"

Bill Clark was facing Vinni and watching Mary over his shoulder. "Yeah, go ahead."

Vinni slowly turned around with his index finger dangling and wiggling through his zipper. Mary lit into one of her screams that bounced off the walls and into the lunchroom. Everyone covered their ears and squatted down. She continued until Mrs. Stout came trotting into the hall from the lunchroom with her eyes half closed and her forefinger on her temple.

"Mary, Mary, please, what in the world is it?"

Mary turned toward the wall and whispered, "Vinni was showing his privates."

Velma Stout had lived in Pleasant Grove most of her adult life and taught for twenty seven years. She had seen it all and heard it all, until Vinni and Mary came along. She gave a huge sigh, shook her head and waved her hand toward the opposite end of the hall. "Let's go." Vinni took his foot off the wall and walked ahead; he knew the way.

Frank Johnson had been the principal for thirty four years and was hoping to retire soon. He was the principal when George was in school and was a good friend with Vinni's grandfather. He was standing up to go to lunch when he saw Velma turn the corner behind Vinni and Mary.

He sat back down in his oak chair and exclaimed in a whisper as he exhaled, "Oh holy shit."

The trio was soon standing outside his door in the secretary's office. Velma was standing behind the students. She just looked at Frank, rolled her eyes, threw her hands up and walked off.

"Okay, Vinni, come in and close the door." This gave Mary great pleasure. She was sure Vinni was already in big trouble. She sat in the chair across from Mrs. Pratt, the school secretary, and strained to hear what was being said. She couldn't wait to report back to her mother.

Knowing there were prying ears on the other side of the door, Frank motioned for Vinni to have a seat. He sat back in his chair and whispered. "Good God, boy, this is twice this week." He opened the second drawer, pulled out a paper bag and tossed it to Vinni. "Here, eat this. I'll be back after lunch." When Mary heard the door handle turn she quickly sat back in the chair and tried to look pitiful. "Let's go back to the lunchroom and get you some lunch, we'll deal with this later."

Mary walked into the lunchroom in front of Mr. Johnson and all eyes followed them. It was obvious to her that everyone knew Vinni was in deep trouble since he didn't return. She took her tray and started to the table beside the window where her girlfriends were sitting. They always sat by the window so they could see what was happening outside.

Before she was a few steps away, Mr. Johnson said in a very stern and loud voice, "Right here, Mary May Crutchfield."

She turned to see him pull a chair out for her to sit on, right between him and Mrs. Stout. It was awful; there she sat for everyone to see at the teacher's table. Only the very worst students had that position. Vinni had been a regular at their table for six years. Why did she have to sit there? She hadn't done anything. It was Vinni's fault and he was out of sight in the principal's office. She could feel her face turn red and her stomach was in such a knot that she couldn't begin to swallow. The half hour that she was there seemed like a day.

What Was That Mrs. Pratt?

Vinni had finished Mr. Johnson's roast beef sandwich in a couple of minutes. He knew Mr. Johnson wouldn't be back before the lunch bell rang, so he just slid out the window. After peeing on one of the bus tires, he walked around the corner and stood under the window of the girl's bathroom. It was too far off the ground to enter without a ladder, he knew from experience, but it was open, giving him an opportunity. He looked around for inspiration and soon saw a dead sparrow on the ground; evidently it had flown against the window. He had hoped to find a snake. He knew the window was actually in the end stall, but it didn't matter since the bottom of the window was eight feet off the ground. You would have to stand on the hood of a car to see inside. He picked the dead bird up by its stiff, curled feet and tossed it up. It bounced across the window sill and fell into the bathroom.

Vinni didn't know what would happen, but he hoped for the best and he got what he hoped for. He had assumed that Mrs. Pratt was in the lunchroom, since she wasn't at her desk. This wasn't the case. Mrs. Pratt was resisting a stomach virus that had plagued the school for a week. She had been able to avoid it and thankfully so because it was the end of the report card period and she had a ton of work to do. Sadly she had contracted the virus just last night and was hoping to stay at school the rest of the day. When she left her desk to visit the bathroom, she expected what was going to happen. But she did not expect a dead sparrow to land in her lap at the very worst time.

This was like a fishing expedition for Vinni. You throw your hook in and wait for something to happen. He threw the bird in the window and got a bite right away. His catch was bigger than he expected. Mrs. Pratt was a large woman, a very large woman. He couldn't understand what was being screamed from the stall, but it sounded like a heard of Holsteins being unloaded at the stock market. There was a lot of banging and moaning and the occasional whoop. He could hear someone frantically trying to unlatch the stall door and decided he should get back to Mr. Johnson's office before the bell rang.

Instead of crawling back through the window, he decided to walk in and scoot around the corner. He was looking over his shoulder to make sure the coast was clear as he approached the door. He was knocked on his back when Mrs. Pratt came busting through the door, heading in a quick trot to her 1940 Ford parked beside the school. She never saw him and the collision didn't slow her down. Vinni wasn't sure what hit him, but while his back was on the ground, he looked over his head and saw Mrs. Pratt. She was leaving in an awkward quick trot, her legs as far apart as her undergarments wrapped around her knees would allow. He jumped up as quickly as he could, trying desperately to erase the vision that was just burned into his brain.

He was back in the principal's office in seconds. Mr. Johnson came around the corner and saw Vinni sitting in his office, pale and sweating. "I need to make notes to put in your file. Have you seen Mrs. Pratt?"

Vinni sat in the chair, resting his elbow on his knee and his forehead in his hand. He was pale and could hardly speak. "I think Mrs. Pratt has shat herself."

Do Something about That Boy

"Thank you for meeting me today. I apologize for having to reschedule the meeting, Mrs. Pratt had to leave early last Friday." The four sat in front of the principal's desk on oak chairs that made them sit at attention. As Mr. Johnson faced them, Edna May was on the left next to Mary May, who was wearing her saddest face. Lidia sat next to Mary May as a human shield between her and Vinni.

"These episodes between you have to end. This last one has iced the cake. In all my years I have never had this complaint. If what Mary reported is true, there will be serious consequences for you, Giovanni Davis. This may involve the county superintendent and even the police department."

Mary May Crutchfield could hardly keep her sad face on. She was suppressing a huge smile, knowing what trouble she had caused for Vinni.

Vinni had been slouching in his chair with his left arm across the back. He sat up and bent forward, putting his elbows on his legs. "That's okay, because it's not true." He looked over at Mary and continued. "And you know it." He wiggled his index finger at her just like he had done in the hall.

Edna May sat on the edge of her chair and slapped Mr. Johnson's desk. "I insist that he be expelled from school. We cannot have the other children exposed to this kind of behavior. Why on Earth would he do such a thing?"

Vinni stood up in a flash, sending his chair over backwards, banging on the wooden floor. He looked down at Edna May. "I'll tell you exactly why I did it. Because she's been staring at my crotch all year. Everybody knows it, too. And besides that, what she said I did was a lie." He wiggled his index finger at Edna May. "Even you should know this ain't a dick!"

Everyone in the room shot to their feet.

"Giovanni!"

"Mother."

"Mary May!"

"Lidia, do something with your child."

"Stop looking at my crotch!"

"Ah, oh, Mother!"

The tension and tempers in the room were at the boiling point and then it happened. Without warning and totally unexpected by everyone in the room, including his mother, Vinni waved the back of his hand at Mary May in a defiant Italian gesture and said, "Mary May Crutchfield che siete una piccolo cagna."

Lidia's reflexes caused her to slap the back of his head. She had never heard Giovanni speak Italian and couldn't believe these was the first words out of his mouth. Mary May screamed like a snake had crawled between her feet and Edna May slapped Mr. Johnson's desk with her hand.

"I insist you call the police and have this boy arrested at once. At once. Do you hear me?" Her insistent words filled the room with hysteria.

Mr. Johnson threw his hands into the air and looked at Edna May in disbelief. "Arrested? For what?"

"You heard what he said! Now call the police."

"Good God, this is a hell of a mess."

Lidia rubbed her forehead and looked at the principal. "Mr. Johnson, please! Giovanni, dear, please control yourself."

Giovanni pointed his middle finger at Mary May's face. "Stop looking at my crotch. She's still doing it!"

Mrs. Pratt was leaning toward the door, hoping to understand every word. When the principal bellowed out his last command she jumped and nearly fell out of her chair. "Edna May, out! Mary May, out! Giovanni, sit! Lidia, oh, just hold on a minute. You two wait in Mrs. Pratt's office while I talk to Giovanni and Mrs. Davis."

Edna May slammed the door behind her, rattling the beaded glass with "Mr. Johnson, Principal" painted in black letters.

Frank Johnson sat heavily down in his chair, causing the front legs to rise and bang back down. He had known the Davis family his entire life and had great respect for them. He had also known the Crutchfields that long. "Giovanni, good God, can't you just reign it in? The year is almost over."

Lidia sighed and rested her hand on Giovanni's forearm. "Giovanni, dear, please keep your hands out of your pants." She looked at Frank with her deep brown eyes. "These boys. What are we going to do? It was the same way in Italy. Maybe it's in his blood."

Frank looked at the round clock above the door separating them from the Crutchfields. It was two seventeen. "Well, I guess I should wait a little longer before we ask them to come back in." He leaned over and opened the bottom desk drawer next to the wall. "I hope you don't mind, but it's been one hell of a day." He sat the brown bag and shot glass on his desk beside the Bible.

Vinni was very understanding. "No, I don't mind, I think I'll have one, too." They didn't see the humor in Vinni's comment.

"I can assure you, Mrs. Crutchfield, that Vinni's behavior will change. Mary May will have no further problems." The combined meeting was finished and Mr. Johnson asked Vinni to give a folder to Mrs. Pratt on the way out. He followed his mother past Mrs. Pratt and out the door, then turned back in.

"Oh, I almost forgot." Mrs. Pratt was staring at him through squinted eyes, her lips were bright red and drawn into a tight knot. When Vinni looked at her, she reminded him of an overgrown, deformed sweet potato. "Mr. Johnson asked me to give you this." He handed it over the desk as he whistled the song of a sparrow. Mrs. Pratt jerked it from his hand, leaving a burning paper cut on his middle finger.

"I'll see you at home." Vinni was walking toward the school buses. The last bell had just rung. Vinni could hear the voices and laughter growing louder as they were about to burst through the double doors and down the steps. "No, you can ride home with me today." Vinni's eyebrows raised and his mouth fell open. It was okay to ride home with your mother if you were sick and left school early, but that was it. Vinni looked at the wave of students getting closer and then at his mother walking away from him toward her car. He noticed their car had been blocked in by the string of cars waiting for the car rider children. He knew he couldn't disobey his mother and was frozen in thought as the wave of students surrounded and rushed by him.

"Hey, come on, Vinni. I've got the back seat. You dropped your papers. Did not, did too! I've already finished my homework, I did it at recess. What was that at lunch today? Somebody told me Nancy peed her pants at first grade lunch. Are we going to have a substitute teacher tomorrow? I'll call after I finish milking. I'm hot. Stop it!"

The voices were pulling him toward the bus, but he had to resist the current. He couldn't let everyone see him get in the car with his mother and he couldn't get on the bus. He fought the weakening crowd and walked toward the schoolhouse. He knew what he had to do and replayed it as he walked up the wide concrete steps past the large white columns into the school. He went past Mrs. Pratt's office on the left where teachers were gathered to pick up report cards. He turned right at the end of the short hall and headed to the side door leading to the parking lot where his mother was waiting. In the corridor just before the door was the girl's bathroom door on the left. He wondered if it would ever be the same after Mrs. Pratt's episode. He turned the white porcelain doorknob and swung open the heavy door. The sun was in his eyes and he pulled his ball cap forward, looking for his car. He spotted it to the left under the girl's bathroom window. He walked over and squatted down beside Lidia's open window.

"Hey mama, If it's okay I thought I would walk home today."

Lidia took a deep breath and closed her eyes. "Giovanni, it's three miles." She opened her eyes and looked down at him and then in her rear view mirror. She had adjusted her mirror to check her make up before the meeting with Mr. Johnson. She saw the same eyes in the mirror that she had seen on her son's face. She realized Giovanni was becoming an adult and needed some freedom. "Giovanni, dear, please be careful and promise you will come straight home. I've had more than I can take for one day. Margaret called earlier."

Vinni saw the worry on his mother's face and knew Genevieve must have had another seizure. "I promise, Mama."

He stood up and started across the parking lot toward the ball field. The sun in his eyes made it even harder to hold back the tears. He loved his sister and the vision of her having a seizure at the church auction years earlier had been recalled and wrapped him in sadness.

Busville

Vinni missed all the action of riding the bus. The bus was like a community of its own. Busville. Instead of a house, you had your seat and your neighbors sat around you. There were some neighbors you liked and some you didn't.

The nicest part of Busville was Front Street. It was quiet, clean and everyone could see what was happening. New members of Busville, first graders, always lived on Front Street. There were no secrets on Front Street. Everyone could see what they were doing, but they were too afraid to turn around and look at those behind them.

Middletown was more diverse. It was where the roughest second graders were neighbors with the third and fourth graders. There was occasional criminal activity in Middletown, gum chewing and kicking seat backs. Candy wrappers and spitballs could be found as evidence of lawlessness.

Dead End Street was the worst area in Busville. A visit to Dead End was only by invitation. Even if all the lots were empty, no outsider would sit there. Scandalous things happened in Dead End. Cigarette smoke would rise from under the seats while farts and cursing could be heard all the way to the edge of Front Street. Gum chewing was an everyday occurrence. A Coke bottle was found

one Friday afternoon by the authorities. The
bottle was spotted in Middletown. They believed
it rolled there from Dead End.

There was only one place more tainted, smoky
and lawless than Dead End. A place where any
rumor was believable. A place most children were
scared to approach. It moved in darkness where
no sin could be seen, as wicked students were
driven far from home by a stranger. It was only
spoken of by Dead Enders, because one day they
would own property on The Activity Bus.

Vinni's Walk Home

Vinni stepped onto the ball field and drug his feet all the way to the pitcher's mound, where he stumped his toe and almost fell. His direct path to the crossroads took him straight over first base. He remembered when he tripped Mary May in a heated game of kick ball. His team won. He had to wait for the cars to pass at the crossroad before he turned right to go home. The car riders stared at him in amazement. They couldn't even ride the bus and he was walking home. Most kids had heard about Vinni; he was famous and getting a glimpse of him was something. A few brave souls gave him a timid wave with their arms hanging out the windows. He just jerked his head upwards, acknowledging their wave. He kept his eyes on the white lined asphalt until he reached the small dirt drive to the left. It led to the old log cabin where Hurley's grandparents lived. Vinni had heard the older boys at Matthew's Garage call it the nigger cabin. He remembered camping out there one Saturday night with Roy. He walked around the evidence of a fresh campfire. Elroy, Herman and Frank had probably camped out there Saturday night.

He followed the path behind the cabin to the woods where the mule trail was still clear. This was the way Swannie and Earl White used to go to church. He remembered his daddy talking about hearing them sing on Sunday nights. It would carry all the way through the woods to their back porch. Sometimes they would turn the radio off and sit on the porch to listen. After he crossed the creek, the path was joined by another one from the left. That path led to Grace Weaver's house, where she lived with her sister, Eva. Vinni was following the path up a steep hill and he heard someone talking. It was Grace walking and talking to herself.

"Yep, I been cleaning the church for fifty years. I don't do it for myself and I never charged a penny. I do it for the Lord. Lord's been good to me, too. I ain't got no money, but I got what I need. I figure if I ain't got it, I don't need it."

Grace was stooped over and had trouble looking up. Vinnie didn't want to scare her by walking up, so he hollered to her. "Hey Miss Grace." Grace's little body leaned backwards so she could see who was down the path. Her eyesight was bad and she didn't recognize him. "It's me Giovanni, George and Lidia's boy."

As they got closer, she recognized him. "Well, so it is, so it is yep, yep, yep."

Vinni looked down at her fragile frame; she was less than five feet tall stooped over. "Been cleaning the church today?"

"Law yeah, been cleaning. Eva helped me last week, but she's been down this week, so I doin' it myself. Left this morning, early, and walked over, stopped and had a mater samich' for lunch, then right back at it. Hard work's good for the soul, you know. I don't do it for money, ain't never charged a penny, but the church folk sure are good to me, gave me a gift for the last seven years." Grace's voice broke and she pulled an old cloth napkin from her skirt pocket and wiped her tears.

"My Mama says we got the cleanest church in the county, even cleaner than First Baptist, and they have a whole cleaning crew every week."

Grace stuffed the dingy napkin back in her pocket. "I member when your daddy brought your mama home, sent everybody to looking and talking. Some folks said she was a colored, some said she was just part colored. I didn't know what she was and I didn't know where he went to get her, but I sure like her. Miss Lidia's always been good to me. She told me to stop by her garden any time and make myself to home. I didn't want people to think I was stealin', so I wouldn't get nothin'. "Then early one mornin' I was on my way to clean the church and Eva was with me then. It was still misty and the grass was wet. I walked past Miss Lidia's garden and there was the purrtist basket ya' ever seen. It had sweet tea and maters, a little loaf o' homemade bread, some soft butter and salt n' pepper. It even had a little cake, all wrapped up in a fancy napkin. I was sayin' to Eva, 'Looks like somebody's goin' be havin' a fancy picnic.' Then I looked and there was a card in the basket. It said 'To: Grace and Eva, Thank you for doing a wonderful job. I hope you'll enjoy this for lunch.' You know, me 'n Eva carried that basket and had a picnic that day in the graveyard, just like we was queens. We took everything back that evenin' on the way home and she told us to keep the rest o' the cake and that fancy napkin. So I did, still got it, right here in my pocket.

"You're a good looking boy, just like your mama and daddy. I member the day you's born, too. Yep, yep March twenty fifth, ninteen thirty

four. That was the month we had that big rain
and they couldn't bury Willis Yow for three
days. He died on my sister Eva's forty-second
birthday. Willis' wife was born the same week
your grandaddy's sister was born, only one day
apart. I might not be much on brains, but I can
member dates. Just ask anybody in the community.
I know when everybody born and died. Don't have
to look at no grave stones either." Grace shook
a little when she laughed. "Some folks says I
must be mighty smart. Don't know about all that.
Ain't had much schoolin', but I can read and
write a little. Mama was so sickly, ya know. Me
and Eva had to take care of 'em both. But they
was good people, Daddy outlived Mama a long time,
a real long time. Me and Eva worked at the mill
for many a year. Folks always gave us a ride. I
never missed a day o' work. It snowed one time
and the cars wouldn't go. I got papa to hitch
the mule to the wagon and drove it to the mill.
Had to leave at daybreak, but got to work."

Vinni liked talking to Grace, or listening to
Grace talk. "You better get on home now, Grace,
you be careful."

"Yep, yep, yep, better watch my step."
Grace's voice faded away without stopping as
they continued home in opposite directions.

The path broke from the edge of the woods into
the edge of George's hay field. The grass was
tall and Vinni knew there would be a good hay
crop this year. It was farming that gave Vinni
his lean toned body. He wasn't interested in
sports, but still had the most athletic body in
his class. He heard the soft roar of an airplane
engine and looked up as it flew above the field.
Vinnie wondered what the field looked like
from an airplane. He wondered about the people

and where they were flying to. He wondered if
Genevieve would ever fly in a plane. He didn't
like to spend time thinking about Genevieve. He
was afraid she was going to die.

Mrs. Lamb's Music Lesson

"There you are. I was afraid something happened." Lidia was putting a loaf of bread in the oven beside the roast.

"Sorry, Mama. I did come straight home, but I came by the nigger cabin. Then I ran into Grace and we talked a while. I guess it would have been quicker to walk on the road."

Lidia was setting the table. "I'm glad you're here, Mrs. Lamb called and changed your piano lesson to this evening at five thirty. Your father said you need to feed the calves before I take you. After dinner we need to talk to George about what happened at school."

They drove up to Viola Lamb's house just in time. Melissa Brewer was just leaving and Mrs. Lamb was ready for Giovanni. He passed Melissa in the den as he headed to the living room. Viola Lamb was a soft spoken, gentle lady who played the organ and piano at Pleasant Grove Methodist church. Her students had to be rescheduled because she and her husband David were leaving to visit her sister in Greenville.

Most people didn't know Giovanni took piano lessons and those who knew assumed it was a torture his mother made him endure. It was true Lidia insisted that he learn to play, but it was not torture. Vinni had studied the workings of a piano while Melissa was playing at school. The top of the old studio piano was left up so the sound would carry across the music room. She played for the eighth graders to sing their spring songs. Giovanni was confined to the music room during recess, as punishment. Typically he had to stay in the lunch room, but they were mopping the floors. Melissa was practicing the piano. Vinni leaned over the piano and watched the hammers hit the metal wires. Then the entire group lifted when Melissa pressed down on the left pedal. It was strictly mechanical and it fascinated him.

When his mother insisted he learn to play, he only objected out of principle. Most adults expected the worst from Vinni, Edna May for example, but not Viola. She believed that children would rise to what others expected of them. Vinni had a natural ability. It came from his grandmother on his mother's side. It has been told that talent and beauty will skip generations and both had hit Vinni dead on.

Lidia had given Vinni some sheet music that her mother had in Italy and Mrs. Lamb was thrilled to see it. Vinni was starting the new piece today and Mrs. Lamb had never seen it. It was from an Italian opera. Vinni began slowly, getting familiar with the notes and timing until he could hear the song breaking through. Once he had the song in his head, his fingers fell into place. It was hard to know if the music was chasing his fingers, or the other way around. Typically music students would work on several pieces at each lesson, but Vinni was allowed to conquer one at a time.

Near the end of the lesson, Viola noticed something uncommon when he played. "Play the third and fourth lines again please." She looked at his hands, the music, his eyes and back at his hands. He was playing notes correctly, that wasn't what she was after. "Continue until I ask you to stop, Vinni." He continued, on time, while her eyes floated across from music to hands to eyes. Each time the music notes were at the end of a line she would ask him to stop. "Please keep your eyes, your hands and head still when I ask you to stop Vinni . . ." Okay continue . . . Now stop." She watched in amazement. When Vinni stopped his eyes were on one line and he was playing the music on the line above. His eyes were always about one measure ahead of his hands. He was remembering the music, not reading it.

By the end of the lesson the Italian opera was floating from the living room into Lidia's car. The heat was familiar, the breeze was familiar and the Italian opera was from her favorite record. She closed her eyes. When Vinni opened the car door he interrupted a memory of the Tyrrhenian Sea.

The Talk

Things were quiet at meal times now. It was always Genevieve who offered the conversations. It was sad. They depended on her to initiate conversations and when she left, the conversations left, too.

They were finishing dinner when George asked Vinni to help him at the barn. The two stood up and walked outside. They enjoyed the meal, but never mentioned it. They just figured Lidia knew. Giovanni followed a few steps behind his daddy and could almost look over his shoulder. They were close to the same height now.

They walked in the barn and it was getting dark. It was still dusk outside, but the barn windows were covered with years of hay dust and the little light available couldn't get through. George flipped the light switch on beside the large sliding door. It was on the wall above the wooden steps that went to the hay loft. The steps were narrow, steep as solid as a rock. Each one held something useful, a few cans of motor oil, a cardboard box of nails, rope and a hammer.

Lidia could see the light from the back door where she was watching. She had to stand there and watch the light. For some reason it called to her like a lighthouse warning of danger if the wrong course was taken. She didn't consider washing the dishes or cleaning the table. After the events of the day, she knew that Giovanni was no longer hers. George would take the reins tonight; the soft light that floated from the barn to the porch was a symbol of Giovanni's new life. He had started on the path to this night years earlier when he spent the day with George, Hurley and Roy. She couldn't move, she couldn't look away from the light and she couldn't stop crying.

"Your mama told me what happened at school the other day and about the meeting today. I haven't mentioned it because I wanted to see what happened at school with Mr. Johnson. Giovanni, you've been in a lot of trouble already, you need to be careful. But here's the thing. You can't be careful, you never have been. Giovanni, you just take the world on, head on, no matter what. You never think about consequences. You never think about other people. You never think if it's a good idea. You just do whatever the hell comes to your mind."

Giovanni had heard his daddy laugh and pray. He had seen him cry. He had seen him work so hard that he could barely walk, but there were two things that he had never heard his daddy do. He had never heard his daddy complain or cuss.

"Now, don't get me wrong, I love you and I'm proud of you. You're just like your mother in some ways."

George Davis wasn't like most men of his generation. He was able to be honest about his emotions. This one thing that Lidia fell in love with.

"I love you, too, Daddy." Giovanni was like his parents in so many ways and so unlike them in others.

"Son, what you did to Mary May Crutchfield at school was wrong. Giovanni, you can't just do whatever comes to your mind. If you don't learn how to control your actions now, you will never learn. Believe me, if you keep this up, one day you will have something far worse than a trip to the principal's office to deal with. Do you understand?"

Giovanni was dealing with his father in a new way now, in the barn, man to man, away from his mama, talking and cussing. Giovanni was leaning against the tractor tire with his arms crossed, looking at the ground between his feet. Then he looked to the side at his daddy. "Mary May's a bitch."

Before he could stop himself, George replied, "I know, her mama's a bitch, too."

There was a freedom that George enjoyed, being a man in front of his son. He didn't have to be perfect. He wasn't a perfect man and this is what he wanted Giovanni to know. He was an honest man, a man who loved his family and was unashamed to let them know.

"Giovanni, the way you treat people is more important than what you think of 'em. It's hard to be nice to people like the Crutchfields and it's not fair. But you have to believe me. You can never win with people like that. You may think you've beat them from time to time, but they will never change and they will never stop. The best you can do is to stay far away from 'em. If you don't stop this fight between you and Mary May now, it will never end. You can move to the other side of the world and she will be there every day if you don't let her go now. And if you insist on winning, then you insist on fighting. If you insist on fighting, you insist on having her by your side. Giovanni, this is something you can't understand. By the time you're able to understand, it will be too late. You have to trust me on this. Stop the feud."

George walked to the other side of the tractor and lifted the seat. In the small metal tool box under the seat were wrenches of all sizes, nuts and bolts needed to attach and repair machinery, oil stained rags from Matthew's Garage and a pack of Winston cigarettes. George picked up the Winston's and took out the pack of matches held inside the cellophane wrapper. He lit a cigarette and put them back in the metal tool box.

Vinni liked being on these terms with his daddy and felt free to say what he wanted. Evidently there were no rules when smoking and cussing were involved.

"Did Mama tell you what Mary May was doin'? Did she tell you the whole story?"

"You mean about her staring at your crotch? She said Mary May's been staring at your crotch all year."

Hearing these words float from his daddy's lips in a cloud of cigarette smoke gave Vinni the freedom he needed to really open up. He stood straight up and lifted both arms in the air. "Hell yeah!"

"Giovanni, watch your mouth. Listen, I know what you're going through. We both know why Mary May might be staring at your crotch. It happens to all boys at your age and it's not something you can control."

Suddenly Giovanni didn't want to have such freedom in conversation. He looked back at the ground and kicked some dirt around. "Oh yeah, well, never mind."

This was like jumping into cold, unchartered waters for George. The only way to avoid pain and dread was to jump in head first. After the initial shock, you would be able to stay in.

"Vinni, I don't know what you've heard about everything that's started happening with you and your friends. I expect you've gotten a bit of information behind Matthew's Garage and at the cabin. You need to know what you're dealing with. First of all, like I said before, you can't control it any more than you can control getting taller. It all comes together. I know you probably call it a hard on, but the medical term is an erection. You need to know that term when you're talking to the doctor. The best way to deal it is baggy pants. The way you feel about Mary May is intense and she makes you madder than hell. There will be a time when a girl will make you have other feelings just as intense. But she won't make you mad and you will react to her in a completely different way. Your body, the way you look at girls, the way they look at you, the way your mind works, the way you sound, even the way you smell means you're getting ready for that moment when a girl will take over your world completely.

"But, Giovanni, there is something far more important you need to learn. You have to listen to something besides your body. There will be no mistaking what your body wants. Your body and emotions will guide you and let you know how to handle things. God made all creatures with this ability. But we are not animals and the most difficult part is dealing with what animals don't have to deal with. Giovanni, as a man, you have to learn to listen to your heart. You can take your body and destroy another person's body. You can take your words and destroy another person's reputation. But the very worst thing you can do is to take your heart and destroy another person's heart. I have seen this done, son, and it happens in an instant, as quick as a gunshot and just as hurtful.

"This is what I am trying to tell you about Mary May. I know you don't like her, and she's a bitch, but the way you two are fighting is by trying to hurt each other's hearts. It seems okay for you two to destroy one another's hearts because they mean nothing to either of you. You care nothing about having her heart, but you have to train your heart to love by protecting hers. I don't believe you will ever have love in your heart for Mary May, but you need to let your heart develop the capacity to love. You can't stop your body from growing and changing. Giovanni, you can't stop your heart from growing and changing, either. But you can control how it turns out. Your heart, the love in your heart is the most powerful thing you will ever have. Use it wisely or it will destroy you and those you love."

Giovanni was staring at the space on the ground between his shoes. His arms were still crossed and his muscles were relaxed. He was glad the tractor tire was there to hold him up. George dropped his cigarette on the ground, tapped out the red ash with his shoe, turned and left Giovanni to his thoughts.

Giovanni heard his daddy's footsteps disappearing as he walked back to the house where Lidia was turning and walking into the kitchen. He was glad to be alone, because his body was experiencing another one of its strange changes. His knees buckled and he sat on the ground, sobbing with his back against the tractor tire.

Lidia finished putting the dishes away and the kitchen was spotless, ready for the next morning. George was lying in bed with his hands supporting the back of his head, staring at the ceiling. Lidia could hear him breathing with heavy sighs when she stretched out beside him. She laid her hand on his chest and she could feel the tension in his body; it was a physical tension and emotional tension. She knew exactly what he needed to relax. She sat up with her back against the headboard and pulled his head onto her lap. Lidia gently raked her fingers through George's hair and soon she could feel his tears on her silk slip.

APRIL 21ST 1948

Genevieve's Decision

"I don't think I'll be able to go. I really need to finish my term paper and Mother can't spend money on a dress. I know the hospital bills were outrageous."

The Spring Gala was coming up next week at The Woman's College and her Aunt Margaret knew it was just what she needed. She missed the old Genevieve, the one who dreamed of Paris and New York, the one never satisfied with the ordinary.

"Genevieve, darling, please, all your friends will be there. You will have a wonderful time. I'm afraid if you don't go, you will regret it the rest of your life. You know, Genevieve, regrets are the very worst things to endure."

Genevieve was staring into her dressing table mirror. It was a reflection of her, of her life. Her face had fine features, French heritage just like her father's. Her vanity was filled with photographs from home. There was one of Giovanni holding a fish he had caught. The photo captured his bare feet and dirty overalls, and somehow the silver frame was appropriate. Other photographs of the family, one of their home and a close shot of Lidia's basket in the garden. The Chanel perfume bottle and a mirrored tray holding Estee Lauder make up were on the opposite side. There was a bouquet of fresh Gardenias left by Miss Mimi resting beside the syringes and insulin bottle. This was her life.

Margaret knew she was afraid and rested her hands on Genevieve's shoulders. "Genevieve, do I love you?"

She was shaken by the question and her eyes jumped up to see the reflection of Margaret standing behind her. Their eyes looked very much alike. People often said Margaret and George could have been twins. "Oh, yes, you love me, you and Uncle Daniel love me like I was your own daughter, and I love you."

"Yes, we do. We love your smile and your grace, we love your sense of adventure, your brilliant mind and your manners, and Genevieve . . ." Margaret leaned over and touched one of the syringes. "We must love this, too, because it keeps you with us. I'm afraid that you will allow your illness to take away your joy in spite of everything we have done. Please reconsider the Spring Gala."

She watched her aunt in the mirror as she closed the door behind her. Her heart was aching with sorrow and sadness. She was angry and helpless. She was embarrassed and ashamed. How could she go to the dance and risk having a seizure? Her body slumped with a deep sigh and her eyes fell on the answer. There it sat, sterile, silver and cold. The insulin was her worst enemy and best friend, the one she was ashamed of and depended on totally, the one that could save her, the one that would escort her to the dance.

"Well, old friend, it looks like it's you and me." She picked up the little bottle and looked at it carefully. She had never paid much attention to the bottle. It would be beautiful if it held anything else, but she resented what was inside and denied it being a part of her life. Then she looked in the mirror and suddenly it all made sense. She had not really looked at the mirror for a long time. There she sat, full of all those emotions, she resented what was inside and denied it being a part of her life. She would have been beautiful if she held anything else inside. She knew Margaret was right. Everyone had helplessly watched her slipping away. They had done all they could to help. Now it was up to her.

She couldn't think about the gala at first. Her mind had been fighting it and the two had to come to terms before she could move forward. Her dreams were empty and it had been years since she looked at a fashion magazine. She walked over to the bookcases that framed a window seat overlooking the stream and ran her fingers across old magazine bindings. Town and Country, she pulled it out and started thumbing through the pages. Then she heard something from her past float over her lips. "Good heavens, what on Earth was she thinking?" There it was in bold print for everyone to see. A photograph of Elizabeth Rothchild at a garden party in upstate New York wearing white shoes, and it was clearly after Labor Day.

This was the spark that ignited her quest for the perfect outfit. She dashed out the carriage house door, through the breezeway and made a quick right turn. She refused to enter a house from the garage, so she trotted around back, across the slate terrace and dashed in the sunroom. "Aunt Margaret!"

Unwelcome News

Edna May was in a frenzy. Gary, her husband, had just called. "Mary May, Mary Maaay, get down here! What are you doing in the attic? Hurry up! Mary May!"

Gary and Edna May had bought an old Victorian house at the end of Old Davis Road. It was the former home of the Ellingtons, who lost it when their yarn mill went under. The house had sat for several years in disrepair and the Crutchfields bought it for a steal. Gary was a contractor and Edna was sure he would fix it up nicely on evenings and weekends, providing her with a showplace. Gary worked tirelessly for three years to make the house livable. When Edna was expecting Mary May, Gary was offered a job as project manager for Quality Steel Structures. It was a firm that subcontracted civil work for state projects, primarily building bridges. His salary was very substantial, but the projects were mostly out of state and usually lasted between one and four years. He only came home every few months and less often if the projects were several states away. His salary meant Edna didn't have to work and she could buy everything she and Mary needed. They both seemed satisfied to have money sent home instead of Gary. He was finishing a large three year project in Kansas and would be getting home Saturday night. This only gave Edna two days to get ready.

"Mary May Crutchfield, get out of that dusty attic. I need your help, your father is coming home Saturday." Mary had heard this announcement many times before and a knot formed in her stomach. The news made her want to stay in the attic forever. The news made the whole community want to crawl in the attic with her.

Gary was a large man, built like a truck. His square head and muscular features were carried over from his years being the star quarterback at Grove High. It was the year after George brought Lidia home when Edna decided she would marry Gary. It took her only two years to leap from the first date to the altar. Gary assumed he was happy because Edna seemed so happy. Ruth Green let it slip that Edna trapped Gary by making him believe she was pregnant. She quietly and privately cried her way through a fantasy miscarriage after the wedding. Gary tried to love Edna, but it was a battle against himself, and the job with Quality Steel Structures was the out he was looking for.

"We have to clean this house top to bottom. You know your father likes a clean house. He is good enough to provide us with a home. The least we can do is have it perfect when he gets here Saturday. You start on your room and I'll start in the kitchen. I wish he had called me sooner. He had a schedule on that project. He must have known when it would be finished. Oh well, I know they depend on him for everything, but that's all right. They pay him accordingly. Lord knows if people around here knew what kind of check I get every month they would drop their teeth, but I'm not one to brag, my mama taught me to be humble."

Edna was in a nervous twitch and the tension could be felt throughout the entire house. It could be felt everywhere she went. The neighbors always knew when Gary was coming home. They didn't have to ask.

"Everything, Mary, everything. Don't kick things under your bed, either. Clean out your closet, dust, vacuum, don't forget to wipe down the baseboards and window seals. Does your mattress need to be turned? Check it after you take your sheets off. Just throw them down here, I'll wash them with mine, ours. I wish we had the yard work done this spring, but I decided to wait until fall. Do you have any friends that could trim the shrubbery and mow the yard? Not that Giovanni Davis. I'll have him nowhere near my property or my daughter, in that case. What about Jake Adams? Lord knows they are off boating or beaching or some such every weekend. Surely he needs some money. Are you cleaning your room, Mary May Crutchfield?"

Mary was not cleaning her room. She was sitting in the attic, frozen in the same spot where she heard the news. The thought of her daddy coming home drained her energy and filled her with dread. The added load of endless housework and her mother's tension weighed heavy on her and she could hardly breathe. She was staring out the oval attic window, taking shallow breaths when Edna belted out from the bottom of the attic stairs. "Mary May, please!"

The Invitation

"George, Margaret just called with wonderful news. Genevieve had decided to go to the Spring Gala. It's next Saturday night. She wants us to come to Greensboro and have dinner with them at the club that night. What do you think, George?"

It had been a long time since Lidia had run to meet him walking up from the barn. He was glad to see the good news lifting her sadness, even if it was only temporary.

"Yeah, that would be great. We could use a night out. So, is Genevieve doing better?"

He could see the answer in her eyes, but wanted to hear it. She put her hands on his arms and quickly nodded her head, raising her eyebrows. "Um hum, I think so, I really do." She turned and put her arm around his waist and her head against his arm and they walked back to the house.

APRIL 23RD 1948

The Fire Drill

It was Friday morning and Lidia prayed that Giovanni would make it through the day with no trouble.

"Bus is coming, gotta go." He jumped up from the table, reached back and grabbed a last swallow of orange juice, popped the last piece of toast in his mouth, grabbed his books and flew out the door. He reached the end of their drive just as the bus door was opening. He immediately looked to the bench seat in Dead End to make sure everyone would be at school. They were all there: Jake Adams, Charlie, Gerald, Tom and David. Vinni's seat was reserved, as always, on the bench. He sat just behind the right seat next to the aisle, where all the guys could talk to him, but the bus driver couldn't see him in the rear view mirror. He walked back, slapping the metal bars on each seat with his left hand and hitting the students with the books in his right hand. Some kids flinched and others just leaned to the side when he passed. He noticed Mary May was sitting next to the window. Her friends were huddled around her forming a protective shield. She was crying. He decided to let it go. When Vinni reached his seat, the guys beside and in front of him leaned in his direction to hear the day's agenda. It was unusually quiet on the bus and the driver knew something was up. There was something sinister being planned on the back seat and something heartbreaking with the girls.

"Now, class, settle down and turn your homework papers in." Mrs. Stout had to speak loudly and knock her desk with her knuckles to get their attention. Papers started rustling and books were slamming shut as the papers were passed from the back to front of the rows.

"As you know, we will have our Friday test this morning, as usual, and then a fire drill." The students on the front rows handed her stacks of papers as she walked by. "Please put your books away and get out a clean piece of paper. You must answer each question with at least two sentences. The test is on Chapter Eleven in your science book. Please do not misuse the word Uranus in a sentence. Believe me, I have heard them all. There will be an automatic ten point deduction for such shenanigans." She waited until the sound of rustling papers and mumbling stopped. The back row resembled the back of the bus, holding Vinni and his friends. The grade averages increased as the rows approached the front. Mary May sat front and center. "What is the orbital relationship between the Earth and Moon?"

The back row was finished in seconds, giving them ample time to whisper and pass notes as the others finished. Mary May completed an eight line paragraph while sniffing and wiping her nose on a brown paper towel from the girl's bathroom. Mr. Johnson waited in the hall for Mrs. Stout's sign to start the fire drill. The test took longer than expected, with Mary May asking permission twice to get extra paper for her answers. Charlie had to sharpen his pencil three times in hopes of seeing a correct answer on his journey. Mrs. Stout finally handed out seven sharpened pencils to the back row.

"Will everyone please pass their papers to the front? Mr. Davis, this includes the notes you have received during the test. I believe there should be five. They will be graded according to grammar and spelling. The scores will be reflected on the grade of the ones who sent them. I hope your friends know how to form complete sentences. I will be giving you an oral exam on the notes after the fire drill. This will also be reflected on your grade."

She turned to the hall and waved her hand to Mr. Johnson. Moments later the loud clanging bell rang across the building. Students rose from their desks and rumbled across the wooden floors toward the side doors.

"Single file, please, and count out as you exit." Mrs. Stout knew her magic number was twenty one. "One, two, three," and so on it went as they filed out the door. "Fifteen, sixteen, eighteen, nineteen." Mrs. Stout put her hand on Gerald's chest. "Hold it number eighteen." She waved the last two by. "Continue on." "Twenty, twenty one." Her students were filing across the gravel parking lot toward the ball field and she gave a quick count, with her index finger bouncing on each head. "Seventeen, eighteen, nineteen, twenty." She pulled her hand from Gerald's chest and let him pass. There was a black head missing and this meant trouble.

The bell stopped ringing and Mr. Johnson filed around the school property verifying that each teacher had a correct count. The superintendent was new and insisted on an accurate report from each principal. She could hear the voices of her fellow teachers. "Yes, all accounted for Mr. Johnson." He was walking to her class on the ball field and she met him in the middle of the parking lot. She was staring at her students in a row snaking across the dirt field.

"One missing." She cut her eyes back at Frank.

"Good God Almighty!" He put his hands on his hips and looked back to the school. "Davis?"

"You know it. What are we supposed to do? He was in class and I have the numbers here on paper for the report."

Mr. Johnson looked at the last remaining class waiting to report. "Well, what they don't know in Central Office can't hurt us."

He was about to continue to the next class and Mrs. Stout heard a car turn in the drive beside the buses. Frank's eyes looked over her shoulder and his hands hit his hips as his eyes rolled to the sky. "Oh, shit!"

Mrs. Stout spun around just in time to see the superintendent close his car door and walk toward them. "I'll leave you to it, Mr. Johnson."

Mrs. Stout quickly headed to her students strung across the ball field. She walked to the back of the line and motioned to Gerald. "Get over here now!" She grabbed him by the arm and turned him so his back would be to the superintendent and she could watch the progress over his shoulder. After a few words with Mr. Johnson, the superintendent escorted him to the head of Mrs. Stout's line of students. She jerked Gerald's sleeve and gave him strict orders. "Listen, buddy-roe. If I ask this class to count off, you better count off exactly like you did coming out. Got it? Eighteen, you're number eighteen, and tell those boys behind you to count off in double time. Now get back in line and don't mess with me. Eighteen!"

Just as she feared, Mr. Johnson was waving for her to join the conversation. "Mrs. Stout, meet Mr. Hawthorn, State Superintendent."

Mrs. Stout's lips quivered and danced around her words. "State Superintendent, oh, oh my, oh my goodness, well it certainly is nice to meet you. Thank you so much for stopping. I trust you will have a safe trip back." Her eyes were in a nervous twitch, desperately wanting to connect with Frank's eyes, and she was scared to death that Mr. Hawthorn would pick up on their dilemma. Her right fingers were dancing across her chest, trying to grasp a necklace she wasn't wearing and for some reason her left hand had started floating away from her side. "I was in the area and thought I'd pop in for a visit. Looks like you're having a fire drill. I trust everything is in order. Let's review. Do you have your attendance record with you?" Her hands regained control and tucked the notebook behind her back in a tight grip. "Oh, certainly, certainly, yes, certainly I do, yes, I do. Thank you for asking."

She looked at Frank standing just behind him and to the side. He looked like a sad clown in a circus, getting ready to be shot from a cannon.

"May I see it, please?" Mrs. Stout gave him the nicest smile, tilted her head to one side and just looked at him. "May I?"

Her response came in breaths, as if they were her last. "Hum, yes, certainly, certainly yes, yes, of course." She looked at her friend and it seemed someone had already put the white make up on the clown. He stood there, no posture, weak, waiting for the cannon to send him to early retirement. She handed the notebook over as they walked to the head of the line. "All here and accounted for."

"Wonderful, let's count off."

Mrs. Stout waved her hand and nodded her head at Mary May. Mary May thought she looked like The Queen of England giving a final decree.

"One, two, three, four . . ." Mr. Hawthorn smiled and nodded at each student as he double checked the list. "Eleven, twelve, thirteen, fourteen . . ." Mrs. Stout was looking Gerald in the eye and fumbling to find her nonexistent necklace. "Fifteen, sixteen . . ."

"Arrgh-skewah-skewah!" Mrs. Stout blasted a sneeze that could be heard across the school yard. "Eighteen, nineteen, twenty, twenty one!" The last four numbers were said so quickly that they sounded like one word. "Oh, heavens me, this dust, excuse me." She looked at Mr. Johnson, and she had scared the color back into his face. He was flushed with relief.

Mr. Hawthorn, on the other hand, was quite pale. Mrs. Stout had planted a scream in his left ear that could raise the dead. Mary May was looking over shoulder at her competition. In her sneezing fit she had kicked dust all over his white shoes, and some had settled in the cuffs of his pants.

She returned the smile, looking at him with her head tilted to one side like before. She began fingering for the missing necklace again. "It must be spring allergies. Don't you think?"

Mr. Hawthorn wasn't sure what she said. "Very well, nice job, continue as you were."

He turned back to his car and it happened. It came out from the window of the girl's bathroom. There was gasping and banging noises. Mr. Hawthorn had regained his hearing and stopped dead in his tracks. Mrs. Stout looked at Mr. Johnson. The students looked at the window. Mr. Hawthorn looked at Mrs. Stout. They knew Vinni Davis was about to step on to the stage. There was another knock from the other side of the window, then a faint cry.

"Help, I'm burning."

Mr. Hawthorn's eyebrows lowered into a vee and he looked at Mr. Johnson. "What was that, coming from the school? Was someone left behind?" His voice had regained the tone of a drill sergeant from years earlier. He looked at the window again.

"Help . . ."

"Arrgh-skewah-skewah." This time Mrs. Stout didn't even pretend to be sneezing. She looked like a bull dog attacking an intruder. She leaned a little closer to his ear with each outburst and didn't give in until he was trotting to his car.

"Help, I'm burning."

"Skewah-skewah-skewah!"

Mr. Johnson had the students filing back into the school, passing by him at the side steps. Mrs. Stout stood beside him, receiving odd glances from fellow teachers as they passed. "What are you going to do about Giovanni?"

Mr. Johnson looked straight ahead and whispered, "Let 'em burn."

"Are all students accounted for, Mrs. Pratt?" She was just writing the final figures down.

"Yes, all accounted for."

"Can you step into my office, please?"

Mrs. Pratt entered the office and sat in an armless chair. She had a bad experience in a student's chair at the lunch room. She preferred a sturdy oak chair with no arms and no casters. "As you probably know, we had a little problem with Vinni this morning. I was wondering if you had any ideas about discipline. I am always willing to hear a fresh point of view."

Mrs. Pratt's barely visible eyes disappeared when she smiled. "Well, as a matter of fact, I have been thinking about what to do with Vinni."

Understanding Neighbors

Tom and Margaret had spoken with Jake Thursday night. "Yes. I know we have planned this weekend for a long time and we know how excited you've been. Please hear me out."

Tom hated to disappoint Jake and hoped he would decide on the side of compassion instead of logic. "I realize Edna May is very difficult to work for and you have never declined. I also know what a mess her yard is in and she needs your help." Tom was trying to talk reason into his adolescent son.

"I know she needs my help and I always help her. But why tomorrow? Can't I do it next weekend, or after school next week? Please, daddy?"

Tom and Margaret didn't want to tell him why it was so urgent. They looked at each other and knew they had to tell Jake. Margaret put her hand on Tom's shoulder, presenting a united front. "Jake, dear, Gary is coming home on Saturday."

Jake's angry eyebrows relaxed into compassion. "Oh." Even Jake knew how Edna and Mary were affected by Gary's visits.

"Jake, we can reschedule everything for next weekend, the skiing, the party, the cook out and the fireworks. I feel sure everyone will still be available and they will understand.

The decision is yours and we won't try to change your mind either way."

Jake was still unbalanced by the news of Gary's return and hadn't really listened to the last sentence. "When did they find out?"

Margaret released a heavy sigh. "Just yesterday evening. Edna has been in a whirlwind trying to get everything perfect. I can only imagine what Mary May is going through."

Jake just stared at his father's desk. "That must have been why Mary was in such a fix at school today. Yeah, sure, I'll help her, no problem, really. Does she need me to come over now?"

Tom looked up from his chair to Margaret, who was standing beside him, and then across the desk to Jake. "Thank you, Jake. I promise to make your birthday party even more special next weekend. Listen, I have seen her yard and it's in a horrible mess. Why don't you see if you can get some help? I'm sure if your friends know what's up they'll be glad to help. Oh, when you talk to them, tell them the party will be next weekend. Not just on Saturday, but all weekend. We will leave as soon as school is out and not be back until Sunday night. I promise I'll make this up to you Jake." Margaret was rubbing Tom's back silently, but he heard every word in her heart. He heard how proud she was of Jake, how much she loved him and how concerned she was for the Crutchfields.

"Hello, Mary?" Jake wasn't sure who answered the phone. Mary's voice was weak, like an old woman's. "Oh, hey this is Jake. Listen, tell your mom that I'll be over in about half an hour and I'm bringing some help. We'll have your yard perfect in no time. Okay, well, anyway, see you later. Bye."

Jake had put the word out like a secret smoke signal and all the guys were ready to work. They were old enough to remember hearing comments about Gary Crutchfield for years. No one talked to them about what went on, but they could see it in Mary's eyes. They called themselves The Tribe. It was a name that started on the playground in third grade and held true through the years. They met two blocks from Old Davis road, carrying shovels, rakes, pruners and even an old sheet to collect leaves on.

Strength was in their numbers. It was time to be men. They all had a secret hatred for Gary and their chosen weapons for battle were garden tools. The work crew consisted of Charlie, Tom, David, and Gerald, who was now called Eighteen. Vinni had asked Roy to help.

Mary May heard a rumbling noise and looked out the oval window in the attic. From high on her perch she saw warriors on bicycles, holding their gardening weapons high and sounding the tribal war cry. They pumped their pedals furiously to the edge of the battlefield. Each boy raised his garden tool toward the oval window and shouted in a single voice, "The Tribe has arrived and we are ready to battle."

Mary May Crutchfield looked down from the attic window and began to cry. She remembered the first time she heard the battle cry. She was stuck on top of the monkey bars during third grade recess and the same boys had rushed from behind a shrubbery hedge to hold her captive.

Getting Ready

"Eloise, quick I need a permanent!" Edna had just burst into Eloise's Beauty Shop with no appointment. "Hurry, I only have two hours. I need a cut too and maybe a color. Yes I need a color, like the one in movie magazine. I know it's around here somewhere."

Edna was darting around the shop picking up magazine piles from the coffee table and the table between the dryers. Velma was under the dryer and could see Edna was in a twitch, but didn't know why. She was looking at a Movie magazine and Edna jerked it from her hands and looked at the cover. "No, that's not the one." She flopped it back down in Velma's lap, angry like it was Velma's fault that she couldn't find the magazine she was looking for.

Velma lifted the hood on her dryer and sat on the edge of the red vinyl chair. "What on earth is wrong with you Edna?"

Edna had spotted a poster on the wall. The ladies' hairstyle was similar t the on in the movie magazine. She pointed at the wall shaking her finger nervously. "That one Eloise. That'll do. Just give me that."

Eloise stopped putting rollers in Ruth Green's hair. Ruth was on the edge of the stylist chair with one foot on the red and white linoleum floor, the other resting on the silver metal foot rest. "Edna, please. What on earth is wrong?"

She stood up wearing the black plastic cape and walked over to Edna. She was staring at the poster on the wall and her hands were trembling. Velma had spun around and turned the large black button on the dryer to the off position. As the roar from the dryer slowed Edna started shaking her head from side to side and her shoulders slumped in exhaustion. She inhaled, and the dreaded truth floated on her breath as she exhaled. "Gary's coming home."

Eloise looked across at Velma and sent a silent message so Edna wouldn't hear. "Oh no."

"Here, honey, take my seat." Ruth turned Edna's shoulders toward the empty chair and started taking out the black bristled curlers that covered half her head. "Here, Edna, now Eloise will fix you right up. Right, Eloise? I think you're right. The do on the poster is perfect, cut, color and all."

Eloise was shaking her head, first up and down then side to side. "Yeah, oh yeah. As a matter of fact, Clairol sent me a sample color with that poster. I thought, well who in the world would I ever be able to use that color on? There aren't many movie stars in here." She threw up her hands, gave a nervous laugh and motioned for the other ladies to join in.

Ruth added her support. "Oh law, Eloise, if you give her that style I'll never be able to walk down the street with her. She will look just like a movie star!" She handed Eloise a handful of pink plastic pins she had removed and started taking her rollers out. "Hand me one of those new round brushed, I think I'll be just fine." Ruth was plunging the brush into her brunette hair and pulling her head to one side as she turned the brush under and out. "I just can't wait to see how it turns out." She was looking across the top of Edna's head into the mirror and saw the tears rolling down her cheeks. Ruth stopped patting her hair and put her hand on Edna's shoulder. "Now, what can I do for you? Do you have a grocery list or laundry to be picked up?"

Ruth had been Edna's best friend since grammar school. There was nothing she didn't know about her best friend and some things she wished she didn't know. Gary had always been rough around the edges and came from a family with an alcoholic father. Edna had assumed that things would be different if Gary had a family of his own. A family he could be proud of with an unstressful life. She knew how harsh Edna could be, even to her best friend, but she understood her pain and refused to stop being her friend.

"Oh, Ruth, would you please? I need to stop by the dry cleaners and pick up some things, they should be ready. Just tell Harry you're picking up my things and put them on my account."

Edna had dried her eyes and was regaining composure as she regained control. "They have my best silk dress, our sheets and a few of Mary's clothes. Oh, and my linen tablecloth and napkins. I asked Harry to please fold my dress, the hangers he uses always leaves a bump on the shoulders. I know he tries, but most people don't have silk and he doesn't know how it's done."

Ruth gave a sigh of relief knowing that Edna was getting back on track. "Absolutely, no problem. I'll drop them at your house this afternoon. Anything else? What about your groceries?"

Eloise had Edna laying back, scrubbing her head in the sink. "No, that's all. I have to get the groceries myself. I'm buying some special items and you wouldn't know where to look. It would take you forever. I have to talk to the butcher anyway. He needs to cut me a standing rib roast. I know you mean well, darling, but that's okay. Just the dry cleaners."

Edna's head was shaking under Eloise's massaging fingers. "Oh, yes you can, I almost forgot. Patsy is fixing a centerpiece for the dining room table. You can pick that up. But be careful not to break any stems. Lord knows I paid a fortune for it."

Velma turned her hair dryer back on, rolled her eyes and shook her head. Ruth dashed out the door without spraying her hair and Eloise took her frustration out on Edna's scalp. "Good Lord, Eloise, calm down. I want some hair left to color!"

Yard Work

The Tribe had broken Edna's yard into quadrants. Jake took the front yard by himself. He thought it was his responsibility for first impressions. The front yard was the smallest and mostly trimming shrubs was involved.

Charlie and Eighteen took the left side of the house. The shrubs didn't need much attention because the shade from the maple tree kept them from overgrowing. It was mostly picking up limbs and raking leaves away from the wrought iron fence that ran down the left side of the property.

Vinnie and Roy had the back yard. It was the largest part of the project, but couldn't be seen from the street. There was a large lawn, perfectly flat and green. It had been cleared when the Ellingtons had a formal garden designed for their daughter's wedding. There was a fountain in the middle, resting in a circular koi pond. The spring flowers were just starting to break through. Daffodil leaves were popping up through the layer of leaves that had blown up last fall. The far back of the yard was anchored by five large magnolia trees. The dogwoods and redbuds were just opening up, with their blooms squeezing between the dark green magnolias. The rectangular back yard was bordered on both sides with Crepe Myrtles that rose above Camilla hedges that desperately needed pruning.

Tom and David had the right side yard under control. It was the same size as the left side, also having maple trees and a wrought iron fence. Mostly raking was needed there, but not as much. The driveway and garage were on their side.

Mary May walked from window to window, watching The Tribe as they worked. She wondered if they were her friends or had she alienated them forever? The thought that they knew about her father was deep in her mind. She had worked for years to keep Gary out of her heart and was very successful. Now she intended to drive him from her mind.

"Vinni!" Mary stuck her head out the utility room door on the back of the house. "I'll bring ya'll some Cokes." She popped back inside and trotted to the kitchen. There was a carton of ten ounce Cokes in the refrigerator on the bottom shelf. She grabbed them and headed out the front door.

"Jake, here's some Cokes." She sat on the bottom of the porch steps and started opening them. As the others came from the sides and back of the house, she handed each one a Coke. Vinni got the last one just as Roy came around the corner.

He handed Roy the last Coke. "Here, I like Pepsi. Got any Pepsis, Mary May?"

Mary noticed the mistake. "Oh, I think so, come in and see." Vinni trotted up the steps and through the front door with an oval frosted glass. Mary heard the door close behind Vinni and realized they were alone. As they walked down the central hall and past the stairs, she could hear his footsteps echo on the wooden floors and then disappear across the oriental rugs. She was

135

suddenly a ball of nerves and could only speak between quick breaths.

"Oh, yeah, we have some Pepsis under the sink, but they're hot." Vinni grabbed one from the lower cabinet. "That's okay, I don't mind. Got an opener?"

Mary turned and fumbled through the drawer she had been leaning against. She handed the opener to Vinni without looking. Their fingers touched with the transfer and Mary gasped. It was the first time they had ever touched. Over the years they had been within fractions of an inch time and time again, but never touched.

They failed to hear Edna's tires crunching across the gravel as she drove up. The sound of her car door slamming jerked their attention.

"Mary, Mary May, Mary May Crutchfield." Her mother's voice grew closer and louder with each shout. "What in the world is going on here?" She was bolting up the back steps. "What are those boys doing here?" They heard the screen door squeak open and slam shut. "There's a colored boy outside Mary, a colored!" She entered the kitchen looking at the floor, shaking her head in disappointment. "What on Earth will people think?"

She looked up and saw Mary May and Giovanni standing there, still holding the Pepsi bottle together. They looked like a picture caught in time and painted on a Norman Rockwell magazine cover. The gasp that Edna inhaled seemed to suck the last bit of air from the room.

"You! What are you doing here? Out, out, out!" She was throwing her arm toward the front door and shaking her finger. "Mary May Crutchfield, what on Earth are you doing? Alone with a yard full of boys and a colored Mary, a colored!"

Ruth had just arrived and was struggling to get out of the car without letting the enormous flower arrangement tilt and break a stem. Roy saw her dilemma, raced around to open the passenger door and hold the flowers until she trotted around to retrieve them.

"Oh my goodness, thank you! Thank you ever so much." She trotted around the front of her car to the passenger's side.

"Yes, ma'am". Roy stepped aside as she picked up the flowers.

"Damnit, damnit, damnit!" Ruth couldn't help herself. She had safely transported the flowers all the way from town and broke the crowning rose bud when she was taking it out of the car.

"She's going to have a hissy fit over this one, I can tell you that. Well, what does she expect?" She looked straight at Roy. "Have you ever seen such a monstrosity?"

"No, ma'am. Here, let me get the door for you. Watch your step now." Roy's hands were hovering underneath the arrangement as Ruth felt her way up the front steps. Roy was reaching for the doorknob when they heard Edna's screams and Vinni's footsteps approaching the double front doors. "Better open 'em both. I don't want to break anymore off."

As Roy was opening the right door, Vinni was opening the left door. In a grand gesture, the enormous arrangement appeared in front of Edna. Roy stepped inside and Vinni stepped back, giving Ruth room to enter. The sight overwhelmed Edna and she completely forgot the rampage she was on.

"Oh my word, ah, well I have never, just look at those flowers, my word."

Ruth's arms were starting to quiver under the strain. "Okay, Edna, okay, can't stand here forever, not your pack mule. Where do I put 'em?".

Edna regained her composure and shook her finger at the dining room. "Oh, in here on the dining room table."

Ruth shuffled her feet off the Oriental rug onto the hardwood dining room floors. "Don't scratch the table!" Ruth slowly sat the arrangement down. The brass feet that supported the cut crystal bowl had felt bottoms so it slid easily and safely to the center.

Edna exhaled and crossed her hands over her heart. "Oh, Ruth, it's . . .". She stopped and squinted her eyes. "Broken! It's broken." Edna was staring at the broken rose bud dangling at the top of the arrangement.

Vinni saw Ruth turning white and Edna turning red. "Excuse me, Ruth."

Vinni stepped by her side to the dining room table. Everyone was too shocked to react as Vinni took the toothpick from his mouth. He stood on his tip toes and stretched across the table, inserting the toothpick down through the center of the rose bud into the stem it dangled from. Everyone watched in amazement at his skill, except Mary who could only stare at his tight butt. "There, good as new. If you have problems with blooms drooping, a hat pin will work, too."

Vinni stepped back and out of the dining room. "Excuse me, Ruth."

Roy nodded his head toward Edna May. "Ma'am."

The two young gentlemen stepped outside and closed the front doors they had just opened.

The Tribe gathered outside were as shocked as the ladies gathered inside. Vinni saw Eighteen grinning and knew he couldn't stop what he was about to say. "Damn, didn't know you were a florist, ma'am." Vinni had no response and laughter ended the conversation.

They had finished their Cokes and were picking up their garden tools when they heard it. The sound turned them toward the house. It sounded like the house was screaming; it belted from every open window.

"What were you thinking? Do you know what you looked like? A common whore, Mary May, a common whore."

"But they were helping, Mama, and they were thirsty. I just gave them something to drink." Mary's words were faint, but as loud as she could make them.

"Edna, please, everything's fine. Just let it go, look how wonderful everything looks. Gary will be so pleased at what you've done."

"Those were his Cokes she gave her little gang of boys!" Edna had turned her anger into hysteria and there was no calming her. "And a colored, Mary May, a colored. I told you I better never see that Giovanni Davis around you and what did I walk in on? It's a good thing I walked in when I did. You, here alone with a yard full of boys, and one in the house. What if your father had driven up? What do you think would have happened if your father had driven up? Do you know what would have happened?"

"I'm sorry, Mama. I'm sorry".

Edna's hysteria had flooded over Mary and she was out of control. "A colored, Mary May, a colored."

"Come on, we'll go get some more Cokes." Ruth's left arm was wrapped around Mary, supporting her as they went down the front steps and to the car.

They passed The Tribe on their bicycles as they slowly headed to town. Mary was too embarrassed to look up. They were too embarrassed to look her way.

Help For Edna May

Ruth and Mary pulled into Green's Grocery parking lot beside George Davis's truck. "Let's get those Cokes and then we'll have some ice cream. Lord knows I've had a day of it." Ruth smiled at Mary and jumped out of the car. They walked through the glass doors and turned to the right. Lidia and George were in the produce department looking at lettuce and carrots.

"Lidia, George, hello." Ruth waved her hand in the air to get their attention. Any visit without drama would be a welcome one today. "Listen, Mary May, you don't have to drag around with me. Just go and look at the magazines for a while. Go ahead and pick one out, my treat. Then we'll have some ice cream." Mary nodded and Ruth could she was in better spirits as she walked to the magazine isle.

"Well, didn't expect to see you here, Ruth." George didn't expect to see anyone at Green's, because he never shopped there.

"Oh, Lidia, have you heard? Well I'm sure you have, since Giovanni was helping." Ruth looked at George, hoping to gain a man's sympathy. She lowered her voice to a whisper and looked around while she spoke. "Well, Gary Crutchfield is due home tomorrow and Edna's about to have a pure breakdown. Those boys were over helping a while ago. Giovanni was there, he's some boy. Well, when Edna got home, excuse my language, all hell broke loose. I've seen her bad before, but not like this. I'm worried, I am, I'm really worried." She continued the saga in a whisper, hoping for some understanding. By the time she had finished telling the whole ordeal, she was out of breath and tired.

Lidia's thoughts were with Mary more than Edna, but she was concerned for them both. "Poor Edna, she drives me crazy, always has, you know that Ruth, but she deserves better than this. I can't blame the boys for leaving; no one should have to listen to that. I don't think I would have stayed either, but I do hope her yard work gets done. Ruth, what time is it?"

Ruth glanced at the large clock hanging in the meat department. "Six twenty two, why?"

"Listen, when you get Mary May back home, please tell Edna that some neighbors wanted to give Gary a welcome home gift and we will be over soon."

Ruth looked at George and George looked at Lidia. There was only one welcome home gift the community would like to give Gary Crutchfield.

"Please, just leave everything to me. Let's go George." George shrugged his shoulders at Ruth and followed Lidia's quick steps out the door.

"Mary Dear, gotcha' magazine? Good, I think I want a double chocolate cone. What about you?"

Ruth was so nervous on the drive back to Old Davis Road that she was biting and pecking at her ice cream, instead of licking it. Mary May watched her attacking her treat then looked up at her wild, half done hair. Ruth had completely forgotten that her hair hadn't been fixed and it was growing wilder and bushier by the second.

The evening humidity didn't help, neither did the wind blowing through the car window.

They pulled up to Edna's. Ruth reached into the back seat and grabbed the Cokes. She was talking to Mary with her teeth holding the ice cream cone. "I'll take these to the kitchen. You just go upstairs and enjoy that magazine." Mary went straight up the stairs. Ruth walked down the hall and turned right into the kitchen.

What she saw made her heart sink. She sat the Cokes down on the counter beside the grocery bag and took the ice cream cone from her mouth. Edna had started unpacking her groceries and only half finished. There on the counter was the empty bag that held the roast and another bag full of groceries. Another small bag was on the floor. This was not like Edna May. Ruth picked up the empty paper bag with red soaking through the bottom and knocked over the medicine bottle. Edna rarely used the pills and Ruth knew exactly how many belonged in the bottle. Her fingers were shaking as she unscrewed the cap. She had taken two, only two. Her doctor had given her permission to take half a pill, only when necessary. Ruth was somehow relieved she had only taken two.

"No, she will be fine, but make sure she doesn't take any more." Dr. Duncan had eased Ruth's worries when he answered her phone call. "She will be out cold for several hours, probably until morning, but I expect she needs the rest. Do me a favor, will you, Ruth? Take the other pills out of the bottle and put them in a safe place. Write a note for her to call me and put it in the bottle. Give her my office and home numbers. Here they are."

Ruth was putting the last of the groceries away and heard a knock on the door. "We're here to help get things ready for tomorrow. I know how difficult Edna May can be, and we don't want to force the issue. Could you talk to her while we get started?" Lidia's brown eyes were full of worry and sincerity.

"Oh, Lord, honey, she took a couple of nerve pills and she's out till the morning. A train running through the house wouldn't wake her up. Bless your heart." Ruth couldn't hold back the tears when she looked over Lidia's shoulder into the front yard.

It was ten thirty and Ruth climbed the stairs with her last burst of energy. She slowly opened Edna's bedroom door to make sure she was all right. She saw that she was okay, better than okay.

Edna was resting on her antique walnut bed like a princess. Her small frame was barely enough to dent the down comforter that she rested on. Her ivory silk sleeping mask matched her night gown and the room smelled like lilac blossoms. The opposite wall held a bay of open windows that almost touched the floor, looking down across the formal lawn. The room was as fresh and clean as a cloud, right down to the silver julep cup on her bedside table, holding white roses. Ruth had never seen her more beautiful, not as homecoming queen or a bride, or even a new mother. The poster on the wall at Eloise's earlier that day was no comparison. There was nothing to compare.

"Sweet dreams, honey." Ruth silently closed the door. She checked on Mary May, turned her light out and made her exhausted way down the stairs and to her car.

"I hope everything goes okay tomorrow." Lidia was resting her head on George's chest and running her fingers across his stomach. His hand was resting in her black hair and his fingers were massaging her scalp. Lidia continued. "Was she always like this?"

George took a deep breath and relaxed. "She's always been dramatic, but not as bad as this. I think something happened to her that summer I came to Italy. I don't know what it was. She seemed different after that."

Lidia held George a little tighter. "Something did happen that summer you came to Italy."

Lidia picked up his hand and kissed his palm, and he kissed her forehead. Their tired bodies wouldn't give strength for passionate sex that night. Making love was softer and they rocked to sleep in each other's arms.

APRIL 24TH 1948

The Big Day

Vinni's alarm clock woke him at five o'clock, just like every other day. Saturdays and Sundays had no respect for the farm. He noticed how tired and sore he was from the work they did at Edna's yesterday. His thoughts went to Mary May; he was concerned for her. What would that day hold for her and Edna?

He pulled on his jeans that were on the floor beside his bed, then the socks that they covered. He heard the screen door close as George left for the barn. He always liked the morning, the sunrise was always soft. His body just naturally rose with the sun, even when he was away from home.

"Vinni, do you want a bite before you milk?" Lidia had asked the same question every morning since he started helping at the barn. She always got up with George, but was the first to the kitchen. The answer was always the same. For the past four years, Vinni had walked to the barn without eating. Today was different.

"Yeah, I think so."

Lidia didn't expect the response that floated down the stairs and wasn't prepared to fix anything. She took a quick breath with intentions of asking what he wanted, then caught herself and exhaled. Lidia's eyes floated around the kitchen and her mind floated back to Italy. She remembered her mother asking her the same question when she was getting ready to tend the goats in the morning. Lidia didn't have to decide what to do, her mother spoke to her heart.

Vinni had finished brushing his teeth and the minty smell of the toothpaste was cut by the aroma rising from the kitchen. It was unfamiliar, wonderful, but different. It was a little like a cake baking, but not as strong or sweet. The sweetness didn't smell like sugar and there was a woodsy aroma. He couldn't imagine what his mama had fixed. He started to go down, but stopped at the top of the stairs and waited. He didn't want to spoil her surprise. He could hear her humming and opening drawers and clicking dishes that were usually reserved for Sunday dinner.

"There, oh, it's wonderful, thank you, Mama."

Vinni heard his mama talking to herself and could envision her hands rubbing across her apron as she gave a final inspection.

"Vinni, dear, it's ready."

His wait at the top of the stairs was finally over and she heard him trotting down instead of shuffling, like other mornings. He turned the corner into the kitchen and there she stood, waiting to serve him. The table was set for one. His placemat was a gift from her aunt on her wedding day; the white plate was an everyday vessel. It held the hand painted bowl that George bought her outside the café where they had their first lunch together.

"It's Greek yogurt, but we don't like to give them credit for it." Lidia's smile broke into a grin, like she was a school girl giving away a treasured secret.

The yogurt was almost as thick as cream cheese and topped with a warm, crunchy granola. Lidia had toasted some oatmeal and coarse bread crumbs from a day old loaf of bread. While they were toasting, she browned some pecans in butter, and added a little brown sugar just as they were starting to roast. A banana was sliced on top of the yogurt and then the warm granola. The treat was finished with two large spoonfuls of honey. This new morning aroma rose with the familiar smell of hot chocolate.

Vinni was shoveling in the breakfast, knowing his daddy was waiting for him at the barn. "Man, this is good. How did you make it again?"

Lidia was leaning against the counter with her arms crossed, tilting her head to one side, watching him shovel in the food. "I'll write it down." Her words came out with a smile. She would write it down and in the years to come she would write down many more. It was a new day.

A New Woman

"Oh Lord, oh my, well, let's see. What time is it?" Edna was still in bed with her satin beauty mask on, patting her hands across the covers hoping to find the answers to her question. She sat straight up with her mask still on. She lifted one corner, tilted her head to the right and looked at the clock. "Eight fifteen!"

Her scream woke Mary May up and within seconds they were standing on the balcony overlooking the foyer. "Okay, okay we're fine. No problems today, ladies." Edna's hands were floating around her head like she was conducting an orchestra. "Nooo problem."

"Mama?" Mary didn't follow with a question, that was the question. She didn't recognize the lady standing in front of her. Yesterday's turmoil hadn't given her time to see her mother. "Mama?" Mary just stared at her mother.

Edna's hands remained in the air, but stood still. "Yes, dear, I'm Mama!"

Mary May took a long look at the new woman standing in front of her. Then she whispered, "You look like a movie star."

Edna whispered back. "Well, maybe I am. Now let's just see what needs to be done today. Shall we?"

Mary watched Edna spin around and float back through her bedroom door. She was afraid to move, afraid it was a dream and she would wake up.

"Hellooo." Ruth enjoyed a much needed rest and didn't expect a phone call this early. Her heart sank when she realized who was calling. "Oh, Mary. How are things, you poor dear? Can I do anything to help? I know your mama was in a terrible fix yesterday." Ruth was shaking her head and her eyebrows were drawn with worry. "Now what? Wait a minute. Can you speak up, honey?" Mary was whispering, afraid her mama would hear the conversation. "She did what? I know she's gorgeous. She said what? Yes, I know it really looks good on her. She's doing what? I don't know, Eloise said it was a free sample, came with the poster. Are you sure, can you actually see her or just hear her? Oh my Lord, honey! I'll be right over. Now tell me again. She said what? About Gary? She doesn't have one does she? Lord, honey, I'm on my way."

Mary hung the phone up and watched Edna walk out the front door. She was still in her nightgown. The morning sun was in her eyes, so she pulled her sleeping mask over one eye and continued, slowly, down the steps. Her hands were floating from side to side as she walked up the drive to get the morning paper. She bent her knees apart, squatted down and picked up the paper. The plastic was still wet with dew and she held it with two fingers, shaking while she turned back to the house. The sun was behind her when she looked up and saw her house. "Oop!" It sounded like she had seen a mouse. She wasn't sure what she had seen, it looked unfamiliar. Edna tilted her head back and peered through her half covered eye in disbelief. After blinking a few times, she reached up and removed the sleeping mask. The morning paper fell by her right foot and her sleeping mask by her left. She looked at her house the same way Mary had looked at her only a few minutes ago. She was afraid to move, fearing it was a dream and she would wake up.

"Oh my, my oh my, well. How in the world?" The memory of the previous day came rushing back to Edna May and she began to cry. Her tears came out of gratitude, out of shame, out of exhaustion and out of pride. She stood in the driveway sobbing when Mary May stepped into the open door.

She saw her mother shaking with tears and Ruth's car driving down Old Davis Road behind her. Mary was frozen. She didn't know if it was the fear or relief that had her bolted to the Oriental rug in the foyer, but she couldn't move. Ruth pulled into the drive and dashed to Edna's side.

"What is it, Edna? Are you okay, darling? Everything's fine now, just fine, now you just calm down and come on in, honey." Ruth picked up the paper and mask and started to guide Edna's elbow toward the house. She wouldn't budge. It was like moving a statue.

Edna was staring at her house and whispering the same thing over and over. "It's so beautiful. It's just beautiful. It's so beautiful."

"What's that?" Ruth was using a very soothing voice; she knew Edna must be a loose cannon.

"The house, Ruth, the house." Edna lifted her hand and pointed her perfectly manicured finger at her house.

"Okay, now . . .". Then Ruth looked at the Victorian house for the first time. She was turned to stone standing beside her best friend, speechless and breathless. "Oh, oh, oh." The only sounds she could make were from the air entering her lungs in gasps as she inhaled. Ruth was finally able to take a deep breath and spoke. "Edna May Crutchfield, you have the most beautiful home I've ever seen." She stepped to the side and looked at Edna. "And you are the most beautiful woman I have ever seen."

Leave Everything to Me

The day before when Ruth had seen George and Lidia in Green's grocery, Lidia said, "Leave everything to me." This seemed like a lifetime ago, but it was all coming back.

Lidia had called all their friends and neighbors and explained the situation. Everyone was on Edna's lawn within an hour. Tom and Margaret arrived with outdoor furniture they had bought for their lake house, along with hanging baskets from their sunroom.

Ed and Velma brought white paint and ladders to freshen up the columns and scroll work on the front porch. Hurley and Daisy White stopped by Green's Grocery and bought all the bedding plants they had. Steve and Fay Duncan loaned the pair of antique cast iron English urns from their front gate. Velma Stout and Frank Johnson loaded his pickup with geraniums being grown by the agriculture class for a fund raiser.

Patsy's Florist had been overrun with flowers. Mr. Holt wasn't expected to live past Wednesday morning and the entire community had ordered funeral arrangements. Mr. Holt made a miraculous recovery, leaving Patsy with a bounty to donate. Mr. Holt's grandson drove him over to watch the others work. The Tribe even returned to the battlefield.

It had taken Ruth almost fifteen minutes to get Edna to the kitchen. "All those people were here yesterday?" Edna May was struggling to take in everything Ruth was telling her.

"Yes, Edna, your yard looked like something being set up to shoot a movie. I have never seen so many people work so hard and so fast, and with such giving hearts. Even those boys, Edna, everyone came back."

Edna looked across her coffee cup at Ruth in amazement. "And all Lidia said was, 'Leave everything to me'?"

"Yes, that's all she said. I didn't ask her to do a thing and had no idea what she had in mind."

"Excuse me a minute, Ruth." Edna got up and walked into the front hall where the phone sat on a little oak table with tobacco twist legs. Ruth couldn't make out everything being said, but knew something grand was being planned.

"Hello, Lidia. Good morning, dear, it's Edna. Edna Crutchfield. Yes. No, it's Edna Crutchfield, dear. I need you to do me a favor. I hate to ask, but it is terribly important. Oh, thank you, yes, in about ten minutes. See you then."

Ruth heard the receiver click down and sat back in her chair, pretending not to be listening. "I have one more call to make, Ruth, then I'll be right with you."

"Okay, take your time."

Ruth thought she might be able to hear better from the dining room and walked through the double doors, pretending to check the flower arrangement.

"Hello, Eloise? Thank you so much for yesterday, you did an outstanding job. Edna, Edna May!" It was getting a little aggravating having to tell her best friends who she was. "Listen I need a favor. I know how busy you are and I wouldn't ask if it wasn't an emergency. It's Ruth, she needs some work. Um, hum, well, it is. Oh, so you understand. Well the closest thing I can think of is a werewolf."

Ruth had completely forgotten about her hair and gasped as her hands flew to her head.

"Thank you, Eloise. I'll tell her." Edna May gently placed the phone back and floated toward the kitchen. Ruth tried to beat Edna back to the breakfast table. She ran across the dining room rug and tip toed across the wooden floor.

"Oh, there you are. Eloise had a cancellation. She said you can pop right over."

Ruth was a little put off the werewolf comment. "No. I think I'll be fine. I'll just wait till next week." Her lips were pursed and her head was bobbing from side to side.

Edna looked at her closest friend. "Honey, I'm not even sure you can wait 'til you get to Eloise, never mind next week!" They were both holding back giggles. "I just hope you don't get caught out with a full moon."

Their laughter shot from their toes and burst through every open window in the house. Edna May Crutchfield's house had spoken once again and this time it was joyful.

Ruth was turning off Old Davis Road just as Lidia was turning on. Ruth leaned out her window and waved Lidia to a stop. When she was trotting around to her window, she could tell Lidia was concerned and a little scared.

"Oh, Lidia, I know you must be confused. Listen, I have to tell you in a hurry. I have to get to an appointment. Remember, Edna took those pills yesterday evening and she was out cold? Well, evidently, they had a real effect on her. She's light as a feather and sweet as a lamb."

Lidia was listening, but couldn't stop staring at her hair.

"She's a different person, but I don't know how long it'll take for the medicine to wear off. If something happens and she goes wacko again, just get Mary and leave, fast as you can. I just don't know what to expect. Better get down there while there's still some good left in the ol' girl. I'll be back soon as I'm done at Eloise's."

"Oh, Eloise's, good!" The words popped out before Lidia could stop them.

"I know, I know." Ruth was rolling her eyes and shaking her head. "It's a long story, tell you later. Listen, have fun, 'gotta go."

Lidia pulled up to Edna's house and was pleased how it looked in the morning sun. She had seen it finished the night before, but it was wonderful this morning. She was admiring everything as she strolled up the walk to the front steps. The fresh coat of paint gave a crisp contrast to the flowers. It was a place anyone would love to be. She rang the doorbell and was looking over her shoulder at the porch when Edna opened the door.

"Lidiaaaaa!" She threw her hands in the air and rushed Lidia with open arms. "Oh, dear, how can I ever thank you?" Her cheek was resting on Lidia's shoulder and the words shot straight into her ear. She stepped back and held Lidia's hand. "No one but you could have done this. You are the most amazing person I have ever met. Now come in, I need your help."

Lidia was flabbergasted at the welcome and didn't move. "Come on, come on." Edna was trotting across the foyer waving her hand for Lidia to follow.

"Edna, you look amazing, I love your hair. Did Eloise do that?"

She turned to Lidia without slowing down. "Yes. Can you believe it? That lady has real potential, just no opportunities. I just love it. Here, have a seat." She patted the breakfast table and nodded for Lidia to sit across from her. "I can't thank you and all the neighbors enough for what you did yesterday evening and last night. You will never know, you'll just never know. Well, here's the deal. I have all this food to cook for Gary." She was resting her elbow on the table and waved her hand in the air. "Why, I'll never know. Anyway, I want to throw a dinner party tonight for everyone who helped. I think I have enough food." She reached across and held Lidia's forearm. "But I need your help."

Lidia was nodding out of confusion and disbelief, and Edna took it for a yes.

"Oh, wonderful, just wonderful! Thank you. Here's what I thought. Let me know what you think."

Thank You for Helping

"Good Lord have mercy, child!" Eloise had seen the worst heads in the county walk in her beauty shop, but this was the worst of the worst.

"Damn, woman, what happened to you?" Eloise's husband, Lester Jenkins, had just walked in with his tool box. Eloise's pipes needed tending to.

Ruth snapped back. "Oh, Lester, don't you have a wrench to twist or something?"

Lester had known Ruth since grade school and they always joked with each other.

Eloise came to Ruth's defense. "Oh, hush, Lester, least she's got something to work with. How you think she would look with your comb over?"

Lester stood shaking his head. "Probably better than I'd look with that." He nodded his head at Ruth's savage hair and they burst out laughing, imagining the combination.

Lidia was sitting across from Edna May. She was confused and stunned by the latest developments and her responsibilities. "Well, everything sounds great to me and of course I'm glad to help. Let me run home for about an hour or so, then I'll be back and we can get started."

Lidia left Edna May's with a long list. She was talking to herself as she walked to the car.

"How in the world are we going to pull this one off? Dio, Dio, Dio!" She wished she was on Edna's medication. Reality wasn't the best place to be right now.

A Missed Phone Call

"Aunt Margaret, did you call Mother?" Genevieve was excited and anxious about the upcoming dance. She had made several plans with her aunt, but hadn't actually spoken to her mother.

"Yes, I called Thursday afternoon and invited them to spend the weekend. She said she thought so, but she had to talk to George. I'm sure everything's fine. I called this morning, but they had already left, or were working in the yard. I'll call back around lunch, maybe catch them in."

Genevieve was on the back terrace overlooking the stream, thumbing through fashion magazines. Margaret was just inside watering houseplants in the sunroom. "I hope it isn't too late to find a dress. Everyone in French class was talking about what they were wearing. Well, at least this way I know what not to buy. I wonder what mother would have worn to a spring dance in Italy?"

She stopped looking at the magazine and pulled the afghan around her shoulders. The morning breeze was cool and she missed being at home and working in the garden. Genevieve's illness had held her prisoner for several years and she was just starting to regain her freedom. She was picking her life up, one piece at a time. Today she would pick up her cool spring mornings on the farm. She could hear the stream roaring at the bottom of the hill. There had been a steady rain the evening before, and all night. The stream was running heavy, carrying the fresh water to Buffalo Creek. The sound and smell reminded her of home. She was in a different place and she loved it here. The sounds were different, but the spring air smelled the same.

"Can I call Mother at lunch?" She tilted her head backward so Margaret could hear.

"Sure, that would be a nice surprise." Margaret was walking back to the utility room to refill her brass watering can.

"I saw a science fiction movie last weekend with Carter Lindley. The office in the movie had an answering machine. That way, when the secretary was away from the desk, the machine would answer the call and take a message. Can you imagine? Wouldn't it be great if people had those at home? Or even in the office, for that matter."

Margaret walked back into the sunroom to finish watering her plants and Genevieve went back to her magazine.

What In the World Is Going On?

"I'll get it." Fay Duncan was downstairs in Steve's study, dusting his desk when the phone rang. "Hello? Oh, hello, Lidia. How are you this morning? I can barely move after last night and Steve is still in bed reading the paper. Well, you're welcome, we were glad to do it. Oh, no, no, that's fine. Really I'll get him."

Fay held the dust cloth over the receiver. "Steve, Lidia's on the phone. Can you pick up?" Fay listened until she heard Steve answer.

"Morning, Lidia. How are you this morning? You must be exhausted. I don't know how you do it. Oh, thanks. I don't feel like we did much at all, but everything looked great. I think, well, I know everyone had a good time."

Steve listened as Lidia explained Edna's call and her plans for the dinner party. "Steve, I don't know what to expect. She, well, we have this list of guests to call, a huge dinner to prepare and she seems to have completely forgotten that Gary is due home anytime. What in the world am I going to do? I was in total shock. I should have told her to enjoy her first week end with Gary and we would have a dinner party another weekend, maybe when she wasn't so busy. Dio, Dio, Dio. I've really stepped in it this time and it's a stinker."

Steve laughed at her comment. "Are you going to be alone with her all day?"

Lidia's eyes darted back and forth, trying to think. "I don't know. Well, maybe, let's see. Oh, Ruth, I'll get Ruth to help. Lord knows I'll need her help on several levels today. Yes, Ruth will be there. That way, I can do the running and she can stay with Edna. What about the way she's acting? Is this going to wear off any time soon? Do we need to give her more medicine? I don't want her out cold like she was yesterday evening and I sure don't want her like she was when the boys were over there. What in the world are we going to do, Steve?"

Steve was trying to remember the dosage on her prescription. He had given it to her last year when Gary was coming home for the weekend. It wasn't just to help her sleep, it was an antidepressant. This was why she was only to take half a pill. *Well,* he thought, *one thing's for sure; she isn't depressed.*

"One thing we need to do is keep her from getting over excited. What about Mary May? Is she at home? She is? Okay, maybe we can help with that. Fay and Mary Alice are going over to the Millhouses this afternoon. I'll get them to invite her. I'll see if Fay can run over and pick her up in a few minutes. When are you going back? Will Ruth be there, too? Okay, good. I think Ruth put her medicine up. Tell her not to let Edna know where it is. If Edna starts acting anxious like she was yesterday, yes, and violent, give her half a pill. You may have to crush it into a drink. I should be close to the phone all day. Call anytime. I think it would look suspicious if I stopped by."

Lidia gave a huge sigh and slumped in her chair at the breakfast table. "Thank you, Steve.

166

I don't know what I'd do without you. Well, I 'gotta go. Wish me luck. Oh, wait. I almost forgot. Can your family be at the dinner party tonight?"

Steve laughed. "We were going to a movie, but I wouldn't miss this for the world."

Lidia shook her head and rolled her eyes. "Really? I'd miss it for a quarter." They laughed their goodbyes.

Lidia finished packing her picnic basket with cooking necessities. Edna had suddenly developed a love of "those wonderful, delicious herbs you use all the time."

She left a note on the refrigerator:

Dinner Party at Edna's tonight.
7 sharp, see you here at 6, not before.
Tell Giovanni.
PRAY!!!

Lester's Wisdom

"Well, when I answered the phone I didn't know who it was. What in the world are you going to do, honey?" Eloise was just finishing Ruth's hair. "There, I gave you a little something extra in the back, since we're going to a dinner party. Look before I spray. That's my motto, keeps the customers happy." She handed Ruth a mirror and stepped aside so she could see the back of her hair in the large mirror.

"Oh, Eloise. Look at me. I look gooood!"

Lester was just finishing his work on the bathroom sink and walked into the room. "Now I been listening and heard the whole story about Edna. I have to say, that's pretty amazing. Just think. All these years everybody thought Edna May was a bitch. Turns out she was just under-medicated!"

"OOhhh, Lester!" Eloise and Ruth hooted and laughed until tears rolled down their cheeks. Lester was overcome with a coughing fit and had to sit down in the hair drying chair.

The three were just regaining their composure and taking deep breaths when the phone rang. Eloise picked up the receiver and exhaled. "Hello. Oh, Lidia, listen to what Lester just said." Their shoulders started shaking again in anticipation of Lester's revelation.

"What on Earth was so funny?" Edna was dashing around the kitchen when Lidia returned from her phone call to Eloise.

"Oh, something Lester said."

Edna waved her hands in the air. "I don't know how in the world she puts up with that man!"

Lidia was afraid the old Edna was creeping back in, but then Edna May let out the silliest giggle and Lidia knew she was safe for a while.

Getting Ready

"Hey Mrs. Crutchfield, is Mary in?" Fay had sent Mary Alice to the door instead of going herself.

Edna May's manicured finger pointed to the top of the stairs. "She's upstairs." Then she gave the sweetest call to her daughter. "Mary May, you got company!" Edna spun around and headed back to the kitchen. Mary Alice was left standing on the front porch, so she stepped inside and closed the door. She heard her friend walking down the stairs from the attic, then saw her walk across the balcony and head down the stairs.

"Hey Mary Alice. What's up?" Mary was relaxed and trying not to think about her father arriving later that evening.

Mary Alice looked down the hall to make sure Edna wasn't listening. "Did your mom tell you I called earlier?"

Mary May crossed her arms and rolled her eyes. She was getting tired of her mother being unpredictable. She answered with a negative nod.

"Oh well, she said it would be okay. Mom and I are going to see my grandparents for a while and wondered if you wanted to go. I think we're having lunch in town first. I called your mom earlier and she said it would be okay."

"Sure, I guess." Mary May shouted toward the kitchen. "Mama, is it okay if I go with the Duncans?"

Edna's cheerful answer came from the busy kitchen. "Of course, have a good time. Remember to be back in time to get ready for the diiiiiner partyyyyyy!" Edna tried to mimic an opera singer.

"Let's get out o' here." Mary took Alice's elbow and rushed her out the door.

Lidia, Edna and Ruth were elbow to elbow in the kitchen. Lidia was volunteering for anything to get her out of the room or even out of the house.

She was taking a verbal inventory of everything that was available. "I think I you have enough china, but I better count, and I'll have to get your grandmother's silver out. It's under the bed in the guest room. I can handle that. Dishes in the butler's pantry and silver upstairs. I have the list so I know what we need. I'll go ahead and put them in the dining room. Do you have a tablecloth?"

Edna's head popped up from the cookbook. "Tablecloth, tablecloth, tablecloth." She snapped her fingers. "Oh, it's at the cleaners. I totally forgot."

"Don't worry, I'll pick it up and grab some sandwiches from the drug store for our lunch."

Edna looked at Ruth, who was peeling potatoes like a machine. "That Lidia is a saint."

Ruth was slapping a potato with a potato peeler. "Community's full of 'em, Edna."

Edna smiled and tilted her head to one side as she stared at the back of Ruth's head. "I do like your hair, especially the back. Eloise

171

is really something if you give her a chance. Honey, you look good coming and going."

Ruth just wanted to look good going at this point. She was almost out of breath and running out of patience. "Edna, do you have another potato peeler?" She was hoping for some help.

"I think so, just look in that top drawer. Why, is that one dull?"

Ruth dropped the potato, put her hands on her hips and whirled around. She raised her eyebrows and pursed her lips. She shook the potato peeler at Edna. "Would you like to help me with these potatoes?"

Edna licked her finger and flipped a page in the cookbook. "No thanks. Did you find the potato peeler?"

Ruth turned around slowly to the pile of unpeeled potatoes. "Yes, Honey. I found the potato peeler. Now where did I put those pills?"

Edna was shaking her foot and flipping pages in the magazine as fast as she could go. "What was that?"

"The spills, the spills. I have to clean up the spills." She was afraid of setting Edna May off and needed to be more careful.

Lidia made her announcement from the dining room. "If I counted right, we will have sixteen adults. That works out perfectly. The dining room table will seat twelve and we can seat four at the game table in the bay window. You have two china settings of twelve. I think I'll mix the settings at each chair. If we arrange correctly using two china patterns, two silver patterns and four clear and color crystal patterns, it will be perfect, just perfect."

Edna stopped flipping pages and looked at Lidia with raised eyebrows. "Well, I've never heard of anything like that, all mixy-matchy!"

Every time Edna said something, they both held their breath. They were waiting for the bomb to explode.

"Can't wait to see it. I know it'll be beautiful. Everything you do turns out just amazing. Just like Ruth's hair. Have you seen her hair? Ruth, run in the dining room and turn around for Lidia. Make sure she sees the back."

"Hey Harry, can I use your phone?" Lidia had run into the cleaners to pick up the tablecloth. She called Steve with an update on Edna's condition. "So far, so good."

"I'll just put it on her bill, don't worry about it. Is there anything else she needs to have picked up?" Harry double checked the C's.

"No, Ruth got everything else yesterday."

"Thanks, Harry." Lidia trotted to her car, whispering to herself. "Dio, Dio, Dio. I've really stepped in it this time."

"I'll have three chicken salad sandwiches on toast, three bags of chips and three Cokes. To go, please. Oh, and three brownies. They look delicious."

Mike Wilkie was in pharmacy school and working in his father's drug store gave him great experience. "They're good, Daisy White just delivered 'em this morning." That name was the answer to her prayers. Daisy White. Why on Earth hadn't she thought of her? "Need to use your phone, Mike." Lidia had to call Ruth and let her know the plan.

Ruth was happy to hear Lidia's idea. "Daisy, of course, I'm sure the Duncan's don't need her today." Ruth was in agreement.

"Okay, I'll call her, no, I'll run over there. It'll be quicker if I give her a ride."

Ruth gave a huge sigh of relief. "Good, good, no, no, no, not good, not good!" Ruth's memory had just been pierced by the scene the day before with Edna and Roy. "Oh, Lord, Lidia, what if Edna goes off on Daisy like she did Roy? When she starts saying a colored, she can't shut up. I don't know if it's safe."

"Leave it to me, I'll explain. I'm sure she'll understand. I just hope she's available. I know they're planning on coming to dinner tonight."

Ruth was surprised and still afraid of Edna May's possible reaction to seeing Roy again. "Oh, you invited the Whites?"

"Well, of course I did. Roy is coming with Giovanni. Listen, I'll see you in 'bout half an hour. Hopefully I'll have Daisy."

"Well, Ruth, I just don't know what's wrong with me. I can barely keep my eyes open. Listen, honey. I'm going to take a little nap, be back down in ten minutes." Edna held the handrail and pushed herself up the stairs.

Ruth watched from the dining room, wondering what the night would hold. Who would return from the bedroom? Would Edna even remember what had happened over the last twenty-four hours? Ruth sat down at the kitchen table and cried. She cried because she was tired. She cried because she was scared and confused. She cried for Edna.

Gary Crutchfield Calls

Lidia came in the back door carrying the tablecloth. Daisy was behind her.

"Here's our lunch." The large paper bag was hidden in her hand under the tablecloth. "Daisy's here. Can you believe our luck? Where's Edna?"

Ruth wiped her eyes and rubbed her hands no her apron. "Taking a nap. Hey Daisy. I finished peeling the potatoes. I think we're in pretty good shape. Oh, those sandwiches look good. I'll pour us some tea."

The three sat eating their sandwiches. Daisy could tell the project had taken its toll on Lidia and Ruth, both emotionally and physically.

"Well, you ladies have really done a nice job here. I know Miss Edna is real proud."

"We all did a nice job, the entire community. We'll never forget all you and Hurly did. Anyway, it was nice for Edna to invite everyone for dinner. I should have said let's just do it next weekend. I just wasn't thinking." Lidia was holding her head in her left hand and rubbing her temples. She was exhausted. "I'll start setting the table and leave the cooking to you two, if that's okay."

Daisy offered the moral support that Lidia and Ruth needed. "Listen, just take your time and relax. I do this every day and love it.

Don't worry about me. Don't worry about the food and don't worry about time. I know the menu and I have everything under control. You ladies have done all the hard work, planning, shopping, peeling and chopping. I'll take care of the easy part. It's the least I can do."

"Daisy you're amazing. Thank you. Ruth, can you help me with the tablecloth in the dining room? I'll hold the flowers up and you put the tablecloth under."

The two had their hands full when the phone rang. They could hear Daisy. "Hello, Crutchfield's residence. No, I'm sorry she isn't available. Daisy, Daisy White. Yes, that's right, Hurley's wife. No sir, just today. Yes sir, she's having a dinner party."

Ruth and Lidia quickly walked to the kitchen without looking at each other. Daisy was holding the phone, listening. They could hear a man's voice shouting from where they were standing.

"Oh, Mr. Crutchfield, I see." Daisy was too embarrassed to look and stared at the floor. They heard the shouting stop and Daisy slowly hung up the receiver.

"Gary?" Ruth tried to look at Daisy, but she looked away.

"Yes, ma'am, it was Mr. Crutchfield. I don't think we'll be able to be at the dinner tonight. You don't need to set a place for us."

Ruth's emotions had been pushed to the limit for the last two days. She had worked, consoled, ran around, spent her money, lost sleep, sacrificed her hair appointment and walked on egg shells. She did all this because of Gary Crutchfield and the terror his return was causing the community. She couldn't hold it any longer. She looked straight at Daisy with her hands on her hips.

Lidia could see something was about to happen, but couldn't imagine what. Then she blasted.

"That son of a bitch. Who the hell, who the hell does he think he is? I have put up with his shit for too many years and this is it. No more. When that phone rings again, just let me answer it. It will ring again, mark my word. I can tell you one thing, Gary Crutchfield can't slap me through the phone line." She pointed upstairs and started to cry.

"He has put that woman through hell, pure hell for years. No wonder she's impossible to get along with. My God, who wouldn't be crazy as a bat, waiting for that red faced, beer gutted asshole to come home? If he ever, ever raises a hand to me, I can tell you one thing. I will kick his nuts through the roof of his mouth! He's had it coming for years. I bet he's not so tough with someone his own size. Screw this, I'm not waiting until he raises a hand to me. I think it's time he knew what his nuts tasted like! I am going to . . ."

The ringing phone stopped her rant. Everyone froze. The phone rang again. Daisy was standing beside it and flinched with each ring. Lidia's hands were in a tight knot and her knuckles were white. Ruth stepped over and jerked the receiver off the hook.

"Crutchfield's residence. May I help you?" She sounded like she had slapped someone's shoulder in a bar and was ready to throw them out. They watched her eyes darting side to side and her jaws tighten. They could almost hear her teeth grinding. She opened her mouth and began to take heavy breaths. "Oh, hello, Doctor Duncan."

Everyone's shoulders relaxed. Daisy stepped over and leaned against the counter. Lidia unclenched her hands and sat at the table. Ruth continued giving Steve information.

"She's taking a nap. I don't know what to expect. Gary just called." Ruth was taking slower breaths and listening. "Did he say what time he would be here, Daisy?"

Daisy was still clearly shaken by his call. "I don't think so. I don't really remember."

Ruth shook her head. "No, he didn't say. She's been upstairs for about three hours. I'm really worried. Oh, that'd be good. Thank you, Doctor Duncan."

Ruth slowly hung the phone up. "He's coming over to check on her." Lidia crossed her arms on the table and rested her head on them. Ruth sat beside her, leaning back and letting her arms hang loose. Daisy stood at the sink and stared at the floor. The phone rang again. They all jumped, but no one answered. It rang, rang again and again. They could feel his anger coming across the phone lines.

All Ready

"I've taken her pulse and blood pressure. She barely woke enough to know I was there." Steve sat his leather case on the counter. "She's very weak. The stress has been too much for her. I think the best thing we can do is let her rest. Has she eaten anything?"

Ruth looked at Lidia and gave her the answer. "As a matter of fact, no. I haven't seen her eat a thing, or take a drink."

Lidia's thoughts went back to Genevieve's illness. "I've seen Genevieve like this. Is it her blood sugar?"

Doctor Duncan shook his head in agreement. "I'm sure it's taken a hit. Let's take some food up, that should help."

"I'll fix her a sandwich and some tea." Daisy was glad to do anything to get past the phone call.

Steve could see all the hard work being done. "Things really look like a party's coming on."

Lidia shook her head. "I should've told her to wait."

Ruth rubbed her shoulder. "We all know it didn't matter what you said, or thought. She didn't even ask you. It was one of her decrees. You're a wonderful friend. If it wasn't for you, she would be doing this all by herself. Now, I don't want to hear another word about it."

Lidia needed the reassurance. She patted her hands on her knees, stood up and helped Daisy with the sandwich.

"Four thirty-five, ladies!" The rest and lunch had brought Edna quickly around. "Well, it looks like everything's about done. The roast and vegetables are on schedule to come out at six forty-five. The tea has been made and Daisy's cakes are beautiful. And the dining room, Lidia. It looks like a photo in a magazine. No, it looks better than anything I have ever seen in a magazine. I can't believe this is my house and my party. I have dreamed of this forever. I think the Ellingtons would be pleased."

She gave a gracious hug to each lady in the kitchen. "Now, go home, rest and be back at seven. Remember, you are the guests and I am the hostess. Plan to relax and enjoy. You deserve it more than I."

She looked at Daisy. "I have the name tags ready and you will be sitting beside me. I think Lidia and George will be in the middle of the table and Gary at the opposite end. He needs to be close to the door. Never know when he'll have to leave." She winked and walked them to the door. "See you at seven, thanks again for everything."

Having the work behind them energized the three as they walked to their cars.

"Hey, Mary May." Fay and Mary Alice had just returned Mary May.

"Bye, Mary Alice, see you tonight." Ruth gave Fay a thumbs up and a smile, letting her know everything went well. "See you at seven. Tell Steve thanks again."

Time to Party

Giovanni ran through the kitchen and saw his mama asleep on the sofa. He had finished his work at the barn and was ready for his bath.

George was milking the last four cows. Then he had to wash down the milking parlor and scrape the lot where cows stood in a small herd, waiting to be milked. The final stage in daily milking was mostly cleaning the wet manure from concrete. George and Giovanni took the same pride at the barn that Lidia took in her kitchen. The Davis dairy had always received the highest score from the inspection department.

George took off his heavy vinyl apron and hung it on the hook beside the door. Just before he left, he turned the radio off that sat on the wide window sill. The country music faded and the metal door closed with a hollow echo. He walked to the house, leaving behind a sanitary milking parlor of concrete and stainless, with a mist rising from the surfaces where hot water had just fallen.

It was six fifteen. Lidia was fighting the urge to get to the party early in case Edna May needed help.

"Giovanni, hurry up please." She was sitting, in the den quickly thumbing a Good Housekeeping magazine. She didn't have time to look at the photos and certainly not read. It was just a method to calm her nerves.

"Is Gary home yet?" George dreaded the answer, but had to prepare himself. He knew from past visits that he may be needed to help control the situation. Especially if there was whisky involved.

"He wasn't there when I left and Edna hadn't mentioned anything. I believe he had called, though." Lidia's foot twitched faster when she thought about the party. "Giovanni!" "Mama, it's not even six thirty. What time do we have to be there?"

Lidia's foot was jerking faster than ever and she wasn't even looking at the pages that she was flipping. "The party starts at seven, but, oh I don't know, just hurry." Lidia's short nap wasn't enough to get her rested. She was running on nervous energy.

George could hear it in her voice. "Got any of Edna's pills with you, honey?"

She stopped taping her foot. "George, please, that's not funny. You didn't see her. That poor woman was pitiful."

"I ran into Lester at Matthew's Garage earlier. He explained what her problem was." George couldn't suppress his laugh and soon, neither could Lidia.

"What on Earth are you doing in the kitchen? It's a dinner party, George."

His answer was muffled by the food he was chewing. "I know. I have to have a snack so I won't embarrass you by eating like a horse at the dinner table. I may be too nervous to eat anyway." He paused and swallowed. "Oh, I almost forgot. Genevieve called earlier. I told her about the party. She wants to hear all about it. She'll call tomorrow around two. Oh, but anyway, about Edna's dinner party. Who in the world gave her this idea?"

Lidia's nerves drove her to the edge of her seat. "George, please. Giovanni!"

Vinni heard his mama's shout over the radio music. He was working on his jet black hair. If The Tribe had seen him, he would never live it down.

"Who's going to be there anyway? I'm going to be bored to death. You know I'm not responsible for my actions when I'm bored."

Lidia heard this truth and prayed. "Ho Dio in cielo e in terra, tieni un vesto bambino fuori dia peri coli." Her foot was bobbing again. "Everyone that helped last night at her, their house."

Giovanni stopped looking in the mirror and shouted out the bathroom door. "Everybody?"

Lidia knew what Giovanni was really asking. "Yes, everybody."

"Even the Whites?" Giovanni didn't mind his friends being there, but he remembered Edna May's screaming rant when she saw Roy at her house with Mary May.

Lidia was tired of the tension about the White's invitation. "Especially the Whites. Daisy is sitting next to Edna May at the dinner table. Giovanni, please."

Vinni parted his hair back to the left and looked in the mirror from the side. "Can I roll up a pack of cigarettes in my t-shirt sleeve?"

Both parents belted out in perfect timing. "No!" Lidia's voice was the clearest one. George was still chewing on a sandwich.

"Just asking, never hurts to ask. That's what Mama always says." Vinni pulled a few strands of hair down over his forehead and tested a one sided grin. "Daddy, where do you keep your . . . ? Never mind, I found it."

George stepped out of the kitchen and looked at Lidia. "Wonder what drawer he found it in?"

Lidia stopped her giggle. "George Davis, he's only fourteen!"

George winked at his beautiful wife and tested the same one sided grin that Giovanni had inherited. "I'll have to check that drawer later."

"Vomini sono amanti, dia da giovani de doi vecchi." She slapped her magazine down on the arm of the sofa. "I'm waiting in the car. George, please, wipe your mouth. Honestly, going to a dinner party with mustard on your lip. Tell him to hurry up." She was walking to the car with the nerves of a school girl on her first date, wondering if she would be able to eat either.

George was checking his mouth in the mirror that hung in the mud room. "Giovanni!"

Giovanni's feet made an unusual beat on the steps. It sounded like someone dancing. "On my way, on my way."

George wasn't expecting what ran down the stairs. "Well, well, well. Somebody special going to be there tonight?"

Vinni tested his one sided grin and shook his head to one side. His black hair rested over one eye. "Yeah, me!"

Several cars were already at Edna May's. George parked beside Velma Stout, who was just getting out.

Giovanni's window was rolled down, but that didn't deter him from making a comment. "Oh, please. Not kraut breath Stout."

George gave him a stern look in the rear view mirror. "Giovanni, she can hear you." George didn't realize she could hear him, too.

"Oh, put a sock in it, Davis, or I'll have you writing an essay on the party to turn in Monday." Velma gave him a quick slap on his arm. "Whoa, look at you, buddyroe. Somebody special going to be here tonight?"

George interrupted before Vinni had his grin set. "Don't ask."

The voices spilling out of the open windows and front door were joyful ones interrupted by laughter.

"Velmaaaaa!" Edna's arms were extended and her head tilted to one side. Velma started fingering her nonexistent necklace. "Oh, well, oh yes, well yes. Ednaaaa."

George watched the very awkward hug and felt like a rubber duck in a shooting gallery.

"And, oh Lidia, you look beautiful." George squeezed by while Lidia got her hug. "You, too." She patted George on the back as they headed in.

"The kids are in the garage office, Vinni. Go on back." Edna May rubbed Vinni's head and he ducked to protect his hair.

Vinni knew exactly where to go. He had just trimmed the jasmine vine away from the door. He looked around before he went in. He wanted to be the last one to get there. Being early at a party made it look like you wanted to be there. The Tribe was already there.

"Hey, Vinni, what's up?" Eighteen was the first one to see him.

Vinni answered as he looked around the room. "Nothing in your pants."

Laughter and pointing broke out in the back of the office where the guys stood. The girls were standing around the desk and threw their heads into a huddle and started giggling. They looked like a flock of nervous chickens with a fox in the hen house. They were.

Vinni stopped at the desk. "Hey, Mary May. Nice party. Hey, Duncan". He thought it was cool to call the other Mary by her last name. "Hey, ya'll."

Mary May had invited a few girls from their class to even out the numbers. Eloise's niece, Sara Jenkins, and Ruby Matthews just giggled at him. The girls wanted to stare at him, but instead stared at everything else.

Roy broke in. "Hey, Vinni, what's up for tonight?" Everyone in the room knew that Vinni would bring the excitement.

"I got a couple of things in mind." He pointed to the corner where the boys were standing. "If you girls ain't too chicken to try 'em." The hens regathered and cackled.

"Does this thing work?" He picked the radio up from the end table beside the leather sofa and turned it on. The music drove the guys into a tight knot in the corner. The girls uncurled from their huddle, crossed their arms and stared at them from across the room. Vinni called their bluff.

"Well, okay then." He snapped his fingers with the music and slid in their direction. This spun them around back into a giggling huddle.

"Thought so." He walked back to the man corner. The hens tilted their heads to one side and watched him walk away.

"Thank you, thank you all for coming." Edna was waving her arms in the air, being as big as possible. "Gary and I want to thank you for coming."

There he stood, red faced, with a beer gut that wasn't there his last visit. His eyes darted around the foyer and into the living room as he nodded his head at visitors. He was clearly out of his element. He was outnumbered and out of control.

"If everyone will please go into the dining room, I have place cards for everyone."

The guests filed in and strolled around the table. No one was looking for their place cards. They were admiring the beautiful room.

The pair of three pronged silver candelabras flanked the flower arrangement. The white table cloth gave a soft reflective glow to the varying china patterns. The table looked like Lidia's summer garden. Colors floated across the room like flower pedals on a lake. The game table in the bay window had a matching tablecloth. The low flower arrangement supported three candles.

Edna May's arms drifted apart and motioned into the room. "Everyone, please have a seat."

The guests started calling out names from the cards, guiding each other to the correct seating arrangement. When the room settled, Edna was at one end of the banquet table. Behind her was the mahogany hunt board. It held Daisy's desserts beside stacks of clear glass plates and silver serving pieces. The oil painting was an original English landscape from 1826. The Ellingtons included it with the sale of the house. Gary sat at the opposite end of the table. He was not visible to Edna because of the flower arrangement. Behind him were the bay window and the game table overlooking the formal garden. The flood lights from the garage gave a soft glow to the lawn and fountain.

A Blessed Evening

The talking softened to a murmur, then silence. "Thank you for being here, but most of all, thank you for being my, our friends. You have all made Gary's homecoming a very special one."

Everyone looked at Gary. Some forced a smile, some did not. Ruth did not.

"Before we begin, I would like to ask George if he would return thanks." This request was never a surprise. Lidia rubbed his back as he stood.

"Let us pray." Everyone bowed their head. Edna May reached over and held Daisy's hand.

"We are gathered before you, Lord, at the table you have set before us. We are gathered with you, Lord, with the friends you have set beside us."

The spirit of fear was broken, peace settled upon the room and tears began to fall. There were tears of joy and comfort. There were tears of relief. Daisy reached for Hurley's right hand and Fay Duncan reached for his left.

"You have given us strength when we were tired and understanding when we were confused."

Tom and Margaret, Ed and Velma joined hands at the game table.

"You have driven the doubt and fear from our hearts and replaced them with joy."

Lidia placed her hand on George's back and Eloise held his hand.

"You have guided us through uncertain paths and brought us together."

The chain continued and ended as Ruth and Eloise placed their hands on Gary's fists resting on the table.

"We are friends who were led together, who followed together and who are blessed together. I pray these blessings that began today will continue forever. For those who prepared the food and set your table before us, we ask for special blessings and strength."

The youth had quietly filed in from outside and stood silently in the kitchen. Vinni was determined not to cry. He hated having his mother's heart.

"For our children, we ask wisdom and guidance." Vinni reached up to clear something from his eye.

"For our bodies, we ask that health and strength be provided by the meal we are about to receive."

Tearful sniffs were peppered across the room, but no one was willing to release their neighbor's hand to wipe the tears.

"We humbly ask in the name of Your Son Jesus, whom we love and honor. Amen."

Glances were kept downward as everyone regained their composure and George sat down. Ruth and Eloise patted Gary's relaxed fists.

"Well, we have a delicious buffet set in the breakfast room and drinks in the kitchen. Everyone please enjoy!"

Edna was standing at the head of the table, holding her hands next to her heart. Gary saw her just above the flowers, flooded in candlelight and couldn't stop staring. He felt Velma tapping his shoulder.

"Please, Gary you start the line. You're the man of honor. Welcome home. I'm right behind you." Her voice carried a sweet authority that even Gary Crutchfield couldn't disobey.

He was still staring at his wife. "Oh, okay." He didn't know why he was smiling.

Paper plates and cups were available for the youth and they wove their way into the line.

Lester patted Roy White's shoulder. "Get right in here, son. You need this more than I do. Daisy, what you been feedin' this boy? He's nearly big as his daddy." The Whites smiled with pride. The inner peace guided Roy correctly this night. He was among friends.

The office was full of talk and laughter, but from two locations. The girls were using the desk as their table. The guys were on the sofa and chairs, eating with their feet on the coffee table. Vinni was the first one finished and carried his paper plate to the trash can in the corner.

"You guys ready for a little excitement?" The guys just grinned and looked at each other. The girls spun around and stared in a trance, nodding their heads in approval.

"I'm not sure, Vinni." Mary May was hesitant, since it was her house. "I don't want any trouble."

Vinni looked at the group of girls and calmed all their fears. "Listen. All you have to do is be quiet and listen. Nothing bad's going to happen. You have to be quiet. If anyone hears you laugh, the whole thing will be ruined. Got it?"

The girls looked at each other and back at Vinni. They all shook their heads in agreement.

"Okay, if you're sure." Mary May wanted one more promise. "Mary May, I'm sure. Just don't worry and don't laugh." Mary couldn't speak and just shook her head.

Vinni pulled a piece of paper from his back pocket with a list on it. "Okay, Roy, here's the information you'll need." He read the list out loud. "The police department number is three five one, zero nine six one. The location is the last house on May Creek Road. It has a red mail box. Your wife's name is Matherina. The woman's husband works at the funeral home, so they can't be called. Be sure and make it sound urgent."

The girls started to giggle. Vinni and The Tribe looked and them and frowned.

"Listen. You are gonna have to shut up or leave. I'm serious. Now what's it gonna be?"

The girls closed their lips tight and nodded for him to go ahead. Vinni put the list on the coffee table in front of Roy and handed him the phone. Everyone in the room held their breath as he dialed the number.

The Prank Call

Sheriff David Lewis and his deputy, Johnny Evans, were on night duty at the station.

"Bill, if any calls come in tonight, you need to take 'em and write reports."

Bill Lewis had just graduated from the law enforcement course in Raleigh. He was Sheriff David's nephew and a position on the small force was waiting for him after graduation.

"Yes, sir, no problem." Roy's call had perfect timing. "I'll get it."

David and Johnny were playing rummy on the other end of the desk. Bill answered the phone. "Hello, Police Department." He picked up a pencil and note pad as he listened.

Roy responded to Bill's answer. "Hello. Is this da' police department? Ah, yes sir, good. No. I's afraid I won't be able to gibe ya' my name. Ya' sees, I's in a bad place right here, an' I needs yo' help, in a might bad way. Oh, yessir, das' right. Well is' a lil' bit hard to explain. Ah, yessir. You sees, I's trapped. Well, yessir. Underneath a woman. Oh, no, no sir. Das' da' problem. No, sir. We's not in bed. We's on da' flo. Oh, she's not my wife. Yessir. We's on May Creek Road. Da' las' house. It's got a red mailbox. Well, I don't rightly know exactly what happened. All I knows is she passed out. Yessir.

An' fell right on me. Well, it's a lil' unusual. Ya' sees my pants is down, an' I's stuck. Yessir. She's a hefty woman, mighty hefty. I's tried ta' move several time. All I could do was pull da' phone cord and call fo' help. No sir, no sir. Can't call no funeral home for da' ambulance. No sir. Her husum' works at da' funeral home. He's workin' now. Can't call da' funeral home. Might as well call da' undertaker as da' funeral home. Might need to call da' undertaker anyways if I don't get home. My wife jus' sent me to da' sto' to get some poke n' beans. I should o' been home by now and I still ain't got no poke n' beans. Matherina. She's my wife, she's a hefty woman, too. Can ya' hurry, sir? I can't feel my legs. Yessir, May Creek Road. Da' las' house, with a red mail box. I'd sure appreciate it if you'd keep 'dis quiet. Hurry now. You hurry on out here. Oh, jus' one thing. Could ya' stop by da' Piggly Wiggly and pick up a couple a' cans a' poke n' beans? Large cans. I'll pay ya' soon as I gets free. Oh well, one last thing, you might need da' kno' . . . Ah well, ya sees, she's a white woman."

The group huddled around Vinni and Roy roared as soon as Roy hung the phone up.

Inside the house, George and Lidia heard the laughter from outside and rolled their eyes at each other. "What in the world has he done now?" George looked out the kitchen door towards the garage.

"Sounds like their having fun. Don't you think?" Edna was pleased with every aspect of her dinner party.

Bill was scanning his notes. "Seems like there's a domestic situation on May Creek Road. I'll ride out and take care of it."

Bill put his pad in his front pocket with his pencil, grabbed his Deputy's hat off the desk and headed toward the door.

David was chewing on a toothpick. "Don't forget to bring a report back."

The door closed behind Bill. Johnny grinned at David. "May Creek Road? Do you know who lives at the end of May Creek Road?"

"Sure do. I might be the Sheriff, but this is a job for the new Deputy." They both chuckled, imagining what Bill had waiting for him.

"There's a big party at Edna May Crutchfield's tonight. Gary's back in town. Hope we don't get a serious call. I think a bunch of teenagers are there."

David was grinning as he laid down four queens. "Is Vinni there?"

Johnny wondered if they were thinking the same thing. David was sure of his answer. "Sounds like he is. Rummy."

Bill turned onto May Creek Road and headed to the end. Just before he reached the red mailbox, the paved road turned to gravel. He knew the sound of his tires crunching toward the house would alert the couple inside that he was approaching.

He stopped the patrol car beside a black 1940 Ford parked behind the house. A yellow light bulb gave a dull glow to the small stoop where the back door was located. He could tell the television was on by the flashing and fading light coming from the window at the end of the small white house.

He stepped onto the stoop where a mop was leaning against the wall. He could still smell the pine scent from the Saturday cleaning. It was hard to see in the yellow light and he squinted to review his notes. He knocked on the door. There were no voices or cries for help and wondered if he should go in. There was no answer and he decided to knock once more before entering.

Bill was guided by his new knowledge from the police academy. He had to put neighborhood etiquette aside. He was reaching for the door knob when he heard footsteps growing louder. Someone was coming through the kitchen to the back porch. He could feel the boards under his feet tremble as the person approached. The light coming from the kitchen presented a large silhouette in front of Bill when the door opened.

"Evening, si, ma . . ." Bill realized he didn't know if it was a man or woman facing him. "Evening, I'm Bill Lewis with the Pleasant Grove Police Department. I'm here to investigate a domestic situation reported at this address."

He was still straining to read his notes in the yellow light. "I have in my report that there was, and I quote, a man trapped underneath a large hefty woman, with his pants down." Bill had to step back as the person stepped forward. He looked up from his notes. When his eyes adjusted to the dim light, he recognized Mrs. Pratt.

She turned slightly to her right. Her arm stiffened and her fist opened to expose her huge palm supporting five oversized, chubby fingers. She gave her body a quick smooth rotation in his direction, lifting her arm on the breeze. Bill's eyes cut from her face to his left just as her ample hand started to lift upward. Mrs. Pratt lifted to her toes giving an upswing to her arm.

Her hand slammed into the left side of his face, full force. Her little finger caught him just below the jaw bone and her thumb crossed between his forehead and hairline. His left

ear received the remaining fingers. Her follow
through was worthy of the Olympics, lifting Bill
to his toes. His right shoulder hit the wall
beside him, knocking the mop to the floor. His
knees hit the wooden stoop below him in perfect
timing with the sound of the door slamming in
his face.

Bill had to give himself a few seconds to
realize what had just happened. When he regained
his bearings, he was on his hands and knees. His
note pad and pencil were on the porch floor.
The drool oozing from his bottom lip puddled
on his note pad and ran onto the wooden planks.
He realized he wasn't breathing and gave a long
gasp for air.

There were sounds of footsteps inside, but
no voices. He realized he was in a vulnerable
position. If Mrs. Pratt returned she could easily
kick his head, sending him tumbling backward
down the steps.

He grabbed the wet notepad and pencil with
his left hand and pressed against the wall with
his right. As he rose, the door and wall swayed
with him. He turned and rested his back against
the wall where the mop had previously stood. His
eyes rolled to his right to make sure no shadows
were approaching before he turned his back on
the house. He stumbled down the four wooden steps
onto the wet grass. His senses were returning
and his feet carried him to the cruiser with a
wobbly trot.

An Evening to Remember

The women were finishing the dishes in the kitchen. Lidia was in charge of returning the china to its origin. Daisy had left enough food for the Crutchfields to have Sunday lunch. She divided the remaining leftovers into paper plates and wrapped them in aluminum foil. Ruth was slicing the remaining desserts and wrapping them in plastic wrap for the guests to take. George and Steve removed the extra leaves from the dining room table and put them under the bed in the guest bedroom.

"Edna May Crutchfield, this has been the most beautiful party I have ever been to." Velma Stout's comments were heartfelt and closed with a loving embrace. She patted Edna on the back and was the first to head toward the door.

"Wait, wait, here, take some leftovers for tomorrow." Lidia was trotting down the hall into the foyer with desserts resting on top of the aluminum foil wrapped plate. "There's a plate for Frank, too, if you don't mind dropping it off. Tell him we missed him, we really did, and thanks for all his work."

Velma took the food with her right hand supporting the dessert on top. "Oh, thank you. I appreciate it. Let's see what time is it?" She leaned back and looked at the grandfather clock in the living room. "Ten forty-five, my word, I didn't realize it was so late. I'll tell you what. I'll drive by Frank's and if his light is still on, I'll drop it off. If not, I'll just call him in the morning. Maybe we'll just have lunch together. Thank you so much again, it was just lovely."

Edna held the door for her and watched her first guest walk down the front steps.

"I don't think she's blocked in." George was approaching the front hall. "We are parked beside her, we need to go, too. It was a great party, Edna. I know you're glad to have Gary back home." George was trying to put a positive spin on the situation and keep Edna's spirits up.

"Are the kids still in the garage?" Lidia was looking around, wondering if they were inside. "I'm sure they are, they were all having such a fun time. I'll go out and tell them the party is winding down."

Edna was headed to the back of the house when George remembered seeing Gary step outside to smoke a cigar. "Wait Edna, I'll go. You better stay inside and say goodbye to your guests." George knew from past experience that Gary kept a stash of Scotch in the garage. He wanted to make sure Edna was going to be okay before he left. He stepped onto the back porch and saw the red glow of Gary's cigar in the back yard beside the fountain.

The prank that Vinni and Roy had played on Bill Lewis had brought all the teens together. New relationships had been formed, in more ways than one. This was something that would be recalled and told to their children and grandchildren. Not all things, however, would be told.

The girls had remained on the leather sofa after the phone call. The Tribe was sitting in arm chairs and on the floor, except Vinni. Vinni was leaning against the wall between the TV and the window, looking toward the house. From this position he could see everyone in the group and the back porch, too. He would warn the others when an adult was approaching.

Sara Jenkins was sitting on the edge of the couch. She was leaning forward, supporting her elbows on her knees. Her arms were pressing her breast together giving her abundant cleavage. No one else in the room was able to see, Vinni was the only one standing.

He stared at his new treasure unashamed and unnoticed. His tongue was running across his bottom lip and his index finger was making small circles on the tip of his thumb. He noticed what his body was doing and remembered how his daddy explained it to him that night in the barn. Vinni was always in control, but this time his body was controlling him.

He noticed Mary May's eyes darting in his direction. She pretended to be looking out the window. She was glancing at his crotch. The conversation was about school, the bus, summer plans and the earlier phone call. Vinni only heard mumbles. His mind was held captive in Sara's bosom.

Gary heard George's footsteps, turned toward the house and gave an upward nod to acknowledge him.

"Nice meal. Are you gonna eat like this every day?" George's question broke the approaching tension. Gary's laugh came as a quick burst of air rushing from his nostrils in a cloud of cigar smoke. "Hope not, I won't be able to fit in my truck."

George's hands came out of his pockets and he crossed his arms. "I know what you mean. I can only take meals like this on holidays." There was an awkward silence while Gary took a long deep drag on his cigar, coaxing the grey ashes to turn red. "Yeah, Edna's gone to a lot of trouble to make your homecoming nice. A lot of people have. Welcome home, Gary." George extended his hand and Gary placed the cigar back in his mouth and accepted with a firm shake.

The handshake wasn't like the handshakes George received at church. Gary's handshake was one that sealed business deals. A handshake from Gary Crutchfield could have millions of dollars depending on it. Gary knew what his neighbors were concerned about and he knew their concern had merit. He remembered his earlier phone conversation when Daisy answered the phone. He refused to feel remorseful, but he had to fight the feeling, especially after spending an evening with the Hurley and Daisy White as Edna's guests. There was an unspoken truth that was understood by both parties.

"Well, listen, I would love to have you and Edna at church tomorrow, but I understand it's been a long several months. Just know you're always welcome. You know how active Edna has always been at church." He looked over his right shoulder at the light coming from the garage office. "Well, guess I better break up the real party. It sounds like they've had a good time tonight. See you around, Gary, g'night."

George lowered his head as he approached the office door. The door had a window and he didn't want Vinni and his friends to think he was spying. He stood with his side to the door and stared at his shoes as he knocked on the glass with his knuckles. He saw wet blades of freshly mown grass sticking to his shoes and was reminded of all the work that was done only a few hours earlier.

"Vinni, time to go. Edna needs everyone inside." George walked back to the house without ever glancing into the office. He was a little afraid of what he might see, but convinced himself he didn't look to be polite.

The unexpected knock startled everyone, even the guys jumped. The girls were the first to stand up and the first to the door.

Instead of going out the door, Mary walked back and gave Eighteen a hug and thanked him for coming. She followed the pattern with each guy and ended with Vinni. The other girls followed her lead. The awkward mix that started earlier had been replaced with closer friendships. The friendship included Roy and the hugs he received were just as genuine as the others. Sara was the last in line and Vinni was the last to get a hug. Sara relaxed her arms after a quick hug. Vinni did not. He liked the way her breasts felt against his chest. Sara tightened her arms briefly and gave Vinni a pat on his shoulder, signaling a release.

"Good night." Sara's voice was low, but not a whisper. Vinni's mouth formed the same words but there was no breath in his body to support the sound.

The string of cars turned right off of Old Davis Road, heading away from town. Bill Lewis met them on his return to the police station. His mouth was hanging open and his eyes were set like stones on the road. He barely noticed the convoy. He was finding it hard to concentrate. The pain on the left side of his face was distracting.

The Wounded Warrior Returns

The sheriff and Johnny were still playing rummy. "Wonder what's happened to Bill? He's been gone a while." Johnny was rolling his toothpick from one side of his mouth to the other, as he decided not to pick up the top six cards on the discard row. He held the ace in the air a few seconds and looked over the cards that had been played before he discarded it.

David leaned up and seized the opportunity Johnny had missed. "I'll take that king if you don't want it." He put his thumb on the bottom of the king of diamonds and his middle on the top, then drew them into a perfect pile with the precision of a Las Vegas dealer.

"Hope Mrs. Pratt hasn't hurt our boy. You think we should'a told him to get the number and call before he went?" David tilted his head back so he could see his cards through his bifocals. His bottom lip rose pointing his toothpick toward the ceiling. "Let's see, I believe I can lay these down." His right hand made smooth arches, removing cards from his hand and placing them neatly on the table. "Three, four, five and six, there's my other jack, oop, an ace on that two, and here's that king you were afraid t' pick up. Rummy!" David rotated his bifocals from his head. "Looks like you owe me another Coke, Johnny boy."

Johnny gave an exhausted sigh as his shoulders slumped and he dropped his cards, face down, on the desk without counting his points. "I hope you enjoy all these Cokes I been buyin' ya'. Hope ya' piss the bed."

Bill slowly pulled into the parking space facing the station. Typically they left this space open for visitors, but Bill wasn't sure he had the strength to walk from the other side of the gravel parking lot.

Johnny stood halfway up, supported on his bended knees so he could see out the half glass of the wooden door. "Looks like Sherlock Holmes is back."

Bill was still weak and a little shocked. His feet hit each step leading to the door and slid forward. The gravel stuck to the bottom of his wet shoes made a scratching sound as they slid across the aged concrete. He was regaining strength in his right arm, but he could feel the soreness setting in from the collision with Mrs. Pratt's wall.

By the time he made it to the top of the steps, David and Johnny were standing inside, looking through the window. Bill stood on the covered stoop and threw his head back with a groan. When he opened his eyes he was looking at the black address numbers painted above the door. He lowered his head and looked through the glass where David and Johnny were standing. What Bill saw was equally strange.

David had put his arm around Johnny's shoulder so they could get closer to see out. Their heads were leaning toward the center of the window, causing David's cheek to rest on Johnny's head. Bill heard David's comment through the glass.

"Good God Almighty." They stepped back, giving him room to come inside. Bill was still stunned at the site of his superiors in each other's arms.

"You boys datin' now?" Johnny quickly stepped to the side and let David's arm fall to his side. David's answer was slow and calm. "Naw, naw, we ain't datin'." His toothpick was perfectly still as his eyes floated across Bill's face. "Here, have a seat."

He grabbed the back of the heavy oak chair he had been sitting in and pivoted it toward Bill. Johnny watched Bill slowly lower himself into the chair. "I'll getcha a Coke." The two men didn't know what happened, but they wanted to take care of their wounded warrior. Bill took the Coke and emptied half the small bottle before setting it on the desk. The left side of his face was turning from red to pink, but the pain was increasing.

David had only heard one side of the phone conversation when the call came into the office. "Now, tell us exactly what was said on the phone and exactly what happened after you left."

Bill started with describing the man, a black man, in a panic because he was trapped under a large, no, a hefty white woman. David and Johnny were shaking with silent chuckles as soon as the story began. He continued telling how the woman's husband worked at the funeral home. He didn't miss a word and told it exactly as it sounded on the phone. The silent chuckles turned to snickers and laughter. When the story ended with a request to pick up two large cans of poke n' beans, the two men roared with laughter and could hardly catch their breath. Johnny was rocking in his desk chair, banging the legs on the wooden floor and David was sitting on the edge of the desk with one foot on the floor and the other swinging and kicking the side of the desk.

David finally regained his composure and inserted a question into the chorus of laughter. "Well, did you get your report?" The question sent the hysteria to a new level.

Bill had endured the laughter to this point, but failed to see the humor of his condition. He stood up and leaned over the desk towards David. He had to scream to be heard above the laughter. Bill shook his finger at the left side of his face and bellowed. "I'm sorry, what did you say? I can't hear out of my left ear!"

The bwahas that followed bounced off the walls and ceiling. As the men tired of laughing, the sounds returned to the silent chuckles that started the concert. David wiped the sweat from his face with a dingy handkerchief. He spoke as he exhaled. "Well, we really do need a report. Especially if people start asking about your bruise and word gets back to headquarters."

Bill's mouth fell open and his eyebrows rose. "A report? You want a report? What the hell do you think I just gave ya'? If you want a damn report, write one yourself. I'm sure it'll be a hoot."

David realized this event would be told for years to come and he couldn't let it rest. "I'm sorry, but we really have to have someone from the residence sign a report, or at least give a statement. You took great pains in logging in the time and general complaint from the phone call. If you don't have something signed to put in the file, it'll look like ya' didn't follow state protocol. That would look bad on your record. I know you did everything possible and the situation was out of control, but if the state auditor stops by, it could be real trouble for you. You want one of us to go back with ya'?"

Bill didn't realize he was being taken for a fool twice in the same night. The phone log could have been thrown in the trash and that would have been the end of it.

"Oh, hell's bells! No, you don't need to go with me. What time is it?"

Johnny looked at his watch. "Eleven twenty. It's getting later every minute."

Bill stood up and walked toward the door. "Shit. I better get back over there before that grizzly bear in pink flannel hibernates. Lord only knows what would happen if I woke her up. Maybe I need to throw a fresh roast on the stoop to calm her down."

He was opening the door when Johnny added his thoughts. "Or maybe a couple cans of poke n' beans." Bill closed the door on the laughter and headed for the cruiser.

When his car drove off the pavement onto the gravel road, his stomach tightened and his head throbbed a little harder. He parked the car in the same tracks he made earlier and gave a quick toot on the horn, letting Mrs. Pratt know he had returned. There was no light in the front room and the television had been turned off. The stoop was even darker without the yellow bulb glowing, but he could see light from the rear falling around the corner of the house.

He wasn't sure if she heard the horn, but decided not to try again. Perhaps his headlights shining on the trees in the back yard would signal his return. He was walking back to the stoop when the neighbor's dog starting barking. His survival training took over and he placed his hand on the holster holding his pistol. His boldness that was derived from anger had been overcome by fear and dread. He felt his hand trembling on the leather holster and his breaths were quick and shallow. His mind searched for reason.

It was less than two years ago when the woman who had just slammed him to his knees was handing him his high school diploma at graduation. He was fighting the feeling of being that fifth grader taken to the principal's office. Mrs. Pratt had stared at him through squinted eyes with pursed lips, making him wish he was already in the safety of Mr. Johnson's office.

It was the same woman who towered over him as a small child when he sat in Sunday school. She was not the one that convicted him of his sins, it was the Lord, but she knew what his sins were. His sins were broadcasted to the entire school every time he had to stand in the hall, or missed recess for misbehavior. She knew every time he cheated on a test, or tried to look up girl's dresses. She was the one who caught him smoking behind the tool shed and kept silent, letting him wait for the news to be told.

It would give him stomach cramps every time his mother would talk with Mrs. Pratt at Green's Grocery. He wondered if she would call the police department and report his list of secret sins. Did she know he had sex with his girlfriend after the senior class dance? Would she tell all the girls he would date in the future? What else did she know? His imagination had transformed Mrs. Pratt into a monster lurking in the shadows, holding his future in the balance.

Maybe he wasn't cut out to be on the police force. What would he do if he faced a man of her stature with a gun? She had left him wounded and crawling away like a kicked puppy. Would she do it again?

He approached the wooden steps he had stumbled down not long before. He was intimidated by the darkness and stood to the left side of the porch. The mop was still resting where it had fallen and his foot kicked something when he reached for the handle. It was his cap. Evidently it had been knocked off and he hadn't missed it. He picked it up and placed it on his head. He held the back with his left hand and pulled the brim over his forehead with his right. As he adjusted it with quick jerks, his confidence was restored. It was like a warrior who had found his shield when returning to battle.

He used the mop handle to give a loud knock on the door. The sound broke the silence and the fear it carried. Bill became annoyed at the situation. He was cowering at the corner of the porch, like that puppy that had been kicked out of the house. He gave another bang with the mop handle. He didn't care if he bothered Mrs. Pratt. He was the one with the authority now. He knocked again.

The vibrations on the wooden porch let him know she was approaching in the darkness. The glow of the yellow bulb let him know she was about to open the door. She didn't ask who was there and didn't hesitate. She opened the door and stuck her head out. He looked up and could see her eyebrows lowered toward her stubby nose. She was irritated. She saw the police cruiser with the headlights on but didn't see Bill standing at the corner of the house.

He tapped the side of the house with the mop handle to get her attention. "It's me, Mrs. Pratt."

She put her fists on her hips and gave a quick
look downward. His head was about the same level
as her knees. "Sorry to bother you, but I have
to get you to sign a report."

She gave a quick snort, like a bull that was
about to charge, and stepped onto the porch.
"Bill Lewis, it is almost midnight. Why didn't
you do this when you were here before?" Bill's
chin lowered and his eyebrows lifted. He looked
up at her standing in the glowing yellow light.

"When I was here before? Why didn't I get it
when I was here before?" His irritation at this
woman outweighed his fear and his professionalism.
He walked back to the steps and up to the porch.
He stood in front of her, holding her mop. The
damp strings covered his hand. "If you recall,
Mrs. Pratt, when I was here before, you slapped
the shit out o' me!"

Mrs. Pratt sucked in the snort that she had
just let out. Her eyes opened wide, but she said
nothing. Bill placed the mop back against the
wall.

"I came here because I had taken a phone call
from someone who said they were in trouble. I
didn't know who lived here and I didn't know who
called. I was trying to explain it to you when
you slammed me against that wall." He nodded his
head to the right where the mop was against the
wall. He was on a holy rant and she offered no
defense so he continued.

"Now, you have two choices. You can sign this
statement, which says there was no situation at
this residence and the call did not come from
here, or I can arrest you for assaulting an
officer. Right now I prefer the second choice.
It's up to you."

Her arms left her sides and crossed over her
chest. She let out another little snort. This

one didn't seem angry, it was longer and more relaxed.

"Well, I am just as irritated as you are. And I do apologize for my outburst. You know that's not like me." She leaned forward and her eyes floated around the yard to make sure nobody was watching. "Well, of course I'll sign your statement. Do you have a pen?"

Bill handed her the clipboard with a pen under the metal handle. "Yes, ma'am, right here. You can sign on that line at the bottom." He pointed to the bottom of the sheet as she held the clipboard.

Her handwriting seemed out of character. Her signature was beautiful and light handed. She handed the clipboard back to the officer. "Do you know who made the phone call?"

He checked over the statement and signature. He needed to make sure another trip wouldn't be necessary.

"No, no, ma'am, I don't know. But you heard what they said." The memory of his last visit was still fresh. He was still studying the report and lowered his voice so she could barely hear his response. "That's when you slammed me to my knees." Bill gave a huge sigh of relief. "Well, I think we're done here. I'm sorry it's so late, but thank you for your help."

His right hand automatically extended to seal the meeting with a handshake. Bill was surprised as he stood in front of her with his hand out. He imagined her crushing grip bringing him to his knees. Mrs. Pratt's fingers lightly touched his fingertips. Her fingers were warm and soft. She gave a gentle squeeze. "I'll see you in Sunday school tomorrow?"

Mrs. Pratt had taken over the young adult class four years ago when pastor Harold Wells resigned. Bill closed his eyes and gave a half hearted nod. "Yes, ma'am, I'll be there."

She gave a quick little squeeze and tilted her head to one side. "Gooood." She released him and he returned to the cruiser.

David and Johnny were waiting at the station for Bill's return. David was almost finished with the last Coke he had won playing rummy. He looked across the desk at Johnny. "Has Pratt ever slapped you?"

Johnny and she were the same age and they spent twelve years together in school. He knew how Bill felt.

"Oh, hell yeah." David shook with a chuckle and waited to hear the story. Johnny's boots were on the edge of the desk and he was rocking his chair on its back legs.

"We were in the sixth grade and had just come in from recess. We were lined up at the water fountain. You know, the one in the back hall beside the music room. That water always tasted like metal. We would line up at the water fountain every day after recess, sweating like a bunch o' pigs. Mrs. Moore would always stand beside the water fountain and count to ten. That's all the water you got. Anyway, I was standing behind Pratt and like I said, we were sweating like a bunch o' pigs. Well, her back was just soaked and her dress was stuck way up in her ass crack. When she got all sweaty and ran aroun' playing kick ball, her ass just ate up her dress. It was like that every day. Well it was a Friday, and nobody really got in trouble on Friday, especially after lunch. So the guy behind me, Jim, reaches around, grabs the bottom of her dress and pops it out of her ass crack."

Both men shook with breathy laughs. Johnny had a hard time finishing the story. Every few words were broken with exhaled chuckles.

"Well Pratt, sheeehe turned around an' loohooked at me straight in the eyes. I knew what was about to haahappen and I tried to baahack up, but I stepped on Jims toohoes. Well he gave me a shove and I landed right on heher cheheest."

By this point, both men were crying with laughter and wiping their eyes.

"Weehel, I jumped baahack just in time to seehee her open her hahand and swing. That girl hit mehee so hard, it knocked mehee off my feeheet. I fell back against Jim and knocked hihim down. The whole line went down like a rohoow o' dominohoes. I'm tellin' youho, that's the truth. I couldn't hehear for 'bout a weheek."

Johnny's feet dropped to the floor and the front legs of his chair landed with a loud bang. His arms were resting on the arms of the chair and his shoulders were shaking uncontrollably.

Bill pulled into the gravel parking lot and parked at the side where he usually parked. He walked in just as the laughter was fading away.

"Well, I got everything taken care of." He let the clipboard drop on the desk with a pop. "Here's the report. I'll file it Monday morning, if that's okay." He dropped his shoulders and tilted his head back. "It's been a hell of a night and my shift was over almost an hour ago. I'm goin' home."

David put his hands on his knees and pushed his self up. "Yep, guess I need to get home, too. Johnny you got my number. Call if you need anything."

It was Johnny's weekend to stay at the station. David followed Bill out the door. The door closed behind them and Johnny could hear their conversation as they walked to their cars.

"Well, guess I'll see you at church tomorrow."

"Yep, see you in th' morning, g'nite." The sound of their boots crunching across the gravel lot stopped and their car doors shut.

Johnny turned on the radio and shuffled the deck of cards for his first game of solitaire. His thoughts were with his wife and six year old daughter, Elizabeth. He wanted to protect her from all the things that had happened that night, but he didn't want to deny her the joy and laughter they brought.

The Perfect End to a Perfect Night

It was eleven thirty and George was already in bed waiting for Lidia to join him. It felt good to stretch his arms above his head and release the tension his muscles had carried the past few hours.

"It was a nice party, turned out better than I thought. You never know what to expect with Gary, maybe he's changed in is old age."

He flexed his toes upward to stretch his calf muscles and watched the white sheet rise and fall. He was reminded of how the air felt when Lidia would let the sheet float down across his back. He could still see how she looked that night, how her silk dress clung to some parts of her body and floated past others. He laughed to himself, remembering the earlier conversation they had about Vinni getting something from George's drawer. He flexed his toes again. This time the sheet fell in a different pattern.

Lidia came into the room and saw her husband stretched under the sheet. His fingers and palms had formed a hammock to rest his head. Everything about his body welcomed his lovely wife. She noticed how the sheet clung to some parts of his body and floated past others. A smile crept across her lips.

"George, it's after eleven thirty and you have to be up at five thirty to milk."

She wasn't denying his wishes, only offering a way out, knowing that sometimes his tired body outweighed his wishes. Not this night. George's grin outweighed Lidia's smile.

"Well, Mrs. Davis, that gives us six hours." His eyebrows danced up and down and stopped with a wink.

Lidia reached behind her head and removed the comb that held her wavy black hair up, letting it fall across her shoulders. George watched her and had trouble speaking. His grin faded and Lidia heard his request in a soft low voice. "Lidia, can you put your hair back up?"

This time when she looked at him, she didn't notice the pattern under the sheets, she only saw his blue eyes. She didn't have the breath to respond, she just smiled and nodded. He watched her long fingers slowly rake her hair from scalp to tip and finish with a twist. Her silk slip tighten around her breast when she reached to put the comb in her hair.

"Vomini sono amarti, nota e giorno, sempre amanti per tutta la vita, sempre amanti."

He didn't know what she had whispered, but it sent blood pulsing through his body. The aggravation and tension that had consumed their lives for a day and a half fueled their lovemaking that night.

George held his breath for several seconds and exhaled. Lidia felt his breath swirl between the pillow and her shoulder. His elbows were at her sides and his palms cradled the backs of her shoulders. He liked the way her fingernails felt, gently raking his scalp through his blonde hair. George wanted to stay there all night, but the strength supporting his legs and arms was waning. He rolled over to his side of the bed, taking most of the sheet with him, then raised back to Lidia. She retrieved the sheet and kissed his cheek.

"I wish the whole world knew what I have, but if I told, the whole world would have it, too."

She felt his breath dance across her shoulder when he spoke. Soon she could tell he was sleeping by the pattern of his breathing. Lidia went to sleep with her fingers in his hair.

A New Beginning

Mary May laid in bed awake. She was exhausted, but too excited to sleep. She replayed the events that took place earlier in the garage. It was the first time she and her friends had really socialized with Vinni and his friends. They had been thrown together their entire lives, on the playground, the school bus and at church. They were always in arm's length of each other and could hear any conversation that wasn't whispered.

Tonight things changed. They were held captive in the garage, unable to break free, bound to live the lives and obey the wishes of The Tribe. It wasn't the garage walls that held them captive, they were free to leave any time. The girls were captivated by freedom. They were free to do as they pleased, free to say what was in their hearts, free to break the rules, free to hug a friend and free to obey or disobey Vinni's demands.

They choose to be part of a world created by men, on men's terms. It was very simple to be in a man's world. No thoughts were whispered, no desires were shamed and telling the truth was natural. They entered this world by the invitation of young men, very young men. The truth was these young men didn't know or understand the rules. The rules in their world changed and grew as they did. Vinni and Ray had entered this world years earlier at Matthew's Garage when they were just boys. Tonight they made it their own. Tonight they set the rules. Tonight they entered uncharted waters, ignorant to what was ahead and unafraid, willing to take a chance and suffer the consequences. It was a secret world where no one could guide them because their desires and their paths were known only to them.

Mary May and her friends were now a part of this world, ignorant of its power and danger, drunk on its spinning freedom. She finally submitted to exhaustion and fell into a deep sleep, a very deep sleep that would usher her into a new life. Tonight the life she once knew was forever gone.

Gary cut his eyes down and stared at Edna while she was sleeping. His power had been taken away. He returned to a home and a wife that was controlled by friends. They had decided what he would do, where he would sit, what he would eat and who he would be friends with. Edna had even decided that they would not be having sex that night. He rested his head against the tall walnut headboard and looked across at the clock on Edna's bedside table.

The green hour and minute hands rested dead on one o'clock. A glowing clock was the only thing familiar to him. They were the same numbers he stared at in motel rooms. The same glowing numbers that reminded him he was alone. One o'clock, he knew where to go.

His movements were calculated and quiet as he redressed. Even the house sounded hollow and unwelcoming when he crept down the staircase. He felt like he was being watched and the house would tell his secret. The only relief came when he closed his truck door and backed to the end of the driveway. He was back in his own world, the world he controlled. His decisions were his own; he had set the rules and was willing to accept the consequences.

His headlights rolled across the front of his house, like the beacon of a lighthouse warning danger. One o'clock, he ignored his conscience and pulled the gear shift down until the green "D" glowed in the dark. He drove into the darkness, dreading the emptiness that pulled him forward. He knew where to go. Regardless of how hard he tried, Gary Crutchfield was not in control.

APRIL 25TH 1948

Edna's Recovery

Edna's throbbing head woke her at five thirty three. It was aggravated by Gary's snoring. She was having trouble concentrating and remembering the extra pills she had taken was driving her insane. What had she done? Her breath was quick and shallow, her mouth was as dry as a bird's nest and the slightest lingering aromas from the party made her queasy.

She slowly raised herself and pivoted to the side of the bed. The height of her antique bed caused her toes to dangle a few inches above the floor. She sat very still for several moments, hoping the extra throbbing caused by her movement would fade. Her silk nightgown made it easy to slide forward until her feet rested on the Oriental carpet. Her eyes remained closed as she slowly slid her right foot in small circles until she felt it hit her ivory bedroom slipper. She had her bearings and slid her small feet into her shoes. Her weight remained against the mattress; she was too tired to move. Her intense thirst was the only reason she pushed herself away from the mattress and dragged her feet toward the bathroom.

The light that was left on in the garage was broken by the faintest morning sun. Using her left eye and the light falling into the tall windows, she guided herself to the bathroom. The mirror on the medicine cabinet above the sink reflected enough light for Edna to find the aspirin and the crystal glass she kept on her mirrored tray beside the sink. She supported herself with one hand then the other as she screwed the top off the bottle and filled her glass with water. Her mouth was so dry that she hardly felt the three white pills on her tongue. The glass of water used to wash down the pills was no match for her thirst and two more glasses followed. She was suddenly aware of her bursting bladder and wondered how a body in extreme drought could be harboring so much fluid.

She had sat with her knees supporting her elbows and her palms and fingertips massaging her forehead for several minutes. She was too weak to stand and dreaded the sound of the loud flushing toilet. The sound of her heart pushing blood across her brain was in timing with her feet sliding toward her bed. She slowly lifted her left knee onto the mattress, letting her slipper fall to the floor and pulled her right leg onto the bed. The slipper remained on her right foot and she pressed her temple into the down pillow, trying to slow her breathing.

It was four minutes after seven when her trembling eyelid lifted again. The pain had lessened to the point where she was not helpless. She needed her husband desperately, but knew that disturbing his sleep would only make matters worse.

Her right slipper had fallen off under the sheet and she pushed it over the edge of the mattress. Her eyesight was available, due to the decreased headache. Her feet lifted slightly as she made her way to the door and down the steps. The grandfather clock in the living room had always run ten minutes slow and would soon

strike the hour. Edna used her extra energy
to detour into the living room and stop the
motion of the large brass pendulum. She could
not endure the sound of the seven o'clock chime.
The morning light was creeping down the entrance
hall through the double leaded glass doors. It
gave enough light for Edna to see as she dialed
the phone.

Steve Duncan had already retrieved the Sunday
paper from the front porch and was reading the
sports page when the phone rang. He didn't want
it to wake Faye, but he had to reach over her to
pick up the receiver. Steve had offered to have
the phone on his nightstand since the late night
and early morning calls were always for him, but
Faye had insisted that it be on her side of the
bed.

"Hello," Steve answered in a low voice, still
hoping to not disturb his wife, however the reach
over and the phone cord across her face made his
attempt worthless. Edna could barely hear him
speak and wasn't sure she had the right number.
Steve answered again after the silence. "Hello,
Duncan residence. Oh, good morning, Edna. Is
everything okay?"

By this time Faye was well awake and listening.
She sat up in bed and the phone cord fell across
her stomach. She listened as Steve continued.
She could tell by his facial expression that the
conversation had him concerned.

Because Steve was the town's doctor and Faye
his nurse, they had knowledge that others didn't.
They were extremely careful to never breech this
confidence, knowing such an act would ruin the
practice. More importantly, it would cause a huge
community breakdown. Edna knew she could trust
and confide in the Duncans, as her doctor and
her friends. Faye wondered what Edna's urgent

morning call was about and feared it involved Gary.

Steve continued. "Of course, yes, sure I will. Are you able to drive?"

Faye inhaled through her mouth and exhaled through her nose as her eyebrow fell to the bridge of her nose. She put her hand on Steve's forearm to offer support. Steve waved his left hand and gave her the okay sign with his fingers as he continued talking.

"Will Gary be bringing you? Now I'll be glad to come over there. Oh, oh I see, right. Fine, I'll see you at the office in about thirty minutes. Are you sure I can't just come over? No, no, that's fine, thirty minutes. Yes. Goodbye."

Steve handed the receiver to Faye. He explained the conversation before she had time to ask questions.

It wasn't often that Steve drove from his house to his office at seven thirty on a Sunday morning. He could tell who was up by the missing papers from the front lawns and driveways. He decided to roll his windows down and the cool air hitting his face readied him for his meeting. He replayed Edna's conversation and symptoms in his head and tried to start on a diagnosis. Was it the overdose of antidepressants? Was it a migraine brought on by stress? Was there really something else causing her to call? Perhaps something she couldn't discuss, fearing Gary would overhear the conversation.

He pulled into the rear parking lot at his office. Edna was already there. She was sitting in her car with her elbow against the window and her left hand supporting her head. Steve closed his car door gently and motioned her to meet him at the back door.

Steve's office was in an older house, similar to Edna's. It was much smaller with a wing added to the rear for examining rooms. Edna followed Steve up the concrete steps, supporting her weak body with the black wrought iron handrail. Steve fumbled with his large set of keys and finally opened the back door. He pushed the white wooden door open and held Edna's left arm as she crossed the threshold in front of him.

The previous back porch had been converted to a small break room with a small round table that once served as Steve and Faye's dining table. The wooden shelves supported by metal brackets that once held plants on the back porch served as a countertop. The only electrical outlet in the room placed the small refrigerator on the left wall as you entered. Steve reached for the light switch, but stopped when he remembered how light affected Edna's headache.

He spoke to Edna in a soft tone worthy of a college library. "We can meet in my office, the chairs are more comfortable, or you could lie on the sofa if you want." Edna didn't speak. She just inhaled and nodded in agreement as she exhaled and followed him down the short hall.

Steve's office was on the back corner of the addition, overlooking the gravel parking lot. The large maple tree was just setting its leaves and the foliage would soon block most of his view. Edna sat on the edge of the leather sofa with her hands woven together as if she was ready to pray. Steve rolled his chair from behind his desk to the front of the sofa. He had to bend down to get Edna's attention.

"I think we have enough outside light. I won't turn the overhead on. Are your symptoms any worse?"

Edna shook her head. "No, no, they seem a little better. Maybe I shouldn't have called you. If Gary wakes up and I'm gone, no tellin' what he'll think." Her voice was low in response to Steve's and her hands were rolling over each other. She inched toward Steve. "Maybe I should go. I'll be okay after a while. I'm sorry I bothered you, especially on a Sunday morning. Gary's probably awake by now. Lord knows what he'll think with me gone. Maybe I should have told him, but I know better than to wake him up. I'll be fine."

She was starting to stand when Steve put his hands on her forearms and gently lowered her back onto the sofa. His response was still soft spoken, but stern. "No, you aren't fine, and you won't be fine until we know what's going on. Now let's just answer a few questions and see if we can get a handle on this. I know you took a couple of your pills, instead of the half that was recommended." Edna's eyes flashed in his direction and her brows lowered. Steve realized she was not aware of Ruth's phone call Friday night explaining Edna's condition. Edna threw her hands in the air. "Oh, you do? You know what I do in my own house?"

Steve realized the effects of the antidepressants were wearing off and Edna was returning to her old self. He knew he couldn't back down and responded with the same sharpness.

"Yes, I do know and you're lucky to have a friend like Ruth Green. You had her scared to death, Edna Crutchfield. She was in tears when she called me Friday night. I know you had reason to take the extra medication, but in your state, the responsibility of your care fell on those around you. Now, if you want to walk out the door, go right ahead, but I suggest we work through what's causing these horrible symptoms."

Edna huffed and crossed her arms. Her eyes darted from Steve to the coat rack beside the window.

Steve continued. "If you were suffering from a reaction to the drug itself, you should have had the symptoms earlier. That leads us to alternate causes. It is very important that you do not use alcohol when taking this medication. Did you have any wine at the party?"

Edna rolled her eyes and answered with an embarrassed glow. "I only put the wine out for ambiance. I poured a couple of glasses and sat them around to make it look like someone may be having a glass. My Lord, Steve, it was practically Sunday. Who in the world do you think would be drinking wine?" She rolled her eyes again.

Steve raised his eyebrows and shook his head. "Well, I had a glass, no, two glasses and Faye had a glass of wine, too. I believe Tom and Margaret had a glass, as well as Lidia. It was very good wine, Edna. Where did you get it?"

Edna's arms had returned to a crossed position and she waved her left hand and answered with closed eyes. "I don't know, Ruth got it somewhere. Lidia probably told her what to get. I think they might drink wine at home. You know being Italian and all." The stress was causing her pain to worsen a little and she rubbed her temples with her index fingers.

Steve asked the question again. "Did you have any wine?"

Edna opened her eyes and tossed her hands in the air again. "Well, looks like I wasn't the only one. At least I didn't flaunt my drinkin' in front of the whole community." She looked at him and shook her head. "Yes, I had some wine.

I had a glass or two just before the party started. There, are you satisfied? Then one just before dinner was served. I don't remember if I had one with dinner. Oh, I'm sure you noticed. Did I have one with dinner, doctor?" Steve could tell her mouth was getting dry. Edna finished her confession. "And I had two glasses after everyone left. Everyone but Gary, that is."

By this time, the softness of the conversation had passed and it sounded more like an argument on the library steps. Edna finished with an appropriate disclaimer. "It was practically Sunday. Of course, I was not going to act like a common lush with a house full of guests. I kept two bottles of wine in my bathroom."

Steve patted her arm as he stood up. "Excuse me for a minute, Edna. I have to double check some research. I may be able to help you."

He left the room and closed the door behind him. Edna was exhausted from a night of pain and little sleep. She fell back on the sofa and was soon asleep. Steve tapped her on the arm.

"I have good news, Edna. I know what your illness is." He handed her a cup of hot coffee. "You, my dear, have a hangover."

Sunday Morning at the Barn

Vinni and George were on the last row of milking. George was inside the milking parlor, putting the milkers on the last four cows. The rest of the herd was slowly walking back to the pasture in single file.

Vinni was in charge of scrapping the wet manure from the concrete pad where the cows had stood in a large group, waiting to be milked. He grabbed the wooden handle of the scrape and started the path he had repeated almost every morning since he was ten. He slid the wide, shallow metal shovel from one side of the cement pad to the other. The wet manure dropped into the shallow ditch when Vinni slapped the shovel on the edge of the concrete. The pattern was repeated twenty two times before he had finished scraping the lot.

He leaned the shovel back against the milking parlor and picked up the green garden hose. His job wasn't finished until he had washed the brownish green film that remained into the ditch. Sheets of brown water flowed to the edge of the concrete and through the thick, tall green grass. When he was finished, the concrete lot was as clean as the basketball court in the school gym.

The men's timing was exact and natural. Vinni was replacing the garden hose in wide loops over the metal hanger while George was releasing the last cow from the suction of the electric milkers. Vinni rolled the large, wide metal door closed as he entered the milking parlor and the last cow exited. George was gathering the stainless steel milkers and taking them into the adjoining room where the milk was being pumped into the large stainless tank. The door closed behind George when Vinni picked up the red hose and began washing the interior of the parlor. The hot water available inside caused the steam to rise and fog the small windows facing the house.

Everything was the same; the sounds, the smells, the wetness. Day after day, year after year, it was always the same. Vinni was growing restless and tired of the routine. He realized that milking was no longer a chore; it was a part of life. It was something he did naturally, without thinking. His body took over his will and he began to work. His mind didn't want to follow and often his muscles were too tired to agree, but his body moved ahead without hesitation, demanding that the task be finished.

He could hear the clanking and banging from the next room as George finished washing the fixtures. It sounded like he was in a giant hollow can as the sound of metal against metal and rushing water echoed in the concrete room. The sound of the radio broke through occasionally with gospel songs from The Grand Olde Opry.

Vinni's thoughts left the milking parlor and returned to the party. He replayed the phone call, the way he looked in the mirror and Sara Jenkin's breasts. He was staring at the wall with his tongue rubbing across his bottom lip.

He was washing the wall instead of the floor when George came back in. The hollow sound of the metal door slamming caught his attention.

"Almost done. I'll close up and be at the house in a minute." The usual routine had the two finishing at the exact same time. Vinni's daydreaming had caused him about two minutes. It was time well spent.

Time for Church

It was a little past nine o'clock and Steve hadn't been home long when the phone rang. His emotions took over his medical creed and he hoped it wasn't Edna May calling again. He sat on the sofa and waited for the next ring. He listened to three more rings before it was answered. He heard Mary Alice pick up in the kitchen.

"Hello. Oh, hey Mary May. Sure, we're going. Yeah, no problem, but I'll ask." There was a pause before he heard his daughter shout across the hall.

"Daddy, can we give Mary May a ride to church today? I think maybe her mama's sick."

Steve's head was resting on the arm of the sofa and he shouted at the ceiling. "Sure, be glad to. Tell 'er we'll be there about ten till." He closed his eyes and waited for a response. There was no response from Mary Alice, but he heard the receiver hit the base and soon he was asleep.

It was nine forty five and Pleasant Grove was in orchestrated motion. Every family had their movements in perfect timing. This dance had been handed down from the previous generations. The birds circling above in lazy circles watched the fine tuned ballet. The movements were smooth and flowing as the cars pulled from their driveways onto the main road. They took their places one by one, meeting at crossroads and falling into line. They would approach the stage from every direction at five minutes before ten. Suddenly, they would turn and swirl into the church parking lot. Cars of every color and size would scatter around the church, landing in their perfect, predestined pattern. Then, the once empty stage would burst forth with dancers, as the car doors opened and families in full Sunday attire swirled around their cars and landed on the front stoop where they were swallowed up by the pair of double red doors.

"Good mownin', chach!" Reverend Simon Kowalski's northern accent cut through the southern air and beckoned a slow southern response. "Mooornin'"

Pleasant Grove Methodists kept their pastors on a regular rotation. Most never lasted more than four or five years. The members who always found fault were strong in voice and few in number. Their Commander in Chief was Edna May Crutchfield. It was under her leadership that the young pastor Harold Wells fell from grace. Harold had stopped Edna from painting the front doors of the church red. Therefore, he had to be taken out at any cost.

Edna found it inconvenient that he had no wife. "Surely any church would benefit by having a husband and wife team to lead the flock." Her casual, well placed comments didn't take root with the congregation who loved their young pastor. It was over coffee at a Bible study where Edna dropped the bomb.

"Harold is just so nice and mannerly, and well spoken. You can tell by the way he dressed that he comes from money. Most men, well, men without wives, couldn't tell a red sock from a blue tie. Not Harold, he's really put together.

It's almost like he has homosexual tendencies." Then she lifted her china cup to her red lips, pinky finger extended, and glanced around the room over the rim of her cup to see if her army had been engaged. Her living room was instantly filled with gasps, darting eyes, pursed lips and arms crossed over chubby stomachs.

"Well, ladies, let's get started on those church cookbooks." Edna had planted the seed, but would not be held responsible for the harvest. Her well planned scheme was progressing as intended, until the enemy changed course. Harold Wells became engaged to a lady he had been dating since college. She had taken a position as a secretary at the Methodist headquarters in Raleigh. They had continued dating, as their busy schedules permitted, and wanted to make sure a married life in the ministry was their calling.

The news of a shift in the enemy's position called for a new plan of attack. It was at the Bible study again. "Well, I didn't even know he had a girlfriend. I've certainly never seen or heard a thing about it. As good looking as he is, you would've thought he would be parading her around like a show horse, unless she's pregnant, of course."

Harold was not willing to expose his new bride to the venom that came from Edna's army and requested a transfer to a Methodist church in Raleigh.

Pastor Kowalski finished the morning announcements, had a short devotional and closed in prayer. They sang the first and last verses of Heavenly Sunlight accompanied by Viola Lamb on the organ, then went to their Sunday school classes.

The attendance book in George and Lidia's class looked much the same as the guest list at

Edna's dinner party the night before. George was relieved not to be teaching. It was his Sunday off. Steve Duncan was not relieved, it was his Sunday on.

Faye raised the windows to let in the morning air. She knew her husband had already worked that morning and hoped it would help keep him awake. Everyone could tell Steve was tired and assumed he had to see a patient in the early morning. Ruth wondered if it had been Edna. There was light small talk while Margaret took the roll.

"Only three missing today. I can understand why Edna would need a rest. What about Clarence and Betty?"

Ed spoke up and said they went to church with Betty's sister. "Her baby was being baptized and the whole family was at the Baptist Church." Steve asked Ruth to open in prayer and the class began.

The young adult class only had a few members. Most were away at college. Bill Lewis was present, just as he had promised on Mrs. Pratt's back stoop only hours earlier. Mike Wilkie was home for the weekend from pharmacy school at Carolina and Lynette Jenkins, Sara's oldest sister, was there. Mike sat beside Bill and noticed his slightly red and swollen face.

"Hey, Bill. Run into some trouble at the police department?" Mike's mind was racing about what kind of ointment would sooth his wound. Bill looked across the room where Lynette was sitting and rubbed his cheek with the back of his hand.

"Yeah, something came up last night." He glanced down at his twill pants and said to himself, "Yeah, Pratt's bear paw hand came up, slammed the hell out 'o me."

Mrs. Pratt sat behind the small wooden desk and looked at Bill. She smiled and tilted her head to one side. "I'm sure you handled yourself and a most professional and Christian manner."

Bill returned the smile and tilted his head to the opposite side. "Oh, absolutely. In the Lord's work, pain is gain. We all have our crosses to bear paw." He coughed as he said the word paw and everyone just thought he was quoting scripture.

Vinni Rises to the Occasion

The youth Sunday school attendees were the same ones who met in the garage office the night before, with exception of Roy White. Roy was attending the Trinity A.M.E. Church with his family and wouldn't be home until after two o'clock. It was difficult to get volunteers to teach their class. Most people didn't want to spend their time trying to keep the class quiet and under control. Velma Stout was different. She had been teaching this age at school for almost ten years. She had learned from years of trial and error how to keep the peace and respect.

The Tribe was seated on one side of the long white table. It had been made in the woodworking class at Grove High. The plywood top was eight feet long and thirty inches wide. The students wanted to leave it the full size of the plywood sheet, but the wood shop teacher had to teach them how to mark a chalk line and use a skill saw. They used the scraps to make the apron nailed to the wooden legs. Vinni was in the middle with his friends seated on either side.

Sara was directly across from Vinni. She had her Bible on the table and her hands in her lap as she leaned over to read the verses that would be discussed. Vinni was thrown back into a trance. His tongue rubbed his bottom lip and his index finger began making small circles on the tip of his thumb.

Ms. Stout banged her knuckles on the table to get their attention. "Okay class, we all had a wonderful time last night and we are so thankful for our friends."

Vinni knew there were other people in the room and someone was speaking, but the only thing he could concentrate on was the way Sara's dress gaped open above her cleavage. He continued to stare as the others closed their eyes and bowed their heads for prayer. He was aware that the lesson had begun by the sound of Ms. Stout's voice. The familiar sound of her knuckles on the plywood table jerked him back to reality.

"Vinni, would you please stand and read the first scripture? It's on page eleven in your book, in the middle of the page." She tilted her head back to focus on the words and waited for Vinni to begin.

Vinni knew exactly what state his body was in and his first reaction was to remain seated. Then his mouth formed a smile to one side and he stood up proudly and unashamed. His problem was at eye level of all those who were seated. The guys turned their head toward opposite walls and covered their mouths to keep from laughing. The girls turned red and wanted to look away, but couldn't. Ms. Stout continued to focus on her book. Vinni lifted his book, just like the pastor, raised onto his toes and arched his back. His hips gave a thrust toward the girls and he began reading with the voice of an evangelist. "Thus saith the Lord your God."

Ms. Stout looked over her glasses to see what was causing such a commotion and immediately saw the problem. "Down, Davis, down!"

Vinni continued. "It was I who brought you out of the land of . . ."

She rapped her knuckles on the table and the sound echoed off the walls. "Vinni Davis, sit down!"

Vinni stopped reading and looked at her, as he remained standing. "Oh, you want me to sit down? When you said down, Davis I thought you were talking about my . . ."

She hit the table with both hands to stop his speech. "Vinni Davis, set yourself down this instant!" She stood straight up and shook her hands at the class. "I will not tolerate such unchristian behavior in the Lord's House. You, every one of you, should be ashamed." Her lips were clinched tight when she stormed out the door. The class heard the bathroom door down the hall slam.

Ruth also heard the door slam and excused herself to see what was happening. She stepped into the bathroom and saw Velma leaning over the sink tears. She walked over and put her hand on her shoulder. "What in the world is wrong, honey?"

Velma raised her head and Ruth saw her tears were caused by laughter. Velma looked at her and tried to stop laughing.

"I have seen it all, Ruth, I have seen it all." She continued to explain the events that had just taken place. Then Velma threw her hips forward and repeated what Vinni had said. Their shouts of laughter could be heard down the hall. George and Lidia exhaled at the same time and shook their heads.

Understanding Velma

Velma Stout loved those children. She loved their spirit and humor. She had to hold a tight line with their discipline, but she wanted them to experience all the joy and laughter they could. Velma remembered her childhood, the parties and sleepovers. She remembered swimming in the pond on hot summer days, working in the garden and long train rides. Velma Stout had always been full of life and was often the one leading the pack.

Velma's grandfather, on her mother's side, made his fortune in the railroad business. His business travels kept him away from home most of the time and he took great joy in spending his fortune and love on his children and grandchildren. Her grandmother was one of the most beautiful and proper ladies she had ever seen. Friends often said Velma was more like her grandmother than anyone else in the family. Her grandmother's family was from Savannah and the ocean tides always pulled her east. They built a cottage at Atlantic Beach large enough to accommodate thirty guests.

Velma and her family spent most of their summers at the cottage. Her father was an accountant, but it was her mother's fortune that supported the family.

The Cottage, as it was referred to by the family, was where Velma met James. James's father was a business associate with her grandfather and was a guest at the cottage most of the summer also.

It was the summer of 1918 on the dance floor at The Lumina Club in Atlantic Beach. The orchestra was playing and the ocean breeze cooled the guests. James whispered in Velma's ear and gave her his heart, pronounced his love for her and asked her to be his wife. She remembered how he had to hold her tighter because the strength left her body and she almost slumped to the floor.

The wedding was to be at The Cottage the following summer. It would be a grand entrance into a new life when James graduated from medical school and married his beloved Velma. Her teaching position at Pleasant Grove allowed her to keep her summer at The Cottage. That summer was spent planning a wedding. The next year was one of the happiest she had known, filled with planning, phone calls to her grandmother and letters from James.

The week of the wedding was spent at The Cottage. The planning had been done and the preparation was taken care of by the staff. It was a time of relaxation, celebration and anticipation. James had finished his exams two weeks earlier and would arrive on Friday night before the wedding on Saturday.

Thursday night, Velma's grandmother asked her to walk on the beach. She told her how proud she was of Velma's work at Pleasant Grove and hoped she would always keep her love for the children. She reached into her dress pocket and lifted out a necklace with a sapphire and diamond pendant. She explained how it was given to her by Velma's grandfather on a trip to Paris. She told Velma the sapphire reminded her of the ocean and the diamonds reminded her of the stars. Her grandmother draped the necklace around her neck and she felt the cool platinum rest on her warm skin. Velma knew she shouldn't play with the pendant, but couldn't keep her fingers from holding it.

Velma fell asleep that night on the wicker chaise lounge in the upstairs sleeping porch. The sounds of the roaring ocean had lulled her to sleep.

The next morning it was her grandmother's fingers on her arm that woke her up. Velma's mother was standing beside her and tears filled their eyes. Her grandmother spoke because her mother couldn't. It was James. There had been a terrible train accident and he had been killed.

The rooms were filled with beautiful flowers. Now they had a new purpose. They celebrated a past life instead of a new beginning. The remainder of the summer was spent at The Cottage, but there were no guests. Velma spent the summer with her mother and grandmother, supported by the staff and occasional weekend visits from her father and grandfather. She spent countless hours holding the pendant that rested on her chest, trying to regain her strength and start a new life.

It was Pleasant Grove that gave her a new life. The Cottage no longer offered her comfort and the reminder of her previous life was painful. Pleasant Grove, North Carolina was as far as she could possibly go away from her pain and she grew to love it as home.

The pendant was put away that summer when she left The Cottage. She hadn't seen it since, but her fingers still dance across her chest, trying to hold it.

The Worship Service

The class of five and six-year-olds ran to the front entrance of the church and pulled the white rope attached to the bell in the bell tower. The sound of the bell and giggling youngsters let the congregation know that Sunday school was over.

People began filing into the sanctuary in groups defined by age. The oldest members gathered on benches close to the front. They were usually seated before the bell rang and offered smiles to the others as they filed in.

The next generation filled the middle of the church on both sides of the aisle. They usually stood and talked with each other for a while as the youth walked past to the back pews of the sanctuary.

The youngest children would fight their way against the arriving tide of teenagers and find their parents.

The sounds and smells were the same almost every Sunday. The hardwood floors echoed hard soled dress shoes while the murmur of voices scattered around the room, broken by spurts of laughter and giggling. A fresh pine scent lingered, thanks to Grace Weaver's cleaning. Viola Lamb's organ music was soft and called everyone to be seated as the choir entered.

Their footsteps could be heard as they made their way from the choir room in the back hall to the door leading into the choir loft. The choir members took their places on three pews as the organ music came to a close. The rustling of their clothes and sheet music gave way to complete silence. The congregation was given one full minute of silence before the pastor entered from the narthex.

Sixty seconds seemed like an hour to the younger attendees, but it was welcomed by the others. This was the only time in the week when they were at complete rest. No one had expectations, no chores, no school work. They were at rest in the Lord's house. This time also gave some tired bodies an opportunity to seek the rest they needed.

Just before heads holding heavy eyes began to nod, the organ would offer a triumphant march and the congregation would rise as the pastor entered from behind them. Reverend Simon Kowalski was the first pastor at Pleasant Grove to wear a robe and the congregation was still adjusting to his grand entrance to organ music. Some of the youth on the back rows would offer a regal bow after he had passed. Often the giggles that followed could be heard by parents and pastor alike.

Regardless of who offered the bows, heads would turn and eyebrows would drop and Vinni was given the silent blame. Edna's army in the choir would lower their heads and peer across the tops of their glasses, straining to see exactly who did what. Their duty was to report to Edna. Velma and Ruth would tap each other's legs and quietly snicker behind smiling lips. The men were too involved in organizing their sheet music to notice the congregation.

There was an unscheduled pause when the pastor reached the pulpit and turned to face the congregation. Simon gave a nod in Viola's direction. She played a few familiar notes and the congregation chimed in singing Happy Birthday to Jake Adams.

It was his fourteenth birthday and he had sacrificed his weekend at the lake to help the community prepare Edna's home for Gary's arrival. Jake's red cheeks showed his embarrassment as he stared at the floor. Vinni and The Tribe were held at bay as the congregation faced the back of the church. The girls used the closing of the song as an excuse to hug Jake and his friends. The congregation was being seated and the last organ note was drifting towards the ceiling before Vinni released Sara Jenkins and her breasts.

Tom and Margaret had trouble concentrating on the sermon. They were writing notes to each other on the back of the bulletins. *Did you remember to take the steaks out of the freezer? Yes, they're marinating. Did you pick up the cake? Oh, damn, I forgot the cake!* Margaret punched Tom's side and marked out his last message. Tom looked at his wife and helplessly raised his palms upward. They tried to refocus on the sermon, but it was harder than ever with the new revelation of no birthday cake.

Simon closed his sermon and asked the ushers to take the morning offering. This released the congregation to smile and whisper among themselves. All was done under the watchful eyes of Edna's army. Their heads were bobbing back and forth to see the congregation's movements and up and down to focus on details.

Tom and Margaret decided to make a quick exit before the last hymn began. The usher's footsteps were echoed by theirs as they nodded for Jake to meet them outside.

Tom used his left hand to shade his eyes when he looked at Bill Lewis's car. "What's that on the hood of Bill's car? It looks like a bag from Piggly Wiggly."

Jake just grinned and kept walking. He expected it was two large cans of poke 'n beans.

Sunday Afternoon

It was a typical Sunday lunch at most homes; sweet tea, fried chicken, pot roast, green beans, butter beans and corn, creamed potatoes, tomatoes, homemade biscuits, gravy and pound cake or chocolate pie for dessert.

The menu was special at the Adams house. Tom was just taking the steaks from the charcoal grill when Margaret answered the phone.

"Oh, Daisy White, you do not have to do that. Listen, I will have Tom run over. He just forgot to pick it up yesterday. I know we had a great time, too. Edna looked lovely. She told me what a life saver you were and you made Jake's birthday cake, too. Really, I can have Tom . . . Okay, Daisy. If you insist, but under one condition. Bring your family and have cake and ice cream with us. No questions. Tom is making a freezer of chocolate. We'll let the boys churn. How's that? Great, let's say around two. See you then. I'm sure the cake will be delicious. Yours always are. Thanks Daisy."

Margaret told Tom and Jake that Daisy was bringing the birthday cake and her family was joining them for cake and ice cream around two.

Jake was glad to hear the news. "Cool, is Roy comin'?"

"Hello, oh Jake, happy birthday. No, he just left for the barn. Can I give him a message? Oh. I know he will hate he missed it. Tell Roy and the Whites we said hello. I'll have Vinni call after milking. Um hum, bye."

Vinni's responsibilities at the dairy were constant. He was beginning to hate being tied down, but wouldn't let himself complain. George gave him a reasonable wage for his work and having spending money lessened the pain.

Lunch at 104 Winterberry Court had been served on the terrace. Miss Mimi had the day off. Genevieve and her Aunt Margaret had fixed the meal. The Longs often had heavy meals during the week at business meetings, so Sunday lunch was usually light. Genevieve made chicken salad the day before and Margaret cut up a cantaloupe to serve with the sandwiches.

"I'll finish here. You go ahead and call your mother. She'll have more time to talk while the men are at the barn."

The dairy barn at Pleasant Grove seemed a million miles from Winterberry Court, but it was where Margaret Long spent some wonderful years with George and their parents. She still planned conversations and visits around milkings. It just came naturally.

Lidia trotted inside and answered the phone on the fifth ring. "Hello. Oh, Genevieve, George told me you called yesterday. Sorry I missed your call. We've had a crazy week end. Never mind that. I'll tell you later. Tell me about the spring dance and all."

The next half hour was filled with Genevieve explaining every detail, every thought and every expectation for the dance. Lidia sat at the kitchen table and listened. It reminded her of the times she sat and listened to Genevieve years before. She had seen her beautiful daughter sink into a depression and wondered if she would ever return. Genevieve Davis was back. After being taken on Genevieve's journey, they said their goodbyes.

"Listen Genevieve, everything sounds great. Tell Margaret I'll call her tomorrow to finalize everything. See you soon. We love you. Bye."

George and Lidia had been talking about Vinni's future for the past several months. It was obvious that college wasn't in his future. The farm was doing well and had potential to support two families. It would mean extra cows and more hours of work, but if Vinni was available full time after he graduated and Hurley was still part of the farm, it was a very sound proposition. George had decided to slowly increase his herd over the next few years and when Vinni graduated it would be large enough to offer him a future in the family business.

Vinni was feeding four new calves that had been born the week before. George had taught him how to milk the cows by hand. Vinni milked the first two cows in the barn to feed the new calves. The first day he fed the calves, he tried a time saving method. The fresh milk was poured into metal buckets with a large rubber nipple attached to the bottom side. Vinni decided to hold one bucket to feed a calf and the other bucket would be supported in the hay trough. This way he could feed two calves at one time. When the buckets were half empty he would switch and feed the last two calves.

His plan was derailed when the milk bucket in the trough was turned over soon after the calf started drinking. Vinni jumped over to save the milk and dropped his bucket. All the milk was lost, along with his first hour of labor. His frustration turned to anger and he kicked one bucket across the barn and grabbed the other one and threw it out the barn door. The calves jumped backwards and ran out the barn doors. George was inside the milking parlor and the sounds outside were loud enough to be heard over the echoes of humming milkers, mooing cows and radio music.

Vinni was chasing the four escaped calves past the parlor door. "Damnit, come back here you little bastards." George quickly looked out the window just as Vinni darted after a calf and tripped over the bucket he had thrown out the door. George took a quick step toward the door then caught himself and stopped. Vinni was in no state of mind to listen. He had to learn this one by experience. He went back to the window and watched. The four calves had separated and trotted in four directions. Vinni stood up, grabbing the bucket by the metal handle and threw it at the calves. When the metal bucket hit the gravel drive, the calves bolted and ran as hard as they could. Vinni ran a few steps in one direction then turned and ran in the opposite. The four calves were disappearing into the corn field, the garden and around the house.

Vinni stopped his useless running and screamed, "Just starve then, you little bastards. To hell with you all. Just starve." He walked over, jerked the bucket off the ground and headed back to the barn.

By this time Lidia was on the back porch wondering what the cursing rant was about. George could see her from the barn window as she covered her mouth and laughed.

Vinni slung the parlor door open and George returned to the milkers, as if he hadn't seen the explosion.

"Calves are out. They kicked the bucket over and ran." Vinni was offering the explanation as he headed to scrape the lot.

George knew he couldn't release Vinni from his duties. "I'll leave the last two cows for you to milk. You'll have to wash and sterilize the buckets." Their voices bounced around the milking parlor, but their eyes never met.

George took the milkers off of his last two cows and left two standing for Vinni. He stepped into the next room to start washing the equipment and saw Lidia walking down from the house.

She carried a bucket full of milk from the refrigerator and the four calves were bumping into her and each other trying to satisfy their hunger. She remembered when the same thing happened to her as a young girl in Italy. Her grandmother had brought the sheep back from the neighbor's vineyard the same way.

Vinni heard the barn door close. Their perfect timing was ruined that evening. The extra time it took George to milk the new cows didn't balance the time it took Vinni to feed the calves and chase them after their escape.

Lidia knew when she heard the milkers shut down that it was time to start putting supper on the table.

Vinni's episode had effected everyone's evening, his, the calves', his parent's and Jake's. It would even effect Sara Jenkin's evening, but Vinni had no idea. All he could see was his frustrating, boring, dead end life.

His chores were finished and he walked back to the house an hour after George. He was walking into the kitchen and the screen door slammed on his words. "I gotta' get outta' here."

Lidia spoke to him from the sink. "Jake called earlier. He wants you to call."

Vinni was heading up stairs. "I'll just ride my bike over after I take a shower." His dark mood lingered in the house. It was like a heavy fog hiding his future.

Vinni was heading toward the back door as George and Lidia were finishing their supper. "Are you sure you don't want to eat before you go?" Lidia had a plate waiting at his seat.

Vinni headed out the door without looking back and answered after the door closed. "No."

Lidia leaned back in her chair and shouted out the door. "It may be dark before you get back. Call before you leave Jake's house. Okay?"

Vinni was walking across the yard and didn't answer. He nodded his head in agreement, but neither parent noticed.

George tilted his chair back toward the wall and rocked on the back legs. Lidia looked at her plate and rubbed the back of her tired neck.

"Oh, I talked to Genevieve today." She gave an extra effort to break the somber mood. "She's so excited about the spring dance. Remember, Margaret invited us up, too. Anyway, I'll talk to Margaret tomorrow to finalize everything. It'll be nice to get away. Don't you think?"

She leaned across the table and held her hand for George to take. His head was resting in the palms of his hands and he was staring at the ceiling and didn't notice. "Um hum."

Lidia knew where his thoughts were. "He's fourteen, George. Everything's changing."

George lowered his chair to the floor. "I know, but I'm not sure it's changing for the best."

Vinni was half way to Jake's house, climbing the hill that ended at the Jenkin's drive. His bike leaned from side to side as he stood up and let his weight pump the pedals. It felt good to work out his frustrations. He wanted to scream, or run, or hit something and the bike ride satisfied his urge. He didn't look up to see where he was. He just stared at his front tire drifting back and forth, waiting to feel the release when he crested the steep hill.

Vinni and Sara

"Hey Vinni!" He didn't expect to hear anyone call his name. When he jumped, he lost his timing and nearly fell off the bike. Sara Jenkins laughed and he put his left foot down and dragged the bike to a stop.

"What the hell, Sara? You scared me to death." Vinni was walking his bike to the end of the gravel drive where she was standing. They were both laughing and Sara walked to meet him on the white line at the edge of the pavement. "I was on my way to Jake's. They had ice cream and cake for his birthday. Roy and his family were over, but they've probably left by now. It took me forever to milk and I'm runnin' late."

Sara was standing in the edge of the grass with her arms crossed rocking back and forth. She was restless in Vinni's presence and he could tell. He watched her as she stared at his bicycle tire.

"Mary Alice said she might go over to Jake's, too. I thought I'd get a ride if she came by. It's getting' kind o' late. She's probably not comin' by. They probably had company at the last minute. A lot o' times they have company from Chapel Hill on Sundays. I wish we had a phone. It's crazy not being able to call anybody. I just talked to Mary Alice after church. I guess she's not comin' by."

Sara was the youngest of four sisters. Their mother worked in the cotton mill before the girls were born. Now it was a full time job keeping up with the family. Lillian and Hank Jenkins led a simple life, mostly dependent on what the small farm could supply. Lillian was the hardest worker in the marriage and was considered a saint to endure Hank's occasional drunken weekends. She was very proud of her daughters and took great joy in sewing matching outfits for them to wear. When the Jenkins girls were seen together in town shopping or at church, they were always dressed the same. Lillian was an excellent seamstress and sewed for the neighborhood ladies for extra money. Lillian's dresses, like Eloise's hairdos, could be easily spotted. Several ladies could be seen wearing the handiwork from both on Sundays.

They would complement each other according to pattern number. "Is that McCalls number four thirty-five? Lillian made me that last year for Easter, but it was supposed to be cold so she added sleeves. When the summer heat set in, I just had her take the sleeves off. Don't you just love it? It looks like a totally different dress in a print instead of a solid. Oh, listen, I overheard someone at the Piggly Wiggly say that the Alliance Store is going to stop selling fabric. Have you ever?"

The ladies would usually buy a dozen eggs when they went for a fitting or dropped some fabric off. Any help for the Jenkins was always welcomed and freely given.

Sara was staring at the ground and Vinni was staring at her breasts. He wasn't sure how to handle the silence. Was he supposed to offer Sara a ride on his bike to Jake's? Was he supposed to walk with her? Was he supposed to offer her the bike? He broke the silence with awkward comments. "Yeah, it's gettin' late. Mama told me Jake called. I didn't call him back, just thought I'd go on over. It's gettin' late. You're probably right. She's probably not comin' by. It's gettin' late."

Their shifting eyes had not met. Sara had her head tilted to one side and was staring at Vinni with one eye closed to block the evening sun. Vinni was staring at his bicycle tire.

Sara shrugged her shoulders. "So, you goin' to Jake's?"

Vinni looked down the road toward Jake's house. "I dunno, it's gettin' late. He probably thinks I'm not comin' anyway."

He rolled his eyes back to Sara and she looked back at the grass. "Guess you could stay here for a while if you're not goin' to Jake's." She tilted her head back and gave him a one eyed gaze.

Vinni's index finger started making circles on the end of his thumb. "Yeah, that sounds good."

Sara turned and headed back to the house without uncrossing her arms. Vinni walked beside her. He could feel her shirt brush against his arm. The Jenkins' house set in the woods and the shade allowed their eyes to refocus. Sara was a little taller than Vinni and a little heavier. It wasn't noticeable until they hugged and it placed her breasts exactly where Vinni wanted them. They were both nervous and the chatter that happened when friends were around was gone. The fact was, they didn't want to talk, they just wanted to be beside each other. When they reached the front porch, Vinni saw Lillian step away from the window. He could tell the rest of the family was inside by the voices. The only words he could understand them say were Vinni Davis.

Sara sat on the porch swing with her hands under her legs. This gave Vinni the peek he had been waiting for. He was aware that he was probably being watched and sat on the swing, leaving as much space as possible between their legs. The swing rocked with their weight and Vinni stared and thumped at the rusty metal chain supporting his end of the swing. Sara held the opposite chain and stared into the woods. Vinni cut his eyes to the left and tried to see inside without turning his head. He was close to the window and didn't like the feeling of someone watching him from the other side.

His eyes were fixed on the window, hoping to see beyond the sheer curtain. "Your folks in tonight?"

"Yeah, they're all here. I thought my sisters had dates tonight, but they didn't. Mama don't like em' goin' out on Saturday and Sunday, too."

Vinni saw the shadows inside float toward the kitchen and soon heard the mumbled sound of the radio. It was darker on the porch in the shade than it was on the road. It seemed later that it really was and Vinni felt uncomfortable. He was in a situation he didn't create, in a strange place without the support of The Tribe and he didn't know what Sara expected. His palms were sweaty and his breath was too shallow to form words. He could almost hear his heart pounding and the pinching bulge in his pants was very uncomfortable.

Sara remained silent as the darkness settled around them. The only things Vinni could hear were the chains squeaking against the hooks in the porch ceiling, frogs croaking and grinding, the mumbled sound of a distant radio and his pounding heart. He wanted to leave more than he wanted to stay, but his body wouldn't move and his mouth wouldn't speak. He was held prisoner.

He felt the weight in the swing shift and then he felt Sara touch his arm. He was too scared to look and stared straight ahead, past the lime green metal chairs on the other end of the porch and into the darkening woods. He could feel her lean closer to him and her breast touched his right arm. He felt her breath on his neck and could smell the chocolate cake she had eaten just before he came.

The message came in a whisper. "I like you, Vinni." There was a long silence, leaving Sara's heart and emotions hanging and unsafe.

Vinni knew he had to respond and the only thing that really worked for him at times like this was to be honest. He lifted his hands a few inches above his legs and turned toward Sara. She didn't move her head and Vinni had to stop just before his nose touched her forehead.

He whispered the reply because his lungs were paralyzed. "I like you, too, Sara, but right now I've gotta' go. 'Cause if I don't, somethin's gonna' explode. It's either going to be my chest or my dick, either way, I gotta' go."

Sara had never been this close to Vinni, or any boy, for that matter. He was the most beautiful creature she had ever seen and the rising moon shortened her breaths. She couldn't stop herself and didn't want to. Her right hand floated up and touched his left cheek. Vinni was completely helpless and weak. He kept his eyes closed. She kept his head from turning away and kissed his cheek. He inhaled in short breaths while she held her lips against his brown cheek. He felt her breath on his eyelashes and sat very still, hoping she wouldn't stop. He liked the touch of her lips as much as the touch of her breasts and at that moment, he had them both.

They were worlds away from that porch swing and didn't hear the approaching footsteps, but the rattling door knob jerked them to attention. When Lillian stepped onto the porch, the swing was bumping against the backs of their legs. Vinni was staring at the side of the house with his hands in his pockets and Sara had her arms crossed and was smiling at her mother.

"Would you like to come inside, children? We have chocolate cake." Lillian had one hand on the door jamb and the other on the door knob. She didn't want to be outside and didn't want to be inside. She only needed to be seen. Lillian Jenkins had been taught the ways of young love by her three older daughters.

"No, thank you, Mrs. Jenkins. I really need to be going. It's getting' dark and I told Mama I wouldn't be out too late." He nodded his head at Lillian, then Sara, shrugged his shoulders and trotted down the front steps with his hands stuck in his pockets. He turned and walked backwards, facing the porch. "Bye, Sara, thanks, see ya at school tomorrow. Happy birthday, oh I mean, never mind." He turned and trotted to the end of the drive and didn't remove his hands until he picked up his bike.

He had struggled to reach the top of that hill. Now his struggle was over. He held his hands in the air and stared at the moonlit clouds as he coasted back down.

"Hey, I'm back." George and Lidia never knew what mood to expect when Vinni appeared. They were glad to hear the happiness in his voice.

"Is everything okay? I called Margaret to see if you had left and she said you didn't get there. We were about to drive down to see what happened."

Vinni was still rising on the wings of his first kiss. "Oh, sorry. I stopped by and visited with Sara instead. They don't have a phone."

Vinni was trotting up the stairs and George looked at Lidia and whispered "Sara Jenkins," pretending to hold two cantaloupes on his chest. Lidia threw a magazine at him.

"Vomanin sono amarti, nota di diorno e sempre amanti a tutta la, sempre amanti."

APRIL 26TH 1948

The Overheard Phone Call

"Hello. Margaret, hello. No, George and Hurley are planting corn and Vinni, of course, is at school." Lidia laughed at the reply from Vinni's Aunt Margaret and shook her head. "Well, no, as a matter of fact, I can't guarantee that he's at school. Honestly, Margaret, was George like this growing up? Sometimes I wonder where that boy gets his character. They say some things skip a generation, but heaven knows our parents were nothing like this. You are so sweet to say that Margaret, and yes, Genevieve is just like her father. I'm glad, too. Thank you for the invitation. It is a blessing to see a light in Genevieve again."

Both Lidia and Margaret could hear the familiar clicks in the background. It was the sound of a neighbor trying to use the party phone line. They both knew which neighbors were on the Davis's party line. They also knew when their conversations were being listened to. There was a click when someone picked up and another click when they hung up. A double click was usual, but an occasional single click gave them reason to be careful what they said. They could even hear noises and voices in the background of the person who was listening to their conversations. No matter how impolite it was for a person to eavesdrop, it was considered even less polite to confront them. Community rules did, however, allow a person to break in on a phone call in case of an emergency.

Lidia had to interrupt conversations occasionally during Genevieve's illness. She would pick up the phone, and if she heard voices she would say, "Excuse me, I apologize for the interruption, but I need the line for an emergency call." The users would always oblige and hang up. There was never eavesdropping on emergency calls.

If there was a single click the conversations were usually shared at Eloise's Beauty Shop. The information was always given with a most concerned tone and accompanied by shaking heads and sad looks all around. "I went to call my neighbor and overheard so and so saying . . ." The long story that followed was always much more than a couple of overheard words. Margaret had a private line in Greensboro and little patience for single clickers in Pleasant Grove.

The single click alerted Lidia and Margaret that they were being listened to and their plans for the following weekend would be repeated at Eloise's.

Lidia offered a remedy to the eavesdropper on the line. "Anyway, Margaret, I'll be in touch."

Margaret wanted the entire community to know about Genevieve and the wonderful weekend being planned. "Nonsense, Lidia. Daniel is at the Country Club playing golf and George is working hard expanding that wonderful farm. It's time for us hens to cluck a while. Genevieve is just beside herself about this Spring Gala and she should be. It's the social event of the year in Greensboro. All the college kids will be at the dance and all the parents will be at the club.

I can't wait. Listen, dear, I want you, no, I insist you come up on Thursday. We'll spend the day shopping. There's no sense in letting the kids have all the fun. We'll give them a run for their money."

Lidia was covering her grin with her fingers, as if the listener could also see her. Margaret paused and listened for the second click. When she didn't hear it, she continued to feed the community gossip mill.

"Well, I might as well tell you. I was in New York a couple of weeks ago and went in Christian Dior's salon. They had the most beautiful spring line I have ever seen. Well, Elizabeth Anne Slater, you've meet Ellie, I graduated with her, anyway, she's the clerk for Dior. I picked out ten outfits and brought them back. Five for me and five for you. She said we could keep any we wanted and return the others. Her brother is stopping by next week on his way up from Atlanta and he'll return what we don't choose. Who knows, maybe I'll just keep them all."

Lidia's mind was spinning at such an idea. She didn't know if Margaret was sincere or presenting a script to be replayed at Eloise's. At this point, there was no reason to listen for a second click.

"Margaret, honestly, I don't know what to say."

Margaret couldn't resist. "Just say you'll be here Thursday morning at ten o'clock. Oh, and Edna May, tell everyone at the beauty shop I said hello."

Her last comment got an immediate second click and the sisters-in-law had a well deserved laugh.

An Appointment to Tell the News

"Hello, Eloise, I need to make an appointment." Eloise's Beauty Shop was closed on Mondays and she answered the phone in the den. Eloise heard the familiar snappy, rude tone in Edna May's voice and knew her medicine had worn off.

"An appointment for what, Edna? Well, you just got one Friday. Well, good Lord. What in the world has gotten into you all of a sudden?" Eloise licked her thumb and started flipping through her appointment book. "How about Thursday? What do you mean Thursday will be too late? Too late for what? Wednesday? Edna, you know Wednesday is my busiest day. Everybody gets their perm on Wednesday so they'll be relaxed by Sunday. Work you in? Edna, if I try to work you in you will have to come in the morning and it will take all day. You'll have to sit between everybody's shampoos and sets, perms and teasings. Well, lordy, lordy, lordy, fine, just fine. Come on Wednesday morning, but I'm telling you, you'll be here all day. I'm not lettin' you jump in front of my appointments."

Eloise threw her appointment book back in the drawer and slammed it shut. Lester lowered his newspaper and shifted his toothpick to the left side of his mouth. "Edna off her medication?"

Eloise rolled her eyes, crossed her arms and jerked her foot. "Sounds like."

Lester chuckled. "Hell, I knew it was too good to last." The newspaper shook when he chuckled.

"Oh, Lester." Eloise brought the book back out and studied her Wednesday appointments to see how she could work Edna in.

School Days

Frank Johnson was keeping Ester Pratt very busy as the end of the school year was nearing. She had no problem keeping up and no complaints.

"Mrs. Pratt, have you finished typing the memo about the May Day celebration and talent show?" Mrs. Pratt leaned her head backwards toward his door. "Yes, sir, I laid it on your desk just before lunch."

He picked up the empty paper bag that held the trash from his lunch. "Oh, here it is. Thanks. Will you make a copy for each class?"

Mrs. Pratt smiled with pride. "I gave one to each teacher at lunch."

She heard his mumbled reply. "Well, I'll be damned."

Frank Johnson was a confirmed bachelor and was dependent on the kindness of ladies in the community. His rugged good looks held up well from his college days on the football team. He had let his body go a bit, but he still enjoyed walking out to the gym and watching the basketball teams practice after school. Even though he was very strict, students knew what he expected and didn't mind obeying his rules. It had taken him several years to reach this relationship with the students.

The only student he had serious trouble with was Vinni. He hoped to retire in a few years and Vinni made him wish he had retired earlier. He had confided to Ms. Stout that he really liked Vinni and things would be a little boring without his antics.

He enjoyed talking to Ms. Stout. He had taken the job as principal the year after her tragic summer and they had grown very close. Velma had always looked after him, making sure he received food after covered dish dinners and never spent holidays alone. Edna had, on several occasions, tried to start rumors of a romance, but they never took root.

The students were heading up the hallway to class after lunch. Their voices and footsteps echoed between the wooden floors and high ceiling. Suddenly, Ms. Stout heard a scream and Vinni's face popped into her head. She quickly walked toward the door leading to the hall. The group of girls that always led the class out of the lunchroom were huddled against the wall, staring at the ceiling and holding their noses. It had caused a traffic jam and the boys in the back were stretching to see what had happened. By the time Mrs. Stout had arrived, The Tribe had discovered the problem.

A first grader had thrown up after lunch. They were trapped. The only way out was to step over the spattered lunch remains that smelled like sour milk. The janitor had sprinkled green sawdust over the chunky liquid, but had not returned to make a final cleaning. Even Ms. Stout's head automatically turned to the side and her eyes closed when she arrived. Without looking in their direction, she waved her hand in the air.

"Back door, just go out the back door and come in by the bathrooms."

The girls hurried back toward the lunchroom, but had to fight against the tide. The guys had to get a closer look. They covered their mouths and nosed with their hands, making it difficult for Mrs. Stout to hear their comments. "Oh hell, look at that shit. It reeks."

Ms. Stout was walking back to the classroom and commented to herself, "If that shit reeks stop looking at it."

She knew that sending Vinni past the girl's bathroom was a gamble and decided to meet the students at the side door. To make extra sure that no one escaped, she asked them to count off as they entered.

Mary May was first, "One, two, three." The count continued without problem until, "thirteen, fourteen, eighteen, sixteen." Gerald had made it a habit to always reply as number eighteen, no matter where he was in line. Ms. Stout picked up the count bobbing her head and finger with each number. "Three short."

She stood at her desk as the students were seated and examined the empty chairs. She was sure Vinni was missing. Who else? As Eighteen sat down, the empty chairs were revealed. Vinni, Jake and Sara Jenkins were not there. "Hum."

Her eyebrows dropped and her lips tightened as she headed back to the side door. She had just turned the corner when she heard a commotion from the hall leading to the lunchroom. She heard quick loud footsteps and stomping, laughter, a pause, a scream and more laughter. She turned and started in the direction of the commotion and stuck her head in the classroom.

"Everyone sit and open your math books to page seventy four. Work problems one through seven. Mary May, take names."

She continued walking and the scene at the end of the hall explained the absent students and the noise. Vinni had decided to take the hall passage back to class and jumped the vomit. He ran from the lunchroom door and sailed through the air with legs extended and arms raised. He slapped the top of the tall cased opening as he flew to safety on the other side. Jake had followed, but with less style. Sara was the last to try. She wanted to impress Vinni and refused to go around the building.

The two guys were watching from safety when she began to run. She couldn't run as fast at the guys and her shoes didn't have the same traction as their tennis shoes. In her nervous haste to get over the green sea of vomit, she jumped sooner than expected. Her jump was long enough, but her timing was off. Instead of leaping with one foot in front of the other, like Vinni and Jake, she jumped with her feet beside each other. She landed about four inches shy of clean hardwood. Her heels landed together leaving skid marks through the green sawdust. Her feet shot into the air and her back slammed into the center of the first grader's lunch. The slick goo let her continue sliding and her dress was pushed up to her waist. When she jumped up, her back was plastered in green, chunky sawdust. Her dress was folded up and stuck to her waist revealing white panties covered in puke.

Vinni and Jake covered their mouths and burst into laughter bending over and pointing at Sara. Ms. Stout arrived just as the hysterical tears began to flow.

"Principal's office." The two guys knew where to go. She looked as Sara, standing in a horrible mess, crying uncontrollably and holding her arms away from her body. "Just go back and step outside, honey. I'll be right there." Sara turned and started walking through the smeared remains on the floor.

"Be careful, don't fall." It was a natural response from Ms. Stout, but it sent Sara over the edge and her cries got louder and echoed down the hall until she walked out the door.

Mrs. Pratt's eyes disappeared behind her round cheeks when Vinni and Jake walked in. "Ms. Stout sent us up." She just snorted and stared as they stood there waiting for a response. She looked at Vinni, then shook her head in disappointment when she looked at Jake.

"I'm surprised at you, Jake Adams." Jake looked at Vinni. Vinni shook his head in the same manner. "I'm surprised at you too, Jake Adams." The snickers that followed enraged Mrs. Pratt and her chair hit the wall when she stood up to report to Mr. Johnson. She gave three quick knocks on the glass of Mr. Johnson's door.

"Trouble again. You know who." Then she gave a disappointed sigh. "And Jake Adams." Vinni shook his head and repeated his response. "I'm disappointed in you, Jake Adams."

Mr. Johnson was on the phone with the county office discussing new bus driver requirements. He decided to leave the two under the watchful eyes of Mrs. Pratt for a while. Unfortunately, that was punishment for all three.

Sara was reduced to sobs and couldn't speak when Ms. Stout arrived with brown paper towels and wet dish cloths from the lunchroom.

Mary May was sitting at her desk on the front row beside Sara's empty desk. Her head was in a constant rotation, looking for any reason to stand, walk to the chalkboard and add a name to the list under Eighteen and Tom. She had also written Vinni and Jake's name in a separate column as a reminder to Mrs. Stout.

Out of fear, one student raised their hand and asked Mary's permission to get help from their friend on a math problem.

Mary closed her eyes and nodded in approval. "Yes, you may."

Eighteen followed close behind by waving his hand frantically in the air. "Oh Miss Crutchfield, Miss Crutchfield." Mary rotated in her desk and stared at him with no response. "Miss Crutchfield, ma'am, Miss Crutchfield." He continued in desperation.

Mary stood, walked to the chalkboard and added a check mark beside his name. Then she turned to the class. "Yes, Eighteen, is there anything else?"

He smiled and batted his eyes, mimicking her style of flirting. "May I please be excused?"

She answered with her hands on her hips. "No you may not be excused."

He accepted the challenge. Now it was a battle of wills. "But Miss Crutchfield, that awful smell has made me sick and I need to be excused. I'm afraid I'm going to throw up on Lisa's back."

He leaned forward and gave a loud heave. Lisa felt his breath on the back of her neck and jumped up with a scream. The remaining Tribe on the back row roared with laughter.

Mary spun around and added three checks beside Eighteen's name and several new names to the list, including Lisa's. By this time, no one was working on their math and the room was out of control. "Everyone please be quiet and finish your work." There was no response, talking and laughter continued to get louder. "Okay that's enough. Be quiet and get back to work." Mary's voice was getting louder to compete with the classroom noise. She had no choice. Mary returned to the chalkboard and started adding to the list of names.

By the time Ms. Stout returned to the classroom, every student's name was on the board. Mary May Crutchfield's name had been added by Eighteen when he was on his way out to the bathroom. Ms. Stout stood beside her desk with her arms crossed, staring silently at the class as the noise softened and students reopened their math books. Eighteen walked in. His head was covered with wet brown paper towels and he was fanning himself with a roll of toilet paper. Ms. Stout cut her eyes in his direction as entered the class. Her lips tightened to avoid a giggle.

"From the looks of the board it seems your medical condition is the least of your worries, sir. Take a seat and see me after class."

"Yes, ma'am." He put the roll of toilet paper on the edge of her desk and returned to his seat.

A Teacher's Wisdom

Ms. Stout leaned against her desk with her hands resting on the edge and looked at the floor as she spoke. "Class, I know this has been an unusual morning and the school year will soon be over, however, we must keep our focus. We still have work to do." She pointed to the door without raising her head. "Believe me, I want the summer to start as much as you. I wish I could just kick off my shoes and walk out that door, but I can't."

Years of experience was giving her speech power. By not looking at the students, she didn't give them an opportunity to respond and couldn't see if any hands were raised, but she could hear if anyone was talking. She continued with her head down.

"This has been a good year and I have enjoyed every one of you, regardless of your occasional outbursts and bad test scores." She could tell by the silence that she had their attention and raised her head. She lifted one leg and slid herself onto her desk and continued as she sat there with her feet crossed and bobbing.

"I can see new friendships being formed and old ones growing stronger. This makes me happy. You see, contrary to what you think, I believe the most important things are not always what you find in a math book or on an English test. Your studies are very important, don't get me wrong, but your friends are, too. We need to learn how to respect our friends. It's been many years since I sat at a desk and I can't remember everything I learned, but I can remember my friends. I remember all the fun we had and wish I could relive those times."

She pointed her thumb at the chalkboard behind her. "This is not something you want to remember. You don't want to remember this day as one you disrespected my wishes, or one where you turned on your friends or laughed at their misfortune. You don't want to remember who made you mad or why. Things like that can follow you the rest of your lives. I know it seems silly now, but it's true."

Velma Stout couldn't hide her love for these children as she continued. "Every day is an opportunity to do something good, to make a difference, to be kind when others are not. You will be remembered for those things, not what you made on the test. There is so much for you to learn and I would be remiss if I didn't teach you the most important things."

She smiled for a few moments of silence and looked at the students. Some of the girls on the front row had tears in their eyes and the guys on the back row were looking at their desks in silence. She slid onto the floor and finished.

"I have to take care of some things outside the class now and this is your assignment. Please close your math books and get out paper and pencils." The mood was broken as students prepared for a test.

"If you will look at the board, you will see that everyone's name has been listed. Eighteen, yours is the first and Mary May's is the last.

I want you to write four or five sentences to the three people listed below your name. Tell them something nice you remember about them, how they helped you or made you laugh. Perhaps you need to offer an apology for something you did or thank them for something they have done for you. If you need to think about it for a while, that's fine. This isn't a test. Please keep your eyes on your own paper and do this very quietly. Put the person's name you are writing to at the top of the page and sign your name at the bottom. Each letter needs to be on a separate page. You may also write a letter to anyone else you wish. I will be gathering these letters when I return. If you are not finished, I will give you as much time as you need. Please give this serious consideration. It will be a lesson you will remember the rest of your lives. Oh, one more thing, please put today's date at the top. April twenty-sixth, nineteen forty six."

She exited, leaving the room in complete silence.

An Emotional End to a Long Day

    Mrs. Pratt was in such a whirl, trying to keep up with the extra year end reports, that she almost forgot about Vinni and Jake sitting in the small room. She had raised the window to give her some relief from the early morning humidity. The fan in the corner carried the aroma of Avon perfume and salty sweat across to the detainees. That aroma, along with the memory of their earlier episode, was making both boys a little queasy.

    When Ms. Stout arrived, she noticed both boys with their heads resting against the wall, looking pale. She had seen this many times before. Mrs. Pratt's office was also the sick room and there was a permanent stain on the wall where the dirty hair of sick students had rested for generations. She shook her head with her hands on her hips. "Oh, dear Lord, not you two. Buddy-row, if you lose your lunch, you better lose it in the trash can. I've had enough for one day."

    She took a couple of steps back and looked out the front door. Mrs. Pratt had propped it open and she could see Sara. She was sitting on the front steps, waiting for a neighbor to pick her up. The school staff had learned who to call in case of emergencies with the Jenkins girls.

Neighbors would usually stop by and tell Lillian they were bringing one of the girls home.

"Being without a phone is an awful trouble, thank you for helpin' out." Lillian's response was always the same.

Mrs. Pratt had decided to call Margaret Adams and ask her to pick up Sara. This would give her an opportunity to deal with her son and perhaps she could persuade her son to tell what really happened. Vinni Davis was not always a reliable source for information.

Mrs. Stout stepped back inside and nodded at the principal's door. "He busy with something?"

Mrs. Pratt nodded without looking up. "County office's new bus regulations. I think he's about finished." She picked up her phone and listened for a couple of seconds, then nodded when she heard Mr. Johnson hang up. "He's ready."

Just before Miss Stout knocked on the frosted glass, Mrs. Pratt offered her assessment. "I think he pushed her down."

Miss Stout turned and looked. Mrs. Pratt was still looking at her work and Vinni raised his middle finger to acknowledge the comment. "You better save the strength in that finger. You have a lot of writin' to do." She rapped on the glass with her knuckles and opened the door.

"Got a minute?" She stepped in and closed the door.

Vinni heard some mumbling, then the sound of a drawer opening and a soft knock on the desk. He knew Mr. Johnson and reached into the bottom drawer for reinforcement. The humidity in the room was increasing and the boys were feeling sicker by the minute. Vinni wanted to walk out, he had done it several times before, but he didn't want to face Sara.

The situation was new to Jake and nerves were adding to his uneasy stomach. "I'm sorry, Mrs. Pratt, but I need to be excused."

She looked up and saw that he was very sincere in his request. "Oh, of course, please go. I'll tell them you weren't feeling well. Go on now." She waved her chubby fingers toward the door. Jake stepped into the hall and Mrs. Pratt shook her head in disappointment at Vinni.

Without raising his head, he replied, "Hope a dead bird don't fly in on em'."

Mrs. Pratt knew she couldn't acknowledge his comment and her temperature quickly rose, so she turned the fan on high. The sudden burst of air slammed the hot aromas against Vinni's face. The papers on Mrs. Pratt's desk were spun into the air and across to Vinni's feet. The two stared at each other in awkward silence. There was absolutely no room for Mrs. Pratt to retrieve her papers and Vinni was not offering any help. The sound of Mr. Johnson's doorknob broke the silence. "Okay, come on in." Ms. Stout stepped into the room and picked up the papers after Vinni stepped by. She handed them to the sweaty secretary. "I'm sorry, but I don't think they're in order." There was a dirty impression of Vinni's tennis shoe on the top sheet.

When Jake returned from the restroom, the meeting was over and his mama was waiting on the front steps beside Sara. Mr. Johnson's door was closed and Vinni was gone. He stepped into Mrs. Pratt's office. "Is everything okay?"

She smiled, glad that he was feeling better. "Yes, dear. Everything's fine. Your mama will explain. Are you feeling okay?"

He looked at Mr. Johnson's closed door and wondered if Vinni was inside. "Yeah, yeah, I'm okay. Thanks. Has Vinni gone?" Mrs. Pratt refused to acknowledge the concern for his friend.

"Your mama will explain."

Jake stepped outside. Sara was sitting at the edge of the porch. Her head was tilted to the left and resting on the large white column. Margaret was standing on the other side of the column. Jake could see large wet patches on Sara's dress where Miss Stout had washed it with a dish cloth and paper towels.

"Hey, Mama."

Margaret uncrossed her arms and turned to face her son. This was the first time he had been in any kind of trouble and neither knew how to react. Margaret had been rehearsing her response since she received the call from Mrs. Pratt earlier. On her drive from home she had recalled some of her high school and college antics and decided to be understanding.

"Oh, hey, Jake. Sara explained everything to Mr. Johnson. It's all right. Listen, I'm going to take Sara home. Just catch the bus. I'll see you at home."

Jake was relieved, still recovering from his upset stomach and almost forgot his plans after school. "Okay, see you later. Oh, wait, almost forgot. Vinni asked me if I could go home with him and help him milk. I was going to call, but forgot. It is okay if I go? I can get off the bus at his house."

Margaret hadn't expected this turn of events and hadn't rehearsed her answer. "What about your homework? How long will you be over there? Will you need to change clothes before you milk?" She could see her son's face harden with each question and his response was sharp.

"I dunno'. It'll take a while, I guess. We can do our homework together. He has to do homework every day, and milk too."

His mama's thoughtfulness and understanding had just avoided one situation and she was thrown into another one. She didn't want to argue and needed to get Sara home, but didn't want to agree to anything that was unnecessary. The Moreheads were good friends with the Davis family, but they had to be increasingly cautious of Vinni and his influence.

"Well, listen. How about this? Ride the bus home, change clothes, then ride your bike over to Vinni's. I'll call Lidia when I get home and confirm everything."

Jake was standing, stiff, with his hands in his pockets. She could tell he was upset and wanted to calm his anger. Her natural response was to kiss his forehead. Her attempt was rejected when Jake leaned back, turned and walked through the double doors into the school. He left his mama standing there, hurt, rejected and confused. She immediately turned her affection to Sara.

"Okay, let's get you home, dear. You've had a rough day." She rubbed the back of Sara's wet dress and they walked to the car.

Vinni was sitting at his desk on the back row between Eighteen and Jake. The mood in the room was very unusual. Ms. Stout had explained what the class was doing and given Vinni his assignment before they left Mr. Johnson's office. Eighteen had two letters finished and was working on the third. Vinni didn't hear the speech that had inspired his classmates and was at a disadvantage.

He looked at the chalkboard and saw where Mary had written his, Sara and Jake's names on the right side of the board. Eighteen had written Mary May's name under Sara's.

The thought of opening up and putting his feelings on paper had Vinni paralyzed. Typically he would wiggle out of the situation by causing a commotion or simply refusing to do the assignment. Today was different. He had not gained control of the situation from the beginning and the class was under the spell of Ms. Stout. He looked around. Everyone was either writing or deep in thought. He couldn't get anyone's attention and he began to feel anxious. He looked at the board again and remembered the assignment. Write something nice about that person, how they helped you or made you laugh or offer an apology. Seeing his name in Mary's handwriting reinforced the fact that she was not nice, she didn't make him laugh and she was the one who needed to apologize.

His mind kicked into gear and he was inspired to write Mary May the first letter, a letter of apology. It was one sentence long and summed up his feelings completely.

The second letter was to Jake and much easier. He wrote as if he were speaking. Jake had been making Vinni laugh for years and was, by far, the nicest of The Tribe. Vinni had been the reason for Jake sitting in Mrs. Pratt's office and he was sorry about that. Vinni's letter to Jake took one and a half pages.

Vinni's three letters had fulfilled his assignment, but the class was continuing deep in thought. Then he remembered that he could write letters to anyone else he wanted to. Vinni had never confronted his feelings. He had always focused on what he planned to do in the near future. The way he felt was present and he had to stop planning the future to deal with it. This sudden and unexpected change in gears gave him a new experience. He realized that his emotions were always present. He didn't have to plan them or work to make them happen. All he had to do was recognize and acknowledge them.

Miss Stout had set the perfect stage. The students were making this journey together; they were all equal and had no basis to ridicule or judge each other. Vinni had his father's heart and his mother's emotions. Hearing the girls on the front row sniffle tugged at his heart. His emotions floated to the top of his character and he was in a sudden and unexpected battle to hold back tears. He began his fifth letter to Sara Jenkins.

Giovanni Davis's emotions and compassion were enormous. They came from watching the way his parents loved, from seeing his sister struggle with a terrible illness and realizing how lucky he was to live in a home that was so very different from his neighbor's. Everything about him was different; his skin, his eyes, his hair. His fingers held music and his voice had the lingering echoes of his mother's Italian accent. His heart was connected to Italy, a place he had never been, yet lived with every day.

He was a vessel made from many clays and molded by the hands of many people. He knew what form his life needed to take, but the people molding his life didn't ask. He was beginning to push and lean, trying to elbow his way out of a future that was being formed. He was trying to make a difference in the shape that was taking form, but his efforts were overwhelmed by the small world he lived in. His dreams were overshadowed by parents hoping they knew what was best for him. He could see his future being planned by others and it was not the future of his heart. It was wrong, but he couldn't resist, deny or refuse this future because it was given in love. He was a person under the watchful eye of God. He knew God, but didn't understand him. He wanted to run from God, but the journey would be tireless and useless. He wanted to love God, but was afraid of what that love would require him to sacrifice.

He felt the soft touch of Velma Stout's hand on his shoulder. The spell he was operating under was broken and he looked up. The light in the room seemed strange and the tears in Miss Stout's eyes spilled over and dripped down her cheeks. Vinni looked around. He was alone, the other students had left. He looked at the large round clock over the bank of windows overlooking the parking lot. Six thirty two. Miss Stout sat in the desk in front of Vinni, her knees were in the aisle and she rested her hand on his hand. She could see the fear in his eyes.

"Everything's okay. I phoned your parents and told them I would give you a ride home." She didn't have a tissue to wipe her tears and let them trail down her face. "You've done a wonderful job, Giovanni. You should be very proud. I know I'm proud of you. Thank you."

He was beginning to grasp reality and looked down onto a stack of letters. Some were several pages long. His body slumped and his hands slid onto his lap, exhausted. The pencil rolled off his leg and clicked onto the floor. Miss Stout straightened and gathered the papers. Some were on the floor, some were lying face down with writing on the backs and there was one sticking out of his math book. She could see where tears had dripped on several, leaving wrinkled dots across the penciled letters.

She noticed the names that defined the letters and fought to hold back the flood of tears weighing heavy in her eyes. Dear Mama, Genevieve,

Dear Daddy, Dear Edna May, Dear Mrs. Pratt, Dear Miss Stout, she was not ashamed of the tears and joined Vinnie. He rested his head in the crook of his arm and his shoulders began to shake, releasing what was left in his heart.

It had taken George an extra hour to finish the milking. He and Lidia were finishing supper when they heard Velma's car drive up. Vinni walked in and mumbled, "Hey," as he walked past the kitchen table. They could tell he was exhausted by the sound of his feet climbing the stairs.

Velma sat at the table, waiting to see if Vinni was coming back downstairs. They heard the toilet flush, then his bedroom door closed and the springs on his bed squeaked, letting them know he wouldn't be returning until morning.

Vinni could hear soft mumbles from the kitchen and wondered what was being said. The wave of emotions that had overtaken him hours earlier was gone and life began to weigh heavy on him again. What had the other kids seen? What had he written in the letters? Would he have to give everyone the letters he had written? What were they talking about downstairs? Why was Mary May such a bitch? He wished he could call Sara. Maybe he would ride his bike over to see her, maybe tomorrow, maybe not.

His mind was leaping ahead and planning what would happen tomorrow. He couldn't leave his future to chance, he had to plan his moves that would dictate the next day. Were any calves born that day and would he have to get up earlier than usual in order to finish milking and get to school on time? What was Sara doing? Was she mad at him? Was Jake in big trouble? Were they still going to the lake over the weekend for Jake's birthday? Was he supposed to make the first move and kiss Sara the next time they were alone? Why did he hate the milking parlor?

The weight of his thoughts sucked the last of the energy from his body and he fell asleep. His dreams took over where his body left off and he struggled until the alarm clock insisted that he get up and go to the barn.

APRIL 28ᵀᴴ 1948

An Appointment with Eloise

It was 10a.m. Wednesday morning and Lidia had just finished talking to her sister-in-law. The excitement of the weekend in Greensboro was being taunted by Vinni's somber mood. Lidia had to focus on the day ahead. She had a 10:30 appointment with Eloise for a cut and set. This would be her first time in Eloise's chair and she was nervous. Edna May's transformation for the dinner party had been amazing and it gave her the confidence needed for a new look.

There was a twenty minute gap and she didn't know how to fill it. The other ladies always arrived at Eloise's a little early to catch up on gossip, but she wasn't in the mood for that. She sat on the couch, quickly flipping through a Ladies' Home Journal. Her waving arm would stop if she noticed an interesting hair style. She didn't know what to tell Eloise and was about to lose her nerve when the kitchen timer dinged, letting her know it was time to leave.

Edna May arrived at Eloise's at nine thirty and sat in the dryer chair, bobbing her foot. She was about to burst waiting to tell about the conversation she had overheard concerning Lidia's weekend in Greensboro. Everyone needed to hear so she had to wait until Eloise finished washing Peg Haith's hair. Peg needed to hear, too. Edna had a way of carrying on a conversation with Eloise in a room full of women. This made it appear that the conversation was private and the ladies in the room were eavesdropping. Her timing had to be perfect, stopping at an important point just before Peg went under the hair dryer. Edna was getting impatient.

"Eloise, are you about done? Good Lord, you're going to scrub her scalp off. I can't be here all day." Eloise looked up and spoke to Edna's reflection in the mirror.

"I told you that Wednesday's were by busiest days and you know that Edna. You know the stores in town close at twelve. Pasty comes in from the florist and the clerks come in from Green's Grocery. If you have to sit there all day, you just have to sit there all day. I can give you an appointment Thursday at four or Friday morning."

Edna just shook her foot and snapped back. "Told you Thursday's too late." Eloise was already getting a dose of Edna. She stopped scrubbing Peg's scalp, rested her sudsy fists on her plastic pink apron and tilted her head to the left.

"Too late for what, Edna May? Is there something I need to know? Good Lord, you act like the rapture's coming tomorrow. Want to look good for the Lord, is that it?"

Edna saw Peg's chest bob with a chuckle and acted like she didn't hear Eloise's comment.

"Time to rinse, Peg." Eloise finished rinsing the thick white suds from Peg's hair and handed her a white hand towel to hold on her forehead. She pulled the lever on the side of the chair and sat her upright. Edna jumped in before Eloise had a chance to pick up another towel to dry Peg's hair.

"Have you talked to Lidia this week?"

Eloise took a deep breath and exhaled. "Not since Sunday at church. She was saying what a nice time she had at your dinner party."

Edna's conversation was almost sidetracked. "Well, glad she did. Evidently that boy of hers had a good time, too. The garage office was a mess, paper plates everywhere, and half empty Coke bottles sittin' on Gary's desk. It's a good thing I got things cleaned up before Gary needed his office."

Peg was holding her head down and her voice was shaking with Eloise's towel strokes. "I heard it was something else Edna, and your hair is just beautiful."

Edna's foot was shaking in anticipation of the news she had to share. "Yeah, well, party's over and I need something a little more sensible." Eloise refused to look at her or acknowledge her comment. "Eloise, have you talked to Lidia this week? Oh yeah at church, never mind. Did she tell you about her plans this weekend?"

Edna was looking at a magazine while she talked. It made the news seem more casual.

"No, she didn't mention anything. I know the Adams are having a party at the lake this weekend for Jake's birthday. They wanted to go last weekend, but plans were cancelled at the last minute. Wonder why?"

Edna closed her eyes and shook her head, "Who knows? Those people do whatever they want to, always popping off to the lake, or Chapel Hill, or visiting friends at who knows where." Then she opened her eyes and shook her finger at Eloise and Peg. "But mark my word, that boy of theirs better watch who he hangs around with. I hear he's in awfully tight with Vinni and that boy is nothing but trouble, nothing but.

Mark my word. Evidently, his parent's aren't too concerned. Did Lidia tell you what her plans are for the weekend? They say that she's going to Greensboro for the weekend. Seems like Genevieve has some big fancy party and Lidia and George are doin' the town with his sister Margaret and that rich husband of hers. What's his name, David Lane, Denny Lang, Ding Dong? Who knows? Anyway, the man's rich as creesies. Well, it's been told that Lidia is going up Thursday morning and they're going, well, I'm sure Margaret is taking her, shopping. Evidently Miss High and Mighty Greensboro Society is ashamed of her poor relations and has to make them presentable at The Club. The way that woman spends money, no wonder her husband has to work night n' day. You know, they say she goes to New York just to buy a dress, or two, or ten. No tellin' how many thousands she spends on party clothes. Well, I guess that's life in the fast lane, Lord knows, she didn't get it from her mama and daddy. They were good people, don't get me wrong, real hard working people, but they didn't raise her to have such carrying on. Poor Lidia. I know she'll feel out of place, little farmer girl at The Club."

Peg wasn't in the mood to hear Lidia bad mouthed so she chimed in. "Oh, Genevieve's going to a party, I'm glad. That poor girl has had a rough time with that diabetes. She is one purty girl. I'm tellin' you, she is one more purty girl. They say she's smart, too. I don't know, but I don't doubt it. I know George was always smart in school. You know he went to Italy."

Edna May knew that George went to Italy. She had hoped he would return into her arms. Instead, he returned with Lidia. Edna added her wisdom to Genevieve's situation. "Yeah, she's pretty enough until she throws down with one of her fits, or seizures, or whatever. I still don't know why they have to keep her locked up in the garage at Margaret's. Surely it's not true what they say about her having a baby."

Peg gasped and looked up in the mirror at Eloise. She saw Eloise turn pink just before she spun around and shook her styling comb at Edna.

"Edna May Crutchfield, I am ashamed of you. I have never, I have never heard such. Now you know there's not a bit of truth in that. You just better nip that one in the bud, lady, nip it in the bud."

She turned and Peg handed her a roller. Eloise took the black bristly roller and wrapped the wet hair around it while she finished her speech. "That poor girl has been through enough without the likes of you stirring up a bunch of lies, the very idea. Who ever heard such? I better never hear that again, I'll tell you that much Edna, better never hear that again."

Peg lowered her eyebrows and shook her head in disgust. Edna sat flipping through a magazine, shaking her foot. She was undaunted by the scorching Eloise had thrown her way. Edna had received similar responses to her news over the years and wasn't affected by people's outrage. She had the perfect response. "I'm just saying, don't know, I'm just saying."

The bell on the door made them look up and Velma Smith walked in. "Morning, ladies, here for my ten o'clock, Eloise. Isn't it nice outside? Morning Eloise, Peg. Hey Edna, I see you're already finished. Your hair is just lovely."

Edna rolled her eyes and didn't respond to the greeting or compliment.

"Hey, Velma. I'll be right with you. Let me put this last roller in and Peg can go under the dryer. Edna, get up. Peg needs that dryer. It's hotter than the other one."

Edna flipped a page and jerked her foot in defiance, refusing to move. Peg could see Eloise turning redder when she saw Edna's reflection in the mirror.

"Oh, the other one's okay, Eloise. I get kinda hot under the other one and I'm not in a hurry today. Dryer number two is fine. Velma may need Edna's dryer." Eloise unsnapped Peg's pink plastic cap and whispered loud enough for Edna to hear. "And Edna may need to take a couple of damn pills."

Edna didn't look up and wasn't influenced by the comment. She simply replied calmly with no anger or surprise. "Heard that."

Edna had a very vivid memory to the effect the slight overdose had on her attitude. She enjoyed the party, but couldn't quickly adjust to the entirely new life that it spawned. Having Gary home was enough of a sudden change without having to deal with losing control of her spiteful character. It had taken years for Edna to reach this level of gossip and offensiveness. The community had grown with her and knew how to respond. Her comments had become benign with little or no effect on the attended target. Under the piercing comments and rolling eyes, in spite of the huffs and crossed arms, along beside the shaking heads and nasal exhales, Edna was loved.

Pleasant Grove was a community of generations and the respect of one's ancestors carried over to those who followed. It was also a community of very caring, understanding and forgiving people. People understood more about Edna than she realized. They knew she needed some way to deal with Gary Crutchfield's shortcomings. They were willing to take the fiery darts that were honed in Edna's anger and fright.

Velma sat in Eloise's chair as the roar of the hairdryer filled the room. Peg was glad to have an oasis from the gossip and closed her eyes and relaxed in her new found freedom.

The ladies had to speak louder to be heard and typically the conversations were much shorter when someone was under the dryer. However, Peg's dryer would only operate on low and was much quieter, allowing easier conversations. Velma had no clue about what had just taken place or the tension that Edna was causing.

"Oh, Edna, Ed said he ran into Gary at Matthew's Garage yesterday. I didn't know he was back in town. I know you're glad to have him and he's glad to be back for a while. It must be hard living out of town so much."

Edna was a champion at turning any comment in the direction she wanted the conversation to take. "Well, some people must not mind being out of town so much. Have you heard about Lidia and George taking off to Greensboro for a big throw down?"

Velma face lit up with excitement and she didn't lean back when Eloise lowered the chair to start her shampoo.

"Oh, isn't that exciting? Ed and I are taking care of the farm while they're gone. Lidia told me about Genevieve's dance and how well she's doing. Lord, I am so glad she is coming back around."

Eloise put her hand on Velma's shoulder and directed her back to the waiting black sink. Velma continued with her comments directed toward the ceiling. "Don't you know Lidia is going to look like a million bucks when they go to the club Saturday night? I hope they take pictures, pictures of everything. I just can't wait to see. Lidia was worried about us having to do all the work without Vinni. He'll be at the lake with the Adams for Jake's birthday. His birthday was last weekend, but for some reason they had to cancel their plans and go this coming weekend. I told Lidia and Ed told George not to worry about a thing. We are glad to help out and don't give it another thought. We're just so excited. They are good people, I'm telling you, they are."

Eloise was massaging her head and spoke softly enough to escape the prying ears across the room. "I know, Lidia called and made an appointment for ten thirty. Lord, honey, she has never set foot in this place. Well, she never needed to, still doesn't in my opinion. Not with . . ."

Edna sat on the edge of her chair and interrupted. "Say what? What did you say about Lidia? Good Lord, speak up, woman. Did you say she was stopping by for something this morning?"

Eloise closed her eyes and exhaled. "Well, yes, as a matter of fact, she has a ten thirty appointment, not that she needs it with that hair she's got. Lord have mercy, I have never seen such a head of beautiful hair. I guess she just wants a shampoo, maybe a set. To tell you the truth, I was so shocked when she called that I didn't even ask."

Edna gave a quick glance at the clock, ten after. She scooted closer to the edge of her chair and dropped her magazine on the green and white speckled linoleum tiles. "Velma, Velmaaaa. What did she tell you about this weekend? Did she say what she was wearing, huh, did she? Because I have from a reliable source that she was almost in tears, not having anything to wear and that sister in law of hers had to go out and buy that poor girl a dress. Now that's just pitiful, pitiful. I guess the farm's not doing so well. Lord, I hope you an' Ed ain't chargin' them for working."

Eloise cut her off. "Edna, I would sure love to know who all your reliable sources are. Evidently we have some government spies in the community. Either that or someone listening in on a party line."

Edna lowered her brows and shook her head. "Hush up, Eloise, I'm talking to Velma. Did she say what she was wearing or when she was going? 'Cause she hasn't told me a thing. I was just wondering, don't matter, I was just wondering."

By this time, Velma had fallen under the spell of Eloise's massaging fingers and was about to doze off. Her answer was soft and slow. "No, not really."

Eloise looked at Edna's reflection in the mirror, raised her eyebrows and gave her a smirk. "Why don't you ask your reliable source?"

Edna fell back in her chair. "Why don't you mind your own business?" She glanced back at the clock, ten fifteen. "Reckon she'll come early?"

The bell on the door tingled and Eloise responded without looking up. "Looks like."

Time for Lidia's Hairdo

    Lidia stopped, holding the door open behind her, not knowing where to go once she stepped inside the room.

    "Hey, everybody. I'm here for my appointment." She could see the entire room in the large mirror, including herself, and she looked out of place already. She stepped in and let the door close behind her.

    Edna bent over and raised her head to the right, giving her a look from top to bottom. "Well, goodness me, what a surprise, Lidiaaaa. What on Earth are you doing here? I thought you did your own hair, or didn't do your hair, whatever." She scooted back into the dryer chair and waved her hand at Eloise.

    "Now I hope you can work me in. I know you were going to have a few minutes between Velma and your ten thirty." She bent over and picked her magazine off the floor and waved it in the direction of a chair against the wall.

    "Sit down, honey. You look like a long tail cat in a room full of rockers. Nothing to be scared of here. I'm getting another style for the week, seems like this party-do that Eloise threw up on my head takes too much time to keep up. I thought it might be when she did it, but I didn't want to say anything. You know how it is.

Anyway, why, I mean what are you having done? How's that son of yours? Is there some special occasion calling for a special hairdo? You know, Eloise was just saying she didn't know why in the world you even made an appointment. Isn't that right, Eloise, honey?"

Velma wasn't able to rest with Eloise taking her frustrations out on her scalp. She raised her hand from underneath the plastic cape and patted Eloise's elbow. "I think we're ready to rinse, don't you?"

Eloise turned the hot and cold levers on and tested the water on her hand until it was a comfortable temperature and began rinsing. "Lidia, now Edna's making it sound all wrong." She was turning to look at Lidia and spraying Velma's forehead as she talked. "I said that you had the most beautiful head of hair that I had ever seen, and yes, I didn't know why you needed to come in here. I can't possibly imagine how I could improve what you have. But, now you know I will do whatever you want."

Edna looked down at her magazine. "I hope she doesn't want to get water logged like Velma."

Velma was waving her right hand over her head and grasping for the towel on the counter. She couldn't speak or open her eyes because there was a steady stream of water flowing over her face.

"Oh, damn!" Eloise noticed what she was doing and turned the water off. "Excuse my language, ladies. Velma, are you okay?" She mopped the water off Velma's face and began rinsing her hair.

Lidia's eyes cut back over to Edna, who was sitting on the edge of her chair again. She held her hand beside her mouth and leaned toward

Lidia. "I don't know what's wrong with her today. She's making a mess out of everything."

Lidia smiled and looked past Edna to Peg, who was fast asleep under the warm dryer. Her nerves took over and she lost control of her English. "Bella giornata, chi bel cielo, nuvole di belle. Cavolo ci faccio seduta qui?"

Edna followed as if she knew exactly what was said. "I know."

Eloise was finishing Velma's rinse and raised her chair to the upright position. "Of course you do, Edna. You know everything. Now what was it she said again? I didn't get that last part."

Edna didn't miss a beat. "She said to hurry up and wash Edna's hair."

School Plans

Vinni and The Tribe stood at the end of the line filing into the lunchroom. The familiar smell of fresh baked rolls was accompanied by the aroma of fresh vegetable soup. The lunch room ladies treated the school children just like family. Their gardens had been planted for this year and the remaining frozen and canned vegetables from their homes were brought in to make soup. The grilled cheese sandwiches had been brushed with fresh butter and toasted to a golden brown.

The third graders were empting their scraps into a metal garbage can and sacking their trays on the table beside the door exiting to the gym. The younger students snaked across the lunchroom and entered the hall where The Tribe stood. They wanted to stare at the young men, but brushed their shoulders against the wall and stared at their shoes instead.

Vinni had been famous since the first grade. Those who were not in is class, or didn't share the playground at the same time, or didn't ride his bus, only knew him by exciting tales of his escapades. Without Vinni Davis, Grove High would be nothing but ordinary and boring. Those who were not fortunate to be involved in his life stood on the sidelines, hoping to see or hear the events.

Without knowing it, Vinni was shaping the lives of many and changing the community. He was changing the rules by breaking them. He was breaking the boundaries of what would be expected of students. He was raising the bar for those who followed in his footsteps, the future leaders of recess and bus riders. His spell had even overpowered the girls in his class. Sara was helpless in his presence. Mary May was in awe of his good looks and nerve. Mary Alice stood in the background, refusing to be influenced, but planning the day when she would join his army.

Vinni Davis was bigger than Pleasant Grove. The community could no longer mold him, he was molding the community. Vinni Davis was the answer to the restless disobedience that lived in the hearts of young and old alike. He fulfilled their need for excitement and romance, for freedom and independence. Vinni Davis's life gave them hope and satisfaction.

This put the community in a very dangerous position. If Vinni Davis left the community, an army would have to be raised to fill their needs. They would have to step up and take responsibility of their own excitement, fulfill their own desires, make their rules and break their rules. If Vinni Davis remained in the community, they would continue to rely on him to feed their restless hearts, letting him take the responsibility and consequences. Some cursed his actions and others prayed he would stay.

Eighteen was staring at the metal garbage can being filled with scraps of food and left over milk. "Hey Vinni, remember that time you had to be punished by Mrs. Pratt? She made you take the slop cans out to Mr. White's truck after school.

If I were you, I would've dumped one can in the front seat of her car. Can't believe she made you do that."

Vinni's mind was about thirty minutes ahead, planning what he would do on the way back to class. His answer was distant and given without much thought.

"Yeah, yeah, that was a truck load o' shit, all right. Nasty, I spilled some on my shoes, they stunk for three weeks. Mama finally made me wash 'em."

"Do you know what he does with that stuff?"

Vinni's thoughts came back to the present and he looked back at Eighteen and answered his negative nod. "He feeds his hogs with it. He's got about twenty hogs, and he feeds it to 'em. I know 'cause I told him I would go home with him and help. It was kinda cool actually. It stunk like skunk ass, but I'd rather do that than milk cows. He takes them to the stock market about every two months, makes pretty good money, too. Don't cost much to raise 'em and they have a whole slew o' babies every time. I guess people don't like raisin' 'em cause they stink so much. Hell, didn't bother me. The way I look at it, don't matter what kind o' shit's up your nose if it smells like money. He makes good money and it's a lot less work than milking, I can tell you that."

Eighteen listened to what Vinni said, he always did. "I don't know, seems kinda' gross to me. I'd rather have motor grease under my fingernails than pig shit."

Eighteen's uncle ran Matthew's Garage and being a mechanic was all he ever considered. He was raised on the smell of a garage and had been helping his uncle since he was big enough to hand him a wrench. His fingernails were already stained with motor oil and his future was being planned by his uncle and parents. Like Vinni's parents, they were sure he wasn't college material and knew what was best for him.

Pleasant Grove was big enough for Eighteen. Being a local mechanic was the biggest dream he could have. There was nothing in his heart or mind that pulled him to places unknown and sights unseen. His life was simple, predictable, comfortable and stable. For Eighteen, no dreams meant no worries, no failures and no regrets. He was willing for Vinni to supply him with the adventures he wasn't willing to take himself.

Jake was listening, but remained quiet. He didn't enter conversations about planning a future. He liked being part of The Tribe, having friends like Vinni, Eighteen, Charlie and Roy, but Jake was different. He had already tasted life outside Pleasant Grove and he liked it. He knew he would be going to college, but didn't mention it. He couldn't join in on most of the conversations with The Tribe because he didn't have the same experiences.

He didn't live on a farm or work on cars. His clothes didn't come from The Farmer's Alliance Store or Sear's and he didn't have chores to do after school. In most ways, Jake was the least like Vinni. That was why Mrs. Pratt was so disappointed to see him sent to the principal's office. However, in one way, Jake was exactly like Vinni. He was like Vinni in the most important way. He understood Vinni like no other friend did. Jake Adams was bigger than Pleasant Grove. He loved Pleasant Grove and the people, he loved the school and church, but he also loved the lake and Chapel Hill. He was raised on the floor of a newspaper office that smelled like ink instead of motor oil, the sound of printing presses instead of milking machines. It was a life that very few knew about and even fewer were interested in, but it was his life and he loved it. He had to keep it close to his heart. He knew that if he shared it, he would risk losing the respect of The Tribe. He had to accept their friendship on their terms; he had nothing to offer that would interest them.

Of course, The Tribe knew what Jake's life was like. They tried not to think about it, knowing they knew they could never experience it. They weren't able to talk to Jake about most things. Jake found himself feeling less a part of The Tribe as they grew older and he filled the void with things outside Pleasant Grove. This weekend would be different, though. This weekend The Tribe would be on his terms, a part of his world. This was the weekend being spent at the lake.

"Okay class, take your seats. Lunch was over fifteen minutes ago and we're behind schedule."

Mrs. Stout was as restless as her students. They were behind schedule because she had been making plans for Saturday night. A gentleman had asked her out for dinner and she was telling a fellow teacher about her plans. This made her late for class. It had been about two years since Velma had been on a date. It wasn't because she didn't have opportunities. There were no men, no summer evenings, no ocean breezes to compare with her youth.

She stood in front of her class and her fingers darted around, searching for a necklace as she spoke. "Quiet, please, quiet, take your seats."

The noises that echoed between the high ceiling and wooden floors softened and disappeared. The students sat quietly, waiting for Mrs. Stout to speak, watching as she stared out the window toward the ball field. Her nervous fingers were dancing across her chest and her mind was chasing her heart.

"Yes, Mrs. Stout?" Mary May broke the awkward silence.

"Oh, yes, Mary May. Class, as you know, our annual bake sale and talent show is coming up. It will be on Friday night, two weeks from this Friday, May seventeenth, at seven o'clock. Several acts have already signed up. If anyone is interested, please send a note to the office by this Friday. That will give Mrs. Pratt enough time to make the programs. There will be a ten dollar prize for the winning contestant. We are asking parents to volunteer for the hot dog dinner. That starts at five o'clock. The proceeds from this dinner will help with the expenses. Please have your parents send a note by this Friday if they are available to help. Are there any questions concerning the talent show?"

Mary May raised her hand immediately. "Miss Stout, I've been in the talent show several times and always won either first or second prize. Do you think it's fair for me to keep entering? I mean, I don't mind, but is it fair for the other students?"

Before Miss Stout could gather her thoughts to answer the unexpected question Vinni raised his hand. "Miss Stout, I think the students are taking advantage of the parents. They have to bring us to rehearsal, cook the meal, clean up the kitchen and buy tickets to the show. I think we could invite someone from the community to be a judge. Don't get me wrong, we really appreciate Mary May's mama being the head judge all these years, but I don't want to take advantage of her good nature."

Miss Stout was still stunned from Mary May's offer and Vinni's comment put the icing on the cake. "Yes, Mary May, I think you should definitely enter the contest if you wish, and yes, Vinni. I agree. It would be an excellent idea to have guest judges. That would give a new dimension to the talent show. How about the pastor of The First Baptist Church, and maybe even the Mayor? Just think. That would be great publicity and bring in a whole new crowd. Vinni Davis, that is an excellent idea. I would have to get approval from the planning committee, of course, but I can't imagine that anyone would object. I will get on this right away so Mrs. Pratt can include it in the advertisements and announcements. Thank you, Vinni."

Mary May's face was beginning to flush when she offered her advice. "I'm sure Mama doesn't mind helping, too."

A Bad Hair Day

The door to Eloise's Beauty Shop had barely closed when Eloise lit into Edna May. "How could you? Did you see what you've done to her hair? What on Earth am I going to do? That beautiful head of hair ruined!"

The two cashiers from Piggly Wiggly sat staring at each other, afraid to look at anyone else in the room. Edna May sat in the dryer chair bobbing her foot and flipping pages in a magazine.

"Me? What do you mean what I did to her hair? You're the beautician. This ain't Edna May's beauty shop." Eloise was almost in tears and too weak to stand. She collapsed in her chair. She used the last of her strength to blast Edna May. "I should have known better than to ask you to set the timer for her perm. Lord knows, anyone with the sense of a monkey could set a kitchen timer to five minutes. Five Edna May, five, not fifteen, five minutes. How could you? Did you see what you did to that poor woman? The most beautiful head of hair I have ever seen and it is ruined. What am I going to do? What in the world am I going to do? The weekend at The Club, Edna May. What in the world?"

The two clerks cut their eyes over to Edna May, waiting for a response. "Oh, good Lord, Eloise, calm down. It's just fine. I didn't hear her complain. She didn't say a word and you could barely see any of her hair under that Italian cloth thing that she tied her head up in. She's fine. God knows, I've seen you make worse messes than that. At least she'll be out of town where nobody knows who you are."

Eloise was able to get a few last words out before she burst into tears. "Just shut the hell up, Edna May, just shut the hell up!" Eloise was almost hysterical as she ran up the steps to the kitchen.

Edna May looked at the two clerks, rolled her eyes, shook her head and simply said, "I don't know why she's got a bee in her bonnet."

George Davis was still the same man with a heart that yearned for romance and adventure. The trip to Italy had not satisfied his heart, it only enhanced it. He wanted Lidia to have a wonderful weekend. The farm had denied them the freedom to take vacations. Lidia felt it wasteful to spend hard earned money on frills. George wanted this weekend to be spectacular and left his desires in a letter on the kitchen table. He was sure Lidia would be excited to find it after her morning at the beauty shop.

Lidia sat in the car and let her hands rest softly on the linen cloth that held her hair captive. She stared past the steering wheel to her knees as she raised her hands and pressed against the tight fabric. When she pressed down, her hair rose back, filling the cloth like a sponge. Eloise didn't let her look in the mirror before she left. She was afraid to look in the rear view mirror. She looked at her watch; twelve fifteen. George would be in for lunch soon. She felt like all the energy in her body had been absorbed by her hair and was fighting to escape through the linen cloth. Her legs were almost too weak to move and her mind was racing.

"What do I look like? What was I thinking? I could have used that money for something reasonable. I guess this is my punishment for being vain. Genevieve will be ashamed of me, so will George. Why do I have to ruin everything? What was I thinking? Poor Eloise, I need to call and let her know I'm okay."

She felt her hand press down on the metal car door handle and the door opened. She was walking to the house and rested her hand against the tight cloth. Her hand rubbed the edge of the cloth and she felt the length of hair that had escaped. It billowed out like a cloud of cotton candy. The unexpected find was more than she could stand and the tears began to puddle in her eyes. She walked into the kitchen, sat down at the table and closed her eyes.

The Letter

She crossed her arms and started to lay her head down when she felt the bulging envelope that George had left. She opened her eyes and tried to focus on the envelope. Her curiosity dried her tears and she saw something that she had seen many years before.

She remembered an envelope like this one from George's trip to Italy. She had found it on her bed one Saturday night. George had written it and asked her grandmother to take it to her room. The handwriting and words on the envelope were the same. *To My Darling Lidia*. She wiped the tears from her cheeks and chin and dried her hands on her skirt before she picked it up.

He had written it with a fountain pen, probably the same one given to him by Margaret when he graduated from high school. The envelope was tied with a pink ribbon from her sewing box. It matched one that Genevieve wore in her hair when she left for college. She pulled the loose ends and the envelope fell open under the pressure of the folded pages that held George's heart.

Lidia,
Please forgive me. Forgive me for not being
able to offer you all the things you deserve.
Please forgive me for having to give most of

my heart to the land. Please forgive me for not telling you how much I love you. Please forgive me for not telling you when I hurt. Please forgive me for expecting you to care for and nurture me more than I care for you. Please forgive me when my prayers for you are in my heart and don't reach your ears. Please forgive me for not telling you how beautiful you are.

Lidia,
Please let me tell you. I could spend my days staring at you, watching your hands float over your work. I could spend my energy following you, just close enough to be in the fragrance of your hair. I could spend my hours working to provide for you. I could spend my memory with our past and be satisfied with what you have given me. I could use my hands to hold yours and let you lead me through life. I could follow your dreams, never ask why and never look back. I could spend my nights wrapped in moonlight and your arms. I could satisfy my hunger with the taste of your lips and my desires with the warmth of your body. I could live as a part of you and sacrifice myself. I could live for you. I could die for you.

Lidia,
You are beautiful, you are amazing. You have something that everyone wants to be a part of. You make even the simplest things magical. Your voice draws me across the oceans and your brown eyes pull me back to my youth. Our children pull me to our future. You have me spellbound and I am helpless.

Lidia,

Let me thank you. Let me thank you for giving up Italy for me. I am forever grateful and indebted. Thank you for the wonderful children you have given me, for your daily sacrifice to make them happy. Thank you for understanding my faults and forgiving my shortcomings. Thank you for loving me like no other could. Thank you for putting others first, when you are more deserving. Thank you for supporting my dreams and desires, even when they seem to crush yours. Thank you for making me the luckiest man alive, just by walking beside me. Thank you for holding my hand when I pray. Thank you for holding my heart when you pray.

Lidia,
I want this weekend to be a wonderful gift. One we will share with Genevieve and our family. I can't offer you trips to New York or dinner parties at The Club, but I can make this weekend special. I look forward to leaving our daily life behind and tasting a new life with you. Let's live this weekend like it's our life and not one we have borrowed for a short time. Please promise me that you will put yourself first. Promise me that you will not feel guilty and enjoy this weekend. Promise me that you will accept this gift with no questions, no concerns and no regrets.

Lidia,
I have left something for you on our bed. Please go upstairs and be happy. You deserve happiness. We both do.

Forever yours,
George

Lidia ran her fingers across the tear stained words, just like she did so many years ago in Italy. She wanted to read them again, but she didn't. She couldn't risk letting them grow old, like a favorite song that grows old when you hear it time after time.

She stood and walked upstairs, forgetting about the dilemma on her head. She opened their bedroom door and gasped when she saw the bed. There was a new black tuxedo with a brightly starched white shirt. A pair of black shoes rested on the floor below. There was another envelope resting on the jacket with the same inscription, *To My Dearest Lidia*. She opened the envelope and stared at the gift in disbelief. Her fingers trembled and she nearly dropped the envelope. Her thoughts were overwhelmed and she couldn't focus.

"Uno, due, tre, quattro. Cosa ha combinato questa volea. Quattro cento dollari?" She examined the envelope again, wondering where the contents came from. Surely this was not the envelope intended for her. The words were too astounding to stay in her mind.

"Four hundred dollars? What on Earth was that man thinking? Four hundred dollars? For what? I couldn't spend that much money in six months. Who in the world does he think I am, The Queen of England? Does he know how many calves he can buy with four hundred dollars? Cose est conminando? Un, due, tre, quattro, cento dollari!"

Her mind couldn't comprehend what was in her hands and she looked around the room to regain some sense of stability and reason. Her eyes fell unexpectedly on the mirror over the dresser and she saw her new hair terror for the first time.

"No, no, no, no non puo essere racconto di sast no, no, no!" Her strength left and she turned and sat on the bed beside the new black tuxedo. How could she overcome this calamity and enjoy the weekend?

The phone rang and jerked her back to reality. It was George.

"Hey, Lidia. Did you get what I left for you? No, now don't say a word. You might break the spell. I'm glad you're happy. Oh, oh, oh not a word. Listen. I'm at Matthew's getting a tire fixed, so I won't be in for lunch, but listen. Margaret called and wanted to know if you could come up to Greensboro this evening instead of tomorrow. I told her you would be glad to. No problem. She is expecting you around five. Do you mind taking my tux? I'm afraid I'll mess it up. I can't wait to see you. This is like a secret affair. I love it. I just wish you were going to be home tonight. You know? Oh, stop with the Italian already. You will probably be gone before I get in so have a great time until I see you. I do love you, Lidia."

Hurley was standing nearby with the other men and shuffled away when the phone conversation got personal. "Okay, see you then. Bye."

George's new schedule and a chance to get out of town early lifted Lidia's spirits. She knew she could depend on Margaret to be discreet about her hair explosion.

Margaret's phone rang. "I'll get it." She was in the kitchen and picked up on the second ring. "Oh, hello, Lidia. Did you get my message? He did? Good. Then you'll be here around five? Okay, what's that? Surely nothing as bad as all that."

There was a familiar click on the line and the ladies waited for the considerate second click. The silence told them their conversation wasn't private. Lidia decided to let Margaret see for herself without giving Edna May the satisfaction of hearing her tragic story. Margaret decided to give Edna May something else to gossip about.

"Oh, by the way, George said he wanted you to bring his tux. Don't forget."

Edna May forgot she could be heard and she automatically exclaimed, "A tux!"

Margaret ended the call. "Lidia, did you hear something? There must be a possum in the junction box. Listen, honey, I'll see you when you get here. Don't forget the tux. Bye now."

Gary and Edna May Go to Lunch

Edna May jumped when she heard the kitchen door slam. Her nerves had been drifting to the edge since Gary arrived. His voice was still harsh, but it seemed more fragile with age. Edna May could see that Gary's drinking was taking its effect on him. His handsome square face was bulging from weight gain and flushed with red. She couldn't tell if it was from alcohol, high blood pressure, or both.

She closed her eyes and waited for his coughing fit to pass, knowing she was about to be blasted again. Living with Gary Crutchfield's anger made the scorching comments from others seem like compliments. His first words were mixed with gasping coughs.

"Get off the damn phone, bitch. Good God, that's all you ever do. You ain't even talking half the time. You must have a bunch 'o yackity friends. You just sit 'n listen. Where's my damn lunch?"

Years of experience had taught her to recognize how much Gary had been drinking by his language. On this visit, Gary's language had become harsher and more vulgar early in the day. She knew he was spending more time in his garage office and wondered how many bottles of whisky were littering the desk and floor, but she wouldn't dare approach the building.

She had begun to hate her husband's drinking, not tolerate it, not accept it, not make excuses for it, just hate it. She could feel the hatred growing and knew, in her heart, that one day the hatred would overtake her feelings for Gary.

She had survived the past fourteen years by pushing her problems to the back of her mind and replacing them with other people's problems. If there weren't enough problems or sadness to fill her mind, she simply created them. The citizens of Pleasant Grove knew what Edna May was dealing with, but never mentioned it. They knew when Edna May's life grew sadder that she had to spread the sadness. This was the only way she could survive. Living with such hatred and bitterness, when her friends had lives filled with joy and happiness, was simply unbearable for Edna May. The truth was, Gary's sickness had overtaken Edna May. It had crept into her life, leaving her bitter and tired. There was no medicine to take away the sickness. It filled her life. It had taken over her body and mind. The only way to rid herself of the awful intruder was by pouring it out on her friends. The only way to escape a life filled with torture was to rid herself of Gary. This was not an option.

She was too weak to respond quickly and jumped again when Gary shouted, "Where's my damn lunch?"

Edna spun around and looked surprised. "Lunch? Oh, I'm sorry. I thought you grabbed a bite to eat in town. I was at Eloise's all morning and I haven't eaten either. Listen, let's run over and grab a burger at Lou's. I'll drive."

Edna knew the only way to stay ahead of Gary's anger was to outrun it. She could make decisions and act on them before he could disagree. She was out the door and headed to the car before he realized what was happening. She had dodged his anger and taken control. He followed several feet behind on the way to the car. Edna heard him mumbling, but didn't respond.

"Lou's? Hell, I thought she died."

Miss Stout's Afternoon Class

Velma Stout wasn't herself the rest of the day. Instead of teaching, she simply told her students to read a chapter in their history books and work on their math homework. She reminded them of their spelling test and math test the next day and encouraged them to go over their notes. This would give any students with poor grades a chance to prepare and pull their averages up with high test scores.

She slowly strolled up and down between their desks making sure they were doing their work. She would hear the noise from the back row steadily increase as she approached her desk and soften when she turned and headed to the back of the room. Instead of looking at her students, she was staring out the long row of windows as she walked. She saw the younger children walk, single file, onto the ball field then run to take their positions for a game of kick ball.

Velma was restless. She couldn't concentrate. She wanted to go outside and run across the ball field; maybe some fresh air would help. She raised some of the windows and the fresh air carried in sounds from the kick ball game.

The windows that remained shut had been closed since the high school students painted the classroom a few summers earlier. The students who took pride in their work raised the windows when they painted them, leaving them up to dry overnight. The lazier students simply painted the windows closed and they would remain closed for the next few years.

Sara Jenkins's hand was raised, but Miss Stout didn't see it. She was staring out the window as her fingers danced across her chest.

"Miss Stout, Miss Stout?"

She kept staring out the window and answered without turning. "Yes, Sara, what is it?"

Sara spoke to the back of her teacher's head. "Miss Stout, I've finished my work and it's almost time for recess. Would it be okay if I went to the gym and took the softball equipment to the field? That way we would have more time to play."

Her permission was given softly. "Yes, that'll be fine. That's a good idea. You go head. Thank you, Sara, that's a good idea."

Miss Stout heard Sara as she closed her book and stood up. She also heard someone on the back row getting up, but she didn't turn to see who.

"I'll help her." Vinni was almost to the door when he made the announcement and there was no objection. The sounds of books closing and pencils clicking into the groves at the top of the wooden desks changed to soft spoken conversations.

Miss Stout saw the youngsters on the ball field pick up the kick ball and form a line that snaked its way back to the school house. She noticed Sara and Vinni as they opened the green wooden door and entered the gym.

Eighteen broke her concentration. "Can we go ahead now?" She shook her head to clear her mind and turned toward the door.

"Just a minute. Let me check." She walked to the door and stepped into the edge of the auditorium.

She could see the young students returning from their recess and lining up at the water fountain. Each one would rest their sweaty head above the arc of the cool water that had the taste of metal pipes. The teacher would count to six and give the drinker a tap, letting them know it was time to move on.

This practice seemed cruel to the students, but the teachers had good reason. Once there was a mother substitute teaching who didn't count. This resulted in very hot children overdosing on cold water. They were all able to hold their full stomachs until they reached the classroom. The mother was taken by surprise when the first child got sick from the mass of water and threw up. She was paralyzed with fear when half the class followed suit and the young class was even more surprised when their substitute teacher heaved her lunch on the teacher's desk. The story was a legend and if the teacher forgot to count, you could be sure the students would be counting.

Miss Stout waited for the last student to finish. "Okay class, you may go outside now." She stepped out of the way as her students walked toward the side door leading to the ball field. A couple of the girls stepped into the restroom while the others exited.

Miss Stout watched her class run and scatter across the field. Then she heard Eighteen. "Hey, where's the equipment? I thought Vinni and Sara were getting it."

She saw Eighteen head toward the gym and regained her composure to take control.

"Hold up. I'll see what's taking so long. You just go back to first base. Charlie, is your team ready to bat? Remember, girl, boy, girl, boy."

She was talking to the students on the ball field and walking backwards toward the gym. "Who's pitching today?" She turned and was almost at the gym door when it opened. Sara walked out carrying two dusty softballs and a canvas bag full of worn and faded gloves. Her face was red and she was staring at the ground. Vinni followed close behind with the leather strap of a canvas bag over his shoulder. He had the bats and catchers equipment. Exiting the dark gym made him squint against the afternoon sun, but Miss Stout could see the grin on his face.

"All right, Davis, let's keep all the playing on the field."

Vinni stopped chewing his pink bubble gum long enough to blow a bubble and wink at Miss Stout when it popped.

She tried not to smile, but couldn't stop. She hoped her date Saturday night would be as exciting.

Lidia Gets Ready For Greensboro

Lidia didn't spend much time packing. She had been planning for several days and knew exactly what to take. She was walking down the stairs with her large suitcase in one hand and her small toiletry case in the other. She would return for her dress that had to be carried on a hanger and George's tuxedo.

She turned onto the main highway that led out of town and remembered her phone conversation that was cut short with Margaret. Her new hair tragedy was still a problem and she needed to warn Margaret. She needed to use a phone, but couldn't decide where. It couldn't be one on Edna's party line. Steve's office had a private line and she made a short detour to borrow his phone.

Since Lidia had agreed to come a day earlier, Margaret had made a trip to the grocery store. Mimi was dusting the mahogany dining room table when the phone rang.

"Hello, Long residence. No, I'm sorry she's not in. Is this Lidia?" Lidia's accent gave her away to most people who answered her calls. "Yes, Miss Lidia. She told me you would be coming this evening. We're so glad you're coming. Genevieve can't wait and I have the guest room ready for you. Can I give Miss Margaret a message?"

Lidia didn't know what to do, but decided to tell Mimi her situation since she would soon know anyway. Mimi listened to her story.

"Um, um, um, you know, she didn't. Oh law, Miss Lidia, you ain't so. Now surely it's not that bad."

Lidia hadn't given herself time to really think about the situation fully and when she finally explained it, she was overwhelmed and burst into tears. Faye Duncan was sitting at her desk while Lidia was using her phone and handed her a box of tissues. The news of Lidia's trip to Eloise's had already spun through the gossip mill and Faye knew what happened.

She put her hand on Lidia's when she gave her the tissues and whispered, "You look fine."

Mimi just kept talking when Lidia started crying. "Now listen, Lidia, sweetie, you just calm down now. Ain't a thing to worry about, just calm yourself. Miss Mimi knows just what to do. Don't you worry 'bout a thing. Lord, honey, listen. If there's one thing us black folk know 'bout, it's how to get the frizz out o' some hair. Now you just believe me when I tell you this. What you need is exactly what all my sisters need every Saturday night. This is what we do to get ready for church on Sunday. Now, honey, you just dry them tears and come on up. I'll have you in fine shape in no time. I got the relaxer and hot iron. I got everything you'll be needin'. It's goin' be just fine now, just fine. I'll tell Miss Margaret you called and you're on your way."

Miss Mimi's news was wonderful and unexpected. Lidia thanked her again and again.

"You're welcome, you are most welcome. Now don't say another word. Yes, ma'am, bye now."

By the time Mimi had finished her conversation, Lidia had regained her composure.

"Faye, I just need to make one more phone call if it's okay."

Faye smiled and reached for her rolodex. "I have Eloise's number on file."

Vinni Goes to the Principal's Office

Miss Stout's class was returning from the ball field when Vinni got the message. "Mr. Johnson wants to see you in his office."

The request was familiar, but this time unexpected. Vinni followed Miss Stout's instructions and went to the principal's office when his classmates returned to the room.

He entered Mrs. Pratt's office to the usual greeting. She drew her red lips into a tight rosebud and shook her head in disappointment.

"I'm not sure why he needs to see you, but I am sure he must have a good reason." She leaned toward the small crack between Mr. Johnson's door and the doorframe. "He's here, Mr. Johnson."

Vinni heard papers being shuffled and the bottom drawer close. "Okay, send him in."

Vinni opened the door and closed it behind him. His actions were familiar and he was comfortable in the principal's office. He took the seat that was reserved for him, slid down until his shoulder blade rested on the back of the chair and rested his right foot on his left knee.

Mr. Johnson was looking over his papers and didn't raise his head. "Thanks for coming in, Vinni, nothing wrong. I just need a favor."

The request caught Vinni by surprise and he sat straight in his chair. "Yeah, I guess, sure. Whatcha need?"

Mr. Johnson finished signing the last forms and called for his secretary. "Mrs. Pratt, the signatures you needed are ready." He handed the papers to Vinni. She reached inside the office, took the papers from Vinni's hand and disappeared.

The principal relaxed with a long exhale and slumped in his chair. "Vinni, Mr. White needs some help and I thought you may be the one for the job. I guess you know the talent show and hot dog supper is coming up. Well, it looks like we need to spruce things up a little. The stage is a little shaky and the back wall could use a coat of paint. There's a few other things, I'm not sure exactly what, but I was hoping you could help with the repairs. I know you have to get home and milk, which eliminates any work after school, but I thought maybe Miss Stout would let you work during lunch and recess. If she approves and your grades are sufficient, you could take some time out of class also. Let me be clear. This is not in any way a punishment. I know you helped him out on a couple of projects previously and he was very pleased with your work. It would only be for a couple of weeks, maybe every day, maybe not. I'm leaving it up Mr. White to coordinate with you, that is, if you're interested. Again, it's nothing required. We just need your help. So just think about it for a day or so and let me know. I guess I'll need to know by Monday morning."

Vinni had never been in Mr. Johnson's office on these terms. He was on equal footing, man to man. He had been chosen because of his good work. This was unexpected and Vinni immediately rose to the task.

"Oh, yeah, sure, I'd like to help. I like Mr. White. He's nice. I don't mind missin' lunch a few times, and recess too. That don't matter. I guess time out of class is up to Miss Stout, but I'd be willing to help then, too. When do I start?"

Mr. Johnson liked interacting with Vinni on this level. He was a tough nut to crack as a teenager, but he gladly stepped up to the plate and took responsibility as a man. The truth was he sometimes welcomed the unexpected antics that Vinni offered. He always kept a stern hand and held him accountable, but he loved Vinni Davis's spirit.

He sat up in his chair and leaned toward Vinni. "If you're sure. You may need to talk it over with your parents."

Vinni was rubbing his hands on his knees. "No, really. I'm sure I can help."

Mr. Johnson stood and extended his hand to Vinni. "Thanks, Vinni. I really appreciate this and I know Mr. White will." Vinni accepted the handshake.

"You know I have to come down on you pretty hard for some things and you know why. But I've noticed what a hard worker you are and you're very smart, Vinni."

Vinni didn't expect this conversation and hadn't planned his response. He was out of his element, out of control, and had no plan. The only thing he had to rely on was honesty.

"Well, thanks. I don't mind hard work. I'm used to it. I don't know about being smart. Jake's the smart one, but thanks anyway." Mr. Johnson patted him on the shoulder.

"Well, I do know about you being smart. I'll have Mr. White get with you on what he needs. I guess you better get back to Miss Stout's now. Thanks again."

Vinni opened the door and walked by Mrs. Pratt's squinted glare. His first thought was to rub his temple with his middle finger but something stopped him. Instead, he tapped the edge of her desk.

"Have a good day, Mrs. Pratt."

The Bus Ride Home

The dynamics on the school bus had shifted and there seemed to be a power shift also. The Tribe remained in control of the rear seat, but the girls had shifted back two rows to be closer. The secrets within sexes were still whispered and kept in confidence, but there were more conversations between the boys and girls. Mary May took the leadership position with the girls and Vinni remained the leading example to the boys. It was common knowledge that Vinni and Sara were forming a bond, but no one dared ask questions. The guys simply approached the situation with vulgar humor.

Eighteen tried to embarrass Sara. "Hey, Sara, were you able to find any balls in the gym before recess?"

The question and laughter caught her off guard. She blushed and stared at the floor.

Vinni came to her rescue. "Hey, Eighteen, did you find any balls when you took a piss after lunch?"

The girls fell into a huddle and giggled, just like they had in the garage office at Edna May's party. They felt a little out of place, but they were bolder as a group. Sara was the only one that had actually broken ranks and dealt with The Tribe by herself.

Laughter broke the tension and they began to talk as one group of friends instead of two. "Mary May, are you going to be in the talent show? You know you'll win. You always do."

Sara was attempting to draw Mary May deeper into the group. Sara felt a little awkward being closer to Vinni than the rest of her friends. Alice spoke up before she could answer. "I think I'm going to enter this year. I've been taking dance lessons on Saturdays. I might do what I've planned for my dance recital."

Vinni offered his wisdom. "It better not be a striptease act. The preacher and the mayor are going to be judges. If you're not careful you may end up getting arrested and baptized in the same night."

The girls covered their giggling mouths and pointed at Alice.

Vinni continued. "Anyway, if I don't help Mr. White with the stage there may not be a talent show. He showed me what he needs help with. The stage is about to fall down." Vinni leaned back in his seat and the conversations shifted back to The Tribe.

The bus came to a jerking stop at Vinni's mailbox. "All volunteers to help milk follow me." Mary May elbowed Sara, daring her to follow Vinni.

Eighteen had gotten off at Matthew's Garage and Sara was the next to be dropped off. Jake was the last stop and he felt awkward riding the last few miles alone. Sometimes he would walk to the front of the bus and sit behind the driver after Sara got off. The feeling was familiar.

Jake would be taking his life further than his friends and he would ride the last few miles alone. Vinni, Eighteen, Charlie and the rest of

The Tribe would be stopping at home and Jake would keep moving.

He stayed on the back seat, wondering what would happen at the lake this weekend. He was a little nervous, afraid his friends would be bored. He was glad his parents had planned the party, but almost wished they hadn't. He had never shared the lake with anyone. It was something he had that no one else did. Vinni had his milking, Eighteen had the garage and Jake had the lake. If The Tribe made fun of it or didn't have a good time, he would be disappointed. What if he showed his friends what he loved to do and they were bored? Would they make fun of him behind his back? Did they really consider him a member of The Tribe or were they being nice because their parents were friends? Did Mary Alice Duncan think he was like the other guys? Did she know he liked her? He and Mary Alice seemed to be much the same. Their personalities fell outside Pleasant Grove, just like their dreams.

"See you tomorrow, Jake." The bus door swung open and he walked to the front. He remembered what he needed to tell the bus driver.

"Oh, I almost forgot. I won't be riding Friday, neither will Vinni, Eighteen and the rest of The Tribe. My Dad's picking us up after school and we're going to the lake for the weekend."

The driver smiled and raised his white eyebrows. "Sounds like a great time. Hope you guys have fun."

Jake heard the rubber edged doors on the bus doors squeeze together and the bus roared away.

Mary May Gets Home

Mary May could feel the tension when she walked in her house. Gary and Edna May were in their bedroom and the sounds were familiar. She didn't want to go upstairs, but she felt so alone downstairs in the big house. She trotted up the stairs, hoping the sound of her steps would be louder than the argument drifting from the master bedroom. She closed her bedroom door, turned on her radio, sat on her bed and drew her knees up to her chest. Her arms were wrapped around her legs and her head rested on her knees.

Her mind kept jumping back to the fight her parents had when she was a little girl. She remembered the sounds that drifted through her bedroom door. Her mother pleading for Gary to please calm down, begging him to be quiet so Mary May wouldn't hear. She remembered sitting on her bed in the same position so many years ago. She wanted to scream loud enough for the world to hear, but she was paralyzed and silenced by fear. She didn't understand what was happening and couldn't explain it. So she would scream, hoping someone would understand, or at least ask why she was screaming.

Mary May had screamed for years, every chance she got. She screamed for help, she screamed out of fear and desperation, looking around to see if anyone was listening. She sang her song of sadness as loud and long as she could. She had screamed until there was no breath left in her body, but no one asked why she was screaming. No one knew her pain. No one cared.

Mary May had stopped screaming years ago and now she stopped the pain with denial.

Gary had continued to drink after their lunch at Lou's. His drinking increased along with his anger and sexual tension. It was a triple force that Edna May had no defense against. She had longed for a husband to love her, someone to be gentle with her and care about how she felt. Gary didn't have that capacity.

"Damn, come on woman. I've been gone for months. What the hell do ya' think a wife's for. Come on baby, come over here to daddy."

Edna said as little as possible. The smell floating from his mouth and his body was a mixture of alcohol and stale cigar smoke. His hands were huge and rough, causing her to flinch when they approached her face. Her breath was weak and she could only whisper.

"Gary, please, I think Mary's home. Let's just wait until later. We'll have a nice dinner and some wine. Yes, I'll have some wine and a nice romantic evening. Please, baby, just give me a chance to relax a little."

She put her small hand over his and tried to move it away from her face. He wouldn't release his position and when her hand slipped, it caused his hand to fall against her face. He didn't slap her, but the force of his hand on her face caused her head to jar. He was looking down at the top of her head and she was afraid to look up.

"Now, see what you made me do, baby? You just need to relax."

She was raising her arms to squeeze some space between their bodies and he held her fists in his hands. He took advantage of her position and continued his pursuit. "Yeah, that's better."

His red face was moving down to her and she tried to escape again. "Don't you think some wine would be nice? I have a bottle in the bathroom under the sink."

She still didn't look up, but she knew the look that came across his face. She had seen it many times before. His teeth were clinched behind an angry tight grin and his eyes were darting around her face. He leaned down and looked into her eyes.

"What's the matter, bitch? You saving your sweet stuff for George Davis? Huh, that it? You think George is gonna' come over since his lady's out o' town? Hell, sweetie, I know you been wantin' him since high school, but he went off and got him that fine little Italian piece. Hell, you can't compete with that fine ass, baby. You might as well settle for big daddy. Now stop fightin' me, baby."

She was being overpowered and her only defense was to keep her head turned and hold her breath. He staggered and swayed as he stumbled out of his clothes. Her trembling hands had to take the opportunity to get undressed, hoping to avoid the unpleasant experience of having her clothes ripped and ruined by his anxious hands. She tried to soothe his anger when he fell into the bed beside her. She rubbed his hair.

"Now, let's just relax a little. We don't have to rush."

Her breath was forced out of her lungs when his clumsy body covered hers. The pain caused her to gasp for air, which Gary interpreted that as sighs of delight. Her eyes were closed and her teeth were clinched, waiting for the unpleasant experience to pass. She tried to rub his hair, but her fist would tighten with pain, leading Gary to think she was participating in his pleasure.

The pounding conclusion was accompanied by his hot breaths of whiskey blowing on her face and hair. It sent tears rolling from her eyes into her ears.

The experience left Gary sweaty and exhausted. Edna was able to slide to the edge of the bed before her partner collapsed on top of her in a drunken sleep. She pressed her arms against his right shoulder and he rolled onto his back.

She could hear his heavy breaths as she closed the bathroom door. The tiles were cold against her feet and she sat naked on the white rug in front of the sink. She drew her knees up to her chest and held her legs with her arms. Her head rested against her knees and she wanted to scream, but she was paralyzed and silenced by fear. The music from Mary May's radio drifted through the walls and she felt her tears roll down her legs.

Wednesday Evening at the Farm

George and Vinni finished milking on schedule and walked back to the house together. The farm could tell Lidia was gone. The sounds were different and the smell of a hot meal being prepared was gone.

"Do you have everything ready for the lake this weekend? Your mama wanted me to make sure you were ready. She had planned to go up to Greensboro tomorrow, but your Aunt Margaret wanted her to come up this afternoon instead. Ed and Velma are taking care of things while we're gone. I'm leaving Friday morning after we finish milking, so nobody will be here after school. Make sure you have what you need. I left some money on your dresser."

Vinni's voice was more confident than the day before. His new responsibilities and respect at school made a difference. "Yeah, I got what I need. I don't need much, so I rolled stuff up in my sleeping bag. I put my clothes inside and zipped it up. Jake said they got fishing poles and everything so I just had to pack my clothes. His daddy's picking us up after school in his truck. Well, I think it's his truck. They used to deliver papers at the office, but he can use it. I guess the school bus'll be 'bout empty

Friday, but that's okay. I bet you wish you were goin' to the lake instead of Greensboro."

George remembered his letter and what he left for Lidia in the bedroom. He imagined how she would look on the dance floor at the club and he smiled.

"Oh, I guess I'll be all right in Greensboro."

Lidia Arrives At Winterberry Court

When Genevieve heard her mother's car turn in at the bottom of the hill, she trotted across the foyer and opened the front door. She had spoken to Lidia by phone, but hadn't seen her in several weeks. Genevieve was making a new life for herself. It was nothing she had planned, or even considered. It just happened. It grew slowly and intentionally, like a seed planted in Lidia's garden. Genevieve's days were filled with school and her evenings with her studies. She had wonderful memories of Pleasant Grove, but she felt more comfortable in Greensboro. Moving to Greensboro gave her a new identity. She wasn't known by anything she had ever said or done in Pleasant Grove. Her history was being forged daily; it was a brief and mysterious history.

Genevieve missed her family and the farm, but she was haunted by the memories of her illness and the years it kept her in darkness. Her life in Pleasant Grove had been redefined. Diabetes had devoured every part of her life. It even robbed her character. She had spent years dreaming of New York and Paris, struggling to bring excitement and glamour to their farm in Pleasant Grove, but the world she lived in and the world she dreamed of were too distant. Genevieve was growing weary in Pleasant Grove and her dreams were slowly changing into fantasies. Genevieve knew there was a great difference between someone who fantasized and someone with dreams.

If Genevieve Davis had remained in Pleasant Grove, she would have become that sick lady who was a little crazy. Pleasant Grove was not broadminded enough to care for Genevieve's character. Her physical needs would have been met, but that wasn't what kept Genevieve sane. Her family and friends would have decided what was best for her, without asking, and provided only that. Genevieve Davis would have been driven to insanity in Pleasant Grove, driven by caring hearts and helping hands, driven by those who loved her most with her best interests at heart. Instead, she had been driven away from those loving hands by a horrible illness, an illness that didn't have her best interests at heart, an illness that didn't love or care for her, an illness that entered and redirected her life, an illness that would remain with her forever.

Genevieve had finally embraced diabetes as her companion and invited it to be a part of her life. The only other option had been to resist it and spend the remainder of her life in a battle.

Lidia didn't see Genevieve standing on the grand front porch. Her eyes were fixed on the driveway, being careful to avoid the freshly watered green grass and lush boxwoods. Genevieve was walking toward her car when she opened her door and stepped onto the concrete driveway.

"Genevieve, oh cara, il mio bambino, Genevieve bella." Their embrace took Genevieve back to her childhood. Her eyes were closed, but she saw her mother hanging clothes in the summer sun with the garden in the background. Everything from her childhood came rushing back and she wanted to hold her mother forever because she knew the memories would be interrupted when she released her grasp.

Their arms relaxed and when Genevieve took a deep breath, the aroma of Lidia's fresh permanent filled her nose. The strong odor caused her to cover her mouth and cough. Lidia saw Genevieve's eyes when they discovered the tragedy on her head.

"Oh, don't worry, dear. It's a long story, but Mimi will take care of everything. I'll explain later. Is Margaret in?"

Margaret opened the door and stepped outside. Mimi was close behind. Margaret waved her arm in the air like she was flagging down an airplane. "Hello, Lidia, glad you made it. Come in, come in."

Genevieve reached into the back seat and picked up Lidia's faded and worn leather suite case. It was the same one she carried when she left Italy.

"Thank you, Genevieve. I'll get the rest out of the trunk."

Genevieve walked across the slate porch and Lidia followed, holding the hangers with George's tux and her dress high in the air. Margaret smiled when she saw Lidia's hair held captive beneath the scarf and shook her head.

"Mimi told me everything. Honestly, that woman, Edna May, has hit a new low with this one."

The weight of the problem had been getting lighter as she drove to Greensboro and by this time Lidia just laughed about her hair.

"Oh well, Mimi's got her work cut out for her. Glad I came a day early, it may take two days to get this head under control."

Mimi joined the laughter and threw her hands on her hips. "We'll show 'em, Miss Lidia, we'll show 'em."

Velma Stout's Phone Call

Velma Stout was glad to see the school day come to an end. Her thoughts were still consumed with her plans for Saturday night. She had just finished supper and was folding a paper towel full of sandwich crumbs when the phone rang. She answered on the second ring.

"Hello, oh, it's you." Her hand floated up and her fingers danced across her chest. She felt weak and sat back down in the metal chair at her kitchen table.

"Well, of course we're still on for Saturday, unless you called to cancel." The words escaped her mouth before she thought and panic flashed across her emotions. If he had called to cancel, she had just made it easier, giving him the perfect opening. Uncontrollable words kept flowing from her mind without pausing.

"But I hope you're not canceling." Her fingers danced faster and her foot began to bounce frantically. She hoped words would come back across the line and give her a chance to stop talking but they didn't come.

"Well, are we still on? Yes, I know that's what you said, that's good, fine. What time? Five? Isn't that a little early? Raleigh? Well, good Lord. Raleigh? No, no Raleigh's fine. Well, it makes no difference to me, five, six, whenever, just let me know. Okay, six. Will I what? Well, I most certainly will not. Honestly, sometimes you do drive me right to the edge. Are you sure this is a good idea?"

His answer caused her hand to drop and her foot rested on the floor. "Oh, that is the sweetest thing. Six o'clock then. Thank you. Oh, oh my, please. Goodbye now."

APRIL 29TH 1948

Plans for Vinni

Mr. Johnson stuck his head into her classroom. "Miss Stout, could I have a word with you, please?" She stepped into the auditorium.

Vinni leaned over and tried to watch the conversation between Miss Stout and the principal. He could tell they were discussing him by the way Mr. Johnson would nod in his direction and then point toward the stage. Miss Stout would nod in agreement and then in disagreement, leaving Vinni wondering what his chances would be in helping Mr. White with the project.

Vinni had to lean further to the edge of his desk as the pair stepped to the side. He could barely see them and didn't realize how far he had tilted his desk when the metal disks on the bottom of the wooden legs slid. Vinni and his desk hit the floor with a loud bang followed by roars of laughter.

Miss Stout stepped back into the room just as Vinni stood up and lifted his chair back into position. She could tell right away that Vinni wasn't trying to cause trouble. He was frantically picking up his papers and was the only one in the class who wasn't laughing. It wasn't Miss Stout's presence that stopped the laughter, it was Vinni's agitated glares at his classmates that shut them up. He looked at Miss

Stout and received a familiar gesture. She was staring at the floor and motioned for him to get up and come to the front of the class by waving her hand in small circles. She turned and walked toward the principal's office. Vinni's heart sank knowing he had just ruined his chances of helping Mr. White.

Mrs. Pratt heard the commotion and shook her head in disapproval when Vinni followed Miss Stout into the principal's office. The mumbled voices coming from behind the glass were familiar and she was sure Vinni was in trouble again. She was very surprised when Miss Stout opened the door and Mr. Johnson was shaking Vinni's hand and thanking him. Miss Stout patted him on the shoulder and added her thanks as he walked out the door. "Will you close the door, Miss Stout?" She closed his door and followed Vinni back to class.

Mrs. Pratt felt very strange about the meeting. She was usually informed about everything that happened in the principal's office. She was even asked to sit in and take notes on some of the meeting concerning Vinni, but she had no clue what was going on this time and felt rejected.

When Miss Stout returned to the classroom without Vinni, the class expected the worst but didn't ask questions.

Vinni had been directed to find Mr. White in the large storage room behind the stage. The stage and storage room was flanked on both sides by hallways and classrooms. The hallway on the right led to the lunchroom with an exterior door and water fountain. The hallway on the left led to the large music room with a water fountain and a door leading to the playground and one entering the storage room behind the stage.

"Mr. White, you back here?" Vinni heard bumping sounds coming from under the stage so he walked over and looked into the open access door. He could see Mr. White crawling back toward him. A sixty watt bulb offered a dim light to the area beneath the stage.

"Yes, sir, yes, sir, right here, be there in a minute. My bones is gettin' too old to crawl around here, yes, sir, be right there."

The access door was about four feet tall. The area under the stage was about five feet tall, but you had to be very careful not to bump your head on the various items that hung from the joist supporting the stage floor. Mr. White rose from his knees and stooped to walk out the small door brushing white dust from the knees of his denim overalls.

"Yes, sir, glad you're here, Vinni, principal told me you could help, sure am glad, sure am glad. Got a lot 'o work to do, lot 'o work."

Mr. White stood straight up with his hands on his hips and looked down at Vinni. "Good help." Mr. White reminded Vinni of Hurley, tall and kind with a friendly smile. There was a slight family resemblance between the first cousins.

"Yeah, I'm glad to help. Better than sittin' in class. Just let me know what I need to do, until school lets out, anyway. I have to catch the bus home and milk after school, or I'd help longer. Just let me know. What're we doin' first, workin' on the stage?"

Mr. White was walking up the short set of stairs leading up to the stage floor. He stopped on the second and third steps and bounced, checking to make sure they were sturdy.

"Yeah, guess we better get this fixed." He motioned for Vinni to follow him across the stage as he bounced on several spots. Vinni noticed the floor sagging and remembered the same problem in their barn loft where hay for the cows was stacked. He followed Mr. White's lead and bounced on areas of the stage.

"Looks like these joists need some extra support. I had to fix somethin' like this in the barn one time. Well, me and Daddy fixed it. Do you have the lumber and tools?"

Mr. White was surprised to hear Vinni talk with such experience and confidence. He put his hands in his pockets and nodded in approval.

"As a matter o' fact, I sure do. Got two by fours, ten pennies, a saw . . ."

Vinni's mind was two steps ahead. "Got a level 'n chalk line?"

Mr. White laughed in approval. "A level and a chalk line? You my kind o' man, Vinni, my kind o' man. Most just throw somethin' up, especially on a project like this. That's why it needs fixin' now. Somebody didn't care how they did it the first time. Yes, sir, a level and chalk line, they're in my truck with the other stuff we need. I went to the hardware store this mornin'. I think we're goin' get along just fine, yes, sir, just fine. I can tell you're a man that does it right the first time. Good boy, good boy."

Vinni started down the short set of stairs on the opposite side of the stage that led to the hallway outside the lunch room. "I'll go get 'em." He knew Mr. White's truck was parked beside the lunchroom.

The morning seemed to go slowly for Miss Stout's class. Vinni's absence made a big difference. Typically the lesson would be interrupted by a pencil flying to the front row and hitting Mary May in the head, or the back row swaying and moaning with covered noses because of a toxic fart. Miss Stout even found herself with extra time because her lesson went quicker than expected. There were a few attempts by Eighteen to get some attention, but without Vinni's encouragement and direction, his efforts fell flat. Miss Stout found herself with free time for herself and the class.

"Okay students, you've done very well this morning. I think we deserve a treat. Everyone please put away your books and straighten your desk."

Before she could finish the assignment, there was a knock on the door. Mr. Johnson opened the door to find Miss Stout sitting on her desk with her ankles crossed and the students removing everything from their desk. Her first reaction was to jump down, straighten her skirt and stand at attention. However, she rejected her thought and simply tilted her head to one side and looked at the principal.

"Yes, can I help you, Mr. Johnson?" The principal stepped back to avoid the inquisitive eyes of her students. He put his hands on his hips and silently mimicked her response. The students wondered what made their teacher grin, then heard Mr. Johnson speak from outside the door.

"You have a phone call Miss Stout, you can take it in the lunchroom." This news was very unexpected and she quickly slid off the desk and headed to the door. "Class, please wait quietly until I get back. If I hear any disturbances, our special treat will be cancelled."

Mary May was waving her hand in the air as Miss Stout walked out the door. "Do you want me to take names?"

The answer came from the other side of the wall. "No, that won't be necessary, Mary May."

The class was left in a strange silence. The Tribe felt obligated to take advantage of the situation, but didn't want to lose their reward and without Vinni's guidance, they were helpless.

Mary May felt alone, scared and vulnerable without the power that came with standing at the front of the class holding a piece of chalk and looking for the slightest reason to begin her list of names. Sara kept looking out the door, hoping to see Vinni. The other students just looked at each other in silence and shrugged their shoulders, wondering what was going on.

Ms. Stout's Phone Call at School

By the time Miss Stout made her quick trip to the lunchroom, her heart was pounding. It was very unusual to get a phone call and only in the case of an emergency. She stepped past the stainless steel buffet line where empty pans were waiting to be filled. The aroma of fresh food baking was very different without the accompanying sounds of clattering children. The yeast rolls were baking and the roar of the giant mixer caused the sweet smell of cake batter to fill the kitchen. Mr. White had raised the windows and the entire room was filled with fresh air. Miss Stout wanted to sit down and enjoy the moment, but motioned to the lunchroom supervisor.

"I have a phone call and Mr. Johnson said I should take it back here."

Instead of shouting over the roar of the mixer, the supervisor just motioned for het to go into the office. The small room was just inside the side door that had been left open. The screen door kept the flies out and let the fresh air in. The small office had a desk against one wall and shelves on the other. Paper supplies and receipt books sat beside the ladies' pocketbooks on the shelves. Miss Stout picked up the black receiver.

"Hello. Oh, hello, my goodness, I didn't expect the call to be from you. No, no that's fine. Is everything okay? Saturday. Is that why you called? Well, yes, I'm still planning on it."

She listened and took a deep breath, closed her eyes and shook her head. "No, don't worry about it, maybe some other time. Well, I don't know, maybe. Well, no, I don't have any plans that I know of. No, I am not telling you no. I'm just saying, well, I don't know what I'm saying, I guess I'm saying I was looking forward to this weekend, but I guess not now. Well, my word, why in the world didn't you just wait and call me at home? Sometimes you just drive me right to the edge, you know that, right to the edge. Well, right now I just don't know about next week, but I do have an opening for Saturday night! What? Well, I never. You better watch yourself, buddyrow. Yes, I know you're not asking me to wait on you, but I do have twenty, no nineteen students who are waiting on me. I really have to go. You know sometimes you drive me right to the edge. Fine, call me tonight. If I don't answer, it's not because I'm not there. Goodbyeeee."

She put the receiver down and slumped into the chair. She was exhausted physically and emotionally. Mr. White's head popped around the corner.

"Here you go, right out of the oven." He sat a plate on the desk with two hot yeast rolls and fresh butter. "Looks like you came at just the right time, Miss Stout."

She smiled at the plate. "Thanks, Mr. White. At least somebody came at just the right time."

Vinni and Mr. White

Vinni had retrieved the materials from Mr. White's truck and carried them to the storage room behind the stage. He positioned two discarded lunch tables to make a saw horse and laid the two by fours on top. Mr. White came in with a couple of hot rolls on a plate.

"Looks like you got this job under control. Here, have some rolls while they're still hot." He sat the plate on the table and Vinni grabbed a roll and stuffed it in his mouth. He didn't have time to swallow before he began explaining his plan to Mr. White.

"I think I'll mark the sagging floor joist every four feet and number the marks. Then I'll take a measurement on each one to see where the floor starts sagging. That way I'll know where I need to nail the supports. All the supports need to be the same length to make the floor even. That makes the job a little easier. I put a baseball on the stage and it didn't roll at the front or back, so those two areas are level. I measured underneath the stage at both locations and the numbers matched. That's how long I need to cut the supports, sixty two inches. We'll need a two by four cut about a foot long for each support. It can be nailed to the floor and the support nailed to it. That should make the repairs permanent."

Vinni had finished the first roll and shoved the second one in. "I can go ahead and start marking and measuring the joist if you want to start cutting the supports, sixty two inches long, and a foot long piece for each support. Or you can measure. It don't matter to me. I just thought it would be easier for me to crawl around under the stage. I might need a flash light, the light's kinda' dim under there."

He swallowed and waited for Mr. White's response. Mr. White's smile faded and he motioned for Vinni to come closer. His response was in a whisper.

"Boy, you better not talk so loud. If they hear all this you plannin' to do, they'll fire me fo' sure and hire you." He slapped Vinni on the back and let out a proud response. "Good boy, good boy. I tell you what, you the best help I ever had, smart, hard working, smart, real smart, you got a natural way about building, you sho' do, got a natural way. Yep, I'll start cuttin' these two by fours and you start measuring."

Vinni opened the access door and stepped under the stage. He had left a pencil, his measuring tape and the level where he could find them. He was making his first measurement and he could hear the sound of wood being sawn and Mr. White talking to himself.

"Smart boy, I tell you what, that's one smart boy. He's gonna' do all right in this ol' world, cause he's a smart boy, hard working, too."

The extra vote of confidence made Vinni work even harder. Vinni Davis had always risen to meet the expectations of others, good or bad, usually bad. Mr. White didn't realize what a difference he made that day.

It was lunch time and Vinni could hear his classmates on the other side of the wall. They didn't realize that he was only a few feet away and could hear what they were saying. Mary May and Sara were leaning against the wall closest to him and he was about to bang on the wall and send them screaming down the hall, but he didn't want to give away his position without careful consideration. He was wondering how he could get a rat or snake and release it on their feet, but didn't want to involve Sara. Mary May's conversation was intense.

"Mama said it was just awful, she's never seen anything like it. She said her hair was as big as a bushel basket and it was all she could do to get it tied up under that Italian rag. Well, she said it served her right anyway. She never has even been to Eloise's. She probably just wanted to brag about goin' to that fancy dance thing, or dinner, or whatever it was in Greensboro. Well, actually, she didn't say anything about it. Mama just overheard when she was trying to make a phone call. Mama said she would love to be a fly on the wall when she walked into that ballroom with a head that looked like a warf rat's nest."

Vinni was drawn closer to the wall, like he was under a spell. He laid his pencil and measuring tape down and walked to the adjoining wall. He could feel his heart beating and his breath sounded like he had been running. He sat down with his back against the wall directly behind Mary May. He tilted his head toward the wall for more information. He could hear the familiar rumble get louder as the younger children lined up in the lunchroom and began walking down the hall. Mary May continued.

"Well, Mama says she acts like she's better than everybody anyway, the way she talks in Italian and never goes to the beauty shop, and grows all those herbs and flowers in her garden. She says she acts like she's too good to be a farmer's wife and she wouldn't be surprised if she ends up with one of those rich men in Greensboro."

Sara could only listen and whisper an occasional disapproval.

"Oh, that's just awful. How could your Mama do such a thing? How could she say such a thing? What if Vinni found out?"

Mr. White stuck his head through the access door and saw Vinni sitting with his back against the wall, breathing very heavy through his nose. He assumed he was sitting, out of breath because he'd been working so hard.

"Okay, Vinni, time for lunch, time for lunch. Your class is linin' up so come on out."

Vinni heard the footsteps on the other side of the wall rumble toward the lunchroom. His answer was vague, like his mind was in another place.

"Yeah, yeah, I'll be there in a minute."

A Day with Margaret

"Oh, Lidia, honestly, how could you just let her get away with it? You know she did it intentionally. Really, one day someone is going to slap that wasp right off her nest. I know poor Eloise just felt horrible. She must have. You know she thinks the world of you, she always has."

Margaret sat her coffee cup down on the glass top coffee table in the sunroom. She leaned forward and glanced past the den and into the entrance hall.

"Mimi should be here soon. Her husband was going to drop her off this morning and she's running a little late. Did she say what time you had an appointment this morning?"

Lidia finished the last sip of coffee and nodded her head.

"No, she just said that her sister would let her use a chair in her beauty parlor to fix my hair."

She pressed the cloth tied around her tight hair. "I know Mimi means well and I appreciate it. Do you really think she can help me? Maybe I should just wash my hair a couple of times a day and let it run its course. I would hate for anything else to go wrong. Mimi would just be beside herself."

She leaned over and whispered to Margaret across the coffee table.

"Now, if you have any doubts at all, please tell me, Margaret. I hate to admit it, but I'm getting a little nervous about this whole relaxer thing."

Before Margaret could answer, the front door opened and they heard Mimi's footsteps on the slate floor.

"Mornin', Miss Margaret, mornin', Miss Lidia, another beautiful day, praise th' Lord, um hum."

Margaret and Lidia stood up. "Back here in the sunroom, Mimi. Grab a cup of coffee and join us."

Margaret motioned toward the kitchen and Lidia rested both hands on her head. Mimi passed the kitchen and headed straight for Lidia.

"No, ma'am, ain't got time for coffee this mornin'. We got to get Miss Lidia taken care of. Now, let's see what we dealin' with."

Mimi reached up and slid the cloth from Lidia's head. Lidia closed her eyes to avoid Margaret's shock, but heard her gasp when the cloth fell on the chair. She opened her eyes and saw Margaret holding her fingers over her mouth.

"Maybe this isn't such a good idea. I appreciate your offer, Mimi, but maybe this is just too much."

Margaret was speechless and just waved her hand in the air. Lidia felt Mimi's hands rub her hair and her shoulders rose in embarrassment. Mimi stroked her hair from top to bottom and then reached to the sides and pulled it back into a ponytail.

"My word, Miss Lidia, your hair must a' been 'bout six inches longer b'fore this perm. It sho' did draw you up, sho' did, um hum. What was that woman thinkin'? Must not 'a been thinkin' much, um hum, not thinkin."

Lidia took a couple of steps toward Margaret and turned to Mimi. "That's okay, Mimi. I know it's worse than anyone expected, maybe I'll just wait it out. Don't you think maybe, Margaret?"

She looked at Margaret for approval and she was staring at her hair with one hand over her mouth and waving the other one in the air. She couldn't keep her comments to herself.

"Wasp, she's just a wasp flying around to see who she can sting."

Mimi didn't understand the meaning of her comment and started slapping the air around her head, dipped and swayed.

"Wasp? I can't stand no wasp. I ain't never seen no wasp in this house. Lord, child, I seen my mama swell up like a pig from a wasp sting. Where you see a wasp?"

Lidia broke into laughter and rested her hand on Mimi's arm. "No, there's not a wasp. Margaret was talking about Edna May. She called her a wasp."

Mimi stopped slapping the air and waved her hand at Margaret. "Child, I think you're right. She is a wasp and I wouldn't mind slapping her either, um hum, Lord forgive me for sayin' so, um hum."

The tension had been broken and Lidia accepted Mimi's invitation to take a ten thirty opening.

"You girls get in the car and I'll drive." Margaret plucked her car keys off the hook in the utility room and followed them to her car.

"Let's go downtown and have lunch at the S and W when we're done. My treat."

Mimi's sister spoke to Margaret first, then Mimi. "And you must be Lidia. Listen, child, Mimi told me everything and you ain't got a thing to worry 'bout, not a thing. Believe you me, honey, nothin' we ain't already seen once and fixed twice."

Lidia smiled and looked at Margaret for support. "I'm sure you're in good hands."

Mimi was looking in the drawer for a plastic cape. "Um hum, that's right, good hands, um hum. I been prayin' 'bout this and yo' in the hands of· th' Lord, um hum, th' hands of the Lord, honey."

Lidia sat in the chair, released a long breath, closed her eyes and added to Mimi's prayer. Margaret sat in a metal yard chair next to the large front window and picked up the Greensboro Daily News.

With Lidia's eyes closed, she focused on the unfamiliar smells and sounds of the shop. The smell of chemicals and creams were strong and the radio played blues and jazz music. She felt the pick float through her cotton candy hair. It reminded her of George's fingers running through her hair on a warm summer night.

"Mimi, again, I can't thank you enough. I love my hair. I never would have dreamed to cut it, but I just love it, I really do."

Mimi was sitting with Margaret and Lidia at the breakfast table. It was three fifteen. Slices of lemon pound cake with lemon glaze sat on glass plates. The iced tea was in tall heavy glasses and the linen napkins were folded across their laps.

"You know, I've learned something from this ordeal. I really think God was in control. He knew everything I was going through. I believe he had a journey planned for me and Edna May sent me on the journey. I had to take a real look at myself."

Margaret laughed and held her fork in mid air. "Lord, Lidia, we had to take a real look at ya', too."

Mimi covered her mouth and tried to conceal her laugh out of respect for Miss Lidia.

"And I must admit. I wasn't sure God was in control." Margaret chewed her cake while she hummed a laugh.

"I know, I know, but seriously, Margaret. I have had a wonderful time getting to know Mimi better and spending the day with her friends in the beauty shop. I saw something that put everything into focus for me today.

"It was when we were leaving S and W after lunch. There was on older lady waiting on the corner of Elm. She didn't look like she needed to cross the street. She was just waiting. Her clothes were old and she looked tired. And she had her hair wrapped up with a red bandana. That red bandana made me feel like I could relate to her. I wondered what wonderful hair was under that bandana and what a wonderful woman was under those clothes.

"I realized that I have always been able to cover up my problems, my heartaches, my fears in some way. Sometimes I hide things until they get fixed, like my hair. But if it's something that can't be fixed, I just refuse to lift the bandana and face it. I'm afraid that's what I've done with Genevieve's diabetes. I can't fix it, so I don't look at it. I never really talked to Genevieve about her illness. I covered it up with doctors and medicine and tried to let the good things about Genevieve outshine the bad. I thought enough happiness could choke out the sadness, but I'm not sure it has. I'm afraid to lift that bandana covering her illness."

She was staring at the window and talking to the trees outside instead of Margaret and Mimi. The touch of Margaret's hand on her arm refocused her attention.

"Lidia, you have been a wonderful mother and caregiver to Genevieve, and yes, maybe you have covered up her diabetes, but it was for your own good. There is only so much a person can deal with and there is nothing wrong with knowing your limitations. Genevieve has had the very best care available and is very fortunate, even with her illness."

She sat back in her chair and wrapped her slim fingers around her tall glass. She noticed that Mimi was uncomfortable with the conversation by the way she was bobbing her knee under the table and looking around the room for something to pick up or dust.

"Mimi, I know the perfect thing for Genevieve. How about fresh flowers for her room in that crystal vase she always talks about. It's in the china cabinet, and you have the most beautiful way with flowers."

Mimi stood up in a hurry. "Yes, ma'am, now that's a good idea, a good idea. Now, you know it's the Lord's work. I don't make the flowers, I just put 'em together and bring 'em in, yes ma'am, I just bring 'em in."

She was half way to the dining room before her comment was finished. Lidia was running her fingers though her soft hair while Margaret continued.

"I have noticed a real change in Genevieve, really since she decided to go to the Spring Gala. I think it took some time for her to come to terms with her illness, but she has. Lidia, I really believe her diabetes is no longer under that bandana. She has accepted that it is part

of who she is and she will make the best of it."
Lidia tried to hold her tears back, but they
were too heavy and rolled down her cheeks.

"Margaret, do you think I abandoned her or
was irresponsible when I let her come here?
Please be honest. Sometimes I think I dumped all
my responsibilities on you and Daniel."

Her eyes were fixed on Margaret, waiting for
her answer when the phone rang. Margaret's tears
followed.

"Lidia, I thank God every day, every day, for
letting Genevieve be a part of my, of our lives.
It is not a burden. It is not a hardship or huge
responsibility. It is a joy to have Genevieve as
part of our lives. While we're on the subject,
I must confess. I understand how you feel. I
also have something I've been hiding under my
bandana. Lidia, sometimes I'm afraid that I have
taken Genevieve away from you. I hope you don't
feel that way, and if you do, please forgive me.
I know she belongs to you, but since Daniel and I
can't have children of our own, I'm afraid I have
taken my responsibility too far emotionally.

Mimi opened the swinging door connecting the
dining room and kitchen and softly broke into
the conversation. "Miss Margaret, Ella Watson is
on the phone about the church bazaar. Should I
tell her you'll call her back later?"

Margaret and Lidia wiped their eyes with linen
napkins. "Yes please, Mimi, thank you."

Lidia took a deep sigh and a sip of tea.
"Margaret, I don't know what we would have done
without your and Daniel's help, and Genevieve
loves you both dearly. I realize that God has
given Genevieve to all of us and we receive
blessings in many ways."

She leaned over and hugged her sister-in-law.
"I'm so glad we took off our bandanas. You know

they really would look silly with our formal gowns at the Club Saturday night."

The evening sun gave a soft glow to the mahogany paneling in the Long's den. Lidia was sitting in the leather club chair with her feet on the ottoman. Daniel's Bible was on her lap and her head was resting on the chair's tufted back. She had dozed off while she was reading from the book of Luke. It was the lesson to be taught in Sunday school and she always felt disconnected when she didn't read the scriptures.

Margaret was upstairs in her bedroom, looking through her jewelry box for the appropriate accessories for Saturday's dinner and dancing.

Mimi was softly humming hymns while she dusted the living room. Most people would complain about Margaret's collection of porcelain figurines in the glass display case, but Mimi always admired them and enjoyed dusting each one. She noticed the clock on the mantel.

"Lord have mercy, look what time it is." She stepped across the room and looked out the long wide window onto the street below. "Okay, he's not here yet. I was 'fraid he'd be waitin' on me, time just slipped away today, just slipped away, um hum."

She untied her apron while she walked across the foyer and into the dining room, then stepped back into the foyer and shouted up the stairs.

"Miss Margaret, I'll be goin' now. I told Jim I'd meet him at the mailbox. He'll be here soon, um hum." She was back in the dining room when Margaret responded.

"Okay, have a good evening. Thanks for everything. See you in the morning."

An Evening with Genevieve

The two didn't realize that Lidia had dozed off and their shouts jarred her awake. It took a few moments to regain her bearings and look at the clock.

Genevieve had a study session in the library after her last class. She told Lidia she didn't know exactly what time she would be home, but no later than five.

It was seven after five and Lidia felt like she had been drugged and was struggling to regain her strength. Daniel's Bible felt heavy on her lap and her left foot had fallen asleep. She put the Bible back on the drum table and rotated her foot to wake it up. The soft car motor could be heard and a car door shut. There were a few moments of conversation, a short pause, a few more words, then the car drove back to the street. Lidia smiled, knowing it was Genevieve, and wondered what the short pause was for. She walked into the kitchen, anxious to see her daughter, but not wanting to look to anxious. The footsteps she expected to hear approaching the utility room door from the garage didn't come.

Suddenly the tables were turned. Lidia felt like a school girl waiting at the back door for a friend to arrive, feeling disappointed and rejected when her friend had something more important to do. Where was Genevieve? Why didn't she run inside and give her mother a hug? What was more important? Was she upset because her mother hadn't spent time with her the night before?

Lidia slowly walked into the utility room and peeped out the door facing Genevieve's carriage house apartment. She felt like she was spying on her daughter and felt distant. There was no sign of her. She wanted to open the door and walk over to the carriage house, but she was frozen with rejection. Lidia stood on her tip toes and took a couple of steps backward, hoping that no one would see her spying on Genevieve.

"Did I hear Genevieve drive up?" Margaret's voice startled her and she jumped and spun around. She felt her hair float behind her body.

"Oh, Margaret, hey, yeah, yeah, she just came in. I think she went to her apartment."

Margaret was much more relaxed that Lidia about Genevieve's actions. "Oh yes, she never comes in until she's taken her books to her apartment and freshened up a little. She likes to wind down a little. I'm glad she takes that few minutes for herself. She told me one time that she has to make the transition between school and family. Sometimes, especially during exams, she just falls on her bed and goes to sleep. You know, Lidia, it's been a few weeks since she's had a seizure. She is very good about pacing herself. Her schedule revolves around her needs instead people's expectations. I wish I was more like that."

Lidia took one last look out the window. "I guess you know her better than I do. Oh, here she comes."

Genevieve's steps bounced past the garage and to the slate terrace behind the sunroom, keeping her rule to never enter through the utility room.

"Mother, I'm back. Are you in?" Margaret followed Lidia into the sunroom. Lidia held her arms out and met Genevieve in the middle of the sunroom.

"Oh, Genevieve, give me a hug, dear. How has your day been?"

Genevieve's response fell into Lidia's newly soft hair as they hugged. "Wonderful, just wonderful. I've had a great day. Well, Carter and I have had a great day."

Genevieve stepped back and held Lidia's hand. "Mother, I can't wait for you to meet him. Oh, he's just the greatest, but, of course, we have to wait until Daddy gets here. When will Daddy be here, is he coming in today? Oh, I can't wait for you to meet him. Aunt Margaret and Uncle Daniel have met him already. I hope you don't mind, but of course they would have to meet him first since he's in and out now and again. Anyway, when is Daddy coming in? How is Giovanni, still making all kinds of mischief? He really is the rascal, you know, but all the royal families in England have one just like him. I can't wait to hear what he's been up to. Has he put Mary May in her place yet? You know, I really do think he's probably the only one who can do that. Lord, I do hope that girl has stopped that crazy screaming. What on Earth makes her act that way? I think it's just to get attention. Guess it works. The apple doesn't fall far from the tree. Oh, mother, your hair is beautiful. I love it, I really do. Did Mimi do this?"

Lidia wasn't prepared for Genevieve's whirlwind and was trying to process all the information and find answers for all the questions. She was having trouble remembering everything Genevieve had just said. It had been years since Lidia had heard one of Genevieve's theatrical speeches, but her instincts kicked in, she changed gears and took control of the conversation.

"Here, let's sit down. I know you must be tired, you work so hard at school and all your studying. Let's just relax for a minute."

Lidia stepped past the leather club chair that had just held her captive and sat on the sofa. Genevieve sat on the opposite end and curled her feel under her dress and settled down like a kitten. Lidia took a deep breath and tried to recall Genevieve's questions.

"Well, let's see. I think your father will be coming in tonight, no wait. What is today, Thursday? He'll be coming in tomorrow, on Friday. I'm not sure what time. Ed and Velma are taking care of the farm for the weekend and it depends on how things go in the morning. I hope all is well and George will be here by lunch. He can't wait to see you. He's so proud of you, Genevieve.

"And Giovanni, everyone calls him Vinni now, well, Vinni is doing just fine. Well, I think he's doing fine. He's always made excellent grades and he still does. He never really studies and doesn't mind going to school. I still get the occasional phone call and have to meet with Mr. Johnson, but it's always just boys being boys. Sometimes I think he has to call because Edna May makes such a fuss about things, but that's okay. Vinni works really hard on the farm, never complains. He still goes for his piano lessons. Sometimes he misses a lesson, but I know he loves music. Very few people know about his music, but he has the most amazing gift. Viola has been

really good to let him take his own direction
and play whatever inspires him."

Genevieve noticed her mother was in a trance.
She was running her fingers through her hair and
staring out the window. It was like Genevieve
wasn't even in the room.

"I remember how he was so protective of you
when you got sick, how he attacked Mary May at
the Harvest Festival that night at church. He's
a passionate man, boy really. I have to confess.
I really don't know what to do with him. I never
have. I just sat back and watched him grow, all
these years, I just watched him. I suppose any
direction has been given by George. He respects
his father for that. I know he does and he loves
his father. But sometimes I can see that far
away look in Vinni's eyes, like he is longing for
Italy. It's really hard to explain, and maybe I'm
wrong, but I can feel Italy tugging at Vinni's
heart. People don't understand Vinni. He's not
like his friends. Sometimes I think adults pull
him into their world so they can judge him and
control him, especially Edna May."

Lidia's gaze turned from the window and rested
on Genevieve. She realized that no one ever
asked about Vinni, maybe no one really cared,
but Genevieve did care. Lidia let her final
thoughts escape her heart and mind.

"Genevieve, there is nothing in this world
that can control your brother, there is nothing.
I've learned the best way to help him is to
guide him. He can't be controlled. Maybe that's
good, I don't know. I try not to think about it
because it scares me. I wonder if Italy could
control him. No, not even Italy."

Genevieve had pulled her knees up to her chest
and her arms were wrapped around her skirt.
Lidia was the only person who could mesmerize

her daughter. All her dreams of faraway places and adventure were fulfilled in Lidia's Italy. "I wish Carter could meet Giovanni, I mean I know he will sometime, I just wish he could meet him soon. Maybe he could come home with me some weekend. I haven't been home in a while. What do you think?"

That statement jarred Lidia to her senses. "Oh, well, that is an idea, a weekend visit, you and Carter. Carter, that's right, isn't it, Carter Lindy? Well, a weekend visit with your boyfriend, Carter. I think George will be in tomorrow. I know you're anxious to see your father. He's so proud of you."

"Lindley, mother, Carter Lindley, not Lindy, Lindley." Genevieve had read her mother's comments well and knew she wasn't thrilled about her daughter bringing a young man to spend the weekend in Pleasant Grove. She dropped her feet to the floor in front of the sofa and stood up.

"Well, I really need to study. I'll see you at dinner. It smells like Mimi put a roast in the oven. Mimi is a fantastic cook, so is Aunt Margaret, actually. I'm so glad you were able to come. I hope you all have a wonderful time at the club Saturday night."

Lidia watched her daughter walk away. She was too astonished to speak. Lidia had, for the first time in her life, been rejected by someone she loved. Most girls feel this pain several times in their youth, losing their first love, having their tender hearts broken, their confidence crushed and left humiliated. Lidia had fallen in love with George on the coast of Italy beside the Tyrrhenian Sea. It was rare and lasting. She had told Genevieve about that summer and over the years her daughter would ask her to tell the story again and again.

Genevieve was a dreamer and loved the fact that her parents were so romantic. She always hoped to find love in Paris, Rome or maybe in Cairo. But she had not. Genevieve Davis fell in love with Carter Lindley at the library on Foster Street in Greensboro, North Carolina. It smelled like musty books instead of salt air. It sounded like whispers instead of crashing waves and their first kiss was by the dim light that crept between the bookcases in the back of the library instead of a sunset.

Genevieve's dream of an amazing summer romance had not happened as she planned, but it did happen and she was in love with Carter Lindley. She offered to share this part of her heart with her mother and her offer wasn't accepted with open arms. Instead of risking further rejection, she protected her tender heart and left her mother alone. Neither one saw what was coming, neither one knew how to deal with their emotions and neither one knew how to move past the unexpected and deep hurt.

Lidia wondered if this weekend would continue to sour. She wished George was there. She wished she was back in Pleasant Grove. She wished she could turn back time. She wished the tears would stop rolling down her cheeks.

APRIL 30TH 1948

The Morning Of The Lake Trip

"Vinni, got your sleeping bag?" George and Vinni were behind schedule and they could hear the bus coming. A calf had been born the night before and the extra time it took caused them to skip their breakfast. Vinni's wet black hair stuck to his forehead as he grabbed the bulky roll in one hand and his suitcase in the other. He struggled to keep his books under his arm and ran out the door just as the bus was slowing in front of his house.

"Have a good weekend, Vinni." George's shout made it out the door just before it slammed.

His sleeping bag was too cumbersome to deal with so he threw it up the steps of the bus and asked the driver to send it back. The first graders in the front seats jumped and tripped over each other in hopes of touching Vinni's sleeping bag.

The youngster next to the aisle lost all control and instead of passing it back, he grabbed the sleeping bag and ran, full speed, to the back of the bus. The bulky roll was almost more than he could carry and it completely blocked his view. In his excitement, he ran into Eighteen, who was sitting in the middle of the bench seat. The collision bounced the little guy backwards and he fell, landing on his back and looking straight up at Vinni.

He had just ran, head first, all the way through Busville from Front Street, through Middletown, onto Dead End street. He was a helpless lamb who had been thrown into a den of wolves. The mumbles faded to whispers, the laughter stopped and the sounds of children spinning around on brown vinyl bus seats led to silence. Vinni Davis was bigger than life to first graders. The stories of his antics in school became legends; he was unapproachable. He looked even bigger and more menacing to the little guy lying on his back.

Vinni looked down at the helpless child and saw tears forming in his wide eyes. Eighteen waited to follow Vinni's lead. He didn't know where to let the helpless kid go free or punish him for invading Dead End street. He looked down at the helpless victim then up at Vinni. Vinni winked at Eighteen and handed him his suitcase and books. Then he looked down at the frozen and helpless child.

"Thanks, little buddy, you're a strong one. Want to sit with us today?" He reached down, picked the smiling child up and sat him in his lap next to the window.

"What's your name, little guy?" His head was shaking because Vinni was rustling his hair.

"Jeff Kidd, Jeff Kidd, sir. I have a little sister named Gracey".

"Well, Jeff Kidd, sir, thanks for carrying my sleeping bag." The bus engine roared and bounced the students down the road to pick up Sara Jenkins.

Vinni stretched his neck to see around Jeff's head and watched Sara walk from her driveway to the bus. She was wearing a thin sweater that hugged her figure and a skirt that her mother had made. He almost forgot that Jeff was in his lap and nearly dumped him on the floor when he stood up and motioned for Sara to come to the seat in front of him.

"Hey, Sara, here's a seat." His tongue started drifting across his bottom lip and his index finger was making small circles on the top of Jeff's head. Sara dropped into the seat and sat with her back to the window.

"Hey, Vinni, hey, Eighteen." Before she could enquire about the first grader, Jeff scooted to the edge of Vinni's lap.

"Hey, I'm Jeff. I'm in the first grade. I carried Vinni's sleeping sack. I have a little sister named Gracey."

Vinni laughed on the top of Jeff's head. "Hey Sara. It's a sleeping bag, little guy, not a sleeping sack."

Jeff felt right at home on Dead End Street by this time and didn't listen to Vinni's comment. "Vinni's got a big sack." Eighteen punched Vinni in the arm. Sara laughed against her hand and raised her eyebrows at Vinni. Vinni took care of his new little friend.

"Hey, buddy, listen, it's a sleeping bag, bag not a sack, a sleeping bag. Got it? Shut up, you guys"

The bus was bouncing toward Jake's house. "You guys are going to the lake with Jake this weekend, right?"

Sara had overheard conversations and wanted to make sure all the guys were going to be gone over the weekend. She had planned to spend the weekend with Mary May and didn't want to jeopardize missing time with Vinni.

Eighteen answered in the excitement. "Yeah, we're going after school. Jake's daddy's picking us up in his truck. We won't be back 'til Sunday evening, so we won't be on the bus after school and won't be at church Sunday. They got a boat 'n everything. We're goin' fishin' 'n swimmin' 'n no tellin' what all. We'll probably cook out on a campfire too, I 'dunno. It's goin' be fun, you can betcha."

The bus came to a slow, jerking stop. Jake grabbed the handrail and jumped from the ground to the top step. He saw Vinni's suitcase and sleeping bag under Eighteen's feet.

"Hey, guys, ready for the weekend? Who's stuff is this?" Vinni leaned over to make sure there was room for Jake on the back seat.

"It's mine, just kick it out of your way." Jeff jumped up on his knees.

"Hey, I'm Jeff. I'm in the first grade. My little sister's name is Gracey. That's Vinni's sleeping bag, I carried it back here for 'im. It's a sleeping bag, a bag."

Jake squeezed past Eighteen's knees and sat against the opposite window.

"That's cool, Jeff. Where's your stuff, Eighteen?" Eighteen looked out the window and turned a little red.

"Oh, yeah, well, I got my clothes in a paper bag from Piggly Wiggly. I ain't go no sleeping bag, but it don't matter."

Vinni agreed. "Yeah, it don't matter."

Jeff agreed. "Yeah, it don't matter."

Jake had the solution. "We got extra sleeping bags 'n stuff at the cabin anyway. If you forgot something, it's okay."

Miss Stout clapped her hands to get everyone's attention. "Settle down, everyone, settle down. I know we all have exciting weekends planned, but we have to get our class work done. Vinni,

Eighteen, Gerald, have a seat. There's nothing outside that you need to be concerned with. Step away from the windows."

The rumbling of the students diminished to a quiet hum, then silenced. Mary May raised her hand and shook it to get Miss Stout's attention. "Miss Stout, Miss Stout."

Velma Stout tried to ignore the request for her attention, expecting Mary May's comment to be self absorbed. She turned to the chalk board and started writing geography test questions. She answered Mary May with her back to the class. "Yes, Mary May, can I help you?"

Even though her back was to Mary May, she could tell that she stood up to make her comment. She turned to face the important comment. Mary May was standing at attention with her hands folded in front.

"Miss Stout, I was speaking to Mother about the talent show next Friday night. Is it true that you have asked the mayor and the pastor from First Baptist to be judges? Mother was under the impression that she would be a judge, but hasn't received a phone call. She asked me to find out if this was an oversight on someone's part, or if had she been replaced."

Miss Stout closed her eyes and shook her head. "Mary May, this is hardly the time or place to discuss such a matter. There is a committee handling the talent show and I suggest that if your mother has any questions, she call the committee chairperson. I'm sure she knows who that is. Now please, have a seat."

Vinni's despise for Mary May's mother had been rising since he overheard what happened at Eloise's Beauty Shop. Typically, he would have offered a comment, but his anger had driven him past speaking and he was planning actions to deal with Mary May and her mother. Vinni Davis would make sure the upcoming talent show would be remembered for a very long time.

Miss Stout addressed the class as she finished the tenth question on the board. "Please get your papers ready. I need your name and date in the top right corners please. These questions are from the last two chapters we have covered on the northern states and Canada. You are not required to write the questions, but if you need extra credit, I will give five extra points if you do. Please keep your answers to no more than three sentences. I don't have time to read essays this weekend."

Everyone knew the comment was directed towards Mary May. Her hand was shaking in the air again.

"Miss Stout, is it possible to get a score of one hundred and five?"

She was looking in her desk drawer for the attendance pad and answered without looking up. "Yes I suppose so. Jake Adams."

The response came from the back row. "Here."

Vinni was passing his test to the front when he saw Miss Stout walk over to the door where Mr. White was standing. He couldn't hear the conversation, but Mr. White kept nodding in Vinni's direction. Miss Stout looked at her watch and made a short comment before Mr. White turned and headed to the stage. He wondered if he would be able to help on the stage, but didn't want to seem anxious.

"Are all papers handed in?" She walked across the front row and collected the stacks of test papers. Mary May's hand shot up again.

"Miss Stout, I'm afraid I may have written more than three sentences a time or two. Will I get extra credit?"

She turned and looked at Mary May and sat the papers on the edge of her desk.

"Well, as a matter of fact, no. Your instructions were to limit your answers to no more than three sentences. If you did not follow instructions, your answer may be considered incorrect."

Mary May's hand dropped like a stone and her face faded from red to white.

Velma Stout leaned against her desk and stared out the window for inspiration. "Let's see class, how about something a little different for our English and writing lessons today? Tell you what. I think we will combine the two. Yes, that's what we'll do. We'll combine our English and writing lessons, extend them until lunch and skip our science today."

She heard sighs and groans from the back row. The Tribe's least favorite lessons were English and writing.

"So please get your English composition books and pencils and follow me." The students were confused and scrambled for their things as Miss Stout walked out the door. She was opening the side door leading to the parking lot beside the ball field before the students caught up with her.

"Please, no running or shoving. We're going down to the ball field. If a class comes out for recess, we'll have to leave. But, for now, let's just gather on the ball field."

The students didn't run in front of her, they didn't know what to do, so they followed in small groups of friends. The Tribe brought up the back, wondering what Vinni would do for entertainment. Miss Stout stood at home plate and faced her class gathered around the pitcher's mound.

"Over the years I have realized that all the great painters and writers have a connection with nature. They are inspired and enticed by the outdoors. We don't limit our lives to the inside of the school and we should not limit our minds to the inside of the school. It's very difficult to describe a tree when you're staring at a wooden desk, or describe what a bird or the wind sounds like when you are behind closed doors. I understand that we have to use our imagination, and that's good, but I think we also need to learn how to capture reality. What is the wind doing when a bird floats by, or what does the tree smell like in the springtime? If we force ourselves to write about these things, we also force ourselves to experience them.

"Life is too short to let things go unappreciated. Now I want you to find a spot where you are comfortable, sitting, standing, it doesn't matter to me. Then I want you to write five sentences about your surroundings. One sentence for each of your senses. Tell me what you see, what you hear, what you smell, what something feels like, and you even have to taste something. Use your imagination. There are no wrong answers and your papers will not be graded. Now, I know this will be more difficult for some than others, just like all things in life, we all have different interests. But maybe, just maybe, there is a budding author in our class, and this little lesson will inspire them. You don't have to hurry, we have until lunchtime to finish. Spend a while experiencing your surroundings. Just relax and enjoy. Like I said, this is not for a grade."

She watched her students as they drifted apart. The Tribe went into the outfield and sat on the grass. Mary May and a couple of her friends sat on the benches at the dugout. A few others just stood or walked around and looked for inspiration before they settled down.

Velma Stout leaned against the tall metal post that held the fence behind the dugout. She closed her eyes and let the morning sun penetrate her chest. The cold metal crept across her back and the breeze picked up a few strands of hair and laid them across her cheek. It all felt so familiar and distant. Her fingers danced across her chest and she wondered what she would be doing for the weekend. Maybe her date that was canceled would be rescheduled.

She looked around to check on progress and noticed that Sara had left the bench and was sitting in the outfield grass with Vinni. Seeing their new relationship grow made her feel awkward. She was having the same feelings that Sara was. She was nervous and sensitive. Afraid to speak or make a move and afraid not to. Why in the world was she going through this at her age?

Suddenly she heard herself speaking. "Sometimes that man drives me right to the edge." She dropped her hand from her chest. "Okay, gather round now, gather round."

The students slowly regrouped and drifted to the pitcher's mound where Miss Stout was now standing.

"I think you're all doing a great job. Now, this is the second part of your assignment. I want you to write down what you expect will happen over this weekend. Write about your plans and how you think they will turn out. We will follow up next week by writing what really happened and compare the two. I think this will be an excellent exercise comparing imagination and reality. If you enjoy our class being outside today, maybe we can do it again next Friday. Okay now, you can go back and continue your writing."

"Miss Stout?"

Velma turned to see Sara's hand raised. "Yes, Sara, what is it?"

Sara dropped her hand and smiled at her teacher. "Are you going to write about your weekend?" Sara walked over and offered her composition book. "Vinni and I can share a notebook."

Her fingers began dancing across her chest. "Oh, well I, oh, I guess I could. Thank you, Sara."

George Leaves For Greensboro

Ed and Velma had just arrived at the barn. George met them at the door to the milking parlor.

"Hey, hey, thanks for helping out. I know this a huge favor to ask, especially with everyone gone. Vinni won't even be around, you know. He's spending the weekend at the lake with the Adams. He won't be back until Sunday evening. We'll probably beat him back. I hope you don't have any problems. Got a new calf, just born this mornin'. He's in the stable with his mother. It's been taking Vinni and me about an hour and a half to get everything done. The milk truck gets here around seven. It may take you a little longer. I believe you know where everything is. If you need to get in the house, you know where the key is."

Ed threw his hand out for a handshake. "Glad to do it, glad to do it. Now listen, you just go off and have a good time. We been helping out on this farm since you was a baby. Now, if we need anything, we know where you'll be and how to get in touch, but don't expect to hear from us." His handshake ended with his comment and Velma stepped up for a hug.

"Tell that lovely wife of yours hello, I hope you kids have a great time."

She stepped back and shook her finger at George and smiled. "Word has it that you even got a tux. You know how things get around." George rolled his eyes and shook his head.

"Oh yeah. Don't we all know how things get around. I wonder if Edna May knows anything about this weekend that I don't know."

Ed chuckled and Velma threw her hands in the air. "Lord, honey, if she don't know it, she'll just make it up."

George stepped past them and offered one more thanks. They watched his quick steps roll into a trot then break into a sprint as he headed to the house.

He was walking across the kitchen with his suitcase and decided to check in with Lidia before he left. He knew she had his tux and she never forgot anything, but just in case, he picked up the phone and dialed.

"Hello, hey, this is George. Oh, hey Mimi. Is Lidia there? Oh, no, that's all right. I was just checking to see if I needed to bring anything extra".

George and Mimi heard a click, then another click. "Do you know what time they'll be back? Oh, I see, uh huh, uh huh, okay. Well, if they're gone until three or four, maybe I'll just wait. Oh, okay, she just has one class today? Great. When she gets back, tell her I'm on my way. That's good, good, we can spend some time together. Oh, sure, that'll be great. I love your chicken salad, a sandwich sounds great. Okay, see you in a while. Thanks, Mimi."

George pushed the back door open with his suitcase and closed it with his foot. His thoughts had already left the farm when he turned past his mailbox onto the road.

It had been years since George had driven away from the farm, leaving Ed and Velma in charge. The last time was that cold stormy night when he drove Lidia to the hospital for Giovanni's birth. The farm and its responsibilities tried to creep back into his mind. George had to fight past his guilt and focus on the weekend ahead. Was it so wrong for him and Lidia to have a short vacation? Was it wrong and irresponsible to give Lidia four hundred dollars for the weekend? Four hundred dollars? Did he need to buy Vinni a few more calves instead of throwing money away on frills? Why didn't he spend more time praying about that decision? Maybe he should ask Lidia to return the money. Surely she would understand; she was the sensible one in the union. Why should Lidia's dreams be crushed by his knee jerk decision?

It was George's quick actions on his dreams that landed him in Italy so many years ago. It was one of the things Lidia loved about her husband. It was also what they loved about their daughter. He was proud to have a beautiful daughter who was so much like him. Genevieve had captured all his best traits and features and paraded them before the world. George Davis was far too reserved to flaunt his character and accomplishments, but took great pride in his daughter. He knew that Genevieve would demand a life of excitement and adventure. Vinni, he thought, was more like his mother, more reserved and content with daily life. Maybe he would surprise Vinni with a couple of new calves.

George Davis spent the remainder of his drive to Greensboro planning the lives of his children. Genevieve was easy, her thoughts were her words. Anyone who knew her could plan her future. It would be filled with fashion and travel, beautiful homes, well educated and proper friends, country clubs, beautiful churches and busy committee work. She would be the center of attention in the world she created.

George was sure he understood his son, what he thought, how he felt, what he desired. Boys were so much easier to understand. Their lives were simple and uncomplicated. George Davis didn't understand his son. As a matter of fact, a very sad fact, he didn't really know his son at all.

Giovanni Davis was born into a world and family that was already established. The course had been set for the Davis family. Their ten-year-old daughter had spent her short life molding everyone and everything to conform to her wishes. Genevieve Davis was born with a very strong character. It was easier for her parents to conform to her wishes than to battle against her will. There were no consequences to this way of life because Genevieve's wishes were admirable and harmless. She wanted the very best of everything for everybody. As she grew and changed, she demanded that her world change with her, and it did.

Giovanni was born with a stronger will and greater sense of adventure. His father saw this when he was a child, but didn't encourage Giovanni to take command of his life. Instead, he did the safe and easy thing by directing Vinni to be a part of his life. He had shaped Vinni into a strong young man with an appreciation and will for hard work. He knew the importance of taking responsibility and the consequences of his actions. These were good and admirable traits, but Vinni had more to offer. A greatness that was overlooked and even denied by others.

Vinni Davis had the mind of a genius. He could watch Eighteen work on a motor at Matthew's Garage and understand how it worked without asking. He would watch birds fly and notice how the air currents would lift them and how they guided their path with the slightest movement of their wings, and understand the flight dynamics of an airplane. He could look at a sheet of piano music and hear the rhythm by looking at the pattern of the notes. He could remember the voice of his school teacher and what was happening outside when she told important facts then recall them when he took a test. He knew the answer, he understood the answer and remembered the exact moment when he gained the knowledge. Vinni didn't have to study because he knew how to observe and understand. Saying Vinni Davis was smart was like saying Claude Monet liked to paint. He had a mind and genius that was very rare. Sadly, this was why it went unnoticed.

George was in a daydream when the people behind him blew their car horn. The light at the corner of Main and Fourth had been green several seconds and George hadn't moved. He sped forward, forgetting that he needed to make a left turn. He tried to watch the street signs, hoping to navigate his way back to Winterberry, but the college students in the car behind him stayed close, urging him to get out of their way. By the time he had an opportunity to pull into a parking spot and let them pass, he was on a one way street on the college campus. The campus was in a buzz. The exciting weekend festivities were just getting started. He could hear music and laughter floating through the tall oak trees on campus.

George was sure he could go to the next light, make a right, then the next right. Then he could follow the street numbers back up to Fourth Street, make another right and continue on to Winterberry.

Another car horn blast stopped him from pulling out. The last classes had just finished and he was surrounded by swarms of guys filled with testosterone and girls filled with giggles. He looked over his left shoulder and pulled onto the busy street. "I need to get the hell outta' here."

The next right led him past a row of Sorority houses. The waves of students thickened and filled the street. He slowly maneuvered his truck past bicycles and students running with arms full of books. He looked for the next street to the right. As the street continued, the houses became smaller and the noise softened. He found himself in a residential area just outside the campus on the opposite side of town. He looked at his watch. Twenty five minutes late already.

There was a black man working in a yard several houses up and he decided to ask for directions. He stopped at the curb where the man was mowing between the sidewalk and low brick wall with a rotary mower. George exited his truck and walked to the back so he could meet the worker at the driveway. "Good afternoon."

George extended his hand for the greeting. After wiping his hand on his stained overalls, the man accepted the handshake. "Howdy, howdy, what can I do fo' ya', sir?"

George was glad to see a friendly face and explained his situation. As he was explaining, the man listened and understood what George needed.

"Um hum, um hum. Oh, Winterberry, yes sir, I know Winterberry. Nice neighborhood, real nice." He looked at George's truck and noticed his callused hands. "You doin' some work for the folks over on Winteberry?"

George looked back at his truck and understood the question. His first response was to tell the truth about his plans for the weekend, Genevieve's dance, the tuxedo and his sister's home on Winterberry.

He felt very comfortable with his new acquaintance and wanted to keep it that way. "Well, you know how it is. They like to keep things looking nice, can't blame 'em for that."

The man smiled and shook his head. "No sir, sho' 'nough can't, sho' 'nough can't. Now, let's see. You want th' shortest way or th' easiest way?"

George looked at his watch. "I better take the easiest way. I've found that's usually the quickest."

"Okay. Easiest way is to go up to the third light, 'bout six blocks, an' take a right. That'll be Frank Street. You turn just before the railroad track. Just follow that and it will turn into Fourth Street just when you get back into the city limits. About eight or ten blocks an' you'll cross back over Main Street. Now, you said you can get to Winterberry from there?"

George was relieved to have such a direct route back. "Right on Frank Street at the railroad tracks. Sounds great, listen, thanks a lot, I gotta' go. Have a nice evening."

When he turned into Margaret's driveway, he felt his muscles relax. It was the same sensation he had after the dentist finished cleaning his teeth. He didn't realize how uptight he was until he turned the ignition off and sank back into his seat. "Thank you, Lord, for safe travels and please bless that nice man who gave me directions."

George let his shoulders slump and leaned his head back, resting it on the edge of the vinyl seat. This posture was familiar to George. He often rested in the hay fields before driving the last truckload of hay back to the barn. The cool breeze that lifted thinning hair across his forehead was the only thing familiar. His eyes were closed, but the sounds were very different and there was no hint of hay in the air. The last recognizable smell he encountered was the aroma of freshly mown grass when he stopped for directions.

George's drive to Greensboro, his labored thought about his children, the ordeal driving onto the college campus and his lengthy trek back around the outskirts of town had left him exhausted.

It was Genevieve's knuckles rapping on his window that broke him from his unexpected nap.

Catching Up With Genevieve

"Oh, Genevieve, hey." His nap had been deep enough to disorient him and he struggled to regain his bearings. "Hey, darling. I must have dozed off. It's been quite a drive up. What time is it anyway?"

Genevieve stepped back so he could open his door. "Twenty five after one, but that's okay. I only had one class this morning. I'm free the rest of the day." She threw her arms around her daddy's neck and gave him a kiss.

"Mimi left some chicken salad in the fridge. I'll make us some sandwiches and we can eat on the terrace. I think there may be some potato salad, too. Aunt Margaret made some to send to church for the family Bible study tonight. Mimi took it over a few minutes ago. Do you want tea or lemonade? I think I'll have lemonade. I usually drink tea, but let's have lemonade."

George sat his suitcase down and opened the front door for Genevieve, then followed in behind her.

"Do you remember how we used to drink lemonade in the summer when we were working in the garden? I can still smell the garden every time I drink lemonade. Can you smell the garden when you drink lemonade? Carter always drinks tea, well, tea or water. His doctor says that water is the healthiest thing to drink and you know Carter. Health first."

George sat his suitcase down behind the soft leather club chair. "Well, actually, no, I don't know Carter. Who's Carter?"

Genevieve's late night talk with Carter Lindley had softened the sting of her mother's disapproval of Carter spending the weekend at their house.

"Oh, that's right. I haven't told you about Carter, only mother. Carter, Carter Lindley's his name and he's just fantastic, Father. Really, he is. He is graduating from the Master's program this spring, in finance. He may be interested in law. I'm not sure. Actually, he isn't sure either. He plans to work in the financial field for a little while, save up some money, then decide if he wants to continue his education."

Genevieve's heart had been caught up in her dreams once again and her lips couldn't cast a net over the thoughts that were pouring from her heart. George saw her staring out the window over the tufted leather sofa, the same window her mother had stared out the day before. Her far away gaze was familiar to her father. It had always yielded dreams, but nothing like this one.

"I love him, Father. I love Carter Lindley. I am hopelessly in love." Her whispered confession drifted through the room like an icy winter breeze, leaving George and his daughter frozen by the confession.

"Well, I better get my things up to the guest room." George looked at his daughter while as she continued her stare out the window. He wanted to hug her, he wanted to tell her he loved her, he wanted to tell her he was afraid of losing her, but he was gripped with fear. His life had suddenly been filled with the unknown. He had driven to spend an exciting weekend to celebrate his daughter's new life. He had landed in the whirlwind of a young woman in love. The Genevieve that he came to see was forever gone and he had missed her farewell.

The small suitcase that he carried to the top of the stairs felt like led. He stepped into the guest room and saw his tux hanging on the edge of the wardrobe. The room smelled like Lidia. He was ashamed of himself. Walking away from Genevieve was painful, but not as painful as dealing with the emotions that were filling their room. He sat his suitcase down beside the wardrobe and turned to go back downstairs. He held the crystal doorknob, but instead of opening the door, he quietly closed it. He couldn't face his daughter so soon. He didn't know what to say. How would he explain why he had walked away? He didn't know how to explain his feelings. He wasn't even sure what they were. Genevieve was his daughter and it was his responsibility to help guide her through these wonderful events. He had failed and needed help.

George Davis had needed help many times in his life and always knew where to find it. He turned from the door and placed this right knee, then his left on the Oriental rug beside the bed. The soft mattress sank beneath the weight of his elbows and his hands formed a cradle that held his chin. His prayer followed his tears.

"Father, I thank you for your blessings and understanding, I thank you for safe travel and for those who helped guide me to my destination. I ask a special blessing on my friend who gave me directions. Lord, please care for and help Ed and Velma take care of your farm. I ask for protection, wisdom and guidance for Vinni and his friends. Thank you for Lidia, I love her so much. Please give her a happy heart and peace, let her enjoy the blessings that you have sent her way, and Lord help her to help me.

"Thank you for Margaret and Daniel, for their hospitality and for everything they've done for Genevieve. Lord, I don't know how to help Genevieve. I'm lost. I don't know how to handle her new life. I'm scared of losing her. I feel like I just got her back. You have given her the joy and excitement that was lost for so many years. I have waited for this time for so long and when it finally arrived, I realized that her hopes and dreams, even her love, was being given to someone else. Lord, forgive me for being selfish and controlling. Forgive me for not embracing her joy. Forgive me for being jealous of the man she loves. Help me be the father she deserves, one who is supportive and excited, one who is compassionate and understanding, one who loves unconditionally.

"Lord, help me release her to a new life and ease the pain in my heart. I pray that you will help me be more like You, Father. Now I lift up my daughter, I offer You her dreams and happiness. I thank you for blessing her and keeping her ever in your sight. Give her joy and peace, fill her life with love and understanding. I pray that you will direct her path and give her courage to follow your direction above all others. When there is pain, comfort her. When there is doubt, give her wisdom and when her life is filled with joy, please Lord, remind her where her joy comes from. I love you, Lord, and I praise You, for all your blessings, for Your forgiveness, for Your faithfulness, I thank You and praise You, my Lord, my savior and redeemer. In Jesus' name I pray. Amen."

His clasped hands fell forward and he rested his face on his forearms. The white cotton bedspread absorbed the last of his tears. He stood and faced a door that needed to be opened.

"Would you like another sandwich?" Genevieve was walking back to the kitchen to refill their tea glasses.

George picked his linen napkin off the slate floor in the sunroom. "No thanks, I . . ." Then he stopped himself and spoke the truth. "Actually, I would love another sandwich. I'm starved. I was so excited about seeing you today that I didn't even eat breakfast. As a matter of fact, let's grill one. Remember how Lidia taught us to grill sandwiches?" He stood up and followed her into the kitchen. "Where did that bread come from?"

Genevieve finished filling her glass and started filling her father's. "Do you want lemon? Mimi made the bread. She makes it for her church when they have communion. She always makes an extra loaf for us. I know. It's good, isn't it?" Genevieve gave a sly grin, cut her eyes back to George and whispered, "Nothing's too good for the Lord and the Longs."

George's surprised snicker broke into a rolling laugh. When Genevieve's laughter joined, it sounded like a hymn from Pleasant Grove Methodist Church. The two were so much alike that their laughter was even harmonious. George looked at his new daughter and the Lord answered his prayer. He was filled with joy and excitement.

"Carter Lindley is a very lucky man and so am I."

Genevieve sat the glasses on the counter and turned to George. He could see the light bounce in her eyes. "Oh, Daddy, be serious. Do you really think so?"

George answered with no hesitation or doubt. He gave a deep nod with his head. "I really do, Genevieve, and I am very happy for you both."

Genevieve's arms spontaneously flew up in the air and she hugged her daddy's neck. "I love you, Daddy. Thank you."

George patted her on the back and she stepped back to the tea glasses. Her excitement about a weekend visit spilled out again.

"I really want him to meet Giovanni sometime. I told Mother that maybe we could come home and visit for a weekend."

George had been caught up in her excitement and agreed. "Oh, for the weekend, okay now, let's see. Why not? I'm sure Ed and Velma would be glad to have him as a guest. That way he would get to know some neighbors and feel a real part of the community. He would spend as much time with you, with us as he wanted, but if he had his own place, he may feel more comfortable. You know, he wouldn't feel like he was living with us. I think it would be great. What do you think?"

Suddenly the tables had been turned on Genevieve. Her father's rant had left her spinning. So many questions and ideas to think about. They had overrun her and tripped her up like a litter of jumping puppies.

"Oh, oh, I guess that would work. Ed and Velma's, meeting the neighbors, well, I never thought about that. I'll have to ask Carter about it, of course, but I don't see any reason why not. For the whole entire weekend, even church, I guess. Oh, well, I'll just have to see about that. I sure will. Ed and Velma and the neighbors."

George didn't miss a beat. "That's right, Ed and Velma's, or maybe he could stay with Edna May, Mary May and Gary. Now how about that grilled chicken salad sandwich?"

The Tribe Leaves for the Lake

Miss Stout was gathering the test papers to grade over the weekend and had to raise her voice to be heard.

"Okay class, okay. Quiet'n down now, quiet'n down. I'd hate to give out extra assignments this close to the final bell. Charlie, will you please close the windows? You boys, please don't forget to pick up your sleeping bags and things on your way out, they're over in the corner. Mr. White moved them when he swept during lunch. Sara, can you please take this report up to the office. I believe Mrs. Pratt needs to file them on Monday. Thank you, Charlie. Did you get the one on the end closed? Sometimes it sticks and I believe they're calling for rain this weekend."

The voices were rising again and Miss Stout had to take control. She slapped a wooden ruler on the edge of her desk to gain attention.

"Thank you, that's better. I wanted to say again what a wonderful job you did writing today. Remember to think about everything you do this weekend, how all of your senses are affected, be very observant. Who know, we may have a famous writer among us. If you enjoyed the extended class outside, I'll ask Mr. Johnson for permission to do it every Friday, weather permitting, until the end of the year. Thank you for taking that up, Sara."

She turned and looked at the large round clock above the chalkboard; a minute and a half until the bell.

"Boys, Vinni, why don't you go ahead and get your equipment together and head out. It will be easier if the other students don't have to maneuver around all that."

The back row stood in unison like the choir on Sunday mornings and their chairs slid across the floor in perfect harmony. Vinni gave the instructions.

"Just grab everything, we can sort it out when we get to the lake."

Sara sadly watched as they grabbed the first things they came to and headed to the door. She wished she was spending her weekend at the lake instead of with Mary May.

"You boys be careful and have a good time." Miss Stout was excited for them and the class chimed in, telling them bye. Sara tried to say something, but only a whisper came out as Vinni exited into the auditorium.

Only a few seconds had passed when she heard Vinni's muffled voice echo back into the room. "Bye, Sara."

Tom Adam's truck was the first one in line. He saw The Tribe lumbering toward his truck and stepped to the back and let the tailgate down.

"Hey, guys. Ready to go? Got everything you need? Here just throw those things in here and jump in."

Vinni threw a sleeping bag into the pick-up bed and jumped in. The other equipment and friends followed. Jake started to open the door and get in the front seat out of habit, but stopped himself and jumped in the back. Vinni tilted his head back and shouted above the final bell alarming.

"What about Roy, still picking him up at Matthew's Garage?"

Adam answered as he cranked the pick-up. "Sure am. I hope we can get ahead of these busses." He shifted from neutral to first gear and jumped into action.

Vinni watched the students pouring into the busses, hoping to see Sara. He was already wondering what she would be doing this weekend and wondered when he would be able to sit with her on her front porch swing again. He laid his head back and looked up at the clouds, noticing the birds circling and rising on air currents and wondered if it would rain over the weekend. He watched the clouds for a while, then closed his eyes and listened to the others talking and laughing. He was anxious to see Roy. He remembered the first time they met, the truck ride to Matthew's Garage and the first time anyone called him Vinni. He started planning the excitement for the weekend at the lake and how Roy would be his right hand man.

"Hey, Mr. Adams, be there in a minute." Roy was talking to Johnny Evans and Bill Lewis from the sheriff's department when Tom pulled up at Matthew's garage.

Vinni sat up and looked to see what was going on. He noticed that Johnny was doing most of the talking and seemed to be asking Roy a lot of questions while Bill was taking notes. He looked around to see if there was any evidence of vandalism and didn't see any.

"Hey, Eighteen, what's going on at the garage? Did you rob the place when your uncle wasn't lookin'? Cops are everywhere. Wonder if they think Roy did something?"

Eighteen was climbing over the tailgate to check out the situation and the other boys were looking around. The usual characters were at Matthew's and there didn't seem to be anything wrong, but it was very unusual to have the deputy and his assistant questioning someone. Roy didn't seem to be upset; Johnny and Bill didn't seem to be very concerned either. It all seemed very routine.

Suddenly, Vinni remembered the phone call from the party at Mary May's. "Oh, shit!"

Eighteen stopped beside the truck and looked up at Vinni. "What, oh, shit what? You know what's going on, Vinni?"

Vinni was staring at his tennis shoes. "I dunno', maybe. I just thought of something, but maybe not, I dunno."

Eighteen backed up and The Tribe watched the interrogation. "What the hell, Vinni? What do you mean maybe, I dunno'."

Eighteen talked without looking at Vinni. Vinni was his friend and he trusted him, but he wondered if Vinni could have something to do with an incident at his Uncle's garage. He was afraid to ask any more questions. Vinni turned and looked back at his tennis shoes.

"Hey, you guys, remember what happened with the phone call at Mary May's party? Roy was the one that made the phone call and Bill was the one who got in trouble with Pratt. Maybe that's what this is all about. I dunno'. Wonder if that's it?"

Charlie looked at Jake, who was turning white. "What do you think, Jake? Reckon' we're in trouble? Any reporters at the newspapers been asking questions?"

Eighteen looked at Vinni. "Hell, if Roy goes down, we all go down. Hey Jake, what kind of trouble could we be in, I mean legally? What could we be charged with?"

Jake's back was to the glass where his father was sitting. He wondered if they were being watched through the rear view mirror. He was afraid to say anything and afraid to keep quiet. Just before he was going to answer he was interrupted by his father opening the door and walking over to the deputies. The Tribe turned back to see what was happening.

"Hey, Bill, hey, Johnny. What's up? Anything newsworthy?"

The two were familiar with Tom Adams and knew they could trust him to be discreet. There were plenty secrets in Pleasant Grove society that were kept in confidence by the sheriff's department and the newspaper editor. Tom knew when news needed to be reported and when it didn't; he had the respect of law enforcement. Bill nodded and waved his note pad.

"Hey Tom, nothing to worry about. Nobody's in trouble. We just had a domestic dispute call and Roy was in the vicinity. We were wondering if he heard anything that may help the case." The news was a great relief to everyone in the pickup bed and the harmonious sigh of relief sounded like a tire going flat. Roy saw the relief in his friend's faces.

"All right, sir. Will that be all, guess I told you 'bout everything I know."

Bill closed his notebook and Johnny shook his head. "Yeah, that's all. If you remember anything else, just give us a ring."

Roy crawled over the tailgate with a paper bag from Piggly Wiggly under his arm. "Hey, guys, sorry you had t' wait. Thanks for invitin' me, Jake. Boy you look whiter than usual, I swear you white boys is gittin' whiter every day, damn."

They all laughed while Eighteen crawled over the tail gate. Vinni took center stage and controlled the conversation.

"Hell, Roy, we all look whiter when you're around."

Tom was chuckling at the comment as he closed his door and cranked the truck. "Okay men, next stop, White Lake."

The sudden movement of the truck shook the passengers into position and they were off to do whatever Vinni was planning.

Vinni had been staring at the sky for almost two hours. He had seen the stop lights and power lines crossing when they inched through small towns and noticed how the oak and maple trees were being replaced by tall pines. An occasional airplane would enter the white cloud formations that were changing from long white trails to rolling white pillows. He had noticed a few shore birds glide by and the smells of musty salt air and sand were growing stronger. His friends were quiet and the only sound was the smooth engine and the muffles sound of country music from the radio. Tom slowed down and turned to the right onto a road with hard packed sand. The boys had to hold on to keep from sliding to the front. Vinni saw everyone looking over the sides of the truck.

"Looks like we're here. The cabin's at the end of this road. There's a couple of other cabins, but I don't think anyone else will be here this weekend."

Jake felt like one of the tour guides he had seen in Charleston. "Sometimes in the fall we see flocks of Canada Geese and even some Mallards. They're pretty cool. My uncle said they saw a black bear here a couple of summers ago, but I haven't ever seen one. We see deer a lot and I did see some wild turkeys a few times. We mostly just fish, we don't hunt any."

The air was strong with the aroma of the tall pines and the rolling drive bumped the boys and their cargo until Tom slowed down and pulled up to the cabin.

Margaret shouted from the kitchen window. "Hey, boys, hey, Tom. How was the ride?"

Tom was reaching over into the pick-up bed and helping with the sleeping bags.

"Hey, Maggie, had a great drive down. What time did you get here?" The Tribe had never heard Margaret Adams referred to as Maggie and felt a little awkward.

"I came down this morning, got here about eleven. I thought I might need to straighten up a little." She walked out of the kitchen onto the screen porch that ran across the back of the cabin and overlooked the lake. The screen door slammed behind her as she started down the wide wooden steps toward the truck. Maggie walked up to Tom and he leaned down for a kiss on the cheek.

"Well, looks like you men have the luggage under control, I'll hold the door."

Each boy nodded and thanked her as they passed into the porch. "Thank you, thank you, Mrs. Adams, thanks, thanks Mrs. Adams. Hey, Mom, what's for dinner?"

The screen porch overlooking the lake was very wide and the length of the cabin. There were several fishing rods hanging on the wall beside the row of windows and life jackets were on the floor. A picnic table was at one end of the porch with an oil lantern, a map of the lake and a paperback novel that Maggie was reading. Rocking chairs sat in a row facing the lake separated by a couple of wrought iron garden tables. The wide floor boards were worn with years of summer vacations and the screen door into the kitchen needed painting.

Vinnie liked the cabin. It reminded him of the barn loft on the farm. Eighteen didn't know what to expect, but thought it would be nicer. Roy was the most uncomfortable of all. He had never spent the weekend away from home and didn't know what to do or say. His instincts kept telling him to offer to do work around the cabin, but he resisted the urging.

Mrs. Adams patted Roy's shoulder. "You guys can leave your things here on the porch. Just put them over beside the picnic table. We can decide where everyone wants to bunk down later. Jake, why don't you take them down to the lake? The oars for the canoe are down there somewhere and the Williams said we could use their canoe, too. It's behind the rhododendron under that big pine tree. I think they said the oars were under it. Life jackets are there on the floor. Dinner should be ready in a couple of hours. Oh, Vinni, I almost forgot. Did your parents get off to Greensboro? Your mom said she had an appointment with Eloise to get her hair done and your dad has a tux. It sounds like a great time."

Vinni's mood worsened when he heard the mention of his mom's hair. "Oh, I guess they're all settled. Ed and Velma are taking care of the milking while we're gone."

Margaret looked at the anxious boys waiting to go to the lake. "You guys scoot and have a good time. I'll blow the whistle when it's time to eat." Her directions were like a bell ringing at a horse race and the guys shot through the screen door.

Jake was paddling at the front of one canoe while Eighteen had the other paddle in the rear.

Vinni was paddling the front of the other canoe with Roy in control of the rear. Charlie noticed a wooden pier jutting from the woods on the other side of the lake and shouted across to Jake's canoe.

"Hey, Jake, what's that pier for?"

Jake picked his oar out of the water and focused on the other side of the lake.

"Oh, that's for the cabins on the other side of the lake. The folks who have cabins over there joined together and built a dock. It's pretty nice, they tie their canoes up and use the end like a diving board. I don't know who they are, but sometimes I hear them over there. Sounds like they have a good time. They have a big bonfire and cookout for the fourth of July."

Vinni squinted against the sun. "Are they over there now?"

Jake pulled his oar out of the water and let his canoe drift in the direction of the pier.

"I dunno', most people don't come for the weekend until school's out. Usually the first weekend of June. I guess they could be there, or maybe not."

Vinni looked across to the pier, then back to Jake's cabin. He could barely see the edge of the screen porch peeking past the pine trees. He figured that by the time they were at the pier, they would be out of Tom and Margaret's sight. He and Roy paddled up and grabbed the side of Jake's drifting canoe.

"Can we go over there? I don't see anybody, but it don't matter anyway. Do you think they would care if we used their dock? Hey we could go fishin' 'n swimmin' 'n all sorts of stuff. You never been over there? Looks pretty deserted to me and I don't hear nothin'."

Jake shaded his eyes with his hand, looked at the pier, then turned and looked at his disappearing cabin. Jake was actually farther out than he had ever been in the canoe, but didn't want the others to know. He looked back and couldn't see his cabin, then looked at his watch. He expected to hear his mom's whistle soon. "Well, I guess we could go over . . ."

Vinni jumped in before he could finish his suggestion of going over tomorrow. "Great, come on Roy, let's see how fast we can get there. Let's race, Jake."

Splashing water from Roy's oar rained into Jake's canoe. Eighteen started paddling quicker than Jake and their canoe rotated in the wrong direction. Jake held his paddle in the water to redirect his craft.

"Hold on, Eighteen, let me catch up." The race was on and Vinni was standing on the dock when Jake arrived. "Let's see who's here."

Vinni was running toward the sandy shore and pine trees. Jake held onto the sides of the rocking canoe while Eighteen and David jumped onto the pier.

Jake noticed that Vinni hadn't tied his canoe to the dock and it was drifting back into the lake. "Whoa, whoa, whoa guys. You gotta tie up."

He leaned over and used his oar to pull the drifting canoe back. Vinni looked back and saw Jake tying his canoe to the dock.

"Come on, Jake." Jake looked up from the rope and saw the others disappearing into the pine trees. He looked back and couldn't see his cabin.

Vinni was winding through the pine trees and everyone followed with Jake several yards behind Charlie. Suddenly, Vinni stopped and squatted down on one knee. He motioned for the others to get down and be quiet.

"Shh, be quiet. I think they're home. Sounds like a bunch o' girls."

Jake saw their heads swaying from side to side and bobbing up and down. He wanted to tell everyone to get back to the canoes, but his heart was beating so hard that he could barely speak. The only sounds were muffled voices and giggling coming from the cabin and the sound of pine needles being crushed beneath their knees and feet. Jake was imagining what would happen if they were discovered spying on a bunch of girls.

Suddenly their stares were interrupted by the far away sound of Maggie's whistle.

Jake quickly began crawling backwards. "Let's go, let's go, that's the whistle for dinner. Come on, let's go."

MAY 1ST 1948

The Morning of the Dance

George's first morning on Winterberry Lane arrived with a kiss from Lidia on his forehead. "Good morning, sleepy head. How does it feel to sleep in and not worry about milking?" George sprang up to his elbows, thinking he was at home and overslept. His heartbeat slowed when he looked around and realized where he was. He fell back on his pillow with his forearm over his eyes. "Oh, it feels wonderful. I had forgotten what it feels like to sleep in without being deathly ill. What time is it?"

Lidia's breasts pressed against his chest when she leaned over to look at the clock on his night stand. "Six thirty two. That's late for us farmers." Lidia fell back onto her down pillow. George smiled at the thought of them sleeping late and laughed.

"Six thirty two on Saturday morning? I bet we're the only people awake in Greensboro. We better be quiet or we'll wake the neighbors. How long do you think we could stay in bed if we didn't have to get up?"

Lidia rolled onto her side and rested her head in her left hand. "Probably until about seven o'clock. I wonder if there's any coffee downstairs."

George sat up in bed and rolled his neck to work out the stiffness caused by his down pillow. "Do we have to get dressed before we go down?"

"No, I don't think so, but you may want to brush your teeth, smells like you brought the barn with you." George's pillow hit her head before her comment was finished.

"Lidia Davis, you should be ashamed, staying in a fine neighborhood like this with a husband whose breath smells like cow shit. I'm calling Edna May!"

Lidia was running her fingers through her soft black hair and rolled her eyes. "Edna May? Lord, if you're calling her, call her something for me. Margaret say's she's just a wasp flying around to see who she can sting. I know I'm a Christian and should rise above carnal thoughts, but I must confess, I do believe she's just a little bitch."

George was shocked to hear such a comment from his wife and turned to see her calmly running her fingers through her hair. "I like the new Lidia."

She smiled and sat up beside him. "Good. Let's get ready to go downstairs, shitty breath."

The aroma of fresh perked coffee met them half way down the stairs. They turned to the left and went through the dining room into the kitchen. Daniel was sitting at the breakfast table in his pajamas and robe. The Saturday morning Greensboro Daily was spread across the table and he was sipping a cup of black coffee. When he saw them, he quickly folded the paper with his left hand.

"Oh, good morning, thought you two would sleep in this morning. Here, let me get my paper out of your way. Grab a cup of coffee, cream and sugar is beside the pot. Did you sleep well?"

George blinked and raised his eyebrows at Lidia. "Morning, Daniel. Well, actually, we did sleep late this morning, we're still on farmin' time. Didn't expect to see you up so early. Here Lidia, you want cream in your coffee? Smells great. I slept like a log, thanks. Here's your coffee, honey. Where did you say the sugar was? Oh, here it is never mind. I hope you didn't get up early and fix coffee because we were here."

Daniel leaned back in his chair and dropped the folded paper over his crossed leg. "Oh, heavens no. I'm always up early on Saturdays. I'm usually at the office by seven during the week and can't seem to sleep late on the weekends. I guess I'm a morning person. I had to be at my dad's grocery store early when I was growing up, guess I never broke the habit. Have a seat. Margaret, well, she's been able to break the sleeping schedule of a farm girl. I expect her down around nine o'clock on Saturdays."

Margaret's voice drifted across the foyer with a chuckle. "Daniel Long, you know I have a full breakfast waiting for you every Saturday morning at six o'clock. Morning all. Did you sleep well?"

She bent over and kissed the top of her husband's head. Lidia smiled at the thought of Margaret Long being a farm girl. "We did sleep well, thanks. I hope you didn't get up because we're here." Margaret tapped her silver spoon on the edge of her coffee cup.

"Oh, Lord no, I was too excited to sleep. I can't wait until tonight. George Davis, I'm telling you, you better look tip top tonight because the dress your wife bought yesterday is going to knock the socks off of every man at The Club. Boy, you better be ready."

Lidia bounced her eyebrows at George across the rim of her coffee cup and George winked at Margaret. "Here, have a seat. Got any gum?"

Lidia kicked George under the table.

Margaret dropped her hands beside the cup on the table. "Gum with coffee? What on Earth? Lidia, let's go back to Montaldo's. I'm still not sure about those shoes I picked up. Maybe we need to bring the black open toed ones home just in case. Did you buy a purse? I can't remember. Lidia Davis, the entire floor stopped working when you stepped out of that dressing room. Even the women at the cosmetics counter turned around, and when you looked in the mirror and started making comments in Italian, they almost dropped their compacts. I cannot wait for tonight, I just can't. I was too excited to sleep. We'll stop by The Club for lunch. What are you boys doing today?"

George looked across the table at Lidia and tilted his head to one side. "Well, as a matter of fact, you ladies may want to invite Genevieve because Daniel and I are having lunch with Carter Lindley."

Lidia stopped her coffee cup in midair and sat it back on the table. Margaret looked at George, then back at Lidia. Lidia sat back in her chair and crossed her arms.

"Carter Lindley? Che cosa e questo grande segreto? Che ne pensate che si stannl facendo impianto segreto? George Davis, Carter Lindley, you and Daniel are having lunch with Carter Lindley?" George and Daniel exchanged a casual look and shrugged their shoulders. "That's right, Carter Lindley, Daniel and I are having lunch with Carter Lindley, I hear he's just dreamy."

Margaret's pursed lips couldn't hold back a snicker, but Lidia wasn't amused. "Carter Lindley?"

George closed his eyes, smiled and nodded in his wife's direction. "Yes, dear, Carter Lindley, I hear he's just simply all that."

Margaret couldn't deny her amusement and just sat back and smiled as she watched the conversation continue. "George Davis, please. Dio, Dio. Does Genevieve know about this?"

Daniel came to George's defense. "Yes, as a matter of fact, she gave me his phone number so I could call and invite him to lunch. He seemed very excited, very excited. He seems like a very excitable young man. Don't you think so, George?"

Suddenly the two men had given Lidia reason to worry about the young man. "Oh quell povero ragazzo, quell povero ragazzo impotente.". "What on Earth are you going to do with Carter Lindley? Why do you need to meet him?"

George and Daniel looked very thoughtfully and seriously at each other, then George explained. "We're going to gag him and tie him to the railroad tracks."

Margaret's laugh seemed sillier than usual and the two men couldn't hold their laughter either. Lidia crossed her arms and bobbed her foot under the table. Suddenly she was the voice of reason. "George Davis, and you, Daniel, really. Oh quell povero ragazzo, quell povero ragazzo impotente. I'll let Genevieve know what time we're leaving. You two and Carter Lindley."

She raised her hands and flipped them outwards like she was directing someone to open a curtain. "Honestamente, perola gli vomini non cueseono mai, sompre ragazzini, sompre amnti, s

Genevieve's insulin shot was interrupted by the phone ringing. She was finally able to answer on the seventh ring. "Hello. Oh, mother, hey. No, I just had some coffee and toast over here. No, really I'm fine. Yes I know. I am taking care of myself. Yes, I know. It is going to be a very exciting night. Um hum, um hum, oh, I see. Well, actually, no he didn't. I knew he had plans, but he isn't supposed to pick me up until seven. That should be nice, having lunch with Daddy and Uncle Daniel. Well, I really didn't have anything planned for today. I have everything ready for tonight. I picked up my dress last Friday and my shoes on Saturday. Oh, I don't know. I guess I'll just put it up. Really, Mother, I appreciate the thought, but there is no way to get an appointment today. The salons have been booked for weeks. He's picking me up at seven. Well, I guess I could go. What time? Oh, what time is it now? Okay, I'll be up in fifteen minutes. Bye."

The trip to Montaldo's was a success. Shoes and purses were taken back to Margaret's car and put in the trunk. Lidia put her arm over the front seat and looked back to Genevieve. "Now for lunch at The Club, then to your hair appointment." Genevieve crossed her arms and looked away from her mother to the sidewalk.

"I know you told me not to worry, but honestly, Mother. How do you expect to get an appointment with this late notice? We have to have lunch at The Club, which I am looking forward to, and I have to start getting ready by five. I don't want to be rushed and I really don't want to waste valuable time waiting for a stylist. Don't get me wrong, I appreciate what you're trying to do, really I do."

Lidia interrupted her daughter with a stern voice. "Genevieve Davis, look at me." Genevieve's brows automatically lowered and her eyes quickly cut from the sidewalk to her mother's gaze. Lidia simply smiled and winked at her irritated daughter. "Just leave it to me, dear, I have more connections in Greensboro than you know."

Margaret was signing the check and telling the waiter to apply it to the Long account while Genevieve was staring at her watch. The waiter was wishing the ladies a happy evening when Genevieve interrupted.

"Thank you, thank you very much. We had a delightful lunch, but we have an appointment to meet. I'm afraid we'll be late." She stood up and slid her chair up to the white linen tablecloth.

Lidia was more interested in finishing her coffee than their appointment. Margaret was looking past her nose into her compact mirror and applying lipstick to her thin lips. Margaret pressed her lips into a tissue. "We'll meet you at the car, dear."

She was barely out of sight when Margaret looked at Lidia, waiting for a response.

"I know, I seem difficult toady, but honestly, Margaret, she needs to be reminded that I am her mother and she can trust me without controlling me. She should be excited about this little adventure we're taking her on. When all is said and done, I'm sure she'll understand and have a whole new outlook on the entire evening. Especially after Mimi's sister gets finished with her hair."

The car was slowing down and drifting into a row of empty parking spaces on Elbert Street.

Genevieve looked up from her magazine and was startled at her location. "What's wrong? Are we having car trouble? Where are we?"

The car came to a stop and Margaret and Lidia stepped out. Genevieve was still trying to grasp the situation.

"Are you going for help? Do you see a policeman? Are we out of gas? What time is it?"

Lidia opened the back door and stuck her head into the car. "It's time for your appointment at the salon." Genevieve looked past her mother to Margaret's smiling face.

Margaret raised her eyebrows and nodded in agreement. "Let's go, I think your chair's ready."

Genevieve looked back to her mother and whispered in desperation, "But the gala, what will I do? What if . . ."

Lidia sat down in the back seat beside her daughter. "What if you have the most fabulous hairdo at the dance? Genevieve, if I can trust her with my hair, you can trust her with yours."

She took her daughter's hand and led her into the salon.

Across the Lake

The Tribe slept late. Their poker game had lasted until three fifteen on Saturday morning. The deck of cards was scattered across the picnic table in the screen porch, sleeping bags filled every available floor space. Tom and Maggie didn't cook the bacon and eggs, instead they just had a bowl of cereal in bed.

It was about eleven o'clock when Eighteen farted and woke Jake up. He jumped up to escape the fumes and tripped over Vinni. The toxic cloud drifted across Vinni's face.

"Damn, what the hell did you eat, Eighteen? Smells like skunk ass. What time is it, Jake?"

Jake stepped into the den and looked beside the door at the clock above the barometer. "Five after eleven. You guys want something to eat? I can fix some bacon 'n eggs."

The rest of The Tribe was stirring and sitting up in their sleeping bags. Their approval came in slow grunts and nods. "Yeah, um hum, sure, I guess, sounds good to me."

They were kicking from underneath sleeping bags, Vinni was peeing on a pine tree, Tom and Maggie were walking down the stairs and the phone was ringing.

Roy was the first to greet the hosts. "Morning Mr. Adams, thanks again for letting us come up to the cabin."

"Glad you could make it, Roy." Tom reached across the kitchen counter and picked up the phone. "Hello, yeah hey, no, no, that's okay. What's up? Yes, yes I remember, no we decided to hold off on that news. Just a minute, let me take this at the phone upstairs."

Maggie could tell something serious had happened by the frown on Tom's brow.

"Maggie, could you help Jake with the eggs? I have to take this upstairs." Jake's mom took the frying pan from the cabinet and Jake set the eggs on the counter beside the stove.

"I tell you what, you guys wash up while I fix breakfast. Now scoot, be ready in about fifteen minutes. Jake, show everyone where the bathroom is."

Vinni was stepping through the screen door. "I found it, it's down at that pine tree."

Maggie smiled at the comment, then she heard Eighteen pipe in.

"Better use that pine tree while it's still alive. Vinni just flooded it out. Oh, sorry Mrs. Adams, I thought Jake was fixin' breakfast."

Maggie was looking in the refrigerator for the bacon. "That's okay, Eighteen, but you boys do need to be careful, I heard someone talking about a skunk this morning." Mouths were covered, fingers pointed and faces turned red. Maggie winked at Eighteen. "Can you get the paper plates out, buddy?"

Eighteen stopped blushing and grinned. "Sure, where are they?"

The canoes were carrying the same passengers as the evening before and they followed the same course. Jake wasn't concerned about the cabin that drifted slowly from sight. He kept his eyes on the pier where they had docked yesterday. Their oars dripped water on the fishing poles at their feet as they alternated sides to keep the canoes heading straight for the shore. Vinni's head was bobbing up and down, hoping to get a peep through the pine trees.

"Wonder if those people are still here? It sounded like a bunch o' girls to me. If they don't like us using their dock, I'll just tell 'em we're with the state wildlife commission. Is it hot enough to go swimming?"

Jake answered quickly, "No, not really. We don't swim until June. The water's really cold until then. Nobody swims this early." He hoped he had stopped any thoughts Vinni was entertaining. "Besides, we didn't bring our bathing suites."

All Vinni heard was a rule that could be broken. He dipped his hand in the water and threw it in Jake's direction. "Don't feel too cold to me." He winked at Roy and started planning his next move. "I might just try it. What do ya' think, Eighteen? You game?"

Eighteen nodded his head in disagreement. "No way, Vinni. You might be okay in the water, but when you get out with soaking wet clothes, you gonna freeze your little balls off. I ain't getting' in the water. I don't think you will either."

Vinni grabbed the edges of his canoe and jerked it to one side. "How about let's all go swimming?" He looked back for Roy's support and saw his sidekick holding onto the sides of the canoe with a terrified grip.

Roy was too scared to speak, but Vinni understood his whisper. "Oh, hell no, Vinni, I can't swim. I'll sink to the bottom like a rock and drowned, I swear to God, I'll drowned.

You better keep your little white ass in this boat."

Vinni changed the course of action. "Race you to the dock, Jake. Loser has to build a campfire."

The campfire that Vinni started was small, but paid his debt. They had been fishing from all sides of the dock for over an hour with no luck. Jake had the most patience and stared at his cork with great anticipation. Eighteen was constantly reeling and casting his line. If he caught a fish, it would have to catch his bait first. Roy was with Charlie and David, throwing pine cones in the fire.

Vinni had left his fishing pole hanging over the side of the pier; he was laying on his back staring at the clouds. He sat up and looked over to the pine trees. "I'm bored. I think I'll go swimming."

Jake answered without breaking his concentration. "Too cold."

Vinni was taking his tennis shoes off and the three friends were walking down from the pile of smoking pine cones.

Eighteen looked at Vinni with one eye closed. "I told you, you're gonna' freeze your ass off when you get out with those wet clothes on. I ain't goin' in with ya'. Call me what you want, but I ain't goin in."

Roy had just stepped onto the pier when Vinni started taking his shirt off and knew what Vinni had in mind. "Oh, hell no you ain't, you know you ain't." Roy was grinning and shaking his head in disbelief. "Boy, you are crazy, you know you ain't."

Jake looked behind him to see what was happening and saw Vinni unzipping his pants. He tried to say something to stop Vinni from stripping, but all he could say was, "Oh, oh, oh, wa, wait, wait, wait a minute, oh, oh, no, no, no." He reeled his line in and looked up just in time to see Vinni's white butt break through the water.

The Tribe exploded in a loud cheer, jumping and chanting Vinni's name. It was like they were watching an Olympic event. Vinni's head popped up several yards away.

Roy shouted from the middle of the pier. "Boy, you are crazy, you know you didn't."

Jake's eyes were darting from Vinni to the pine trees across the lake, back to the campfire then to the pine trees leading to the cabin.

Eighteen crossed his arms and nodded his head at Vinni. "Gonna' freeze your little balls off, Davis. Is it cold enough for ya' now?"

Vinni slipped back under the surface and bobbed back up beside the canoes. "Come on, guys, it ain't cold, really. When you jump in, it really ain't bad."

He saw Roy with his hands tucked in his pockets, whispering and shaking his head. "Oh, hell no, ain't no way. I'll sink like a rock and drowned, ain't no way in hell. I don't care how hot or cold that water is, it's still water. Ain't no way in hell."

Vinni fanned his arm and threw water into the canoes, across the pier and over everyone's legs. They all ran to the end of the pier and continued to the smoldering fire. Vinni pushed off from the canoes and drifted back into the lake. He shouted back to the shore. "That's okay, sit up there by the fire. Be careful, don't toast your marshmallows." He shook his middle finger in the air and dipped back into the water.

Eighteen shouted back, "You're gonna' freeze your ass off."

Everyone was laughing, but Jake was keeping a constant watch on their surroundings. He thought he heard something in the pine trees and cut his eyes in that direction. He saw something white flash behind a tree and heard shuffling in the leaves.

He jerked at Roy's shirt and whispered, "Hey, hey, I think something's over there."

Roy turned toward the trees and saw the white object move again. He shook Eighteen's arm. "Shh, shh, be quiet. Something's in the woods."

The Tribe had stopped watching Vinni and was quietly staring into the pine trees. The white object dashed from one tree to the next and they heard girls giggling.

Vinni noticed them staring at the woods and shouted. "Hey, what's up? You guys set the woods on fire? Get Eighteen to piss on it."

The giggles that came from the pine trees made it clear to The Tribe that they were being spied on by some girls. They instantly looked at Vinni, then back at the pine trees. The giggling got louder and the white shirt moved again. Roy broke from the group and trotted down to the pier, bent over like he was under fire.

"Vinni, Vinni, there's some girls up in the woods watching you."

Roy's loud whisper wasn't loud enough for Vinni to hear over his sounds of treading water. Roy trotted onto the pier and continued to the end, holding his crouched posture. He kneeled down at the end next to the canoes and motioned for Vinni to swim over. The Tribe turned from the woods and watched the pier, waiting for instructions from their naked leader. They, and the girls in the woods, watched as Roy continued to lean over the end of the pier, having a conversation with Vinni.

The girls stood up and stepped from behind the trees into the path that led to the lake, giving them a better view. They saw Roy motion for his friends to join him where Vinni was holding on to the end of the pier. When The Tribe turned and ran to the pier, the girls tiptoed to the edge of the woods where the pine needles meet the sandy shore.

Vinni looked past the legs of his friends running to rescue him and saw three girls squatting beside the smoldering campfire, hoping to get a glimpse of him when he crawled onto the pier. The group of guys huddled at the end of the pier, looking down while Vinni gave them instructions. To the girls it looked like a football team huddling around their quarterback.

Vinni looked up at Roy and raised his eyebrows, "Okay, you got it, Roy?"

Roy looked down at him, then leaned backwards and looked at the girls. "Are ya' sure, Vinni? Maybe you better not, I mean, there could be somebody else in the woods. Did anybody see their parents?"

Eighteen encouraged Vinni, "No man, they're by themselves. If their parents were anywhere around, you think they'd be watching you? Do it man, just go ahead."

Roy looked back at Vinni, stood up with the rest of the guys and faced the girls.

The girls saw the U shaped formation as the guys turned and faced them, then they heard the water swoosh when Vinni pulled himself up onto the pier. There were no secrets, no spying and no denying what was going on. The three girls stood beside the dying campfire and stared at the pier hoping, without denial, to see Vinni's naked body.

The guys slowly started walking in tight formation toward the shore, keeping their naked comrade tightly hidden. When they reached the pile of Vinni's clothes they stepped over them and stopped when Vinni could reach them. They stood at attention and watched the girls tilting their heads up and down, from side to side hoping to get one last peek at Vinni before he got dressed.

After a few moments, Vinni gave the orders. "Okay men, I'm ready."

The Tribe resumed their slow regimented march toward the end of the pier.

Roy tilted his head back towards Vinni and whispered, "You sure? Not too late to back out."

Vinni whispered orders to the back of the heads surrounding him, "Keep in formation until I'm at the end of the pier, then give me room."

The three girls stood with their arms crossed, staring at what seemed to be a ridiculous war game. The heavy beat of the march on the wooden pier softened as each soldier stepped onto the sand. The girls continued their stare as The Tribe stood for a moment in the sand; there was still no sign of the naked swimmer.

Vinni Meets Joy

The girls looked back to where Vinni's clothes once laid and saw that he had redressed. They were giggling, shaking their heads and looking at each other when it happened. Suddenly and forcefully, the war cry rose from the middle of the formation. "Chaaaarge!"

The Tribe gave a supportive war whoop and quickly stepped to the sides as Vinni burst out, threw his clothes in the air and charged towards the girls.

The unexpected shock left them paralyzed. Vinni's jeans and shirt seemed to slowly rise through the air then float down with his white underwear. The naked boy they had spied on was racing toward them at high speed, backed up by loud war cries from his soldiers. Their feet started moving before their arms were uncrossed, leaving them off balance and causing them to trip in the sand. They could hear Vinni's shout growing louder as he rapidly approached their backs. The sand was slowing their efforts to escape the naked madman running at them. The three girls were tripping and running on all fours until they reached the edge of the pine trees, where they finally broke into a full run.

The cover of pine trees gave them a safe haven and they slowed to a trot. Their hearts were beating and their legs were tired from the sudden burst of exercise. When they were sure that Vinni had stopped at the edge of the woods, they stopped to catch their breath.

Surprisingly, Vinni had not stopped, he had been slowed down when he tripped over a pair of sandals lost by the youngest girl. They heard his scream before they heard his footsteps. "Arrrugh!"

The smallest girl was the last and closest to the quickly approaching nude maniac. She screamed and started running, without looking up. Her foot slipped and she fell on her knees, pulling on her sister's white shirt. Being jerked from behind caused her sister to stop running and fall back. The third sister continued running several yards, but stopped when she realized her two younger sisters were in trouble. By the time the two fallen sisters were able to get up, Vinni had arrived.

He stood underneath the pines wearing nothing but his tennis shoes. The girl in the white shirt was standing up and brushing pine needles and sand from her arms. The youngest was on her knees, facing the other two with Vinni standing over her. His tennis shoes were only inches from her bare feet. It was her sandals that had tripped Vinni and slowed her down. Suddenly the four stood, and kneeled, in silence.

Vinni had planned everything but the collision. The three girls were supposed to run to the end of the pine trees and disappear into the cabin while Vinni returned to his clothes. He looked down at the youngest on her knees with her backside up in the air. Her green cotton skirt had been displaced in the fall and she was trembling and frightened with her eyes closed and tears forming. She could feel the sand on her feet that Vinni kicked up when he stopped running. Her soft plea was helpless and fragile, offered like a prayer while she was on her knees. "I'm a virgin."

Vinni looked down and simply replied, "I see your panties, virgin."

The last bit of adrenaline pulsing through her body erupted and she kicked sand on his legs when she bolted past her sister's white shirt.

Her arms were brushed clean of sand and pine needles and she brushed off her white shirt. She looked back to the edge of the woods where her oldest sister was hugging the youngest. She looked back at Vinni and crossed her arms. His nudity had lost its power, the shock was over, the battle had been surrendered by both parties.

The Tribe was standing at the edge of the woods where the sandy shore met the pine needles. They were tilting their heads up and down, leaning from side to side, hoping to get a glimpse of what was happening.

Vinni watched as the brave, strange girl crossed her arms and tilted her head to one side. She didn't speak and didn't move.

Vinni crossed his arms and returned the same posture. He nodded at the girls standing at the edge of the woods. "Is that your little sister?"

She twisted at her waist and looked backwards then looked back at Vinni. "Yeah, that's my little sister and my big sister." Her eyes looked down at his tennis shoes then slowly rose to meet his dark brown eyes with strands of wet black hair falling across his eyelids. Then she looked back down and nodded at his crotch. "Is that your little brother?"

Vinni suddenly remembered his swim in the cold lake and realized he was standing with his feet at shoulder width and his arms were crossed over his chest. He looked at her for the first time. Her blonde hair was pulled behind her left ear and stopped short of her shoulders. Her white shirt was light enough to reveal a bra that was about the same size as Sara Jenkin's. He started rubbing his bottom lip with his tongue and his forefinger was making circles around his thumb. He looked back into her blue eyes and answered. "Yeah, sometimes it's my little brother and sometimes it's my big brother. My name's Vinni."

She unfolded her arms and rested her hands on her hips. "My name's Joy."

Vinni closed his eyes and nodded his head in approval. "Well, okay then, Joy. I guess I'll be seeing you around. Be okay if we stay over here at th' pier for a while? I thought we might catch some fish 'n maybe have a cookout."

Joy twisted back toward the cabin then back to Vinni. "I guess so, if not my daddy'll run you off."

Vinni uncrossed his arms, tilted his head down, ran his fingers through his wet hair and looked up at Joy. "Well, okay, thanks. Tell ya' little sister I'm sorry if I scared 'er."

She watched him trot back to the edge of the woods. Just before he reached the sand he turned around, took a few steps backwards and waved his left hand in the air. "See ya' around, Joy."

JUNE 1ST 1948

The Last Day of School

The school sounded different that morning.
Voices were louder, laughter was unchecked and
the sounds echoed off empty desks. Their school
books had been handed in two days earlier. Mary
May had assisted Miss Stout in inspecting the
books and deciding which ones should be sent
to the discard section of the library. Several
students had to pay a five or ten cent fine for
damage to their books. A few had slipped by with
unflattering drawings of Mrs. Pratt added to the
dinosaur section of world history. The Tribe had
stacked the books on the stage where tables were
arranged by subject.

Sara Jenkins was uninterested in the
conversations on the front row. She was sitting
at her desk with her knees in the aisle, looking
toward the back row. She was hoping that Vinni
would look her way and offer a wink or a smile.
She would accept any excuse to believe that
Vinni still liked her. Things had been very
different since the weekend at the lake and she
didn't understand why. Sara Jenkins had entered
Vinni's world and accepted all the conditions
with the privilege of being in his close circle.
There was no way out.

Eighteen was explaining to The Tribe how he
was going to rebuild a motor in an old Chevy and

it would be his to drive when he finished. His future had been set and he had gladly accepted his fate without consideration. Matthew's Garage would be his life from this summer forward.

Miss Stout was standing with her back to the class, gazing across the ball field. Her comments to the class sounded more like she was talking to herself and went unheard by most. "Okay students, let's not let our talking get out of hand. We are still in school and will remain so until the bell rings."

She was staring out the window past the ball field into the clouds. Something was tugging at her heart, something she hadn't felt for many years. Her hand was dancing across her chest and her mind was drifting back to the ocean. She had not spent a summer in the ocean breeze since that summer of sorrow. Why on Earth was it calling her back now?

"Mrs. Pratt, have all the teachers given you the final report card grades? You know the new county regulations are making us have two copies. I don't know why in the hell." Mr. Johnson's voice came from behind his closed door, but Mrs. Stout understood his mumbled question.

She was glad his door was closed because the heat was overtaking her and she had taken the small fan from her desk and placed it on the floor. The cool breeze was wafting past her ample calves and lifting her cotton dress off her knees. "Yes, sir, Miss Stout was the last to give me the grades this morning. I don't know what's got into her. I thought she would be the first to finish, but she was the last." Then the secretary looked to make sure no one was in the hall and leaned toward Mr. Johnson's door. "I've heard that she's been dating someone, but that's just hear-say. But that could explain it."

She heard Mr. Johnson's drawer close and a double knock sounded on the desk with his reply. "Oh, hell."

Vinni's desk was tilted onto the back legs and he was rocking in small jerks. He couldn't wait for the bell to ring. His mind was spinning in reverse, going over everything that happened that year. It was a good year on the farm. His talk with his daddy in the barn had made him wonder more than he expected. People were still talking about the party at Edna May's. Lidia had told him about Carter Lindley and the visit he would be making.

This had been an interesting year. It was the year when new friendships had been started. It was the year when girls were allowed to enter Vinni's world. It was a year when everything had changed with his body and mind. It was the year when Vinni met Joy.

More To Come

My how things change.
Life in Pleasant Grove carries on with new
faces, new situations and new generations.
What will happen over the next few years?
You just can't imagine.

NOT THE END

CPSIA information can be obtained at www.ICGtesting.com
Printed in the USA
BVOW012342111011

273386BV00001B/1/P